George W. Bush Buys Coke in *Mid-Eternity*

George W. Bush Buys Coke

in

Mid-Eternity

Liam Mac Sheóinín

A Menippean Satire

SERVING HOUSE BOOKS

George W. Bush Buys Coke in Mid-Eternity

Cover by Walter Cummins

Serving House Books logo by Barry Lereng Wilmont

ISBN: 978-0-9826921-3-4

Published by Serving House Books

www.servinghousebooks.com

First Serving House Books Edition 2011

The pity is the public will demand and find a moral in my book—or worse they may take it in some serious way, and on the honor of a gentleman, there is not a single serious line in it.

— James Joyce to Djuna Barnes in an interview published in *Vanity Fair* (March 1922)

To my beloved parents and brother Gary and my sisters, Kathleen, Denise, and Maureen

Liam Mac Sheóinín is publishing his first novel. He has received three Pushcart Prize nominations and in 2007 was an Eric Hoffer finalist.

CHAPTER 1

sixbuildingsablur, the seventh we see through a glass, darkly. All action then shifts to room 107 of the Traveler Inn, 7 Eccles Street, Ocean City, New Jersey, where the soulmates are registered under an alias:

Mr. and Mrs. B. Boylan,

619 Molly Lane,

Lindalindo, Eire.

When joined, our Hellenic monarchs—a stolen lover will steal your heart away—are Adam and Eve happy enough, but in the words of the very first murdered playwright:

Her lips suck forth my soul: see, where it flies!

"Is this not the most beautiful day the world has ever witnessed, Mrs. Boylan?"

"Mrs. Boylan," Rachel echoed, trying hard to suppress laughter. "If you…" She laughs uncontrollably for a few seconds before gaining composure. "Tell me you're boiling for me, I'm leaving."

"So what else is new?" Brian asked angrily. "You enjoy leaving me."

"I don't."

"I think you do."

"You know my situation," she snapped, prior to taking his right hand, tenderly. "Though I promise when I stay … it will be forever."

What's time? Leave NOW for dogs and apes! Man has forever.

"Are you hungry?" he inquired.

"Of course."

"Where then? What about room service?"

"Isn't it bad enough we're stuck on the first floor?"

They are, in a mere moment, seated in the on-premises restaurant—The Gibraltar Room, a less than elegant establishment, musty and eclectic, yet a place with an interesting feel.

An appetite, a feeling and a love.

Her deep-set, liquid eyes flowed the gaudy room in blue excitement: noticing the faded prints dotting the smudged alabaster walls—but not the equally faded lone gilt-framed oil on canvas depicting the Battle of Waterloo with Wellington commanding from atop a tall bay steed.

His bardic ear lists joyously to the buzzing, pinging, and all other manner of onomatopoeia:

O! it came o'er my ear like the sweet sound

That breathes upon a bank of violets

Stealing and giving odor!

En attendant Godot—their appositely named tardy waiter—they share a kiss over the wobbly table spatially dividing them. *Her lips: Statement of the mass-energy equivalence relationship: Energy equals mass times the speed of light squared.*

"Do you know what you want?" he asked, feeling stupid that he didn't mitigate his question with an endearment: love, honey, Desdemon, etc.

"Really Brian," she chided, looking with blue-eyed perplexion at the rose-colored menu.

Hers: Swordfish and salad awash in wintery spring water.

His: Filet mignon, bluddlefilth rare. Baked, blighted potato.

Leaving the restaurant, Brian and Rachel and their ghosts start back to their room. He walks with a loftiness she finds oddly amusing. Her walk is a verse of steps he adores:

She walks in beauty like the night,

Yeah, Yeah, Yeah.

On a pedestal of white marble, she waited for him. Her inanimate eyes fixing on the passionate pelagos of his heart.

O pallid bust of Pallas, source of my source, guide me on my travels, for I am lost in the memory of many lives.

Take the snotgreen sea of carpet to the flamming corridor of dreams, whirl yourself, like Aeolus on speed, past monster and the stench of chlorine, there, you will find, somewhere on this meager side of paradise, foamy tenseven, where nymphs and satyrs copulate.

Still fled he forward, looking back still. What does he see? The answer: Malbecco seeth glass Hellenores everywhere. Veritable unholy apparitions constructed of undiffused light that he can't seem to escape. Fear buile! But histologically, molecularly, socially, and deeper, he's more than a oneeyed, hooknosed voyeur, sometimes potatopocketed secular saint; he's the chief of all his tribe, a bluesoxclockolder, sperm whale of a man, spilling his copious seed in the belly of his callused hand.

He walks a stony path to her heart, vowing to climb the mountain which is her soul later. *Whatsoever parteth ... hoofbeats in the solarium.* When bovine Brian stumbles, she whets her knives.

"You're such a clod," she kinched.

"I'm a good ballplayer," he defended jejunely.

"I'm a good ballplayer," she mimicked nasally.

Apologise, O, if not ...

"I find love to be clumsy emotion," he offered, *no takers*, looking down at his smart tan Rockports.

"We're here," she crowed, setteclesian dubhdoor recalled, dimly.

The keys to. A way a lone a last loved a long the

Standing an instant from the bliss promised to them by the loin-inspired pennings of a madman (*Dearest Rachel, Forget Platonic love! It's a scam. Because when my engorgan does finally implode within your diminutive cavern of joy, it will, in a burst of light and love, fuse our long separated souls*), these modern pagans pause, almost reverently, as if preparing to enter a cathedral.

Rachel smiled when she noticed her ursine companion unexpectedly frowning.

"What?" she asked, sensing something amiss.

"The keys are in there," he answered, pointing to the door.

"OK! Let's just go back to the lobby and ask for a duplicate."

Behind the marble counter in the lobby, the night manager, a caramel-colored man with an island accent, corrected vision, and a knowing manner (the telepathy of poets), tosses our hero a duplicate key without much inquisition. "*Catchitmon!*"

We can say nothing but what hath been said. Our poets steal from Homer ...

Back in their room, no time at all appears to pass before the speed of light couple are unclothed and frantically falling into each other's arms. Soon we hear the drone of intercourse: Essere o non essere essere o non essere essere o non essere essere o non essere essere o non essere ...

In truth, it is a melancholy whisper of a maddening proposition, but exponentially more maddening is the ceaseless, soundless Cartesian voice traveling through space and time on the reticent rocket we call our innermost self.

Blooming anemone emits a sweet scent and even a sweeter sound from winedark lips. O! the world hath not a sweeter creature; she might lie by an emperor's side and command him tasks. But, alas, a Spenserian stream of nectambrosia refused to flow into his imperial bed. On her white breast she wore a sparking ankh, he kissed it adoringly. Put me on earth again, and I would rather be a serf in the house of a landless man ... than king (of all these dead men that have done with life).

"Shamie," she screamed softly.

"What, Rachel?" he needlessly asked, somewhat bothered by the fact she had called him by his secret name.

Dispatch from the Freeman's Journal 6-19-1988

Spring Lake, New Jersey—In a private ceremony, here, on Sunday, Princess Rachel Scota Neal, the only direct descendant of Niall of the Nine Hostages (and whispered to be a distant cousin—on her Yiddisher momma's side—to that miracle worker with wood—Josh ben Joseph), married Irish American Gangster Brian William Seamus Jordan. The marriage, however, was quickly annulled when the Bride learned (details to come) that her erstwhile husband had been victimized by self-incest on their wedding day (he apparently used the mini- penknife on his keychain to bore a passage through the right hip pocket of his pants in order to have—romantically speaking—a honeymoon in the hand).

Docket No. 88-1222-310

Interrogatories

re annulment proceedings

1.   List the name of the last sexual partner with whom you reached climax.

Mlle La Main.

2.   Were you at least thinking of moi?

Relatively speaking. But I shall try to come to that later.

I now unpronounce you man and wife of mikveh baths. Chapel bells unring. Rice returns to throwers' hands. The Maid of Honor degenerates into a diseased prostitute with the Best Man as her only paying client; the Bride enters a nunnery; the Groom fights a fatal duel with annulled Brother-in-Law. Thus proving Plato wrong when he declared: The Past is immutable.

"Rachel," he cried timidly, realizing he was beginning to fail her.

"What?"

"I take a long time getting started," he began, "and an even longer time finishing. Does it bother you?"

"Well," she exclaimed, "it's different."

Diffident dicked. Less man, more Pan. *Hwaenne* secret secretions seep out of the dells of desire:

Never turn over, I hear.

Never turn over, my dear.

For a really lot of hell will break loose,

If you let him stick it in your caboose.

So I say—olé!

Olé—So I say!

Her brother, my catamite.

Her brother, my catamite.

Sexual intercourse between them ends quietly (zero panting).

This is the way the world ends

Not with a bang but a whimper.

13

I whimpered her! Whimpered her real good. And in the name of the other scions of heaven such as Achilles, Fionn Mac Cumhaill, Beowulf et al., I, Whimpering Willy, alias Bill Bang, gave one of the prized daughters of man (previously Pharaoh's daughter) a good you know what!

In a state of quasi-reality, the defeated Brian plucked himself from the mattress-planted Rachel, and without hesitation sonorously intoned,

"I promise it will be better next time."

"It was fine," she exhaled, lying through her fine white teeth.

He wanted to kiss her for her manifestly kind prevarication, but feared such a gesture might escalate into dreaded intercourse,

Liaress to sexual lie: When that vaguely handsome, six-twoish, nix Jewish, two hundred twenty pound leucodermic god (of course a Jewish American Princess has a very low standard of apotheosis) fucks me (not obscene because I love him), he's announcing with each pelvic thrust that he owns every inch (62" horizontally) of my body.

Sexual lie to liaress: A lump of organized matter that impedes access to your soul.

Liaress to sexual lie: A woman's sexual engine is fueled by the libidinous gasoline of animal magnetism, and not, as you latent faigelehs think, by the fluid words of a water-logged poet.

"Thank you," he replied belatedly. "You know how much I need to know that I'm good enough for you."

"I never said you were good enough for me," she a kidling kidded. "So why are you thanking me?"

"I'm thanking you for tolerating me. Thank you. Thank you. Thank you."

"One thank you will suffice, thank you very much."

"Rachel, an eternity of thanking you wouldn't suffice. You know why?"

"Why?"

"I shall keep my words to a minimum."

"Sure."

Brian playfully surrounded Rachel, his huge arms draped over

14

her like fond restraints. "On that fleshly stage of Eros known as physical love, I play an impotent Paris to your hapless Helen ... all right a tepid Blazes to your Molten Molly."

Rachel smiled at the effusive Brian. "Molten Molly?" she asked with a less than affable voice.

"Euphonious, don't you think?"

"Shut up and kiss me," Rachel demanded in a quiet Chandlerese.

I'll kiss her a dead awakening kiss, draw her soul through her lips, mingle it with mine, and thereby unite our souls in space and spit.

After his determined lips had made their way across the perfidious terrain of her fuchsia-colored mouth, and after their gladiatorial tongues had met and clashed in the Gallic arena, Brian's libido looked south, and for an eternal moment he gave her to hold in her fiery fist the trembling tongue of his passion.

What is this thing exhibiting such a Faustian hold on men? Multiple choice (A) circle of Judas (B) piece of heaven (C) peehole (D) most precious square of sense ...

"Kissing—more than anything else—connects two souls," he said, speaking first, as was his habit.

He who speaks first loses! exclaimed the ad canvasser in him, after the fact.

"I guess so," she granted stolidly as she cleverly inched her way out of Brian's passionate snare.

"It is not like you to mince."

"You stopped."

Brian sat up and rested his dark-haired head against a dark wild purporting to be a headboard. A bemused Rachel embedded her gellerish head in his barreltone chest.All and all , as comfortable a pillow as the one Othello had used to smother Desdemona.

Kill me tomorrow, let me live tonight. Bore me to death tomorrow.

"We have kissed kingdoms away," Brian proclaimed cheerfully.

"In our past lives perhaps," she conjectured in between a yawn.

"I have seen slaves riding on horseback," he pedantically shouted. "While princes walked on the ground like slaves … to quote a great king."

"King Arthur," she foolishly guessed.

"No," he corrected. "Solomon ben David."

CHAPTER 2

When faux Boylan awoke the next morning it was not to vociferous sunlight but whispering darkness. And although she had vacated his bed hours before the moon's argent coin had been spent by the prodigal night, it was only now, his cheeks damp with sorrow, that he remembered the prophetic words of the noblest African of them all:

Hinc illae lacrimae.

Those tears of the sky for the loss of the sun. Which means: alldarkhidden: the only light continuing to shine is the blue memory of heaven blazing in god's eyes.

Who cut down the heaventree of stars

in mid-eternity?

She's to blame.

Her body the ax handle, her eyes the blade.

Which brings us to the esseric consideration

of existing in a universe as obscure

as God's heart.

God's heart is a rose with a bloody thorn.

Drip.

    Drip.

        Drip.

It's a long way to nullus locus.

My coil unravels. Yours. Ours.

One spool at a time!

saith the grandsire of all

the living and dead mattering.

Irish Nobodaddy?

Cad?

Tat tvam asi: Who sees all things

and hears all things.

I'm sorry, son. I wasn't listening.

What do I do without her?

'Tis Pity She's a Whore.

All harlots were virgins once.

Vergine madre, figlia di tuo figlio.

I recognize a metalogical statement

of truth even though I'm only polygnostic.

Are you calling me a pangnost?

Boylan, a false man, begotten by a false god in a lachrymal dream, died the death of a waking mind. Which allowed Jordan, the forsaken spirit, to resume his quondam life by donning the decedent's discarded skin. Complicated? Confusing? Or just a case of gangster metempsychosis?

God!

Cad?

The void is showing.

The rainbow comes and goes.

Let me see.

Jordan closed his eyes before aiming them at the white telephone on the cherrywood night table.

Did she call?

I'm not your answering service, boyeen.

I fear she didn't.

Man is fear.

God is a concept.

Marxist–Lennonist.

Gaseous vertebrate.

Nobo?

Yes, my love.

I thought I heard you boom

a nova fiat during the dried up
consciousness of halfdeath, did you?
I didn't. But, for you, Brianeen,
I'll rewind Time, and, like
the old days, croak one out.
Go raibh maith agat.
Let there be a red flashing light!

Feasting on the blob of light, Jordan picked up the phone and called the front desk.

"This is ten seven. You have a message for me?"

"Hold on," exclaimed a marginally male voice.

Life is a message scribbledehobbled in the dark. Who else could it be? She's a light, a glory, a fair luminous cloud enveloping Tir na Brian. How did it start? It always begins the same way : in a mist. Or in something that rhymes with mist. Marcel produced a woman from his own thigh. I also followed scripture: Behold, there ariseth a little néal out of my scumsilted hand. Kings play with themselves the same as bondsmen. When the viscous star goes forth in heaven, I wield the sword of Blake's Angel King.

"Mr. Boylan, I'm sorry for the delay. A Mr. Frank Dentelupo phoned at Seven, requesting you call him at your earliest convenience. He said you would know where to reach him."

"Thank you," Jordan said, slamming the phone down. Monday morning. Another day, another drachma to be made. Guinea Sisyphus wants me to help him push the rock. How did he find me? Knows my alias. Apt name for a concupiscent. *Nullius filius* found me amidst the nothingness of n.l. Roused me from blackbed of darkdeath. Good for him.

Jordan rushed into the bathroom. His thoughts read like a poem: alliterative, assonant, a symphony of verbal music, as he stood over the edge of a makeshift Aegean. Cries of drowned men. All these. He kicked the toilet seat up with his left foot, liberated his foolish thing, and felt as if he would never stop pissing. The chartreuse stream amused him so much that he punctuated it with a fart. A few moments later, he dialed Hades.

"May I help you?"

"Frank."

"Bry? Where you at?"

"The hotel."

"Is Rachel—"

"She went home to Rick."

"I'm sorry, Bry."

"It drives me crazy, Frank. Waiting for her to decide, I mean. I think she's ready to leave him."

"She will. Fuck! Diane is on hold. Can you—"

"Sure."

As Jordan awaited Dentelupo's return to the line, he played with the silver cross dangling from his left ear. The Celts certainly have it in wonderful measure. They look better dying than most do living. I'd rather be a dead Celt than a live Anglo-Saxon. Jordan cleared his throat and intoned:

> The Great Gents of England
>
> Are the men God made sexually inferior;
>
> For all their wives are beautiful,
>
> And yet they still prefer a boy's posterior.

Am I part? No. God no! I'm pure Gael except for a Norman eponym. Not a drop of the murky Thames in the MacSuirtáin. If she only could love me. Multiple choice. Not that again, Brian. Percy Bysshe gave up his quest to roam the female soul. The filthy John was instead content to cause Dottore Polidori to quelph in dark Italian selvi. Perhaps they took turns making one another exclaim? Should I bugger a boy? Or should a boy bugger me? He was supposedly straight. Heterosexual Englishman is a contradiction in terms. A convert to the one true faith, as Tyrone père called it. I say Catholics are born, not made. Like any good sinning Catholic, I feel the winds of hell blowing me towards the bright abyss. For once you feel his fiery breath in your ear, you are spiritually doomed. Yet all is not lost, boyo, because you are materialistically saved. Languishing on this plastic rood, I wonder if I am goniff one or goniff two? I am certainly not the anointed one. When on marathon calls to

Rachel, I always think: Am I talking into eternity along the Jersey Shore? Nobo, why have you forsaken me? Frank, you fucking hobbit. What's taking you? The old hag must be pulverizing his pistachios. He fucks her in the ass. Like an Eskimo, he offers her to his friends. No takers. Women have become as sexually adventurous as their late sister Regina Pasiphaë. I'm your white bull, Rachel. Alas, one with a s.d. I'm centimetering closer to the abyss. It smells like cuntstink or a whiff of Rachel's perfume. I can't decide which? It's glowing like a cunt. Who said it had to be a black adiaphane? Nothing might be Sahara sunny. You know what they say? Too much sunshine makes a desert. The porchists declared nothing passes unexplained. They spoke of an active force which is everywhere coexistent with matter. Were they speaking of energy? They're equivalents, mutually convertible according to Einstein. Alright, you've told me about something. Now I want to know everything about nothing! Some will say I already do. We'll all know soon enough, won't we? Or perhaps this call will last the eternity? Where is that microcosm of humanity? Literal ewescrewer!

"Bry?"

"I'm here."

"Sorry about the wait."

"That's alright. How's Di?"

"I'd like to shoot her in the twat!"

"By what you say, Frank, it wouldn't take a marksman to hit that target."

"As easy as hitting Fat Joe in the ass."

The partners convulsed in protracted, high-pitched laughter.

"We're too tough on her," Jordan offered, somewhat composed.

"The fuck we are! No good fuckin' bitch scratched my face to pieces last night," Dentelupo replied.

"Why?"

"Calls on our bill to Alison. Di thinks I'm fuckin' her."

"You are trying, aren't you?"

"That's not the point. Whose side are you on?"

"Do you have to ask? Why the call? A problem in the office?

How the fuck did you find me?"

"Everything's alright. Hundsheim wants a meeting."

"What? To zign zome papeers?"

"Yeah. Nazi bastard! Told him you were taking the day off. He said: Yunior von't mindt."

"At his office, Frank?"

"No, Bry. He wants to have lunch and discuss a few things."

"Where?"

"Klitzer's at One."

"Kitzler's, Frank."

"Yeah, that Kraut place in the Highlands."

"Tell him Two-thirty. I have to catch our friend at his ristorante."

"Rocky? Tell him we need—"

"Not on the phone," Jordan interrupted.

"You're right."

"You never told me how you found me, you sneaky fuck."

"Carrick told me you were planning on staying in Ocean City. I know your alias, so I called around until I found you. You really should stay in touch, Bry."

"I've got to change my alias."

"Should I meet you at the restaurant?"

"No. I'll drop by the office. Don't ever shave!"

Jordan began mentally composing an itinerary for this 20th day of June 1988. Sustenance first. But what did he want to eat? He called room service and ordered white toast, a pot of coffee, and orange juice. Paid in cash. Twenty dollars, tip included. He pulled the arid toast apart and fed himself bits of it. A birdman like Thoth. I hear the soaring parole of a similar creature: Knowledge is a ravenous bird feeding on the soul. Jordan smiled Irishly. I hope mine tastes better than this burnt offering. It was meant for a really, really cool false pseudogod. No pseudogod at all! Since two negatives equal a positive. He raised his cup to his svelte but shapely lips. I drink the milk of madderness. The coffee made him thirsty. Orange juice slaked his thirst. He felt a loosening of his bowels. Charging into the bathroom, he lowered the toilet seat, dropped his underwear, and promptly sat down. A sound not dissimilar to the discharge of a musket caused his head to jerk forward prior to the noisome exiting of the transmogrified meals of the past weekend. One's filth smells sweet to oneself, if one is of that touchy race of cloacal obsessed poets. I am not. Swoosh! I hear waves battering a skiff. The last curragh! Not the last unless this was the final disgusting launch. Like a god, I could've fished it out of the Great Ouse. Eat brown fish and your teeth will be stained for eternity. Jordan cackled, his smug expression turning pained, as he felt, heard, and smelled another discharge of his bowels. Headline: Balaklava: Russian General Brian Brennusovitch was shot dead today while squatting to defecate. The Irish proverb goes: If you shit like a wild goose, you're liable to be shot by one. Jordan dethroned and vigorously wiped himself. Enough paper to wipe a Cyclops' arse. He tossed the paper into the bowl and flushed it away to a familiar voice chanting:

Me cago en Ernesto!

Farewell you Carribean Mariner!

Your shit looks like brown elephants!

Jordan put his yesterday clothes in a large department store bag. His today clothes had been purchased yesterday in the Mall. He carried the bag with him as he set out in search of a mislaid volume of Proust— also purchased yesterday in the Mall. As his size elevens traversed Hades, the bright galaxy of mirrors—like the stellic eyes of God—visually echoed the molecular movements of a lonely thirty-five year old male with Bressantly styled cokedark hair and a dangling argency. He finally located the aforesaid volume at the bottom of a trash pail brimming with discarded packaging. Jordan stuck his nose in the bag. The smell and taste of things remained. A medley of scents, one of which, is hers. His tongue swept his lips in vain for a taste of his Basherter. Expunged from the labial record by Crest. He opened the creaky top drawer of the night table and stuck the volume of Proust alongside the Gideon. Stretched out on the bed, he shut his eyes. Looking through the window of sound, he saw her departing words blossom into a rosebush. I think I love you but I will never leave him. Jordan wept. My ballonish head deflated by a diadem fashioned out of thorny branches. My heart like a flame turned upside down. He went into the bathroom, made a substantial withdrawal from the tissue box, and blew his nose. Stepping back from the glass, he appraised his appearance. His silver skin laced with his golden blood. I should have brought my Braun. I nearly beheaded myself with those crappy razors bought in the gift shop. He wet a towel and washed away the necklace of coagulated blood. A decapitated saint lugging around his head while preaching the logos of J. It's snowing in the devil's stomach. I first met you on the street of stars. That place where life is not flattened into three dimensions.

CHAPTER 3

He pushed open the lobby door and advanced into the haze. Staring at the ensellure of the steaming bitch, he cackled. Her scoliotic, tessellated back held no attraction for his traveling eyes. Turn, turn around, let me see your most precious sensate square. Turning, turning around, the whore Dana (anagrammatically revealing according to Jorge Berkeley), scented by the brilliant beds of useless loveliness throughout the courtyard, showed him her nest of spicery. Uninterested, he looked away and continued, like the ultimate drop of hemowine being drained from the sacred chalice by thirsty Eternity, on his descent, his downward spiral to nothing. Down, down the sensual slope of the severed throat of the universe, also known as Eccles Street, he went. From anear he saw his car: its eurhythmy pleased him. He kicked its right front tire with the force of Dr. Johnson's refuting foot.

"I have seen bondsmen driving Vets, while princes waited for the bus," he intoned in a foppish British accent that made him laugh uncontrollably.

Composing himself, he unlocked his car and sat behind the wheel. Her lips suck forth a buck in change, a 1974 Impala ignition key, lots of lint, and three bent paper clips. His fiberglass chariot ready to take him over burning hillocks, out of order omphalos, obdurate heart, to the milkingplace. Right teat out. Left teat too. Powdered milk again, for the boyo! The whore halfloves and halfhates her sonlover in the thirty thousand dollar machine. 'Tis a pity he's a whoreson! All harlots' sons will be virgins' sons again.

The engine exclaims and he's off. Swarming highway, a highway gorged with dream, where motorists are accosted by ghosts. Even when she walks she seems to dance. My pale tears redden. Fuck her! My thoughts gnaw at the heart of life. Fuck the French Greek style! The windshield bombarded by dark reflections of the Veggie World, a high-speed Rorschach test (I see a cunt, nother cunt, nother...), as he parkwayed to riverine Ithaca. Halfloved, halfhated, at halftime, equals what? Allloved but totally despised? Launched from eternal circumstances, with the secrets of God in his eyes, he a blinking-star blinked. Voyaging heedlessly beyond the stifling bounds of possibility to the splendid corridors of impossibility. The impossible made possible to God or an ad canvasser. Fractal patterns. Everywhere. Other moutains visible in the mountain. (The one he vows to climb someday!) Man is a fractal pattern of Frost's awful God! The latter's DNA found at the primal crime scene. Ad canvassers are fractal patterns of man. And yet, often they stroll down splendid corridors. Hello Mr. Mooch? Yes? Give me some money for a useless—that word again—ad. Alright. How much? Same as always. By the by, your secretary has a nice voice. May I fuck her? Why not? Thank you, Mr. M. Don't mention it. And, by the way, she likes it up the culo when she does coke. That's great! My dick is shy around vaginas. I had heard that.

Halfloved, halfhated, with only black foam laid out to meet him, Jordan drove away from the latitude of his brilliant failure. Would he find the theoretical borne on the other side of a scrotumtightening sea of troubles? He daringly approached it many times, as he bodkineth through traffic in a conceited attempt to negate spatial-temporal considerations. Godlike in his sportscar, heading Erewhon fast, weary and scornful of the grass and trees lining life, he shut his eyes: a moment of black heaven ensued. Opening them, the ride to nowhere continued. Milemarker upon milemarker, filthy green blur upon filthy green blur, the eidetic torture increased until the trip began to resemble a verdic nightmare. One subtle turn of the wheel and the horrible pain of life might be terminated. Pusillanimous, the unbravest d'Exeter of them all. *Le bheith nó gan bheith.* He stopped to render a realmic coin to an outstretched palm. Thank you! And onward he drove in his speedy red machine. A cuntcatcher going zero to sixty in seven seconds. A loss of a second due to the drag on the engine caused by maxing the air. Since he hated life, why not squander time? Slide in a tape. Relax, man. The Furs reminding him why he hated life:

> The ghost in you
>
> She don't fade…

Your ears devour the food that increases your hunger. Stop listening, Brian.

British accented sons of Ormonde. Shining servants. Wild geese. Hating their gall tir by using smack, he hating his by selling shite. Keyes to the kingdom in his briefcase. Rocky Ferro, Mafioso poseur, ordered due chili. If he doesn't pay, he'll stick his greasy, meatballish head in a pizza oven.

> She don't fade…
> The ghost in you
> She don't fade
> Don't fade…
> fade…

Jordan emerged from the träumenwelt of the G.S.P. and drove to Ferro's on Route 37 in Toms River. With the word heaven being repeatedly sung, he parked next to Rocky Ferro's 500 E. O.G.M. His grandfather was a M.D. who came here after the Great War. His father practices law in town. Why this? Lowest thing you can do. Brags of a nefarious nexus. I tell him I'm IRA.Para-military beats crime family. Jordan knew in business dealings with the mob the seller loses. They either turn you into compost for your product; refuse to pay the set price; Sicilian you down; or pay you half on delivery with a promise to pay you the rest when they move the groove. Either way you get a sore posterior orifice. He didn't see the compost scenario taking place. Latta would have been a more appropriate metallurgical surname for Rocky. He's a greaseball. They cheat, steal, lie. Thus Jordan swaggered into Ferro's garlicky nest wary of guineary. They'd step over their morte mammas to assfuck their mezza morte sisters.Up your ass their recurring malediction. He tightly gripped the Agenbite of Inwit in his left hand, sighing, as he crossed the narrow bridge of green outdoor carpet dividing a cortile loud with lunching Riverians. The poetry of knife and fork rang out in stereo. The scent of aglio, as anticipated, dominated the courtyard. Not even the rich perfume of freshly cut flowers adorning the tables could erase the tribal odor of his tribe's ancient old enemy. Vercingetorix abú! He frowned as the door mysteriously opened. Voidward! Who were those Martians? Thankfully, he didn't recognize a skin. Witnesses to a crime in progress. Miniature humans to his Lemuelly self.

Jordan approached a young woman posted, like a sentry, at the entrance of the dining room. Fauxly smiling, an overbite made her otherwise pretty face seem horsey. Jordan returned the phony smile. White dress clinging to troublesome geometry. The rings of Venus around her neck, signature of promiscuity according to the promiscuous Romans. Disqualified a girl from entering the Vestal sisterhood.

"I'm Bry Jordan. Tell Rocky I'm here."

Without hesitating, the hostess picked up the phone resting on a stand a few inches north-east of her haute heels. Turning charmingly on said heels as she talked on the phone.

Mr. Ferro asked if you could wait for him at the restaurant's brown orifice. He'll be out in a few minutes.

She didn't exactly say that. I hear you, babe. What did you say? *I said take a gander at this.* The hostess bent over, lifted her dress, exposed her bare ass. Pseudoblebsia like Jacob's ladder. None of this is really taking place. Yet the reality of experience is all that matters! With proctological aplomb, the hostess spreads her ass cheeks.

–Winedark lips! Creepycrawling over huh butt, where am I after? Satan's anus is the entrance to hell?

Jordan nodded and took off in the direction of the bar. He always seemed to be walking to some fucking bar! Why not? Bars are similar in configuration, color, disposition, etc., to that of a puckered anus. Very bardic, very skaldic description. Jordan could smell that the bar had been recently revarnished. Shitstained like the nastiest bum in the universe!

On his way to the bar, its lips curling in a brownish lie, he stopped. Perfidious lips waiting, Jordan's creaky tan shoes continued barward. Moments later, he glimpsed Rocky's father sitting at a table—breaking pane, wind, laws—with three men in expensive suits. One suit: tastefully British; the other two: Italic flashy. Ferroflab undulating beneath a sheer, powder blue shirt, as he assaulted a piece of ultra-tough veal. The specialty of the house. Scarpa Parmigian. Quanto devo pagare? Dodici Americani. Va bene! Jordan recognized the gentleman sitting directly to the right of Ferro père as Superior Court Judge Mark Kernow. A fine fellow. Someone who had sponsored parvenu Jordan into a very exclusive Country Club. (In return, Jordan retained his wife, then girlfriend, Joanna, as his decorator.) But someone who had—in theory—

become—with the enlisted aid of Jordan—a monster. Obviously, the monsterization had failed. The Judge looked fit, tan, happy. The other two suitwearers were—at first—as dark to him as Poldy must've seemed to Ms MacDowell. Dark stranger she called him. Her surname means son of the dark stranger in Irish. Coincidentally, Rachel's late father's middle name was Doyle which is cognate with Dowell. I do know them! Java the Hut and his cousin. Why are they dressed up? They belong in guinea tees. Look at them. Their dirty eyes repulse me. Not a glint of light in their entire beings. As aphotic as the black olives crowning their salads. Darkness risible in their Armani suits. Fatso must be testifying locally. Or maybe he's back from a Convention. How can Kernow bear such table manners? Like a reptile, Ginese's tongue snaps up its prey: a slimey conveyor belt transporting a large percentage of the world's food supply to the interminable pit above his belt. Chubby hands pocketed in unison. Are they pulling themselves off into their fazzoletti? The cousin has one in tonight. Armbro Grease. Eunymic. I'd bet my cock that Ginese is the real owner. Fat fuck has stolen a zil from the Prick Benevolent Association.

Jordan halted, closed his eyes, and the video preplay of the seventh race of tonight's Meadowlands card projected on the dark innerside of his eyelids:

HN	PP	¼	½	¾	St	Fin		
7 Armbro Grease	7	1	1	1	1^{10}	1^{10}		1:54
								10/00

Fat G. and (if possible) his fatter cugino jumping up and down in the kelly-green carpeted Winner's Circle. Jackie Mo being congratulated by them for an excellent steering. Wait. Mo bought an eight ball Satsun in the Club. Sorry, fat boys. Mo never wins a race after a coke binge. The preplay replayed. Different results:

HN	PP	¼	½	¾	St	Fin		
7 Armbro Grease	7	7	7	7	7^{10}	?		1:56
								3/00

Not always the shining seven! Maybe I should hook her on gambling. That way Rick wouldn't be able to afford her. Jordan's nose trickled blood. He pulled out a crumpled handkerchief from his shirt pocket and raised it to his nose. The ichor escaping the white grasp of linen fell to the rug in red silence.

A different Ferro's since my last alkaloid delivery. I gave him her number. Gone were the chromatic echoes of Garibaldi's flag. Instead, seafoam blue surged throughout the restaurant like the booming Aegean. Jordan's mouth twisted in anger. Fucko owes me thousands and fucking redecorates this brown elephant! How can he dis his H.E. like that?

JORDAN DENTELUPO & ASSOCIATES, P.C.

HEDONIC ENGINEERS

HUXLEY CENTER BLDG 34

777 STELLI STREET

KEYPORT, NJ 07735

908-888-COKE

PRES., BRIAN W.S. JORDAN

The Incas revered their supplier. Ferro's no Inca (although he's short, squat, and swarthy). They believed coke casts a magical shadow on the mind (the shadow of the Inca's soul). Fucking cokeheads! No wonder why they lost their empire. Guineas lost theirs because they imbibed vino from plumbum cups. And, of course, their obsession for building roads didn't help. The fact that all roads led to Nova Sodom fucked them in the arse. The Conquistadors must not have thought very much of the Inca's soul. The scion of the sun, emperor God. They hanged him in his sacred citadel. My kind of town, Machu Picchu is. Nothing godly about groove. It blocks the reuptake of the neurotransmitter dopamine in midbrain. Rise up, Race of Cain, and cast God down onto earth. Call him the son of man and let him forage in the wilderness like a wolf. Or perhaps he'll become a spiritual restauranteur and attempt to feed the infinity we all bear within. And in his second advent, let him try ad canvassing and drug pushing. Thou shalt not push drugs! Assonant, yes, but not something found in the decalogue. As long as I tithe, it's alright. I estimate I owe the Church 200 large. Did give my local parish a grand during Christmas. Tuism: thoughts intended for a second, or other, self. Let him pay the other 199,000. I'm Nobody! Who are you? I'm Nobody too! May you live all the days of your life. And the same to you, sirrah.

The fuchsia-colored synthetic lips of the bar served as a mnemonic of what? Don't answer. Never say. Jordan bellied up to the not so dark wood, placing his briefcase on the chrome-legged stool behind him. An accidental elbowing of the Agenbite of Inwit caused it to wobble. The sands on which my fortune and castle rests shift and sink like a Dantesque hellscape. Heavenscape, perhaps? For there is nothing either good or bad, but thinking makes it so. White gold. White guilt. White shite! Agenbuyer. Agenseller. The wallpaper pattern—a galaxy of iced-blue metaforms—seemed too New Age for a ristorante. Joanna's doing. Jordan resolved that Ferro also had—in theory—assisted in turning Kernow into a monster.

Never turn over, Jo-Jo-Jo-Jo-anna,

When in the vicin of a Nappy's banana...

The Counselor, an ethnocentric friend of Jordan's family, used to warn: Beware of the Neapolitans. They're Greeker than the Greeks! After all, Naples was founded by the Spartans.

Beads of sweat formed on his forehead. Ice-blue. Fractals. He wiped them away with a napkin appropriated from a midnight blue plastic tray on the bar. He unclipped the stainless steel Cross pen from the bright green t-shirt underneath his baggy, olive-green, made-in-India, disappointed shirt. With fiery quickness, he appropriated another napkin, and in a fine, neat hand inked a rocketing by thought upon a remote ancestor of un selva oscura.

The artist reveals the secret laws of nature in order to create beauty. He instantly despised the blue child of his brain affixed to the makeshift page. Epigrams: the refuse of literature. He crumpled the napkin and threw up a three-pointer. Jordan shoots! He saw his shot fall short of the garbage pail. Hoofleather gliding over a throwaway. Relate beauty. Art is relating. The Giocondic smile of a certain faccia brutta. The hellenising of the sow that eats her own farrow. Why as a woodcock to my own springe. Smeller of rot unfold yourself! Eat a crocodile and wash it down with vinegar.

Jordan's upcast eyes, jealous gems, tracked the ascent of the geometric curiosities forming the restaurant's firmament. Metaforms, Mountjoy. Metaforms! Heaventreely magnif. Or as the duck of Stratford would quack:

The bejewelled vault of the gods!

The soul is a metaform! That too sounds very quacky. Two dimensions appearing like three. If I gaze at them long enough will they transport me to the *sráid na réaltaí*? Suppose it's the abyss that I'm staring at? Doesn't the abyss—with the unblinking eyes of a German shepherd—stare back?

Jordan blinked. Continuity broken. I need a drink. Jamie neat chased by a cold one. He massaged his eyeballs with the thumb and forefinger of his left hand. I should've done a line or two in the hotel. How many lines did I do yesterday? My memory and my eloquence are not their best today, never use herculanita and rum. En attendant Guinea. Wop! Dago! Cokewhore Joanna. Is she around? Did coke with me on Groundhog Day. What college did she tell me she attended? Slippery Rock State College? Studied literature under Edward A. Kopper, Jr. Ph.D. How she became a decorator is absolutely anecdotal. Jordan smiled at seeing a postmodern portrait of Sinatra hanging exactly where a conventional one had once hung. The singer's eyes purging thick amber and plum-tree gum. The air in here smells of faults. Joanna and Rachel believe in Tarot cards, captromancy, past life regression. Joanna believes in nothing. She's a liar. One day she told me her father's a MD, the next, that he owns a carpet warehouse. Felt like asking the stupid cunt: What is he *un tappeto dottore*? Joyceday I fucked her repeatedly. My ejaculations were as colorless as her bloodless heart. When I finally fully fuck Rachel, my ejaculations will be red orange yellow green blue indigo-violet. We'll light up the sky with a come rainbow.

Jordan ordered a glass of cranberry juice from a barmaid wearing tight black shorts and a white top. Somatic critique: Stallion legs, silicone breasts, platinum excrements. Spiritual critique: a pseudo-übersoul. Overall: Just the trannie next door. An eonist like Willie Hughes. Why not? Aren't you a de Vere of shreds and patches? All I can say is life ran very high in those days. When Jordan allowed the barmaid to keep the change from a twenty, her tenebrous mouth brightened. How do you make a whore moan? Don't pay her! The Chairman of the board's fucked up eyes grooving on her mesial groove. Drinking, grinning, Jordan admired Sinatra's wall companion: a severed horse's head donning a Yankee cap. The fosh of Di Magge. Clamn dever. Jordan strained his eyes to read the pinxits. Pietro Amillo. A modern day Wop with imagination. At least there's no *l'ultima cena*, modern or postmodern, haunting us with a beacon of Gisic eyes. Rocky Ferro tapped Jordan on the shoulder. The men hugged like brother gangsters.

"I see you brought the papers," Ferro said, winking at Jordan's black leather briefcase.

Jordan smiled boyishly. They were the same age but Ferro's furrowed face made him appear much older.

"This is my oldest friend, Toni," Ferro announced to the barmaid. "Never take his money."

Toni made a motion to return Jordan's twenty but he waved it away. Ferro inspected Jordan's glass.

"What the hell are you drinking?"

"Cranberry juice."

"Have a real drink."

They clepe us. Fuck them! Fuck you! The barmaid departed for another barstander. He's been to the Club, I think. Who is he? Might be a Narc that's onto Ferro. Or maybe he's here to help Rocky kill me. Ferro. Fuck him! The big queer is cuntocentric—culocentric, to be precise. Take your eyes off her fat ass and tell me who's watching us. Watching me, really. Should I say something? Is he in love with her? Seems a cunt. A cunt without strickly having one. Asspussy, someone called it. Same someone who first called coke groove. After God, Shakespeare, Joyce, Monsieur Quelqu'un has created the most. She must be a woman. Maybe she had a penectomy or maybe hormones has rendered it a shrunken treasure to wet Ferro's mouth. Egad! *La ragazza del giacinto.* I must be wrong. I know him since we're kids.

"What a sweet ass," Ferro declared, as he ducked under an opening in the bar and crossed over to the other side, still harping on her ass.

Ferro picked up a bottle of whiskey and poured himself a shot. Striped Lifshitz strategically buttoned third from the top in order to better advertise a gold horn glittering amidst a black jungle of chest hair.

Ferro's thick mauve-colored lips animated in commands to speeding by waitresses. Tarquin and his plebes. The thud of molecules: waitresses through kitchen door, hinges discordant, aromas escape: a winedark wine sauce, clams drowned in marinara, foaming formaggio. Jordan desired the fiberglass cocoon of his car. Traveling the Constant, tape deck player turned all the freaking way up, the street of the stars just around the cornhole, there you feel free.

"I hate this place," Ferro admitted, downing a shot (his second): his mouth succumbing to the friendly fire of straight Jack.

"I hate everywhere," Jordan one-upped.

Ferro smiled, as he crossed back to the civilian side, hands laden with bottle and glasses. "Jack alright?"

Jordan nodded. Ferro poured a shot for both of them. They touched glasses and drank. Corno, short for cornhole. Cunto or culo irrelevant to the wearer of the horn. It proclaims he's a penetrator. Penis-traitor. Manroot of all evil. Pop. Don't get popped! Double entendre perhaps? Gold. So-called precious metal. A chuck of junk hanging from his simian neck and that makes him a man? The Christian device dangling from my ear, not a signature of Christianity, but of Irishity. There's a terrible smell to that word. Celticity, I mean.

> If it dangles from wrong ear
>
> It means that you are queer

I may be a Quare fellow but I'm not queer. Jordan checked his earring. Perhaps they've changed that. Toni bent over and Ferro elbowed Jordan. We all know, it would seem, about the ass that dare not speak its name.

"Let's go back to my office," Rocky said, stagely adding, "It will be easier to concentrate on the contract."

Jordan smiled at Ferro's contrivance: Why not consult his father who's a lawyer? Jordan sensed the barmaid knew their true business in the back. Fakes are always the hardest to fool. Jordan followed Ferro to his private office. Once inside, a bit of frivolity: Jordan crowed and Ferro hopped around in childish enthusiasm.

"Cocaine. Cocaine. Cocaine," Ferro sang, as he played air guitar. Still playing, he sat behind his desk and with an imperial gesture asked,

"What did you bring us?"

"Wine coolers," Jordan snapped.

"How much?"

"Rock."

"Alright," Ferro said, igniting a Marlboro with a gold lighter studded with colorful jewels.

Jordan shielded his eyes from its green sun. Mnemonic of what? In all their conquest, they never set sandal on my sireland. Belated conquest. Anxiety of Influence. We were a happy lot of heathens before Paddy Breathnach showed up with his magic stick. Ferro, let my people go! Jordan placed his briefcase on Ferro's desk, dialed its combination, shining sevens, and clanged it open. Ferro's pop-eyes popping out of darksome sockets at the sight of a white princess exposing her soul to him. The darkeyed foreigner with a swarthy anti-intellectual face jerking off as she sits there noseteasing. Ferro's expensive noserag added a blood stain.

"What is that, a tampon or a handkerchief, Rock?"

"The pitfalls of the trade," Ferro said, burying his handkerchief in his back pocket.

Jordan pensively ran his fingers through waves of cokedark hair. Now he'll try to Sicilian me down. Neapolitan me down. Guinea me down. Erect photographs of Ferro, wife, and their genes' recipient—Rocco Ferro III—looked out over the desk's red precipice, as if tempted by the floor. How many times had those framed similes been knocked over the red precipice as Ferro fucked—presumably doggy-style—one of his employees? Jordan inhaled Ferro's crooked smokes. He fanned them away with his right hand. Ferro smiled. He couldn't understand the misocapny of his colleague. Apotheosis or an attempt at incremental homicide? Theocidal maniacs. No matter how they try, they'll never get that bastard Dio boia. Who killed Christ? They did and blamed it on *gli ebrei*. I'm not worried. I'm not puba Christ, I'm the holy buttterfly. I count not moments but millennia!

"I know I owe you," Ferro said, ending the verbal moratorium. "Ten thousand, right?"

"Eleven. I loaned you a thousand in Atlantic City a couple of weeks ago."

You are still you. Not enough time has passed to say I loaned it to a different cannoli.

"That's a personal loan."

"What's the difference?"

"You're right. Business has really been slow."

Buyers are liars.

"I can wait for the thousand, Rocky. But Frank is adamant that you should settle up. So if you can give me the ten—"

"I knew it was Frank."

Telepathy of guineas.

"He's a brokester," Ferro said, with anger, adding, "The little shit wouldn't have a pot to piss in if—"

"Rock, calm down. I hate to press you but Frankie needs the money. I wouldn't mind my half either. I can wait. So give him his five and I'll let the rest dangle."

"Why doesn't Frankie come here and demand it. You know why? He hasn't got the cogliones."

"Are you going to pay or not? I'll just sell this shit," Jordan said, shutting his briefcase. "To someone else. You know I could sell if for twice what you're paying."

"You wouldn't have the security."

"What does that mean, Rocky?"

"Calm down, Bry. I'm not blaming you. It's that pompino partner of yours. He doesn't respect nothing."

"We're all partners now. And not just in the Club."

"Why don't you let me meet your supplier. I think they're extraterrestrials the way you talk."

"They are," Jordan emphasized. "Not the kind of people to fuck with. I'm not making anything off you. Really, I'm not!"

"Of course you are, Bry. But I don't begrudge that. You're taking a risk. What's that blowjob Frankie doing?"

"Rock, stop the *ad hominem* attacks. Pay me or don't? I'll take the ten thousand dollar lost and we can cease being in business together. I—I really don't want to exacerbate my ulcer."

Ferro scowling, snapped, "Do you want to end our Club relationship as well?"

"That's different. You, Frank, and I can remain partners in the Club."

"I never wanted him as a partner. He's my partner because he was yours. That's why!"

Beware of verderous guinea.

"Sicilian fuck has no class," Ferro grumbled.

"His parents are from Naples," Jordan informed.

"They're the worst kind of Sicilians," Ferro confessed, laughing.

"You're Neapolitan, right?"

"That's right," Ferro said, still laughing. "We're all hotheads," he added, grasping and shaking Jordan's hand.

"So you can wait for the ten?"

"I guess."

"*Grazie tanto, Signore Giordano.*"

If he calls me Bruno, I swear by St. Patrick that I'll double the price and kick him in his cunt. Poor Nolan. They burnt him like baccky, so Dio boia could enjoy a postprandial cigar.

"I really appreciate it, Bry. Last week Pete was ripped off in Asbury Park."

"What?"

"Some Mooley held him up in Fat Joe's parking lot."

"You believe him?"

"I have the family looking for the eggplant motherfucker and when they find him he'll wish he'd never been born. You know how LCN is when they find you?"

"I don't," Jordan said, as if he didn't believe Ferro. "I think Pete's scamming you."

"I'll find out," Ferro said. "And if he is," he paused, to rub out his cigarette in a crystal ashtray, "I'll crush him like an ant. He looks like an ant, doesn't he?"

"I suppose. What's the Italian for ant?"

"Mosca?"

"That's not it," Jordan said, "that means fly. Formica."

"Jesus! You're sure your name isn't really Giordano?"

"I'm cento percento Mick. Asbury fucking Park! What a cesspool."

"Bruce can shove it up his Jew ass."

"How much did Pete get ripped off?"

"Ten thousand."

"Jesus Christ! What the fuck is he doing in Asbury Park? He can't handle himself in Seaside Park. Frankie deals directly to Fat Joe. It's our territory. What was Pete doing in that shit hole?"

"He deals a few grams to a couple girls who dance there. One of them beeped him—"

"He was set up. Do I know her?"

"Rosa something. Italian. You and Frankie know her, Pete says."

"I know them all. She's actually a nice girl. I don't know why she'd deal with Petey? She really isn't into it."

"They all do it, Bry."

Shit. Frankie! He got his brother-in-law to hold up Pete. He'll fuck everything up!

"What did the guy look like?"

"They all look alike to me, Bry."

"Age, weight, the car he was driving?"

"He was a rubber head."

"Did he have an accent?"

"He was a Rastafarian."

"He's through."

"I should fire him from the Club."

"Don't. I just don't trust him dealing anymore."

"I'll take care of this, Bry."

"I think it's all coming to pieces, Rocky. You remember the

Town & Country bust?"

"Butch was stupid."

"It started the same way. One of his dealers were ripped off, but actually the police busted him and he agreed to wear a wire. How do you know—"

"I have an in at the P.O. Nothing's coming down. We're safe!"

"Pete's through. He can stay on at the bar."

"I think you're taking this worse than I am, Bry. It's my money."

Did Frank do this? No. Rosa wouldn't get involved. Watch everybody. Never trust a greaser.

"So you're taking care of it?"

"Bry, I told you my famiglia is taking care of it."

Gobshite. You might be in on it with Pete. No hold up. I'll talk to Fat Joe. He also might be in on it. There's an aglic stench to it.

"Alright. Let's get this over with, Rock. I'm late for a meeting with Hundsheim."

Ferro took down a DiMaggio lithograph hanging on the wall and revealed a safe. His thick fingers caressed the black dial. Blur on the way to Nirvana. Not as blurry for those of us with additional ocularity and the telepathy of ethnocentrics. 19 left, 41 right, 56 right. Pop! Ferro swung the safe open, pulled out a pistol, and with gunslinger ease shot Jordan in the Agen. Actually, he removed stacks of cash and handed them to Jordan. Ferro transferred most of the coke to the safe. He reached into a desk drawer and removed a box of baby laxative. Jordan stowed the cash away in his briefcase. Just say Reaganomics. Ice cream and tobacco kills more people than groove. Not the lowest thing, after all. We don't sell to kids, do we? Jordan recalled the lousy meal served to him last time he had dined here. Selling lousy Italian may be the worst thing you can do.

"Going to try it out for yourself," Jordan said, fingering the box of baby laxative.

"Best thing to cut it with. Do you want to do a few lines?"

"No. I'm trying to give it up."

Ferro laughed. "Do a few lines with me, Bry. Never better to do after a shot or two of Jack."

"I have to give that up as well. I'm starting a new policy: only whores and horses."

"That reminds me. Ginese has one in tonight that's a lock."

Jordan produced two new hundred dollar bills and tossed them on Ferro's desk.

"Put the bet in for me, Rock. Tell them I bet on their horse. Say hello to your father. Is he going to drive to the Meadowlands or bet it at Freehold?"

"Don't know yet. The horse is an Oil Burner."

"I hope he's not a money burner."

"You said it. I'll see you in the Club this weekend. I'll see if I can get you to reverse your new policy."

"So you'll have the cash?"

"No problem, Bry. I mean unless something drastically changes."

Ferro squeezed Jordan's outstretched hand. The brightest angel has fallen. Allbright, look like an innocent flower, but be the schlange under it. Ferro opened the door for Jordan, patting his apparitional back. It's snowing in the devil's heart. Zeta Reticuli, here I come!

CHAPTER 4

He navigated through a room of gray cubes and salesy voices thinking of the one waiting for him in Ithaca. A hand out to the skin-shrivelers. A cryptic message telling them: Point your misshapen phallic symbols to the popcorn firmament and greet the world with love and keep calling like merry fools. I need the bread, you whining fucks. Lynch them with its tangled chord—the Lucifer noose—and collect their bones in a mound.

His phosphorous hand mechanically managed another acknowledgement. An effete sign that they existed. Translated: I, Boylan, the white hand of Connacht, not one born of woman, wish you St Vitus' choreography on your face, drinks on me, for the metallic music you make after every sale, tintinnabulation, is the sweet jangling of coin in my pocket. And when my colorless heart, during those rare sunlit days of my soul, blossoms into a red rose, I, Boylan, now called Bloom, will sing you a song of thanks:

> The bells of Hell
>
> go ring a-ling a-ling
>
> for you but not for me

A salesman stood up.

"Bry," the salesman canorously called out from a glaucous meadow.

The straits of mesial groove. Subordinates always begrudge an override. I need to take a whiz. Popped a water pill when thou arose from temporary grave, didn't thou? Are you speaking to me? Je suis, Brustere. This is a gentile house. First thing you do, after a night out, is to pop a pisspill. The mirrors along the purple carpeted corridor of the hotel made you look brawny, Brian. Thin to win, my friend. Ingredients include Potassium and extracts of Buchu, Uva Ursi, Juniper. Parley sans sage too. Leaves of extracts trampled by grossbooted draymen rolling dullthudding barrels. Wonder if the water pill caused you to deflate last night amid coitus? What a big penis you have, grandma. Better to whimper you. I mean, bang you.

Derailed from his appointed course, he floated back to the sales area: eleven hundred celestial square feet that he felt stupidly attached to like some dumbwitted expatriate. Upon reaching the meadow gray cubicle, he switched his briefcase to his left hand.

"What," he exclaimed, awarding his right hand to the salesman.

"I need to borrow a hundred."

"For what?"

"My rent cleaned me out."

Don't neither nor him as the shishkabobbed courtier of Dumbmark would. Hamlet mac Hamlet, I am thy father's speranza. Cad?

"Alright," Jordan said, excavating five wrinkly twenties from his pocket.

The salesman grabbed the cash.

A coistrel who thinks he's a lordling. One of my spongy officers, his manners are that of a lakin. Called Tenny because he's (a) wellhung (b) owes everybody at least ten dollars (c) was a poetaster in his past life.

Thanks, Bry. I really appreciate it."

"I need a week from you. Don't let me down, Tenny."

The salesman nodded the tiny orb stuck to the sleek neck of an androgyne. Often halting, loitering, straying, delaying, returning, yet following no other way, the borrower sat down on a task chair in front of a desk littered with three-by-five cards and computer read outs.

*

Jordan locked himself in his office. It was a stupid cell with beige carpet and a Birnam wood desk. Execuchaired, he forgot all and remembered everything, rocking pensively, rocking. The resultant noise recalled the bawk of bats and the cries of gulls. The shabbiness of his surroundings dismayed him. He'd summon the decorator next week. The leggy, arsey decorator of his lonely Howth. What the fuck is a divan, anyway? He'd pay her with drug money. Reaching over to the Rolodex on his desk, he flipped to the letter P for Pompini. He had repeatedly fucked said decorator on the afternoon of the one hundred and sixth birthday of the exalted father. That cold, shadowy day warmed by her alien flesh. She had bought her client, in appreciation of his generosity (he willingly overpaid), a rare hard cover edition of Finnegans Wake. It looked spiffy in the maplewood bookcase in the den. Through the glass, greenly. His Howth complete. Drug money had purchased the waterfront manor, the gray Toms River standing in for the dark Liffey, a living quarters for servants with piney accents instead of brogues. A Fenian uprising in his pants that day. He has avoided her since that spermy February day (he came four times). That day he gave her back to Mark. (A judge, therefore, king of lawyers.) He knew them from the Club. The blotter's calendar had the eleventh circled as the lawyer's king's and decorator slut's wedding day. He'd forget her. In fact, he easily forgot her. Rachel, he'd never ever forget. Alcohol, cocaine, and other brain cell killing pursuits, turned out to be inverse nepenthes for him. Most nights, he'd lean up against some bar, morbidly intoxicated, his dream gray gaze a sad reminder of her absence. Why then, did he—a renowned sexual übermensch—fail phallically? Didn't he once boast:

Conquer their precious square and you win all!

Was the Cyclops blinded by the sharp light of self-reflection? Well, something poked out the mofo's eye! Did he lose the penisolate war to a raging army marching furtively along the lines of a confused identity? Perhaps the epitaph scrawled in the blood of last night's rare filet mignon will tell us:

B. Boylan 1953-1988

I was killed on belated Boylansday, in the white, wonderful arms of milady, by the suffocating field of hyacinths growing in my mind.

Explanation of said epitaph: fioric cravings, for want of a better term, had blinded him with its cerebral stalkings, had choked him to death with the daintiness of its scent, making it, Bloomsday again.

Love is like a rose

blooming in your heart.

Love is like a cunt

sitting on your face.

Sometimes thorny!

Sometimes stinky!

He searched for something to erase Boylan's epitaph. His brother under the soul. One kiss from her atom splitting lips would cleanse the blood from the Celtic Cross hastily mounted in Glasnevin. The stone crumbling out of existence. Light creeping back into the sky. Dark night finally over. Boylan lives again.

Jesus McChrist! Our boyo came back a day earlier than his Da. He's the savior of our race. Six to five he's back in the bike tonight! He won't get parked like last night. Ah, boyos, I see him winning at odds-on like a champion.

As he cockily contemplated ramming his ewe, plowing his Millyish Molly, the field of hyacinths that had blossomed in his mind wilted. But it would take more to extirpate the rank flower of unnatural desire from the mind than mere contemplation. He'd first have to undread intercourse with the flesh Rachel. This could be achieved by unawkwarding her awkward fist. How? A pledge from him to unpocket his naughty hand forever. And, of course, she would have to abandon the five via position for a better way. The a tergo position would provide him with the sight of terra fime while swimming in her lovely lady lake. By doing this, Squire Blazes, the once and future king, will pluck the fair sword from the hand sticking out of the water. Wielderfighting for good! Splash. Splash. Splash. Had she ever splashed her soul?

*

Jordan heard a knock amidst the splashing of his soul's blood. His partner's Neapolitan knuckles rapping at the door. Rapping at the door. Soon they're snorting coke on his desk. The speed of light partners! A mirror off the wall serving as a shining topography of cnocs of white stuff. A mountain of groove—their tribal name for coke—chopped into hills with the perfection of a razor blade artist. Sculpsit Dentelupo! The artist strawed first, using a hundred dollar bill rolled up into a funnel, a newly minted Ben Franklin snatched from Jordan's fingers, to suck a mound of powder up his paura inspiring, widening nasoscuro. *La chimica delle stelle!* Jordan, using a different bill, snorted a cnoc up his left nostril. Three taps on the nose in order to speed the zauberhill to the village of thought. A redclad doll dancing in his eyes. He felt his shirt pocket for the squeeze bottle of Visine that he always carried with him.

44

A talisman lighter than a potato. It wasn't there. Irishmen see omens in everything. He had left it back in the hotel room on the top of the dresser. May it not be an omen. Let it be meaningless. Let it be nothing. She was technically nothing. His nothing and her own nothing. He rubbed his eyes. Glaring beauty of a blade out of its scabbard, slicing, dicing, much-mentioned brilliance, groove. The scraping sound of metal against glass bothered Jordan. He saw the sound in the terms of rats' feet scurrying across his brain. He rubbed his eyes again. A suction noise: two hills had ascended Dentelupo's hirsute nasal passages.

"Great shit," Dentelupo proclaimed.

A snorting Jordan stopped. "A better brand of baby laxative."

"At least it keeps you regular," Dentelupo replied, laughing hysterically at his own joke.

Jordan resumed snorting. Dentelupo snorted after him. Pisspot. Wolfteeth. Pisspot. Wolfteeth.

"A small eightball," Dentelupo bemoaned. His sloped forehead creased with disillusionment. His shining world reduced to a dull glass plain.

"You're not going to Gionse," Jordan said, smiling.

"No," Dentelupo replied angrily. "One fucking time and you bust my balls every time we do coke. You Irish prick!"

"Frank, every time you do coke, it ends up with you calling me five in the morning. I can't breathe! I'm dying!"

Dentelupo smiled at Jordan's imitation. "You prick! You make me sound like a whining bitch."

"I don't care," Jordan said, "that you become a Taffy every time you do coke. I hate it, however, when you get mushy and tell me you love me."

Jordan whitenosed, laughing.

"Wipe your nose," Dentelupo groused, adding, "You Irish prick! I do love you."

Jordan peered into the glass, produced a handkerchief, sans snot and sans strawberries, from his back pants' pocket, and proceeded to wipe white residue from the wings of his dainty nose.

"*Fazzoletto! Fazzoletto! Fazzoletto!*" he screamed in a mock operatic voice that annoyed Dentelupo.

"Bry," Dentelupo said sotto voce, taking a cushiony seat in front of his partner's unmanned fortress.

"What, my love?"

"Do you know Argo?"

Jordan sat down at his desk, his eyes dancing in disgust. "Not that again," he said. "Alright. Argo who?"

"Argo fuck yourself!"

"Thank you, Frank. Do you have anything else enlightening to say before our meeting with Hundsheim?"

"Gunther changed the meeting to Five. He's waiting for T.J. to come in from Houston. That's what I came to tell you."

"Fucking German asshole, asshole German," Jordan said.

"I fucking told him."

Jordan raised the mirror into the air and handed it to Dentelupo. "All we see or seem." His partner hung it back on the wall. Jordan reclined in his chair, closed his eyes, as Dentelupian fingers squeaked across the mirror, lifting residue at every discordant touch. Per cocaine user usual, he rubbed the residue on his gums.

"Do you want to go to the ship for a drink," Dentelupo asked.

"I'll meet you there," Jordan said hoarsely. "I have to call Rachel."

Oneitalianablur. Alone with his phantoms, Jordan punched in the numbers of Rachel's work telephone. Round numbers are false as water.

"Petite Cadeau!"

Her voice.

"Rachel."

"I can't talk now."

"I need to talk to you."

"I'll call you back. Are you in work?"

"Yes. When?"

"In a few minutes."

Waiting for the callback, Jordan attacked a legal pad with his Cross pen. The peristalses of its silvery body ooze a cosmos of doodles onto a greenlined, canary yellow sheet of paper. Then, in a pile of caps, there appeared amid the chaos of mindless creation, the words:

THE

CHEMISTRY

OF

STARS

He ogled the black bank of letters trying to extract its meaning. A Catholic term but also a way of expressing a cocaine high. He continued to scribble, mostly imperfect stars, before a chiming phone stymied his pen.

"Jordan."

"Bry," Rachel cried. "I don't have much time."

"I realize that. Can you see me tonight?"

"I can't. I'm working an iron."

"Quit your job."

"I need the money."

"Why? I pay your car payment and insurance as it is. Move in with me and I'll buy you a shop."

"I can't see you. I need to take some time off from our relationship. I'm confused."

"About what?"

"I'm engaged to Rick and I'm running all over the place with you. It's not right."

"It's not right to jerk me around. Don't say you can't see me. Be honest. Say you won't. Tell me the truth. Tell me you hate me."

"I don't hate you."

"You must."

"Stop it, Bry."

"Why won't you see me tonight?"

"I can't see you because I still have feelings for Rick. I love him."

"You're playing fucking games again, Rachel. I think you've been fucking with me all along. You selfish, selfish little bitch. I hate you! I hate you. Fuck you! Fuck you!"

The rustling sound a phone makes when being seized by a stronger entity.

"Why don't you leave her alone?"

Jordan recognized the strident voice as belonging to Rachel's friend and co-worker, Dawn the Yenta, former whore of Babylon, N.Y. A moment of silence. Her dark, plump hand squeezed the phone in anticipation of Jordan's reply.

"Who is this," he asked, with the pretense that he hadn't recognized her voice.

"Dawn," she answered angrily.

"Put Rachel back on the phone. This isn't your business."

"It is so my business. You're torturing my best friend. We're like sisters."

"Hyperbole. Put Rachel back on the phone."

"I won't."

"Get off the phone, salesgirl."

"I won't let you hurt my friend."

"What a cliché you are! I'm warning you," Jordan said with force. "Put Rachel back on the phone."

"And what a creep you are! Rick is your friend and you're trying to steal his girlfriend."

"You don't know a fucking thing."

"Rachel tells me everything."

Another pause. Another approach. "Listen, Dawn. I've never done anything to you. So why the belligerence? I noticed it the first time I met you."

"I hate fakes."

"Fake?"

"You're a drug pusher masquerading as a legitimate businessman."

"You're the fake. Look at your nose."

"Fuck you, Brian."

A mean electronic mantra pulsed in his ape-ear. Spiritual disconnection. Clinks, rings, followed by a voice of a woman demanding him to act:

If you'd like to kill her, please hang up. Drive home to Howth, retrieve Chum from his hiding place, inside the hollowed out hardcover of Lolita locked away in the previously alluded to maplewood bookcase. Get back in your red machine and speed south on the G.S.P. Listen to lugubrious songs on the way, pinch your nose, the salt marshes of the Mullica River, turn off at Exit 44, head west approximately ten miles until you see a sign on the left for the Mall, make a left there, go four traffic lights, two of them four way stops, first you'll pass Stockton State College, where your fat friend Charley received a degree in Criminology, then you'll pass a so-called airport, finally, you'll come to the Atlantic City Race Course, built by Olympic gold medalist in sculling and sire of a Princess, not to mention the handsomest man F.D.R. said he had ever met, Philadelphia's Jack Kelly. The Mall, where Rachel works, is adjacent to the track's parking lot. Be sure to park in front of the main entrance, her shop is the first one on the right. Good luck and good hunting.

Poison in the porches. He hung up and tilted his head to the right. He knew how to play his role artistically. To recite howling his public tirades. He pressed redial.

"Petite Cadeau!"

A South Shore Accent.

"You're right, Dawn. I'm going to stop being a fake. I'm going to call Rick and tell him about Rachel and me."

She the Babylonian tried to babel, but he terminated the call before a single intelligible word had escaped her mouth. By now, her sour lips were at the sweet ear he had whispered love into last night. If she didn't call momentarily, alright in a few minutes, he would have to make that call to Rick. Dawn had called him his friend, but he didn't really like him. The fuck face called him a Mick gangster every time they saw each other. And he rooted against Notre Dame. He wondered what Rick's reaction would be when he told him he had fucked her. Half-fucked her. Penetrated her at least. Rick would most likely threaten to kill him. If he tried anything, Jordan vowed to spill his mutt English-German-French blood all over the streets of Lindalindo.

But what if she really did love him? She'd hate him for hurting him. She might refuse to see him again. Perhaps he had never been anything more than a Penelopian suitor. Her palaver of their shared past lives, a past life marriage gone awry, a sham, a bogus tapestry of words, designed to entrance him. He remembered her telling him that Rick had been her son in a past life. Echoes of Jocasta and Oedipus. He seriously doubted that he could overthrow her son-lover. He didn't know what to believe. Massive night began to settle in his soul, as a cacophony of doubt continued unabated in his mind, interring him in a solid tomb of blackness from which no mortal rises. Yes, no mortal rises from a grave of unrequited love.

Take the stone away!

The phone rang.

Perhaps Christ's call to Lazarus?

"What," he answered, breathing deeply, his grave clothes unwrapping.

"Are you alright," Rachel inquired.

"You turn me into a monster," he sobbed; then, composing himself a bit asked, "Do you tell Dawn everything?"

"She's exaggerating. You have to grab hold of your emotions, Brian. You're losing control."

"Do you love Rick?"

"I love you."

"Why do you stay with him?"

"It's complicated. I care for him."

"See me tonight."

"It will have to be late."

"Where should we meet?"

"In Atlantic City. One of the casinos Rick doesn't like."

"He hates Resorts. I'll register there."

"I love you, Bry."

CHAPTER 5

Jordan jumped out of the car. The brilliant turquoise of the bay surprised him. A sunny summer breeze, Athena's gift, caressed his back, as he ascended a hilly patch of green leading to the Gangplank, the shiply bar, where his partner awaited him. A foot away from his destination, a disturbing optical echo: a clump of purplish pink flowers. He trampled them, blindly, and planked aboard the musty vessel. A drumming of feet: leather, cellulose, and lignin combined to produce mnemonic percussion. Seafarers enter the harbor. The DNA of Rolf or Rollo, Abbey plunderer, getter of kings, reverberated in his useless adolescent heart. Where my heart lies, let my brain also lie. Which brings us to the monomachy of Celt and Worse. Celt: poet of pastures. Worse: freebooter and city conditor. Celt: ancient wisdom. Worse: polypsychic. Celt: Jacobite. Worse: pragmatist. Celt: macrodont. Worse: macrophallic.

Jordan, smiling, touched the worse part of himself: a signal to a sparkling chrysophilist leaning against a bar ninety large Rockports away.

"Partner!" the chrysophilist screamed.

80. 70. Jordan accelerated his locomotion. 40. 30. 20. Ten. Five. One. Shoulder to face.

"Speak fewer, Frank," Jordan commanded, briefly diverting his eyes from Dentelupo. "This isn't a Jersey City tenement."

"What, are you ashamed to have me as your partner?" Dentelupo asked.

Wife beater! Sheep shagger! No. I'm delighted.

"For fuck sake, Frank. Stop acting like a cunt. You should—"

Unfinisher. Halffucker.

"It's the coke," Jordan whispered. "It makes you paranoid and turns me into a maniac. More of a maniac," he chuckled.

"You're right. I'm sorry too. We shouldn't do it."

Dentelupo rolled up the sleeves of his white sports jacket, revealing darkly tanned, muscular forearms. He smiled Moorishly. *Mia figlia! Mia figlia!* I prove by algebra the Dark Lady of the Sonnets was Desdemona's bonus genitalic daughter by Othello (sent with fiery quickness to England). *Je suis sans pitié.*

"What a fucking day," Jordan exclaimed. "No wonder why I have an ulcer. Fucking Rocky! I hate dealing with him. Always crying poverty."

"Don't believe him. He's got money coming out of his ass. Whines like a Jew when it's time to pay," Dentelupo snorted.

Jordan winced, clutched army conveyance, clutched again. Agenbite of duodenum.

"What's wrong?" Dentelupo queried.

"My ulcer," Jordan surmised. "It's telling me that I should have something to eat."

"Have a drink before you eat," Dentelupo said earnestly. "Alcohol, they say, helps with digestion."

"I'll have a Tab," Jordan spouted to anonymous ears.

"Don't drink that poison, Bry."

Jordan looked away and observed groups and groups of piscavores occupying the wide belly of the creaky establishment. Jonesin' Jonah! A mad Pisces.

"Poisson is French for fish," Jordan wistfully offered. "Eat—"

"Poison fish? Sounds like Diane's pussy," Dentelupo interrupted, heaving with laughter.

Fool! Feste! Yorick! I refuse to laugh at your gibes, sirrah. Pwason, you stupe! Clean the shite out of your monkey ears or I'll pour a flagon of rhenish on your head. Poisson distribution: the number of idiots at a few meters of this fucking bar; the number of pines in daily verdic commute; the number of stars with planets where one can obtain, for a great price, a James Joyce tenner and two JFK halves and perhaps a rectal probe, exemplary yeyo and decent Chinese, no Monosodium

Glutamate a must; the number of hits in a gram of Bolivia's National Product. He's right, of course. Her little fish will become a big she-cat.

"Eat fish and their beady eyes will pursue you through eternity," Jordan postulated.

Jonesin' through eternity. Mid-eternity now. Forever Now. It will be forever.

Dentelupo frowned.

"Alright, have a salad."

Salade jetée en l'air.

"That sounds good."

Anonymous waited for their order.

"Two garden salads, please," Dentelupo shouted. "Oil and vinegar on the side for mine and French for his." He pointed an unoffensive thumb at his partner. "No croutons on mine, please."

Please! Please! Jordan tasted his drink. Filet mignon battlefield nasty and great potato mused by dying soldier.

"You're right, Frank. This stuff is poison. Please," Jordan said to the still scribbling bartender, "when you get a chance, I'll have a cranberry juice with a spurt of seltzer."

Dentelupo sampled a rum and Coke served to him by a different anonymous.

"Gunther told me," Dentelupo said. "He expects us to do great importing used Beemers and—"

"They'll need catalytic converters. And by the way, never call them that again. Only yuppies talk that way." Jordan leaned both elbows on the bar. "Fuck the yuppies."

"Anthony says he knows a guy who can install them for about half what it costs anywhere else." Dentelupo thrust forward his underjaw and uttered an abbreviated cough.

"We'll need someone to sell them."

"We'll get someone, Bry."

"Whom are we going to get? I'm not going to sell cars. Even a coke dealer has a limit to how far he'll stoop, my friend."

Dentelupo compressed his lips.

"We'll get someone," Dentelupo said, with a tinge of anger, as anonymous placed their salads on the bar. Dentelupo anointed his with oil and vinegar, impaled a soaked leaf of lettuce on his fork and started eating. Jordan neatly dripped French dressing on his, speared a crouton, and ate with relish. Toasted manna for the would-be King of the Irish-Israelites.

"What's a tabby, Bry?"

"What a fucking non sequitur?"

"What? A nun sexure? What the hell is that? Are you mocking God again? You should be more respectful."

The Omniboss of the Cosmos strike me down. The guy up apples and pears doesn't like it when you blaspheme. It's alright to blaspheme as long as one doesn't blaspheme the holy gaseous vertebrate. Fucking moron! Your partner. Why, boyo? He's a snake! I'm a caiman. As that Scotch lepidopterist McNab used to say, then you are the noblest izmena of them all. Is that Gaelic or Godlic? It's Serpentinish or Lizard Vulgate. That jeween bawn, Sunny Jim, is as cold and false as ice water. She's always saying: J'ai sang-froid. Your French is worse than your similes. *Je suis sans pitié,* Irish Nobodaddy. T'underin' Jaysus! She'll take your bread and her leaven and leave you with matzoh balls the color of her glazzies, the conniving little jewess. The zeugma on you, Nobo. She's a conniving little jewmickess. During my university days, they used to call it syllepsis. Go, University College! Ecphonesis. Where language reigns, I'm the wearer of the crown. Metonymy. The eyes blue rolled in her head pretty. Chiasmus. More Joycean than Joyce, Gospodin Nabokov. Antanaclasis. Dumb Dentelupe, dumb Dentelupe. Apocope and epimone and alliterations. My soul is aching. Consulting the Institutio Oratoria by the mighty Quintilian, I credit you with a very worn metaphor. A piss poor one. Alliteration. It is also a solecism or a faulty concord in a single fucking atomic sentence. So we fight to a draw again. If you want to draw the cashier use the head of a mastiff or a pointer, the eyes of a cat, the ears of Richard III, the beg srón of Lolita Haze, the temples of a cock, and the neck of a tortoise. How is the poet to convince like literature, and not like nature? Your cerebral aqueduct is backed up with the down castings of your retroconsciousness. You were told that by the Southie leading The Forum, the new est, held at the Philly Area Center last year. Are you thinking your thoughts or are they thinking you? You didn't make it through the whole thing, did you? You had a date with a chupacabra. Billygoatsucker, I mean.

"It's a cat with mottled fur," Jordan revealed.

"Why did you call me a tabby?" Dentelupo's compact forehead registered confusion.

Jordan laughed sonorously and speared another crouton.

"Not a tabby. A Taffy. A Welshman. Jones is a common Welsh name. Get it?" Jordan tapped his own forehead for emphasis.

"Get what? I'm a dumb motherfucker." Dentelupo dabbed at his mouth with his napkin and scowled dumbly.

"Dumb," Jordan said, chewing a crouton. "Like a fox."

Dentelupo forced a smile that metamorphosed into a frown upon glimpsing a disagreeable sight in the mirror: an italophobic friend of Jordan's family.

"The counselor is coming over," Dentelupo warned. "Time for me to take a piss."

"You're not going to get out of seeing him. He'll be here when you get back." Jordan whirled around for a preview of Dentelupo's bête blanc.

"I won't wash my hands." Dentelupo scratched his head.

"Whatever makes you happy, Frank. I'm glad he's here. I need to get some free legal advice from the big fuck."

Fool, speak a prophecy: Beware of language, for it is often a cheat.

Dentelupo rushed away, carefully saluting an approaching monobrowed giant arrayed in a seeming acre of Irish linen. Six six squared.

"Cue!" Jordan exclaimed affably.

Agon of metacarpi: the counselor's monstrous paw prevailing slightly.

"How are you, Brian?"

Jordan opened and closed his smarting right hand.

"Excellent and you, sir?"

"Don't knight me, Brian."

Ard rí Michael Cusack Sullivan, Esquire, Emperor of the Irish Riviera. President of the Spring Lake Country Club.

"Then, as the Bard says, you are benighted."

The counselor shook his mighty head.

"We have our own bards to create the conscience of our race," the counselor barked. "Shakespeare was the descendant of Sephardic Jews and an eonist to boot. His warped philosophy in the guise of poetry is like a toxin seeping into the soul and murdering it."

If his words are toxins, I'll immerse myself in their honeyed poison.

"That is the best denunciation of Shakespeare I have ever heard," Jordan said, putting his hands together. "I think Bernard Shaw would be proud of you."

Face purpling, optical echo, the counselor finished the drink curled up in his enormous hand. Still apoplectic, he plunked the glass on the bar.

"Jameson," he boomed. "And you, Brian?"

"Cranberry with a spurt of seltzer."

"We'll have to check your lineage for some Jew." Smug joy propelled the counselor's lips to quasi-poetry:

> The great Jordans of Mayo
>
> are the men God made screwy!
>
> Because for all their Celtic charm,
>
> *they can't help appearing Jewy.*

The counselor paid and tipped anonymous.

"Very funny. Give him a drink on me," Jordan requested. Anonymous placed a capsized shot glass on the bar grained and hued like his grandfather's casket.

"*Sláinte!*" the counselor said.

"*Sláinte,*" Jordan echoed amidst a xylophonic ring.

"Here, like an Injun, is your partner." The counselor slapped a palm on his knee, laughing.

"Hello," Dentelupo said unctuously. "How have you been?"

Ad canvassers, drug pushers, publicans lose another metacarpi agon. The counselor deriving pleasure from the pain inflicted on Dentelupo. *Vae victis!*

"Fine, Frank. And you—or should I say youse? Meaning your lovely pack of brothers and sisters. Their various activities have been very good for business. I've represented just about all of them, thanks to you. Is Michael behaving himself? Balked at receiving probation but it was the best I could do for him. He could have been sentenced to five stiff, but Judge Barton, a former associate of mine, suspended the sentence. He won't be so lucky the next time. He still owes me a thousand but I feel confident that he'll pay me."

"You'll have to take that up with him, Mr. Sullivan."

"Cue, Frankie. Quite a tan you have. Perhaps you can do some brotherly leaning. Quite a tan!"

"I'll do what I can."

"I'd appreciate if you could speak to him about it, Frankie. Brian's dad, whom I know my entire life, tells me you're an alright guinea."

"First of all, I don't believe Bry's dad would say that. His son, my best friend, calls me a guinea on a regular basis. I'm not offended. Are you alright? You look like you're about to croak. You should get some sun."

"Tell your partner, Brian," the counselor said loudly, stowing two fingers in his waistcoat pocket, "that he should stay out of the sun." He paused to swallow a mouthful of Irish amniotic fluid. "Or else he might be mistaken for a lawn ornament. One of those black jockeys that used to be popular in Rumson. Now a bunch of hippies live there."

Italian food: Dentelupo swallowed whole along with the water of life. Wait a moment, a little trouble getting his greasy, meatballish head down the esophagus. Ironic that he consumed what he supposedly conspued. Maybe natural. Irony, according to Carrick Jordan, the most misused word in the language. Jordan, the boyo of many resources, laughed at his friend's unusual departure. The Jerries call taking pleasure in others' misfortune *schadenfreude*. I confess I enjoyed it. Did you? I also enjoyed it and will enjoy the indigestion the swallower will undoubtedly suffer. Agita, the wops call it.

"Another, counselor?"

"At least have a Baileys with me, Brian," the counselor softly urged. "Your grandda and I used to drink together here in the old days. Your father, a fine man in every respect, never drinks. Eamon was bothered that his son wouldn't indulge. He couldn't bear the fact that he had sired a teetotaler."

"He'd be proud of me. Alright. Two Baileys. My tab."

"A *dubh pishogue* on our enemies," the counselor toasted.

Ersehole.

They lifted their glasses in unison. The counselor drank with one eye closed: a magical kiss to his thin lips. Jordan's glass remained inexplicably suspended in mid-heaven. No matter how much I imbibe, how much I snort, fuck, eat, worse ... the ghost in you she doesn't fade.

The counselor placed his glass on the bar for refilling. "You don't like Irish cream?" the counselor asked as he examined the tip of the linen snake strangling him.

"Next round," Jordan answered, pushing his glass in the counselor's direction. "I haven't touched this. Take it."

The counselor gratefully received the glass. "As the ancient ginzos used to say: *Nunc est bibendum*!"

Gunkgunkgunk!

Jordan laughed, ordered another round with a mere fillip.

"Thank you, Brian," the counselor said, gulping down the liqueur. He smiled obliquely and wiped his gob with a sleeve. "What are you waiting for, Father Mathew? Drink at least one!" The counselor smirked. "Perhaps you'd prefer a glass of Goldwasser? I'm kidding. You have the map of Ireland on your face!"

"I'm driving to Atlantic City tonight." Jordan augmented his excuse by pointing south. "Have mine, Cue."

"If you insist." The counselor elevated the acquired glass, bellowed, "Death to the tendon strainers!"

Never turn over!

"I find your toasts refreshing, Cue. None of those stereotypical Irish May you toasts."

"It's from the Inferno," the counselor needlessly informed. "Remember what I told you about those no good guineas? They're Greeker than the Greeks!"

Jordan chomped on a straw. "So you've read Dante?" Bovine Jordan asked with bovine astonishment. "I have read the Inferno a few times and sort of remember the tendon strainer line. Mandelbaum's, not Ciardi's translation," Jordan submitted.

Did Durante di Firenze cross a stony, rosestrewn ponte to the undiscovered city state from whose bourn no pilgrim, save Gis, returns? It's a long way to Minus Eternity. Happiness is a wormhole. Yes it is.

"I prefer the Irish poets."

"Yeats must be your favorite," Jordan presumed. "Eliot called him the pavior of literature's *via moderna*."

"No. Mangan's my favorite. He was right to proclaim that his soul was mated with song." The counselor made a sweeping gesture.

"Knowest thou the castle that beetles over the wine-dark sea," Jordan recited.

Nameless one rolling like a complete unknown.

"Is that Mangan? I don't know it per se but can see it's very Mangan. Homerically Shakespearean," the counselor strummed. "Probably a contribution to The Comet."

Jack Shakespeare and Nick Omeros? I seem to know the names. I know not, sir, whether Bacon wrote the works of Shakespeare, but if he did not, it seems to me, he missed the opportunity of his life. Exit, pursued by a bear. I dote on his very absence. Our poets steal from the author of The Tale of One Burg, we mean, that chap often called the Hellenic Milton, and if he didn't write it, or to be more precise, sing it, it being also titled The Case of the Purloined Beauty Contestant, well, then, my love, some other cat with the same by-line must've.

"I fear those big words that make us sad," Jordan said with buoyancy as he wrapped his fingers around a polished brass rail. He briefly critiqued the deck of the ship. Patina adds cells to the wood. Protects it from liquids: water, whiskey, spit. Bad sales are called wood. Good ones patina. Under the leafy awning of a tree, elm twigs against the gold patina of sky, a blinding Joycean checkerwork of dancing coins, gobs lipsward in quest of protokiss.

"I'm an attorney, Brian. Those big words engendering sadness have made me wealthy. And the saddest one of all," the counselor said, laughing with sadistic delight, "is incarceration."

"Especially," Jordan quickly rejoined, "when one is tossed in with the tendon strainers. Never turn over, my dear."

The counselor laughed, coughed, and began choking. He snagged from his top pocket a green handkerchief and covered his glistening mouth.

"Are you alright?"

"Yes, thank you. Just the remnants of a bronchial cold. You'll have to stop cracking me up, Brian."

The counselor drank a glass of water before drinking a whiskey. Jordan snapped his fingers. Another Baileys for the counselor. Close the mead hall! I have seen croppies drinking at the bar, while princes bartended.

"Cue," Jordan cooed.

"What, Brianeen?" the counselor cooed back.

Good time. Overflowing with the cream of Irish kindness. Blinded by the stuff! Jordan sifted through a bowl of mixed nuts. He slid a few cashews on his tongue and began to chew. "I need a favor," he said, swallowing.

"Anything, boyo," the counselor slurred.

Jordan lurched forward, the ship of his mind under the sway of Gus Aeolus. Two blatherskiting men passed close behind him. One of the voices somewhat familiar, but he decided not to turn around. Instead, he stationed his eyes on the creature from the kellygreen lagoon.

"You have a son with the DEA," Jordan confirmed.

"My eldest, Mike, is the chief of the Metro task force. Why do you ask? What kind of favor?"

"I wish to provide Mike with information."

"On a drug dealer? You an informant? I can't see it, Brian."

"I want to get this pusher and I think the safest approach would be to go through you. Someone I can trust completely."

"Is he mafia? A Gambino? The gang who couldn't shoot straight," the counselor smirked. "The true story of Don Vito Corleone," he smirked on.

"He claims to be a part of the Genovese family," Jordan scoffed.

"I don't know what you want me to do. Is it personal?"

"What isn't personal?" Jordan asked back. He stroked the giant's rounded shoulders, viddied him in the eye.

"Are you in business with him? You know a lot of people say you're a drug dealer," the counselor cross-examined.

"They lie!" Jordan cried. "I dress like one," he admitted, laughing: "And God knows, I spend like one."

"It's understandable. You're in the bar business and have to act the ludicrous part. How is that going, anyway?"

"Better than expected." Jordan rapped the bar, laughing.

"So what do you want me to tell my son?" The counselor's voice evinced concern.

"It's a major deal involving a local crime family," Jordan reported. "I"ll give you the details next week."

"Are you sure? I mean—"

"You don't have to worry," Jordan said calmly. "The information will be totally accurate."

"Is there a girl—"

"You're misreading the situation," Jordan rejoined.

"Who should I say I got this tip from?" The counselor's monobrow arched with the inquiry.

"Tell Mike it's from a low level pusher named Niemand. Promise me my name won't be mentioned."

"Promise me you won't compromise my son's career. After all, he'll be going out on a limb."

"I promise my information will be as treeless as Portugal."

"I'll tell him it's from a kike named Niemand who owes the guineas money." The counselor displayed, with some help of zygomaticus major, a terrifying macrodontia.

"Swear by Saint Patrick," Jordan winked.

"Why swear by that foreigner? I'll swear by Saint Senan." Coming out of his bar slouch, the counselor stood tall, unfurled his arms in solicitation of a hug. They embraced like reunited brothers.

Anonymous watched, listened, ran his aristocratic fingers through a thicket of palehair.

"Excuse me, sir," he said haltingly, "are you Brian Jordan?"

"Sometimes. I'm sorry," Jordan said. "I'm Brian."

"You have a call in the back," Anonymous screamed in competition with the climax of an Irish classic.

It was Brennan on the Moor, Brennan on the Moor…

Jordan cupped his hand to his ear. "Where?"

"Mr. Kiernan's office. He's the owner. It's on his private line. He called up front to say you have a call in the back. For some reason the call can't be transferred up front."

"Thank you," Jordan said, extending his hand. "What's your name?"

"Rory O'Connor," he said, shaking Jordan's hand.

"The name of a king," the counselor interjected, adding: "Albeit not a very able one. Sold Ireland out for a mess of pottage."

Go down in the mud! Nobody's listening.

"Did Mr. Kiernan happen to tell you who was calling?"

"A young woman."

"Probably my secretary," Jordan mused, tipping the rough rugheaded kern a drug dealer's tip.

"That's not necessary, sir," Rory O'Connor exclaimed.

"Take the money, Rory. Brian is loaded. He owns two bars. One a go-go bar!"

Jordan laughed and put his hand on the counselor's arm, opining: "This is the richest Mick I know. Will you be here when I get back?"

"I'm not going anywhere, boyo."

Scudding cloudage greyly conceals a bomber flying unannounced. I'll find refuge in a strait and dark shelter. A reeking place of lonedarkness, where all the garbage of my consciousness has settled. There, I'll burn, with the fire that gives no light, the fungus separating me from my soul. Jordan slid a hand into a pocket. The white warmth he felt with the mere touch of a shining thing caused him to perspire.

The snortorium beckoned him. He pushed its knotty pine door open. At the sink, a tallish, thinnish man peered into a mirror sporting a cobweblike crack. The symbol of Irish Riviera art! He assumed some drunk (Worse: alcohol allergy) had punched the mirror in a Calibanic rage. The peerer peering around the crack, dragged a comb through sparse blondness.

"Bry," the peerer exclaimed. "Where have you been hiding yourself, old sport?"

"Robert Francis Armagh! How are things in the Riviera?" Jordan asked.

Thalatta! Thalatta! Warm sunshine merrying over the winedark sea.

"Who would know better than you," Armagh responded amid a lingering handshake and smile.

"How's the Shamrock flying, Bob?"

"A lot of winners but, alas, still no major stakes. I have a few babies that look promising," Armagh asserted.

"One day we'll see you in the winner circle at the big one," Tout Jordan touted.

You used to medicate your horses illegally. A bowed tendon responds better to bute than a god awful poultice.

"Someday," Armagh said, crossing his fingers. "Larry told me I might find you here."

"The bathroom?" Jordan smiled.

"No, Brian. The Gangplank! He told me he saw you here last week with some greaseball."

"Frank, my partner, likes this place. He thinks he's a pirate." Jordan smiled at the lilt of Armagh's laughter.

"Jesus! Are you still carrying that cross? He's as dumb as Yogi Berra," Armagh sneered.

"It only proves Christ was a Mick, doesn't it?" Jordan spread his arms out in a silly imitation of à Kempis.

The serpent sleeping in the mazy folds of Milton has opened its vicious eyes. Matching nods. Derisive laughy. Isopraxism. The dusky race of Killer Cain!

"I need a favor, Brian," Armagh said, looking away. "Hey George! There's someone I want you to meet."

Seconds later, an exurban cowboy burst through a squeaky stall door, forefinger and thumb compressing his flared nostrils.

"This is Brian, George. The guy Larry and I told you about."

"Nice to meet you, Brian. I'm George W. Bush."

The vice president's son's simian brow corrugated. If you want to give a natural appearance to one of them, a Bush for example, use the fosh of an ape, the eyes of a lizard, the ears of a chimp, the schnoz of a redtail hawk, the smile of a Danish villain, the temples of a rattlesnake, and the neck of a tortoise.

"I need to buy some blow, Brian. Can you help me out, partner?" the vice president's son pleaded, texascombing his rebellious snakeblacklocks.

"I have an eightball in my pocket that you can have free of charge." Jordan smiled uncomfortably, adding: "I'm a loyal Republican."

"Did you hear that, Roberto?" Dubya cried incredulously, his dusky face oscillating in Bushian fashion. "What a guy! I think it's great you'd do that, Brian, but I insist on paying for it. It's the Republican way, partner."

Look at his eyes: reptilegreen. Any closer and he'd be a monopt. His pupils screaming: Fuck Nancy Reagan and Just Say No in her faux royal Taffy arse!

"Alright," Jordan said. "If you insist."

"Brian," Armagh said. "I want to talk to you about helping us raise money for Vice President Bush's campaign. Do you have a few minutes to discuss it over a drink?"

"I have a call in Barney's office that I have to take care of first, Bob. But sure, I'd be delighted to have a drink and discuss it." Drugs and money exchanged hands. "I'll see you in a few," Jordan vowed. The Republicans communicated so-longs. I love you in dactylology or fuck god or Go, Longhorns! After a trip to Moloch Park, you are inclined to think it was meant as a figo to Nobo! Jordan flashed il cornuti back. The trinity suppressed by the horns of the god of this world.

As Jordan pushed his way out of the bathroom, the vice president's son proclaimed:

"God is great!"

Eliyahu-ha Navi is coming. Conundrum: When is a door not a door? Syllogism: Other men die, I am not another, therefore I'll not die. An exiguous light attempts to brighten a bleak hallway. Kiernan's *céad míle fáilte* to a prophet. Light seeking light. A brief spiritual questionnaire, Monsieur. Does God have a soul? And if so, is all light the result of a propitious fissure in God's soul? And finally, crawling over Blake's buns, where are you after? I'll answer all by saying: Only nihilum knows—and doesn't know. Light beguiling light. More light. This lamp upon my face is but a pisscolored guide to a preexistent future. I stop. Momentarily futureless, I continue belatedly. I come under a Celtolume's neamhly blue gaze and instantly feel like a loodheramaun. Senan we hardly knew ye! Pinxit: M.C. Sullivan. I smile. I didn't know he painted. Turning my mind from the eidetic to the auricular, I hear the son of a wandering Dubliner singing:

isn't it good, Norwegian wood

All wood is stained with the sin of the Cross! Where did the wood for the Cross come from? Palestine is as treeless as Iar Connacht. Judas, the true incarnate God of the desert, at least according to Borges's tragic Danish philosophaster, Runeberg, hanged himself from an arbusto branch. I wonder if they have the cross hidden in the Vatican's vault? Or did the Romans burn it afterwards in order to laud their gods? Their lupine eyes following the dirty clouds as they slowly climb to invisible nostrils.

"Mr. Kiernan?"

"Come in, Brian," the addressee spat out the side of his mouth not occupied by contraband.

"I apologize for the inconvenience, Mr. Kiernan."

"Barney, Brian. No inconvenience at all. There's a young lady holding for you," the ghostfaced publican informed, his deranged eyes pointing to the phone on his desk. He has seen the inside of Marlboro.

The grounds puts one in mind of an Irish manor. "I'm sorry the call couldn't be transferred up front. The new system they put in here last month is driving me crazy. Line one, boyo. Tap it twice. Remember to lock up. I'll be at the bar if you need anything."

"Thanks again, Barney."

A blob of light promised to explicate the meaning of the call, pluck out the heart of its mystery. A long shiver of fear flowed over his body. The unforeheard terrified him. Appear, appear, whatso your shape or name! Ox, snake, god, fiend, marvel, mystery, come. The Feds just searched the premises, Bry. They asked a lot of questions. They carted away the financial records … He pounced toward the phone, floorboards moananoaning. He raised the lifewand, cleared his bronchials tubes.

"Hello."

"Brian."

"Rachel? I thought it was my office. You sound funny. Are you alright?"

"Carrick gave me this number. I hope that's alright."

"Of course. What's wrong?" Jordan gazed appreciatively at the framed Dublinscape across the darkly lit room. He imagined he perceived amid clouds of angels, devils too, a prophet ascending to the glorious brightness at an angle of fortyfive degrees over Little Britain Street.

"Nothing. Don't get mad but I can't see you tonight. I'm working an iron. I'm tired. I need sleep. I'll see you tomorrow. Alright?"

Mañana. Demain. Morgen. Amárach. If there is no time for you and me in the Land of the Space of Today, then, my love, I'll conquer the Heavens, where Time meets Space in God's infinite heart. Rest. Sleep. Dream. Your sheathed speed of light eyes two blue wheels on the chariot transporting me to Paradise.

CHAPTER 6

Precious Squares: a dark wooden O crammed with bibulous oscuraphiles condemned by McFate to wear porcine epidermis on this summery daynight. Syncopated light and a sphygmodic beat hurry their hearts.

I'll stop the world and melt with you

Dentelupo walks in holding the door for Jordan. They see their men at the back of the hall. Corkscrew tails wag as they approach.

"I'll have a Perrier," Jordan screamed to a barmaid, adding, "And give these animals what they want."

Abstemious Dionysus commandeth the dark air be filled with polugêthês.

Jordan detached a crisp bill from his bronze money clip and placed it on the bar. The bill's hellfire eyes stared up at him in amusement. Pannage was his right. Aye, Arden.

"You're not drinking," Dentelupo grunted.

"After they leave," Jordan answered, trying to hear above the static of his AM brain. Temporary hydropot. Nunc est bibendum. I'd like to, after all, it's a good man's failing, but I've recently been put in charge of the thinking machine and Lully's operational instructions are quite clear: no bibulousity. What's its ultimate goal? Truth, right? I suppose. But it's a little more complicated than that. Bah! In vino veritas. True, true. But what's truth without bonitas? Vinic veritas is a kind of gallows' god's truth, isn't it? May you be in parthas an hour before the devil knows you're dead! Our enemies clepe us drunkards. Nunc est bibendum. A familiar paw offers me a plumbum demise embossed with Roman stupidity. Fuck you!

"Rosa's dancin," Dentelupo enthused, chomping on an ice cube.

"I see her," Jordan said coolly.

A dago in a Day-Glo gamma-string greets us from a stainless

steel pole. (Would it be daga because she's a bitch?) Her fellow dago waves back with a desperate roundness of hand. I, however, show her the indifferent palm of a hyperborean. Turning and turning in a widening gyre. The center cannot hold. Thus she falls from the heavens: manna or god's shite? Eat me, eat me, eat me, her dark eyes seem to cry with each delicious sway.

"Look at that ass," Dentelupo howled. Jordan laughed to himself. The paragon of podices, hethinks. Two roads diverged in a yellow woods, and though it sounds obscene, I took the boreen. The narrow road of Belialdom stares me in the face (to similify) like a loaded Chum. Simile is the slow cousin of metaphor and the harlot of cliché. Belialdom (a federation of plain conurbation) is a hazy, sterile tir. Years ago, I used to travel beyond the haze to a nicer place. It even smelled nicer. No stinking weeds to tear up, only beautiful country to plant your seeds.

Patricia, peanut butter stuck to my palate. My sandwich, my supper.

I dream of Quiltyville. She's only a few years older than Rachel. Her Dalcassian surname appealed to me. Ugly head? MacLysaght must be wrong.

"I need to get something from the car," Jordan said to Dentelupo.

"What?"

"The contract."

"Get us a gram, too, baby," Mike Campy croaked, his voice, music's sworn enemy, a rape of sound.

"I'll pretend you didn't broadcast that all over the fucking place, Campy," Jordan said with cool anger.

"You dumb shit," Mike Jerky squeaked to Mike Campy. "Don't worry, Bry. I'll see he behaves."

The two Mikes, Campy, a scruffy middleweight, Jerky, a sloppy superheavyweight, play at combat. Campy crounched like a boxer. Jerky affected karate kicks. They stop when they notice Jordan's ocular disapproval.

Rosa bent over in front of them. Jordan halted his departure. When swinish eyes are smiling. Why not? She has, to put it in their words, a nice shitter. A golden mnemonic of every culoteer's dream of discovering a small hidden door at the deepest and most intimate sanctum of a woman.

There's nothing you and I won't do
I'll stop the world and melt with you

"Brown eye," Mike Campy camped.

"Peehole," Mike Jerky jerked.

"Show me your brown eye," Mike Campy recamped.

We're pigs! We desire to possess the soulshaped arse of the Dark Lady of the Sonnets or Dark Rosaleen or a ewe or a catamite or a palm with a crack. What we don't know or understand, but may have started to feel, is that sin's magnet is drawing us voidward. Leave, Brian. Get out! The pale stars light the way to God! Don't you know? The skies are perpetually starless to the blind.

She straightened, whirled around, glided over to Dentelupo.

"Hello, Rosa," he gushed, handing her a twenty from Jordan's change. She kissed him on the lips and cried:

"Missed you, Frank."

Tapping down the line, she playfully widened the mountain pass leading to her supposed heart. Jordan, grinning, shoved a bill between said pass. His retracted fingers, bony pachyderms, escaped the onslaught of avalanching Appian flesh. She kissed the son of Baal on the cheek, asking:

"Did she move in, Brian?"

La Streg wants me to tell her everything. I can't. I'm only.

"Who?"

She scratched her pointy chin and looked to Dentelupo for help.

"Brian," she exclaimed.

Acrylic like Rachel's. Fuchsia! Fakes! Frauds! Fucks! They smear their face with mud. God hath given you one face and you make yourself another. He freed his eyes from her harpy claws and answered:

"Oh, you mean that cunning little bitch I told you about."

"Not nice," she scolded, "but we understand because we love you."

Dentelupo smiled uneasily.

"These guys," he said, facing the drunken contingent to his left, "work for us."

The drunken contingent introduced themselves with Jordan's small change.

"I'll come over after my set," she called out, whirling away in libido-accelerating fashion. Hip. Butt. Thigh. Her Day-Glo g-string, like a visual spoor, helped Dentelupo to track her through a tunnel of fickle light to the other side of the wooden **O**.

"She has such a sweet ass," Dentelupo sweetly mused, lifting his dark glass.

Jordan lifted his bright glass and toasted:

"For thy sweet ass remembered! Everyman his own wife! Drink up, Francesco!"

Dentelupo downed his rum and coke, the glass brightening in the act, his mind buoyed by the demonic distilment, as blackness filled his soul.

"Another," a barmaid asked.

He studied his glass, like an amateur captromancer, before handing it to the barmaid for refilling. He divined Bry would pay. The Fianna Pledge. Jordan's curriculum differed significantly. Still harping on my daughter. Floor work, they call it. Supine one, slutty, millionairess of erotic moves, opening her legs, like any good daughter of man, for one of the Elohim (or if she's Tralala, all of them) or a Pelican. Prone one, ass smiling, seems to be getting it a tergo from a different kind of visitant. One from Zeta Reticuli. That place where coke is accepted as cheese.

The barmaid snatched the bill from the dusky air, danced to the stainless steel cash register, peplos showcasing an exquisite blue bubble, rang up the sale, returned with the change. Before she could deposit his forty-six dollars on the counter, an alert Jordan displayed a halting palm.

"Keep it," he confirmed, her tunicity tugging at his manroot with the dirty fingers of Eros.

"Are you sure, Mr. Jordan?"

Vulture hours circling carrion day as a red hand prepares to unbar the gates of so-called light.

"Bry. Call me Bry! I'm very sure. Don't ever turn down money. Dawn, right? Dae's friend? I'm glad you decided to come to work for us."

"Thanks, Bry. It's very generous of you. I'm glad too. I was planning on going back to Ulster County to work at a local place but Dae convinced me to stay. I'll be working at O on the weekends."

"That's great. This is my partner Frank."

"Nice to meet you, Frank. Why do you guys pay for your drinks? Most owners—"

"It's a Corporation and it wouldn't be fair to our partners."

"Nice to meet you, Dawn. Maybe you'll hang out with us later," Dentelupo proposed.

"Yeah, cool. I'd better take care of these guys (she pointed to a group of customers along the bar). If you need—"

"We'll call you," Jordan interrupted.

When Dawn had moved out of ear range, Dentelupo cracked (thoroughly cracking himself up):

"I need to put my dick in your ass!"

Praxis Sodomiticus Dentelupus Rex Rectum, I need to adjust my antenna and tune in a different station. The brute music this one's playing causes me to see the skull beneath the skin. Outside, though I am blind to the stars, my brain will receive better reception. The gods will be heard. I may even attempt to tune in mañana.

Each day is a wave in th'ocean of Time.

Just say fucking no to epigrams. Especially those composed in pseudo-iambic pentameter. And always say no to Pope!

To wake the hole by tender gropes of arse,
To raise the penis and to mend the cunt.

71

And, of course, resist Learic limericks:

There once was a hurling Mick,

who had a diffident dick.

Too shy to make a goal,

he dug a little hole,

and promptly buried his stick.

"I better get the contract," Jordan said to his partner, "before I get too fucked up to tell if Gunther is fucking us."

His partner, who had been drinking, lowered his glass.

"What does Allen say?"

"He wants us to hold off signing anything until he sees us."

Jordan rubbed out a cigarette left burning in an ashtray, directed his voice to his men:

"I'll be back in a few minutes. Try not to burn the place down."

"Bry, get my Oakleys," Dentelupo requested.

"I wear my sunglasses at night," the bird lips of Mike Jerky tweeted.

Dentelupo smiled reluctantly.

"Do a line for us, baby," Mike Campy suggested hoarsely. The remark infuriated Jordan but he kept walking to the exit.

Bar personnel scurried for the honor of getting the door for the Irish Pablo Escobar. The victor, muscle-heads Dentelupo called such types, a figurative and sartorial advertisement for a popular gym, prematurely flung the door open. Jordan had stopped to watch a replay. Safe. Mets screwed again. Diverting his eyes from the game, he observed how ghostly his surroundings appeared. Gleaming across the stage are those who are known by their dance. Incursions into the solid world by those whose wayward and flickering existence mystify us. Remistry or reality? Who knows? Not the contadino mattoid whom I call partner.

Standing there as still as plastic, eyes affixed to the grainy picture of the projection television crowning the wooden O, his soul swooned. Not trusting its form and color, in a word, hyacinthine, though by definish it should be amorphous and acromatic (like a f.p. of S.S.), he trampled it and walked out of the door. It shambled after him.

With a rebel yell—she cried

more, more, more

Blackened eidolons disappearing from the sight of the gods! Aphotic souls crashing into devouring nothingness. Terrestrials cru- beenically tapping to a dithyramb sung by a soul like theirs:

And with a rebel yell—she cried

more, more, more...

Silently, in the friendship of the ruddy moon, he cast his thoughts to all the points of the compass. Sparks of silver showered the planet with heavenly brilliance. His neo-Berkeleyan cosmography would change all: the flesh would become word again. As the great poet had intended. All else would fade into purplish nothingness. What's the difference? Nothing is really lost if you believe as doubting George did, that everything is a hue Hancocked on the air. Does the air even exist? Jordan took a profound breath and exhaled loudly. The hubris of philos- ophers to think they have all the answers. Only one was honest enough to forge his philosophy out of posing questions. And they killed him for it. I won't allow them to press their dagger definitions to my throat. Nor will I succumb to the bludgeoning harangue of theology. The Angelic Doctor's shotgun marriage of reason and faith sickens me. Aquinastotle at his most Aquinastotelian. My cousin told me back in his seminary days in Ireland, he was constrained to read Too Tall Tom in the original. His instructor, in brogued Latin, summed it up in two words: Respice fi- nem. That's what the fine swine are doing inside. One night I sat ugliness on my knees. The Devil Doctor called all French poetry a boast. That's an anti-boast, isn't it? Aboard, aboard, for shame, Shamie. The wind sits in the shoulder of your sail, and you are stayed for. Not yet. Things to do. The drunken boat will continue its stayance. Tarnally, if I wish. Jordan approached his car. Shining thinghood. No one cares about the afflu- ence of your soul. Jordan retrieved the contract (visor, passenger side) and started back to the bar. La porte noire opening and closing, like the nasty orifice of a gross goddess. He waved a biker by. Noblesse oblige. Before going in, he paused. I'll be destroyed in its maw, but I must, in the tradition of Jonah and Abbot, enter the belly of the nameless one. The amethyst-eyed demophagist enjoys us Celts. Bluddlefilth rare. First however, because I'm übereared, I'll peer into the mind of that swarthy halfling, faux brother, uncle-cousin, future Ephialtes, and glimpse what's before me:

I just swallowed a gobful of poison. Blessed. Blessed. Blessed.

I paraphrase, of course. Are his thoughts the cracked looking-glass of my preexistent future?

Jordan weaved his way through the penned-in throng and re-joined his partner and their men. Not men at all: chattering chattel. A fucking waste of molecules.

Mike Campy: dually-addicted convicted rapist (statuatory).

Mike Jerky: dually-addicted anti-Semitic bully (Hakenkreuz wearer).

Tenny Richards: dually-addicted deadbeat (self-hater).

And his partner: dually-addicted wife beater. Not men at all! Fly infested wanton boys. What about you, Mr. Chadcagoshite? I am all too andric. Your names mock you as excrement, Monsieur. The Kennisto-nian definition of a man, actually. I pass the baton.

What made him think he was any better than his companions? Isn't he just a Mick drugpusher from the suburbs? To his fucking credit, the smuck expects to be struck down any moment by a fiery arrow from the Panmighty.

Instant Karma gonna get you!

How fucking conceited, how Brian. Earlier in the reverie of what this putz calls his life, he had proclaimed himself mac Priam:

"I play a hapless Paris…"

Now the petseleh wishes to be viewed as the about to be slain Achilles. Oy! What a megalomaniac! Because by being both slayer and the slain, one may achieve a modicum of godity. You draw a semi-auto-matic pistol from the waistband of your pants and shoot your unapolo-getic self in the eye. You fall to the floor like a horrid simile falls onto the page: loud and discordant. Your obit reads:

Brian "Shamie" Jordan, 35, of Howth Castle and Environs, BKA, the Riverrun section of Toms River, died as he wallowed in libidic slop at a go-go bar in Old Bridge. Jordan was President and C.E.O. of Odyssey Advertising, Inc., Dover, Delaware (a dummy corporation under investigation by the Internal Revenue Service). He was also owner of two bars, Precious Squares (the place of his demise) and Club Oscura in Seaside Heights (an establishment with ties to the Camorra). At the time of his death, the DEA was closing in on his cocaine distribution ring. He is survived by...

There's the rub, as some Fabianist once remarked. To uncoil and leave behind the stain of loodheramaun. No angels will weep for his shade.

You are not killed. You imagine things. Jordan watched a barmaid pour his companions shots of whiskey. The dragon of the Liffey smiling up at them. He turned his gaze from his companions and pored over the contract. The inky pages gave him control. Control was ownership according to Josephson. (Who would doubt a person with the same surname, albeit anglicized, as the main attraction of Golgotha?) Not a superstitious Catholic like Jordan. In essence, his partners now worked for him. Dentelupo gestured for the contract. Take it! Dentelupo perused the document, not understanding it any better than if it were written in Sinogreco. Abandoning pretense, he rolled it up and lanced Jordan in the side. Coup de grâce? No! I'm like that mad Russian hierophant, I won't be killed easily. Nova agnus dei, I'm not. Try again, Centurion.

"Do you want to order a bar pie," his would-be assassin asked.

If they can't kill me with their lance, they'll do it with their greasy victuals.

"I suppose," Jordan said, "I could force myself to eat a slice of red slop."

"Wop slop," Mike Jerky redacted.

"We'll get one with a topping of Polish sausage for you, Mike," Dentelupo fumed, adding, "Or shit. A Polack can't tell the difference."

"I keep tellin' you, Frankie," Mike Jerky whined, "I'm Hungarian."

"Yeah, right," Dentelupo exclaimed, "and I'm Irish."

An old fellow, dressed for the tropics, with a walking stick at his side, approached them. His ginny breath preceding him by seconds.

"I'm sorry, gentlemen," the old fellow bellowed in an accent Jordan correctly discerned as upper Mancunian, "but did one of you say you're Hungarian?"

"He did," Dentelupo answered, pointing to Mike Jerky.

"We shall see," the old man promised, as he used the pewter tip of his walking stick to raise the yellow flap of hair draping Mike Jerky's nape. Not satisfied with the ocular proof, the old fellow proceeded to grope the back of his subject's head in order to determine the existence of the so-called badge of Attila, that is, the unusually distinct occipital protuberance found amongst those of Hungarian descent. Mike Jerky suffered the inspection by giggling, not knowing how to react without a sign from Jordan et al.

"He's an imposter," the old fellow declared. "He's Polo-Teutonic. A German-Polack, I mean."

A chain of derisive laughter rattled in Mike Jerky's pinkening ears. Infuriated, the fascist pig, Mike Jerky, decided to have his revenge by breaking the ancient phrenologist's walking stick over his knee, but before he could act, the old fellow had vanished like a Druid.

"Crazy fuck," Mike Jerky muttered, still looking around for his prey.

"Told you he's a Polack," Dentelupo announced proudly.

"And you're a fucking Moor," Mike Jerky countered, laughing.

"What about Campy," Tenny Richards asked Mike Jerky. "He's Italian too."

"He's a mulatto like you, Tenny," Mike Jerky said, smiling, rubbing Tenny Richards's back.

"Ain't nothing but a thing, baby," Mike Campy replied, the poor quality of prison dentistry apparent when he smiled.

They all laugh at Mike Campy's Campyese except Tenny Richards.

"I'm actually Scots-African," Tenny Richards informed. "My great-great-grandfather on my mother's side was Angus Bruce, a descendant of the King of Scotland, who owned a plantation in Georgia."

"So," Mike Jerky said, "you're a smoked Scotchman."

"My skin is lighter than Frankie's," Tenny Richards cried, grabbing Dentelupo's hand. "See!"

"That makes Frankie a pigmy," Mike Jerky said, smiling.

"Do you know Argo," Dentelupo asked angrily.

"Not that again," Mike Jerky whined. "Bry, will you—"

"Leave me the fuck alone, Mike," Jordan moaned. "I'm sick of this whole fucking conversation. As far as I'm concerned, you guys belong in nursery school."

Tenny Richards affectionately hooked arms with Jordan.

"Bry, chill. You're the man! Forget about her tonight. Have some fun with your buds."

Entertained, Jordan laughed.

"Do a shot with us, Bry," Mike Jerky pleaded.

"I suppose," Jordan said, "you want me to buy?"

"Fuck yes!" they all screamed in unison.

A blurmaid places a blur in front of you and blurs away.

"Make a toast," Tenny Richards requested loudly.

"You make one," Jordan replied, turning to Dentelupo.

"You," Dentelupo said. "I don't know none."

Jordan made a relenting face and chanted:

"Yesterday's sand, yesterday's rain!

Today's joy, tomorrow's pain."

"That's corny, Bry," Dentelupo said, drinking.

"I'm not Robbie Burns," Jordan said, laughing. "So the next time you can make your own fucking toasts. What the fuck are we, a bunch of old Mickeys? I'm the only Mick here tonight."

"I'm half Irish," Mike Jerky revealed.

"Poland ain't nowhere near Ireland," Dentelupo said. "I'm a stupid motherfucker and I know that."

"Look at you," Mike Jerky exclaimed, amused at Dentelupo's adamance.

"Make another, Bry," Tenny Richards said, again hooking arms with Jordan.

"You mean you want me to buy again," Jordan asked, unfettering himself from Richards. The Defiant Ones. I don't hate him because of his epicolor, but because of the contentlessness of his character.

Dentelupo smirked his usual smirk, saying:

"That's why everybody loves you, Bry. That's why nothing bad will ever happen to you."

Memento mori. But is that so bad?

Jordan held up his refilled glass and toasted in an Irish accent:

"Fuck the cops! And eat their daughters!"

The Mikes cowboyishly whooped, stuck out their tongues, made lewd gestures to a dancer across from them. Tenny Richards smiled. Dentelupo smirked.

"That's much, much better," Tenny Richards said, continuing to smile.

"Much," Dentelupo seconded.

Jordan quizzed his legs. Two shots of Jamey had left them uncertain. Who's walking anywhere? Not Sultan Ali Jordan! At closing time, your highness' blackamoors will litter you to your highness' harem (no longer—because of your highness' percentage here—consisting only of Rosa Palma and her five faccia brutta daughters). If only sheep were better looking. If only our palms had cracks. Concentrate, Brian. You're about to be resomething. I don't want to be reanything. I want to be renothing. Can't do that, Bry. Here it goes:

You peck yourself through a mundane shell, chirping like a mofo, beating your angel's or devil's wings in vain, for paradise is not to be found on this side of your mother's cunt.

*

Jordan locked the contract in the bottom drawer of a filing cabinet. Fluidly, solidly, otherly, he gravitated to the cushiony swivel chair behind his desk. Domestic wild. Carpentry of words tamed us. We were a happy lot of heathens before Taffy Pat showed up on greaseless shores. Oakwise no more. Using the blueprints of McIntire, the master joiner, he hammered us into a cil. This Druid pines for an oaken altar. Playing the top of the desk with his piano fingers, he observed with slight amusement, as Dentelupo emptied dirty ashtrays into a trashpail underneath the mini-bar's stainless steel sink.

"I've got to put up a no smoking sign," Dentelupo huffed, as he mixed himself a rum and coke, belatedly adding: "It's the whores. They all smoke."

"If you do that," Jordan said, "you'll also be posting a no blowing sign."

"I see what you mean."

"We have," Jordan said, "people to clean up around here. Don't we?"

They apply polished lips to the attentive spigots of our soul. See, where.

"Rosa smokes like a fiend."

"She likes something in her mouth," Jordan said, smiling.

Dentelupo groped himself.

"My big Italian sausage!"

"You mean your limp cannoli," Jordan needled.

"Wise fuck. Do you want a drink," Dentelupo asked, holding up his glass.

Desidero cento. Who is he? Those are the streaming locks of somebody? I know. I know. He's ben Zeus covering strange barfellows in forgetful blue snow. A mad whoreson of a fellow partying like it's 1999.

"Nah," Jordan answered, preoccupied with a stack of legal documents. "It seems," he added, "we get a different directive from the state every day."

No matter how bloated the bureaucracy, no matter how many badges come around, Old Dinny will conduct his revels. Otherwise, Aphrodite, the mother of all freedom, will pierce the blue air with shrill-shrieks.

"What do you hear on that matter with the A.G.," Dentelupo asked creaseheadedly.

"Allen assures me it's being shitcanned."

"That's great," Dentelupo exhaled, coming out from behind the mini-bar.

Jordan reclined in the chair until only a small percentage of his partner remained visible. The obdurate web of black hair framing Dentelupo's swarthy, angular face and irregular smile conjured for him Nabokov's two pitch eternities sandwiching the dab of light deemed existence. Hold the Mayo! Das beste wäre, nie geboren sein.

As Dentelupo moved about the room, the ice cubes in his glass broadcasted their vain attempt to escape Dantean confines.

All is not sweet, all is not music.

Stopping to scoop up the black remote from the freckled counter of the bar, Dentelupo switched on the television. Heaveneye chromatically twinkling. No glorious spines to ogle in this crypt. Paneled in shitbrown. Long Kesh chic. New symbol of Irish Art. Videotapes to the left of them, videotapes to the right of them, videotapes in front of them volleyed and thundered. Like evil seizing the soul, they have taken dominion over the bookshelves. (Similic hyperbole.) Leave the debate to social engineers. (Cliché.) As a Berkeleyan, I find it unnecessary to redact the illusion. (Pretentious.) White noise? The gamut of sound? I think so. (Further pretension.) The cochlea-shattering noise a loaded VCR makes before you press play. Perhaps I'm confused? (Stating the fucking obvious.) FM sound revolutionized television. Sarnoff had its inventor murdered. (Conspiracy nut.) I'll ask Jack Kenniston. He'll know. A technician of some sort. I saw him out there nestled between two lumps of matter whose gstrings are impeding his penis-finger's progress to their holes. Right now, of course, he's more interested in different hued noise. Pink noise, pussy farts.

Jordan leaned forward, his eyes straining to take in the faint semblance of life: obscene gestures on the air. A figo to thee! Maestro, aiuto! Bianco pioppi! Der Geist in du. Kenniston would no doubt Kennistonianly explain: Electromagnetic cathode-ray tube et cetera, et cetera. Then, I would translate the Kennistonese into Brianese: A stream of fucking electrons. Hocus focus!

"The Mets are winning," Dentelupo announced. "Cone's pitching a shutout."

Is he smiling because he's happy or is he happy because he's a smiling motherfucker? Signal bouncing like a super spaldeen off the sun and the other stars. I see Mookie run, dive, make the catch. No replay.

They go to a commercial. He's raving about the play. A backfisch in cut-offs drinking the Surreal Thing. He raves about her ass. If I wish to see Mookie's leather magic again, I'll have to take a space ship to where the game airs much later in Mid-Eternity. And we dance and we dance and we dance between God's naked soul and the black adiaphane, choreographed by philosophers regarded holy by their followers. I can't dance. Don't make me. A fiery bush belching a fiat none of us are capable of obeying:

Thou shalt not commit a faux pas!

Life is what? Eternal, if you believe in him. I do! I do! I confess, I don't, really. The lattice-eared priesteen demands that I leave the box. You're doomed if you refuse to be his fiancée, says he. And who is he when he's at home, says I. The Lord thy God, says he. I know two, no three, gods with mothers named Mary, says I. You're fucked, says he. Only bitches get fucked, beeatch, says I.

"I have that thing in the City tomorrow," Jordan said, dragging along with his words a rattling chain of mucous. Coughing uncontrolla-bly, Jordan coerced a wad of phlegm into a crumpled handkerchief. The noserag of a metempsychotic. He folded the handkerchief into an apt configuration and returned it to its former space: the right leg pocket of his cargo pants. Diagnosis: Jacob Deasy: You have bronchitis. Contract it and you have it for life. Life is what? It's a lightning-flash and in its brief illumination I shall attempt to see what lies between the bibleblack space of molecules. Tomorrow I'll either fly or fall to my… Do Geese see God?

"Do you want me to drive you in," Dentelupo inquired, fussing with the sleeves of his darkcolored sports jacket.

"I've arranged for a limo. With the stop off, it's safer."

Shakespeare & Company downtown. Must pick up Annotated Juanita Dark. What's playing at the Angelica?

"What time are they expected?"

"Late afternoon, early evening. Depending on the traffic," Jordan answered.

"They're driving in all the way from Boston?"

"You can't carry guns on a plane, can you?"

Dentelupo smirked. He opened his jacket and exposed a holstered nine millimeter Beretta.

"You need something like this," he said, drawing the pistol, twirling it on his diminutive forefinger. Jordan smiled scornfully. Allopenis. Di claims he's hung like a hampster. One may simile and simile and be a Grillparzer! The true writer has nothing to say. It's the fucking way he says it. All I can see at the far side of the bloodblack sky is an enormous canine chewing on the bonewhite moon. Eusaid! But what does it mean? Its meaning can only be arrived at after lengthy exegesial debate. Fuck that! I want immediate intellectual gratification. Alright, ceannchad, I'll give you what you want: meaning. All kinds. I'm full of good meanings and good wishes. Though if it were up to me, I'd produce a blund'ring melody devoid of sense, free of meaning. In a word, heroically mad. But before I dip my quill in the black lough, I'll slake my thirst with a few jars, as I am sure Johnny Irish must have before starting a scholarly disquisition. A million words or my name isn't Blazes Boylan. As an homage of Séamus of Rathgar, I'll write it in lookingglass Eurish, and just like Technical Sergeant Eliot, a.k.a. the hyacinth girleen, I'll include a section of explanatory notes:

Note one: Don't read these notes.

Note two: Don't fucking read them!

Note three: !reeuq ma I

"Put it away before you blow your fucking balls off!"

Words plow the pastures of my mind, furrowing them with joy. I could take him hunting. Nobody would suspect. We're putative buddies. I could fall, my gun accidentally discharging. His blood crying out from the ground to the highest court, like a call for justice. Translators are traitors, they say in solic Italy. Or I could just fucking shoot him in the cock. What's to stop me? I'm already damned. Pynchon's obsession with preterition bothers me. Wasn't he brought up Irish Catholic? We believe there's always hope. Not that I think there's any hope for an ad canvasser/drug pusher. Make the check out to the Lucifer News. The phone rang, Jordan picked it up.

"Hello."

"Yunior?"

"Hi, Gunther."

"Yunior, I left the account number on da ding."

"My answering machine?"

"Ya."

"Thanks, Gunther."

"Is Frankie—"

"He's here."

"Tell him if his vife finds him dere, she'll cut off his balls."

"I'll tell him, Gunther. I'll tell him."

"Don't drink zo much tonight, yunior."

"I won't."

Auf wiedersehen, der scheisseführer.

"German fuck," Dentelupo exclaimed, lovingly pressing his pistol to the side of his face.

Pistol packing farce. Too chummy with chum. Feu! Maybe I'll shoot him with his pistol. His fingerprints. Frame him like a film noir. They hate each other.

"Frank, put that thing away," Jordan pleaded. Dentelupo smiled and took aim at a Madonna as Marilyn poster. His inaccurate mimicking of gunfire infuriated Jordan.

"I hope the fuckin' safety's on," Jordan moaned, as he surreptitiously glanced at a photograph in his right hand, The Queen of Azure and the fool of the void drive past a half dozen buildings on their way to the shining seventh; to where eyes rage, tongues twist, to where the sky flows into the nostrils of the macrosoul. Jordan slipped the photograph underneath the blotter. If he shot me, where would my microsoul transmigrate?

Dentelupo holstered his pistol and sat down on the edge of the desk.

"How much is Whitey interested in?"

"A suitcase full," Jordan informed, highfiving his partner.

"You think it's safe," Dentelupo said. "I mean, look at all the cash?"

"I've done it before," Jordan replied. "And I told you," he said with increased energy, "there's not going to be any cash. The money's going to be wired to our bank in Zurich. When the deposit's confirmed, I'll turn over the groove."

"How do you know they won't fuck us? Just take the groove."

Defenesomething? Fly or fall? A wild beast flying to paradise. Waxwings not an issue in a universe where the sun is a block of ice.

"Would you fuck the . . . ," Jordan said, with purposeful incompletion. IRPBA. Judases summarily patellacaped! He believes me. He believes. If he knew, I lie like thou.

"No," Dentelupo answered meekly, adding: "What about the bank? Can we trust a Kraut bank?"

Jordan smiled. They don't trust anybody. They'd step over their morte mamma to fuck their mezza morte sorella.

"Swiss, actually. I'd trust Fluntern Bank with Christ's beautiful blue balls. Or something more valuable."

"You're trusting them with our balls," Dentelupo said, his voice deepening with every breath. "And you shouldn't say such horrible things. You know," he exhaled sadly, "that you believe."

I believe. Help my unbelief.

"Cut me a break, Frank. We're doomed motherfuckers. I see Dante building an additional circle in hell just for us: the cocaine dealers."

"Dante? My uncle?"

"The poet," Jordan answered, laughing hysterically.

"Oh, him. I thought you meant my uncle Dante because he owned a construction company in Jersey City."

"Is he retired?"

"You could say that. He's dead."

Jordan continued to laugh.

"So you thought—"

"My father says," Dentelupo interrupted, "his brother Dante is rotting in hell. Because he cheated him out of the family business."

"Didn't your family own a bakery?"

"Yeah," Dentelupo said. "Dante sold it and with the profits went into the construction business."

"So you thought I was being literal."

"I guess."

"You have never heard of the Inferno or Dante Alighieri, have you?"

"Yeah. So what?"

"You're right. Who cares?"

"Bry?"

"What?"

"Do you know Argo?"

"I know. Argo fuck yourself."

Dentelupo giggled as he channel surfed. Jordan gestured for the black device in Dentelupo's palm. Dentelupo reluctantly handed him the remote and Jordan promptly muted the television.

"Listen," Jordan commanded, "the sound of capitalism."

"What?"

"The sweet voice of money, Frank."

He doesn't get it, boyo. And when did you become a Republican? I'm an apostle of Adam Smith. It says here in the Revenant Journal (in very blurry print, mind you) that you've gone over to the GOP. The grand old protestants! How could you vote for that hennahaired (quondam Catholic, quondam Democrat) cadaver? Read revelations, grandda. He's the 666! He whispered in my ear: Sell! Buy! Sell! Buy! Trickle down down down. Put but punts in thy purse! Dentelupo prepared a glistening cokespoon. A line drive to left! He offers me a turn at bat but I decline. Introibo ad altare Bacchus. What in whiskey did Jordan, spiritopot, pourer of the craythure, transporter of the water of life, returning to the desk, admire? Its democracy of destruction, Shiva of liquids. Dentelupo rubbed his economical forehead as if to facilitate the rush of coke.

"Fucking Ferro," Dentelupo screamed, his eyes black with anger. "We give him the best deal in the universe and he wants credit."

Jordan's eyes agreed.

"How do we cut him off, Franky?"

"You'll think of something."

"It won't be that easy."

"You're not afraid of him?"

"You mean that greaseball connected shit? I told you."

"Alright. Alright, Bry. Didn't mean. He's a fuckin' pussy. Why don't you turn him over to your people?"

"I wouldn't bother them. I never wanted to sell to him. Always playing the big fucking shot! He tells everybody. He's an asshole and he has a bunch of assholes working for him. One of them is liable to get popped and then it's Town and Country all over again. How the fuck did we escape that shitstorm?"

"Relax, Bry. Nobody's gonna get popped."

"Are you kidding? People are getting popped every day, Frank. Don't you read the papers or watch television?"

"We're protected. Look at our client list. Judges. For fuck sake we sell to Judges."

Jordan gave his partner a disgusted look.

"You're an out of style motherfucker," he said. "Do you know that? Throw that notion out with the white capezios you wore last night."

"That's cold. Mike's the capezio wearer. Relax, buddy. Nobody's after us. You paranoid motherfucker!"

"Everybody's going to rehabs. Jerry is at Carrier. Eddie O. The Just Say No Movement—"

"Fuck Nancy Reagan!"

"As Jim Merry used to say, not with your dick."

"Jerry went in for heroin. I'd never deal that shit."

His brother, Buster, hooked his brother Michael.

"Unless," Dentelupo continued, "it's completely unavoidable."

"I think they should shoot heroin dealers. Like they—"

"You're right. Coke's different."

"They probably should shoot coke dealers too," Jordan said. "I just hope," he added, "it isn't tomorrow."

"Never," Dentelupo said forcibly. "I think, to go back to Rocky, that we have to cut him off until he pays up. We have to run this like a business."

"I don't think the Chamber wants us."

"Bry, I'm serious."

"I told you I didn't want to sell to him."

"I know. He's an old friend and you hate leaning on him. I told you that I'd handle him."

"I only agreed to sell to him because he owned the Club. He's losin' his balls in A.C. We should buy him out. The Club is a great place to Maytag cash, Frank. What's ten thousand? We'll buy him out. I'll tell him to forget the ten thousand."

"Don't tell him that."

"That's peanuts, Frankie."

"He has to pay us everything," Dentelupo said, raising a monogrammed golden spoon to his nose. "It's the guinea in me," he continued. "I can't stand another guinea gettin' over on me. The ten, if he agrees to sell out, will go on the purchase price of the Club. If he doesn't sell, I'll beat the spaghetti sauce out of him. Dirty greaseball."

Jordan smiled at his friend's self-hatred.

"Do you want a hit, Brian?"

The telepathy of the dually addicted. Jordan unspooned Dentelupo, appraised the garish utensil as if it were an ancient artifact, snorted an enormous line. F.D. Fucking dumb! Chrysophilism is a disease. What we do is an example of chrysopoetics. Shite into gold! White shite. White shitening. Grooveshiners. Who was it that first called it that? Was it the Easter boys? Not I. Perhaps Carrick?

"Get rid of it, Frank," Jordan huffed, giving the spoon back to his partner.

"Why?"

"Are you kidding?"

Dentelupo grinned.

"Alright."

"Give it to one of the whores," Jordan said, laughing. "Any one of them will blow you for it. For the residue alone!"

"I'm going back out," Dentelupo announced. "Are you coming?"

Anon. Anon. Anonly. Coming is a polyseme, isn't it? Jordan ogled the whiskey left in his glass. My parents are nephalists and hyperdulic. I drink and worship Magog!

"Yeah, in a few."

Petty pace accelerated, fast forward to tomorrow, by definition a falser time than today. You're registered in the Waldorf-Astoria, which scratches the groin of Manhattan. In fact, you hear its rumbling prostate out your window. A glimpse down and you see a colony of marching sensual insects. Your job is to turn them into insensate shadows. The keycard holder on the Grecian marble night table is marked 1941. So if you were to suffer defenestration, how long—at the approximate rate of falling bodies—would it take for you to osculate the sidewalk? Time enough and floors enough for repentance, my coy mistress. Your eyes change direction. They fix upon a large blue suitcase resting on the bed. The one your supplier had stored early this morning in a locker at Port Authority. You don't have to open it to see the seeming myriad of diaphanous bags of uncut cocaine piled within like ghostly bodies. With a smug, silly expression, you sing: co-caine, co-caine, co-caine!

You take a long, soothing shower. It gives you the appearance of a scattered, dying hallucination. You stare into a steamy mirror, visageless, until you take a washcloth and rub your face back into existence. Euge! Euge! Ding an sich! The phone rings. Not so much a ring but an electronic aria. You answer it using your deepest voice. The drug lord and his hounds will be there in an hour.

Nobody suspects Micks of selling drugs like guineas. We're cops, firemen, priests, politicians. You drink a diet coke and nosh on cashews. The cashews will no doubt exacerbate your diverticulitis, and the caffeine, your ulcer. You glance over at the sammy full of coke. You'll buy yourself a new digestive system. If you get busted, you'll tell them you're working for Ferro. They're just as interested in getting the fake mafia as the real one. It will be the witness relocation program for you. To enter heaven, travel hell. You want to pray but the sails of faith are limp. The Irish word for rosary implodes in your brain and explodes from your lips:

Paidrín.

Kate Jordan, your sainted nanna, taught you the rosary in the language of the saints, as she called it, but you no longer remember it. Oh, you're such a loodheramaun. A disgrace! Kate was a saint married to an ain't, my uncle Shane opined often.

You put on your armor of respectability: a gray suit. The material breathes according to the onion breathed salesman. You wish, you could. You loosen your tie. You slip on your black Bostonians. An homage to the Southies. As impossible as it seems, you can hear your watch ticking. You dredge a beer out of the mini-bar and sit, sip, wait.

*

"Hello again," Rosa said, shoulders parting for her along the bar. Dentelupo presented her with a stool and she sat down among the cinders. On the fleshly stage of Eros, he plays a dumb Durante to her debased Bice. Debased Bice? Euph, don't you think? French slang for troublesome geometry.

"Do you want a drink," Dentelupo asked, his hand on her bare thigh.

"I'll have a white wine," she replied. Dentelupo sought the attention of a barmaid. Jordan watched his partner's diva being served. Rosa, along with Dentelupo, tipped the barmaid. Fingering the rim of the fluted glass, Rosa asked:

"So what's up, guys?"

"Frank's celebrating his pending divorce."

"Is that true, Frank?"

"Yeah, I just can't stand the abuse no more."

"What about your son?"

"I'm gonna fight for custody."

She caressed his beardless cheek, lingering on a prominent scratch, and cried:

"Good! I hope you win. You're such a good father."

No irony. She believes he's a saint. Do saints fuck you in the ass? She turned her labrose lips to Jordan: a nasty prefigurement took life in his mind. She lit a cigarette.

"What's up with you, Brian," she asked, exhaling a smelly cloud in his face. He stuck out his palm and futilely redirected the dancing gray murderess.

"Nothing," he coughed.

"So you're out of love," Rosa asked.

"She's too ugly to love," Jordan answered bitterly.

"No, she's not. You showed me a picture. She's beautiful."

"She's not as beautiful as she looks," Jordan rejoined.

"You're quoting somebody."

"Marcel Proust."

"Who?"

"Yogi Berra's cousin."

"I love Yogi. Did this Marcel dude play baseball?"

"He played hockey."

"You're lying. Show me her picture again. What's her name? Rachel, right?"

"Rachel," Dentelupo confirmed.

Jordan extended his arm downward to the puffy leg pocket of his cargo pants, reached in, and retrieved a weighty, black leather wallet. He extricated a snapshot of Rachel from a clear plastic photograph holder and offered it to Rosa.

She snatched the photograph from him, examined it, and handed it back.

"She's beautiful, Brian."

Blue eyes dotted with red. Feathered golden hair of Locklear. Her teeth too large for a petite mouth. A nose erected in the face like a flesh and bone monument to her ancestors.

"To burn or not to burn," Hamlet Jordan intoned. "Pass me your lighter, Campy."

Mike Campy slid the lighter over to him.

"Thanks, Campy."

"Don't mention it, baby."

Jordan flicked the lighter on, holding the photograph up to its flame.

"Don't," Rosa pleaded.

Monolithic chin.

"Bry," Dentelupo called out sternly.

One sublime face can't save you from the shit.

"Bry, you'll regret it afterwards," Dentelupo cautioned.

A tongue of light, paradoxically, transforming a rosy visage into a grayblack bouquet. His singed fingers directing an array of beautiful dark flowers to an ashtray.

CHAPTER 7

Hard my knees sinking below sea level of our waterbed silk sheets like Aegean waves bought them at Bams with Brys gold card he handed me it last week unexpectedly saying anything for pharaohs daughter I hate when he says things like that it makes him appear older than he is thirty five going on fifty lately hes been going on about reincarnation which he calls metempsychosis like Im supposed to be impressed my fault for giving him WE ARE ONE ANOTHER for Christmas bad enough hes bugging me all the time about what and who I saw during my regressions hes too chicken to go through it himself shouldve never mentioned I was an ancient Egyptian he somehow took it to mean I was royalty because it makes him feel important and it made him sad when I told him we were a pioneer couple and he constantly abused me and this is why I tell him I feel uncertain in this life about our relationship he swears hed never abuse me and I tell him I know but its difficult to get by what he did to me in that life hes really fascinated with one in particular he a Cathar priest I a priestess burned at the stake together during the inquisition a hesitating hesoul and hesitating shesoul uniting in space and smoke what an image he enthused enthused over nothing because I saw nothing faked it like I fake everything hard I dont think I have a soul the hypnotist bearded like Freud took off his nerdy thick glasses and asked us to picture ourselves wading through a shallow stream only thing I saw was a roomful of zombies and the hypnotist counted backwards and it was all over quicker than it had started afterwards the subjects happily recounted their experiences and I waited for my turn at lying it wouldve been great if I had something honest to share but I didnt even see a heap of broken images

hes so gullible Irish Catholics they believe in the little people dont they maybe he believes me because Im so little believes Im having a difficult time leaving Rick because as I tell him Rick was my son in another life jesus christ does he believe I believe he makes all that cash just selling ads Dawn swears hes a coke dealer claims his incessant sniffling the night we all had dinner a few weeks ago proves it the girl he brought along jewish and Irish like me seemed really high Rick had to work joined us later in the casino I was jealous showed up at the door with what was her name Debbie Debbie does Bry the big macher Dawn came with us said afterwards hes a drug pusher show off gave the waitress a two hundred dollar tip without blinking whats wrong with him his date seemed really really high Ricks gullible too thinks Im out shopping all the time that I go to see my aunt in Pennsylvania Rick he doesnt mind my disappearances too busy gambling away our future he never calls my aunt to check up on me he hates her thinks shes a nervy noisy jew hes right my aunt hates him tells me I should get rid of him my mother too she thinks hes a pisk doesnt think he can offer me security Bry attended Columbia education impresses her I make him happy by not leaving Rick gives him an excuse to drink and do coke and cry hes a poet god made everything from water thus our love was made of tears he loves ghosts always humming the ghost in you by the Furs annoying sometimes Ricks a bore Brys boring in a different way the way he looks at me excites me he has bedroom eyes and Elvis lips makes me want to fuck him last week we almost did it leaning up against the car in the parking lot of Sir Kyles if he could I mean looking up at the night sky he whispered you are fairer than the evening clad in a thousand stars corny shit but I sighed hoping hed do it to me right there people traipsing in and out of the restaurant a balmy night I didnt care if anyone saw I wanted it hard I wonder what the problem is most guys premature he takes a long time so long it never happens becomes soft as a mushroom Dawns theory which I dont necessarily go along with is he goes with the dancers old men she says only have so many orgasms a week his thingy sapped by the end by the whores sexually burnt out maybe he masturbates Ill try acting slutty scream curses when hes fucking me the way I do when Rick fucks me coke supposedly causes impotency not in the Houston Cowboy who fucked me when I went there last year to visit Billie who I hate she said things about me Jackie says I think she liked Steve jealous that he liked me he turned out to be a jerk we got high together he fucked me four times in one night no problem with his cock hard hes a grease monkey for a dealership in Katy Texas Bry puts me on a pedestal doesnt know how wild I can be the club he owns with the mafia has a great dance floor sound system and lights makes you feel like youre a ghost fleeing perverted gods more of a spiritual experience than my socalled regression usually dance for hours some of the time with him but he cant keep up with me hes a terrible dancer doesnt move his hips sweats like a faucet usually retreats to the bar after a few minutes where he drinks and gabs with the staff Dee his ex bartends she seems nice they remain friends cant see that happening when I drop him once when I had finished dancing he shouted to her water water water for my little hydropot she laughed but I dont think she knew what it meant either water drinker he explained when I asked I dont know why he says things like that embarrassing but hes sweet and loves me licked the sweat off my neck and shoulders and the way he looks at me hard its a shame to torture him I know I shouldnt be with either Ricks a gambler Brys a criminal I dont think he saves or invests like he should the Club he boasts will make us rich are we an us from our first kiss outside the Moorish Wall Spanish restaurant he has referred to us as if we were hell never be really really rich the way he spends gives it away like Robin Hood maybe he has millions who knows I really must ask him more about his finances King Brian as I call him sometimes tells me that he was named for King Brian the last high king of Ireland hes certainly that no concept of the bottom line how much does he make selling coke expensive shit lent Rick eleven hundred for the security for our apartment usually spends that much every time I see him seldom uses plastic first time I laid eyes on him I knew he had fallen for me his eyes a mysterious gray or hushed blue darted wildly when I mentioned it to him after our first kiss he said it was a case of spiritual tachycardia he said he knew wed be together the money a finders fee Rick never intends to pay him back calls him a Westie says theyre worse than the guinea mafia chemical Brys reaction after youve had a taste of nothingness how can you believe in more than flesh and fluid the dazed futility of life all of us trying to figure out the puzzling space around us angels or devils helping us to locate that dreamed of paradise

my knees sinking like Atlantis Cayces blue pantied amant Bry called me in a letter why blue I asked the color of your eyes what does he see in me a cold hook nosed jew bitch he should find himself a nice Catholic girl he likes my ass sticks out almost as far as my nose thinks

I have soulful jewish eyes I think jews have a sick look on their face Id never fuck one big nose big ass whats wrong with him yatatata all the time about how much he adores my nose sometimes hes such a yold he likes jews I feel like screaming at him when hes fucking me gait gait thinks hes an honorary yid because hes dating me uses Yiddish planted a tree in Israel in my mothers name riboynoy shel oylom Raefela Hebe screamed upon receiving the plaque from the Jewish Journal documenting her tree doesnt see him as a shtarker what nudniks Rick Bry Rae gai kacken ahfen yam to all of them my fatty friends Dawn and Nancy you too he likes me because I remind him of a little girl with an ass big tits threaten him just fat really both of them seem to like minichested girls or girleens as Bry sometimes calls them pervs perhaps little girl chasers Brys monstrous cock toig ahf kapores as grandma Levy would say cant keep it hard very long giant cock like a dry blintz Ricks a small dildo how do you win oy

told him how weve been lovers down through the ages after all we reincarnate with the same people over and over in order to pay karmic debts hes a Pisces means its the last time around the wheel for him this I tell him accounts for his desperate state must get it right this time or no chance at Nirvana hes so Catholic Ricks a bad Catholic I hate when Bry calls me his Jewish American Princess and he wonders why I wont come and live in that big drafty house Id never give up stiffness for size Rick teases him calls him an Irish gangster he smiles but I dont think he likes it dresses like a drug pusher hard Dawn says Ive never seen him in the same shirt twice yesterday in his bedroom he opened two hulking patent cabinets which held his massed suits and ties and shirts piled like bricks in stacks a dozen high he took out a pile of shirts and began throwing them like a fool one by one shirts of sheer linen and thick silk and fine flannel which lost their folds and covered the table in a colorful mess I called him a fool and he kissed me the way only he can if he only could fuck like he kisses he handed me a vanilla envelope last week filled with hundreds twenty thousand dollars told me to put it away for us my knees went weak we tried to fuck but he had problems again he has a nice mouth Rick has an ugly one too gummy didnt like the stunt he pulled today Ill get back at him make him sit up like a dog says hes gonna buy me his soulmate a condo or townhouse he claims hes gonna give me fifty thousand this weekend Ill grab the cash and run wont do anything he loves me should steal everything he has only gonna piss it all away caught a glimpse of his safe last weekend piles of cash and bonds I think hard

met him in eighty five on the street below the boards very cocky came right up to me and asked my name he said I was beautiful asked if I wanted to hang out with him at the arcade I didnt find him attractive but he was older thin as a rail then we played a few games of Donkey Kong I think the last time I had been in the arcade was when I was fourteen my first poet brought me there a better poet than Brian William Seamus Jordan by far didnt flaunt it Rick was living in a boarding house his room had an old smell he lit some incense he kissed me Crazy For You playing on the radio he put his hand under my top slid a finger underneath my panties and into my cunt I lost control when he sucked on my fingers and fucked me with that hard rod of his ugly and stupid Brys right hes an autophile but at least his cock is hard at least hes not up my ass all the time I try to tell him I see you more than I see the guy I live with Dawn says shes obsessed with Bry if hes not going with the dancers hes jerking off she claims to have caught Alan playing with himself Rick says he probably prefers Rosie Palm and her five daughters than that Yenta at least his hand has no cellulite I laugh but shouldnt Ill never let myself go Dawn could because of her fathers money Rick says they seem as if theyre in love he says Alans in love with Mr Katzs bank account Brys cock starts out as hard as a diamond but after a while especially when he sucks on my tits it becomes soft Freud would have a field day with that Mark says hes gay but nobody has ever kissed me like the way he does a gay man couldnt kiss a woman like the way he kisses me big teddy bear screaming at me one moment sobbing the next hard Rick tells me everybodys scared of him has a mean looking crew working for him hes always so polite Rick says he has seen him beat a guys brains in for a casual remark a violent poet I think he steals some of his stuff first poet told me my eyes reflect the sunset and the dawn that I scatter scents like a windy night your kisses are a drug Bry wrote the same thing to me one day with a few variations signed Brian Flowers Esq

does he come with the others if there are others as Dawn suspects why would she care maybe shes hot for him love hidden in her hatred unreasonable since he never had words with her before today

96

mentioned her nose job but she deserved it theres no proof hes a drug dealer suppose he is he could have her killed make it look like an accident he had that sound in his voice today got me hot Alpha males always cheat she says Alan what a ballless dweeb her jew money Rick says financed his parlors so what if he does theyre whores hard with tit jobs he seems to like mine just fine small but perky he called them sucking on them like a whiskey bottle felt like telling him and your dick is large and limp like a blackmans wonder what hed say how do you know have you been with any no but Dawn told me she fucked a few when she lived in Long Island tells me Alans cock is huge hurts her Brys thing is not only long but fat does that mean hell turn into a fat man Ricks belly keeps getting bigger Brys lost twenty pounds I dont think hes two hundred anymore he cant eat just drinks and does coke I guess I have that effect on men hes wasting away hardly touched his steak last night tipped the waiter over a hundred bucks a gay Frenchman with bedroom eyes like Brys terrible service kept us waiting Bry thinks Im irresistible thought the gay waiter wanted me hes grown so pale and thin in the last month never sleeps glad we got some sun yesterday fathers day on the boardwalk in Seaside dont remember mine very well he was tired hung out Saturday night at Squares what a lousy name for a go go bar says its an allusion to King Lear Regan or was it Goneril calls her vagina her most precious square of sense I told him you should call it Boobs for the customers who go there only kidding I told him put him on the defensive replied Ill sell it if it bothers you you make money dont you and whats the harm he appreciated my understanding last night in bed he fell asleep snoring like Rip Van Winkle kept me awake heard him mutter in between a snore Linda Linda a dancer hes fucking or someone he once was involved with if she can get him to come to come good for her good for her

blinking his useless lids at nothingness I guess Linda Linda what does the echo signify Ill consult my dream book as soon as Im finished here whats taking him taking longer than Bry that is if King Dong ever came Rick says I give the greatest blow job on the planet at least hes never gotten any better and that counts the gay men who he let blow him when he was desperate for money while working at Studio 54 says I suck cock like a gay superman hes so uncouth asks afterwards with a smirk how did the sperm flavored pop rocks taste I should bite it off for the time he brought that little jew whore into our bed too cheap to pay for a motel Ill get Bry off next time and go home to him and kiss him on the mouth that swallowed an Irish gangsters come Ill suck him like a vampire at his own veins last night Bry channel surfing we caught a few minutes of a vampire movie with David Bowie Bry said it was a great movie adapted from a novel by Strieber Communions one of my favorites Bry thinks the authors lying I let him think I believe this way hell believe it when I tell him I love him only him loves impossible a species joke we love only ourselves Ricks an autophile according to Bry cant he see I am too care a better word I care for my mother sometimes my brother Merlin sometimes too Mark never I care for Bry and even the no good motherfucker Im presently hard at work sucking off my first poet was so refined knew how to set a table and prepare French food and when we went to the Rams Head Inn ordered in French to the French waiter I shouldve known he was that way Bry has a lot of nerve to call Rick names hes a drug pusher isnt that self love shouldve guessed poets or pizza delivery boys all let you down poet one like Bry compared my kisses to a vampires wonder whos stealing from who when poet one left he whispered in my ear a line from a French poet which he translated in a goodbye letter only those who leave for the sake of leaving are travelers sometimes Id like to pick up and leave reinvent myself Dana Nothing of the New Port Nothings or maybe I should try to hook up with Steve in Houston a jerk but spoke to him a few times in the last year and I think he might be ready money Brys money Id like to have it but without him he thinks if I go and live with him hell own me hes not a good investment the life he leads is dangerous but anything would be better than servicing this pizza delivery boy in a dingy little room my head hurts to think of the shit Ive created Hard.

CHAPTER 8

Poured forth from stradic aphros, a blazing sea of tar and macadam, they enter, arseways, Precious Squares. Bonhams happily rooting in plump space as time emaciates. Farther off, pink square tiles proclaim the heat of the Circle of Judas.

AWKWARD FIST

You're in like O'Flynn.

MANROOT OF ALL EVIL

I amn't, you smelly piece of fish flesh.

DON HAROLD BLOOM

(dressed in borrowed robes and adult diapers)

Does it have—and please excuse the alliterative framing of my words—I lifted them from a pogromer of poetry whom epistles me later this century, I repeat, does it have the signature scent of sisterhood?

A second best bed takes center stage, two figures wrestle underdarkneath. A bare head pops out, presumably, for the gas of life. Old Nobodaddy's wind.

BIG WILL SHAKEFORK

(raises covers and points proboscis south)

Heaven's breath smells wooingly:

A very ancient and fishlike smell.

DON HAROLD BLOOM

(dances a tango with himself)

To a latent faigeleh like our hero, sorry for the eye cocking, Don Mark Jay Mirsky, it's hell's breath.

BRIAN WILLIAM SEAMUS JORDAN

(hereafter BWSJ)

Someone check his diapers. The brunic air is something out of the Inferno.

DON MARK JAY MIRSKY

(scowls, holds up photocopy of a story by a long-deceased Russo-Judaic fictioneer)

Some of your moments are wonderful, but others are a bit too cute and obvious to hold my attention.

LIAM MAC SHEÓINÍN

(paring his fingernails)

Sorry, boyo. I have premature ejaculation of the pen.

BWSJ

(humping the bar)

I take a long time. I'd say, if I had the words, that I'm diffident dicked.

A tall, balding myope, in a gray sports jacket, walks over to a g-stringed Bloom and hands him twenty bucks. The man pulls up a chair, sits down, whereupon Bloom proceeds to give the man a topless lap dance. The man reaches over Bloom's flabby back and grabs hold of the professor's enormous hooters. Bloom turns around and the man buries his face in the professor's tits. Bloom pats the man's head as he suckles him.

PHIL LAPOTE

(coming up for air)

I wish he weren't so fey.

FRANK FLATULENZA

(waving a calumet)

He's defeated by his words.

BWSJ

I don't know who you are yet, sirrah. But I think you're a bit of a weeny.

FRANK DENTELUPO

I will destroy him.

LITTLE WILSON

(feeling the back of Flatulenza's head)

Judging by this occipital protuberance, he's the lateral descendant of little father, the scourge of God.

Dentelupo pulls Flatulenza off a barstool, causing him to fall—thirty-two feet per sec precious squared—to the floor. The calumet flies from Flatulenza's baby hand, bouncing iambically a few meters from his prostrate body. Dentelupo scurries over to pick it up, breaks it over his knee, flings the severed parts in Flatulenza's direction.

FRANK DENTELUPO

(out of breath)

Smoke that, you queer cocksucker. What the fuck is a hippie doin' in here?

FRANK FLATULENZA

(gets up, glares at his assaulter)

You bunch of latent moes! You should have been home schooled. I'll never patronize a place like this again.

Jordan holds Dentelupo back. He walks over and knocks Flatulenza down with a straight right hand. Dentelupo's nostrils flare. He peers through the bright skin of O'Seoigh's ghost to the other side of the wooden O. He signals to his crew for help. His crew, Mike Campy and Mike Jerky, outfitted as droogs, pointy faux noses and all, athletically scale the bar and join Dentelupo.

FRANK DENTELUPO

(approaches Flatulenza's sprawled body)

Let's show this hippie motherfucker who owns this place.

MIKE JERKY

(slips a Nazi armband on, blondly goosesteps around Flatulenza's body)

Nogoodjewhebekikesheenymockychristkillingcommiepinkofagtrannie.

MIKE CAMPY

(adjusts codpiece)

Fagtrannie, baby? I'll fuck herhim!

As Flatulenza begins crawling for the exit, Dentelupo places his boot on his back, stopping his progress.

FRANK DENTELUPO

Fuckin' mouse!

Dentelupo and his droogs begin to kick and stomp Flatulenza. Blood flies ubiquitously. Flatulenza's cries of agony resound through the bar. Dentelupo and his droogs cackle.

LITTLE WILSON

(tears in his hemoglobin rife eyes)

Lasciate ogni speranza voi ch'entrate, I screamed to him as he passed through the door.

Jordan's ceanndubh darkly turns to the sound of a naked lass tumbling thumpingly out of so-called second best bed.

RACHEL NEAL

(holding up a black merkin)

He threw me out of bed, he did, when he found out I was a lass and fair.

LITTLE WILSON

(a glass of gin in his hand)

Will is like all Stratford men, he likes dark ladies and fair boys.

DON HAROLD BLOOM

(sitting in front of vanity, habited as the Dark Lady of the Sonnets, applying makeup, plucking brows)

You're wrong, Anthony. Stratford men are all for wenches!

LITTLE WILSON

(holds up glass) Sláinte everyone! Sorry, Bloomy. Stratford men are all for boys! *Bloo me. Bloo me. Bli me. Bloo me in second best bed.*

DON HAROLD BLOOM

(looking radiant) Is that the plain truth, Will?

OSCAR WILDE

The truth is never plain and hardly ever pure.

DON HAROLD BLOOM

What about Heidegger's truth as untruth?

OLIVER ST. JOHN GOGARTY, M.D.

(dressed in surgical scrubs) Let's Hellenise this pub, Kinch.

DON HAROLD BLOOM

(exposes buttocks, bends over) Come and get it, Will.

BIG WILL SHAKEFORK

I have heard of your paintings too, well enough. God hath given you one face and you make yourself another. Get thee to a nunnery.

DON HAROLD BLOOM

(crying, mascara a mess)

I was the more deceived.

Jordan uneyes the Bard's and Bonny Bloom's lover's spat. Instead, with considerable trepidation, he eyes the lifeless body of Flatulenza.

BWSJ

Who was he? This man with an Italian fosh and Hungarian fej. I killed him. Well, I helped. But I only helped to kill his body. Whitman is wrong. The soul is worth ten thousand bodies. This hombre—for the moment shade—will live again. He will receive another chance to be turbulent, fleshy, sensual, eating, drinking, breeding. The What's-his-name Cosmos.

LIAM MAC SHEÓINÍN

(drinking Coca-Cola from a mug)

Actually, the Frank Flatulenza Cosmos.

DON HAROLD BLOOM

I surmised that Flatulenza was the issue of Will's second best bedding of Josh ben Joseph's distant cousin.

LIAM MAC SHEÓINÍN

(putting down mug) Conceived through buggery. Which would account for his ciaricity.

DON HAROLD BLOOM

All of this is like we've fallen through a wormhole. My second best theory on his genesis is that he's the result of an intestinal indiscretion on the part of Old Nobodaddy.

LIAM MAC SHEÓINÍN

You'll never be a poet, Cousin Bloom.

BWSJ

(pointing to Flatulenza's body)

Is he?

FRANK DENTELUPO

(pouring a glass of Jameson over Flatulenza)

Fuck yes!

Flatulenza revives. He attempts to get up but is too weak.

FRANK FLATULENZA

(raising his head)

Nobody can kill me. I'm invincible. You murky blooded…

Jordan shakes his head. He then runs over and kicks Flatulenza's head off his neck.

BWSJ

The soul is worth a thousand heads!

DON HAROLD BLOOM

(speaks into an old-fashioned play-by-play microphone)

The kick is a beauty, end over end, a lot of fucking hang time. It finally comes down near center stage as a skull. Big Will Shakefork rushes over to pick it up.

BIG WILL SHAKEFORK

(the skull rolls off the tips of his fingers as he examines it)

Shite!

EARL OF OXFORD

(gathers up chapless remnant of Flatulenza)

Alas, poor What's-his-name, I knew him not, Liam.

Big Will Shakefork laughs profusely at his ghost writer's joke. Prancing, snickering at the world, the Earl hurls the object into outer space, a la Kubrick's bone-throwing primate, Moonwatcher, and it is never seen again.

LIAM MAC SHEÓINÍN

Who knows? It may well be seen again. Perhaps it will become a meteoroid or some other space garbage.

BWSJ

(taking center stage)

What a piece of work is man, how noble in reason, how infinite in fac-
ulties, in form and moving how express and admirable; in action how
like an angel, in apprehension how like a god.

JACK KENNISTON

(bouncing a go-go dancer on each knee)

That speech is the verbal birth of humanism. You dodo! Man is in-
nately a shit. Do you agree with me, Denty?

FRANK DENTELUPO

(squatting to defecate)

Does a Dentelupo shit in the woods?

*Dentelupo admires his work. Then something wondrous strange occurs:
his feces transmogrifies into a gold brick. After nosing it, he dutifully
brings it over to his creator.*

LIAM MAC SHEÓINÍN

Nice work, Frank. Fuck the Gardnerites! No words more than seven
letters, my arse!

*Dentelupo defecates again. This time when the feces transmogrifies into
gold, Dentelupo thinks about keeping it for himself, but his creator—as
one might expect—knows his mind, thus the gold is transported thauma-
turgically to his creator's outstretched palms.*

LIAM MAC SHEÓINÍN

(atop a golden wall)

And fuck the agent who sat on the edge of a desk in a short skirt (sans
undies), opening her porcine legs for a better view of her ugly hole, as
her other ugly hole poured forth clichés like shite from a goose.

BWSJ

(laughing)

I am made in my creator's image: a tongue of light.

IAGO

(darkly)

Mine made me out of the worser part of his heart.

FRANK DENTELUPO

(smiling amberly)

Mine made me out of the stupiter part of his brain.

JUANITA DARK

(passively)

I was redacted by the Russo-American lepidopterist, and only found life within a few lines of an unfinished poem.

BWSJ

(emotionally)

You mean: Satan's little sister, Juanita Dark?

Jordan orally pleasures Juanita Dark.

JUANITA DARK

(orgasmic) Don't! Don't! Don't! Don't stop!

BWSJ

(intermittently going and ungoing down on her)

Mangiare o non mangiare mangiare o non mangiare...

Jordan stops when he realizes he has been performing oral sex on Dolores Haze's stillborn sister. Dentelupo hands him a bottle of Jameson. Jordan gargles some whiskey and spits it out in the direction of his creator. As the creator tries to avoid the spray, he falls, bringing most of the wall down with him.

LIAM MAC SHEOININ

(sans accent) What are you trying to do? I'm allergic to the stuff. Bad for the brain cells.

BWSJ

Where's your accent?

LIAM MAC SHEOININ

(terrified, looking high and low)

It must've shaken off during the fall.

BWSJ

(pointing to a speck on the floor)

There.

The creator runs over and picks the fadas off the floor. He examines them, blows on them to remove any dust and dirt, and places them over the appropriate letters. He smiles as he climbs back atop the glistening erection.

LIAM MAC SHEÓINÍN

Thanks to the Jordan eye all the luster of the immediate jewel of my soul has been returned. *(whispers)* Don't go down on the floor, boyo. It's paved with zealot shite.

BWSJ

(reading from MacLysaght's The Surnames of Ireland)

The Mac Siúrtain never goes down.

LIAM MAC SHEÓINÍN

Spit uisce beatha at me again, boyo, and I promise that I'll turn you queerer than a treeful of monkeys.

BWSJ

(loudly) You can have me sucking horse cocks. I don't care. They'll never publish it. To quote R.R., the poet laureate of Erewhon, it's chad.

VIRGINIA WOOLF

(a haughty look on her equine face)

I finished Chadograph and think it a mis-fire. The book is diffuse. It is brackish. It is pretentious. It is underbred, not only in the obvious sense, but in the literary sense. A first-rate writer, I mean, respects writing too much to be tricky. One more thing. May I eat Rachel's pussy? I hear it has a very ancient and fishlike smell.

DEAN SWIFT

(foaming at the mouth) When genius appears in the world, you can always tell by the Confederacy of dunces against him.

SÉAN O'SEOIGH

They give me a heartburn on the arse, Joe Nathan.

The creator, dressed in a tux, runs through a banquet hall to a podium, where a bearded man in a sailor suit holds a copy of Bari Wood's The Tribe in one hand and a statuette in the other.

LIAM MAC SHEÓINÍN

(out of breath, attempting to wrest the statuette from the man in the sailor suit) I wish to thank Madamonsieur Woolf for coming up with

the title. It's perfect for a book by a scatologicalligrapher who copro-rites all he shites. If you hadn't popped your capallic noggin through the polla á pheiste leading to my consciousness and suggested it, I might have called it Ulysses II. Which, of course, all the anti-Ulysseans would have hated.

PETE HAMILL

(*managing to keep the statuette away from the creator*) Before I award Best in Show to Chadograph, I have to ask: Where did you steal the idea of a talking dog from?

LIAM MAC SHEÓINÍN

(*finally wrests the statuette from Hamill, hugs it to his breast, blows kisses to the audience*) I think you're confusing my book with that of some other genius. And, by the way, the C, like the one in Chanukah, is silent. If you weren't such a self-hater, bent on noting the accom-plishments of alloethnics, perhaps you'd know that. I did steal the idea of the peristalsis of the pen from the divine Dubliner.

JOSH BEN JOSEPH

(*nailed to a cross constructed from strands of dark wood ripped from the bar*) Four faigelehs stole my life story and I wasn't paid a shekel in royalties.

Campy and Jerky, now Roman legionaries, play dice at the foot of the cross. Campy wagers ben Joseph's torn, blood-stained robe.

CAMPY

(*tossing the dice high into the dark air*)

Come on, baby.

The mottled cubes touch down on the robe a millionth of a second apart. Each die displays one marking.

JERKY

Craps! You lose.

Jerky and Campy conduct a tug-of-war over the robe. Jordan tears the robe from them with minimal struggle, drapes it over his head, and be-comes an Irish washer woman.

BWSJ

(*with a brogue you can cut with a kinch*)

Terrible what this boy on the cross did to his mother. He fell in love with a Jew whore and him from a respectable Catholic family.

Shakefork, outfitted as a centurion, sits down on a skull, the remnant of a long-deceased fool or prophet, and begins chiseling lean unlovely English onto a stone tablet.

BIG WILL SHAKEFORK

Othoulovelyboywhointhypowerdostholdtimesfickleglass.

JOSH BEN JOSEPH

(writhing in pain) Not the sonnets, Will. I'd rather be Pilate's irrumator. Save for seventy-one! *No longer mourn for me when I am dead for a ducat. (laughs)* The hudibrastic Hebe in me desires to rhyme the next line with succoth. But the Mickey half—my mother hailing, no pun intended—from that gravitated piece of heaven—that golfers and tenors adore—hates rhyme. *(chuckles)* You know, when I get home in a few days, I'm going to hit flatulent Nobodaddy with: *Say thou didst forsake me for some fault. (guffaws)* He'll like that. His taste is, as you Micks say, in his arse.

Shakefork dashes the stone tablet to the ground, shattering it into eighteen hundred pieces.

JOSH BEN JOSEPH

(laughing through pain) Hey Moses! Who's gonna clean up the mess? I gave Martha the day off.

Shakefork sneaks around to the back of the cross.

BIG WILL SHAKEFORK

What a lovely bum.

JOSH BEN JOSEPH

(trying to look back)

Don't go Marlovian on me, Will.

Shakefork thrusts a spear into ben Joseph's left buttock.

JOSH BEN JOSEPH

(screaming) Are you fucking nuts?

Shakefork removes the spear and walks to the front of the cross. He is met there by Oxford.

EARL OF OXFORD

(unsuccessfully whispering to Shakefork)

Tell him one has to be cruel to be kind.

Oxford disappears into a cesious cloud that is the creator's eye. Shakefork and Jordan assume the roles of the crucified thieves. Looking down, ben Joseph becomes polypneic when he sees a naked Rachel Neal, smooth shaven and unmerkined, displaying in her dainty little fist a scroll containing the dirty penetralia of a thief called BWSJ. She removes the scroll from her vagina.

RACHEL NEAL

(unrolls the scroll and reads)

He is the product of polymyth. Concupiscent, parvenu, jejune Jesuit. He was given by his creator, who will never wear the diffuse matter of a god, a hankering for catamite.

Flitting onto the stage is Mark Neal, Rachel's erstwhile brother. Standing there, nude and fully erect, the girl from Ipanema with a penis the size of Rachel's uncircumcised nose, he smiles enigmatically at the three crucified men.

DON HAROLD BLOOM

(screeching) Not one a god! Men. Just men. The scions of the mud such as Billy of Normandy, Cormac Cas, Joey ben David. Not one a god! Save one.

LITTLE WILSON

(shouting) BWSJ: latent Irish gangster with literary pretensions, half cuckolder with an alcoholic personality and a limp tongue.

GEORGE BERNARD SHAW

Shakefork: Capitalistic Humanist who hated Jews, Blacks and women.

Mark Neal removes the scroll from his sister's clenched fist, rolls it up tightly, bends over, and shoves it between his butt cheeks.

MARK NEAL

(peering through bent legs)

A golden mnemonic of every culoteer's dream. Shamie's ladder. The way to parthas is through this glistening tuckus. *(sings)* I'll always bend over, you queer. Her brother, your catamite. Her brother, your guilty masturbatory fantasy.

JOSH BEN JOSEPH

(foreskin magically restored, he masturbates without hands, like a horse)
I think I'm going to spirit!

A beautiful wave travels through him: spiritual peristalsis: the soul of the son of man forcing its way through the dark air of earth to the shining space of heaven.

BWSJ

(dead dicked)

I take a long time. I'm diffident dicked. Meaning: it's shy around vaginas.

BIG WILL SHAKEFORK

(ejaculating Shakesperm onto the rocks)

Two words, boyo: prostate massage. I was introduced to it by the Dark Lady of the Sonnets.

DON HAROLD BLOOM

(snapping off a latex glove)

You could have waited until I mouthed you. For it is—according to the Yahwist—better to spill your seed into the belly of a whore than onto the rocks.

BIG WILL SHAKEFORK

Cad? I mean, what?

DON HAROLD BLOOM

Did you think I meant country matters?

Rachel struts over to Mark, yanks the scroll out of his anus, and pushes him off the stage.

BWSJ

His aphotic soul crashes into devouring nothingness. Isn't nothingness something? Thus it actually crashes into somethingness.

RACHEL NEAL

(unrolls the scroll)

A beautiful ineffectual angel, beating in the void his luminous wings in vain.

DON HAROLD BLOOM

(wearing a dirty, torn doublet)

Quillets aside. Our hero is not what one would call a flying sthup.

As Bloom curtsies to the wooden Oers, he is set upon by Don Mark Jay Mirsky, who appears out of Erewhon wielding half a shillelagh, befitting the half Mick status all Boston Jews enjoy. John Updike, another unexpected Erewhonian arriving on the scene, saves Bloom's life by pushing Mirsky into the devouring maybe. Updike helps a slightly battered Bloom to his feet. Bloom dabs away the blood trickling into his eyes as he awaits medical attention. Orderlies Campy and Jerky gurney Bloom to the wings. Rachel Neal, M.D. treats Bloom's injuries by urinating on him. Bloom whimpers as she administers a pleasant enema. She tosses a bluddle filthy dildo to the groundlings.

DON HAROLD BLOOM

(dismounts gurney)

Why did I ever turn over?

JOHN UPDIKE

(reading from the Abiko Quarterly)

It says here, Brewster, that you lack the telepathy of poets.

Bloom picks his nose, examines his boogies.

DON HAROLD BLOOM

(flicks a boogie in Updike's direction)

Begone Updike!

Updike casts himself into the devouring nothsomaythingness. Rachel again takes center stage. She reads the final words of the aforesaid penetralia, rolls it up, and sticks it in her womanly cave.

RACHEL NEAL

(nods to the scroll-penis sticking out of her vagina) It says he's not Bill Bang, he's whimpering Willy. A sexual liar from as far back as the womb. His sainted mother's womb.

DON HAROLD BLOOM

(crying) Did he at least deliver on the boast of a dead awakening spatial-spitial kiss? Of course, how would you know something like that unless you were dead? And, if you were dead, how would you know it?

It is only possible to know life. The bulldog Aquin is quite emphatic on this point.

RACHEL NEAL, M.D.

(listens to Jordan's penis with a stethoscope)

In my opinion, it's dead.

Maybe's prodigal son, Mirsky the Great, returns with a thick manuscript lodged under his arm. He hands it to his teaching assistant, Jen, the flower of his Jewish studies course.

MIRSKY THE GREAT

(wearing a diadem fashioned out of toilet paper) I hear a story winding through *BELATED* BOYLANSDAY, but its verbal minefield blows the narrative to caca.

LIAM MAC SHEÓINÍN

There's no love story between those two cretins, professor. It's the love story of Mac Sheóinín and O'Seoigh.

BWSJ

All I knew is that we loved in vain.

RACHEL NEAL

I have written a novelette about that June day titled The Boylans of Eccles Street. It begins: To fuck to fuck to really fuck!

DON HAROLD BLOOM

(snaking his hand down the back of his pants)

The greatest piece of writing, dismissing the split infinitive, from a great piece of ass, since that Hittite babe composed the juiciest part of the Pentateuch.

REDACTOR

Stop pulling things out of your ass, Bloom. She didn't write a word of the Torah. And it was Uriah, her first husband, who was the Hittite. She was a JAP!

A dismayed Bloom bravely excavates his bowels with his stubby, unprofessory fingers, the digits of a daylaborer, producing out of his labor a document he perceives to be the undeniable proof of his claim.

DON HAROLD BLOOM

(holds up excrement-stained document)

Here's my proof, big R. The heretofore undiscovered Dead Sea Scrolls assigning authorship of what I call The Portrait of Yahweh as a Young God, but what you call the Torah, to none other than the mother of a great king, Bathsheba the Hittitess.

REDACTOR

(angrily snatches the document from Bloom's fat, fecal fingers and begins to read right to left) The (sic) hesitency the King felt over his Hittite wivey's plan of writing the definitive history of his people manifested itself in his inability to maintain an erection during intercourse with her.

The Redactor consults the fire-fretted ceiling for an answer.

DON HAROLD BLOOM

The Bloom is right again.

REDACTOR

You know I find it strange such an important document isn't cuprous.

DON HAROLD BLOOM

What?

REDACTOR

(tears the scroll into eighty-two pieces)

I shan't bother to read the psalm assigned to David ben Jesse addressing his own impotency and weird sexual fantasy.

BWSJ

Does it begin: Never turn over?

REDACTOR

It does.

Bloom weeps for a moment.

DON HAROLD BLOOM

Fuck! Will, darling. I need some sticky.

REDACTOR

The word hesitancy is incorrectly spelled. The word of Yahweh isn't anything if not orthographical. I declare the scroll a fraud!

Bloom feverishly masturbates Shakefork, collects his sperm in an out-

stretched palm, and proceeds to glue the pieces of the scroll together.

DON HAROLD BLOOM

Almost as good as new except for a lacuna here and there. If we only had a superior writer to fill in the missing parts. Someone who knows in excess of twenty ancient languages. Someone who is never self-regarding. Someone who is moral. Someone who could lull us back into the fictive dream.

John Gardner is placed down on center stage in a sedan chair lugged there by anonymous academics.

JOHN GARDNER

(handling the broken calumet of the late Frank Flatulenza) Get me some glue, Jew.

DON HAROLD BLOOM

(again fiercely jerking off Shakefork)

Shakesperm coming right up.

The bard erupts prolifically and the Bloom catches it in a golden cup which he, in turn, hands to Gardner. The beastly, greyauburned man sniffs the contents of the cup before using the magical substance contained within to glue the calumet back together.

JOHN GARDNER

(lighting up) I gaze on the dark Satanic mills; I shake my head; they vanish.

ANONYMOUS ACADEMIC

(resembling Charles Johnson)

That he sees them proves he's human; that they vanish proves he's divine.

DON HAROLD BLOOM

Theandric Gardner meet mortal god Shakefork. I would have introduced you to ben Joseph, also a divine human, but he has already been sung to his rest by flights of mad, bad Mac Sheóinínian metaphors.

JOHN GARDNER

(amid a foul and pestilent congregation of vapors) My eyes are red verbs slaying evil, and its proclaimed brother, illusion. This is why I am clothed in clouds: the diffused matter of a god.

Jordan dies on the cross. Shakefork unghosts as well. Terpsichore go-goes around the crosses in a Free State tricolor g-string emblazoned with a Mogen David.

TERPSICHORE

(bends over, slaps her own ass)

Dance, Rachel, dance around all these dead men that have done with life.

Rachel ignores the musings of the Muse, and instead points the makeshift penis between her legs to the heavens in wishful expectation of revivifying Jordan.

RACHEL NEAL

(chants) This is what you desire: the plant of life: bulbous with a long narrow leaf, a hyacinth, pinkish purple, whose juices taste as sweet and warm as the milk of God's heart. Suck God's spirit back into you and be like a god.

The said makeshift penis presses against heaven's amethyst lips. The spirit flows back into Jordan and he arises two days, twenty-three hours and fifty-seven minutes earlier than the carpenter's son did some nineteen hundred and fifty-five years ago.

CHAPTER 9

The wheel of life in the lobby pointed you in the right direction. So here you are in the place you imagined you would be today. As anticipated, prostatic rumblings abound. Everything exactly as you saw it last night: Sammy on bed, keycard on night table. Like Kreskin, you accurately predicted your room number. Does the aforementioned successful prognostication increase the chances of a defenstration? You hear yourself screaming on the way down:

Out

of

the

depths

have

I

cried

unto

thee,

O,

Lord.

You note the irony and realize, being acquainted with Virag's Law, that you'd never finish the psalter's line. Unless, that is, you speed scream. You peer out the window. A glance down and you see the progeny of men. Your mission—as one of the Elohim—is to turn them into painless shadows.

You disappeared for hours. Not just your smooth shaven countenance, as indicated in your projection, but the rest of you. Did you travel—with the aid of your friends from Planet X—to another dimension? Not four, as commonly speculated, but a finger's counter dilemma. Eleven is the number dear to the wedders of general relativity to quantum mechanics.

Strung out superstringists of the world unite!

Alright, no magic, no dimension hopping. You simply took a limo drive downtown. You commanded your driver to stop in front of your favorite bookstore:

Shakespeare & Company

There, you purchased, as premulled, the Annotated Juanita Dark. You also blew an Alistair on something Rachel would enjoy:

The Regression Manual

Dana Niente

Its title and subject intrigued you less than the name of its author. Speaking of said book, you wanted nuffing to do wif such nonsense before you met her. You were a militant R.C. (albeit you never attended Mass).

Ung roy! Ung foi! Ung loi!

Your Hiberno-Norman sept's motto and answer to the Protestant's protest. What are they protesting? The One True Faith? After all, Peter Piscatore got the keys, not Hank Tudor.

Peccavi! Peccavi! Go and sin no mas, Jimmy Lee. Impossible unless you chop your Avernus pavior off. In other words, you must become, as prophesied by the melancholy Dubliner, a fucking androgynous angel. Or, as they say in the vernacular, a dickless wonder.

He took a Commie's sickle

and cut off his own pickle.

It rolled like Antoinette's head

til it stopped completely dead.

A dickless wonder!

A dickless wonder!

Quo Vadis? Furor poeticus. Ignis fatuus. Vox et praeterea nihil. Tu quoque. Bono vox! Bono vox! Cacoëthes loquendi. Cacoëthes carpendi. Quos Deus vult perdere prius dementat. Tangere ulcus. Insanus omnis furere credit ceteros. Who cut down the heaventree of stars?

When he realized what he had left.

He cut off what seemed so bereft.

A ballless wonder!

A ballless wonder!

Exiting the bookstore, bag in hand, sports jacket folded over an aloof arm, a handkerchief damming the flow of perspiration from your forehead, you strolled down Broadway. Why do you sweat like a fat man doing jumping jacks in an attic? Because of the heat—anything above sixty is regarded warm by your standards—you decided to go pieceless. Yes, despite last night's charade, you do own one. You acquired it last year from a friend of Campy's. Five bills (silencer included). Campy called it a pug-nosed 38. He can't sell his ass for a hole in the ground but you keep him around for laughs. You call him Mrs. Malaprop but only Carrick gets the joke.

To go back to the defenestration scenario, who, if you screamed, would hear you among those resting their arses on creepy stools in *parthas*? Dunno, brother? And if one of them suddenly pressed you against his heart, wouldn't you fade in the strength of stronger existence? Dunno, brother?

Whitey wants you to help him eliminate the Gambinos. He operates under the assumption that you're Irish Republican Army and that you can get a cell member handy with C4 or plastique—or whatever the fuck they call it—to blow the Ravenite to smithereens (or the Bergen, if he's there, he being, the so-called Teflon Don).

NEW YORK POST

MAFIA MEATBALLS COOKED IN RAVENITE EXPLOSION

NEW YORK DAILY NEWS

AUTHORITIES SEARCH FOR CLUES TO MOB HANGOUT BOMB-
ING

Don't clear up any misconceptions. That way you'll never be dewindowed. Nobody fucks with the boys! To be honest, you'd love to see the guineas sleeping with the swimming awkward fists. You'd think a Boston Mickey like Whitey would be able to talk to them himself? The I.R.A. is everywhere you look in Boston. But what's the use? The guineas are like the Fuzzy Wuzzies, kill a hundred and a thousand zips take their place. Sicily is almost third world. Naples isn't much better. So many failed governments. Socialism hasn't helped. The siggies have controlled smack since the fifties. The Godfather's a lot of shit. A Sicilian would eat their children for money. What an overrated film. Due's just as bad. Il Apocalipso Adesso sucks too. If they were satires, they'd be masterpiec-es. It's his pretension to be a serious commentator on history. Besides, he has poor taste. The Hollow Men is as bad as the hyacinth girleen gets. Conrad's a bloody bore. Cheech's wife's maiden name was Neal. They met while working on a film in Ireland. A horror picture. Herbert George in his autogbiog says his mother, Sarah Neal, was remotely Irish. Perhaps they're all related?

Weren't you once interested in writing a book on Irish sur-names? You keep a page of O'Hart's in your wallet that lists the names of the gentric hounds who came out of the continent and exile with Séamus an Chad to fight in Ireland against the Williamites. Circled in the honor roll is the name Sir Brian Jordan. Your noble ancestor.

The Southies will be arriving soon. Whitey Anglim, their Mick-ey (honorific akin to Don) suffers from megalomania, delusions of gran-deur. Sees himself as the second coming of Vercingetorix. Thinks he can unite the Micks against the guineas. Whitey Bulger, Blackie O'Neal, Sandy Sullivan, Brownie Dunne, Red Smith, Red Foley, Rusty Regan, Rory Boyd, Don O'Connor, Roe O'Connor, Fionn Doody, Howdy Doody, Red Green, Red Down, Red Skelton, Robert Redford, Mickey Mahoney, Jock Mahoney, Mickey Maloney, Mickey Spillane, Mickey Mantle, Mutt McGruff, Mutt Mantle, McGruff the Crime Dog, Doghouse Reilly, Moon Mullens, Buck Mulligan, Spike Milligan, Studs Lonigan, Hoodo Flynn, Cake Blake, the Mighty Casey, the old Billy Boru, the man who got away, the man who broke Brooke Shields' hymen, the Man from U.N.C.L.E., Napoleon Solo, Han Solo, Mad Anthony Wayne, Duke Wayne, Duke Mantee, Mack the Knife, Peter Gunn, Shem the Pen, Shaun the Post, Tail Gunner Joe, Machine Gun Kelly, Ned Irish, Fibber McGee, Dan McGrew, Mack McFate, Art McFart, Buck McFuck, Whitey McDark, Blackie McLight, Spanky McFarlane, Skinny Skinner, Fatty Farnell, Corny Keleher, Lamppost Farrell, the citizen, the counselor, A.E., Blazes Boylan, Dan Boylan, Duff Macbeth, Dutch Reagan, Buffalo Bill Cody, Cody Jarrett, Mat Dillon, Marshal MacMahon, Marshall McLuhan, McGeorge Bundy, Al Bundy, Mac McCurdy, Father John Conmee, Father Flanagan, Father Pat Feely, Father Coughlin, Mother Jones, Brother Loftus, Sister Carrie, Redmond Barry, Sudden Sam McDowell, Nolan Ryan, Jim Ryun, Brian Ryan, Brian Mulroney, Brian Jordan, Brian Cryan, Bull Connor, Jimmy Connors, John McEnroe, Little Mo Connolly, Pop Gleason, Babe McRuth, Lou McGehrig, King Kong Kelly, Red Hugh O'Neill, Owen Roe O'Neill, Buck O'Neal, Hugh Duffy, Ed Delahanty, Denny McLain, Don McLean, Vincent MacGogh, Michelangelo Bunratty, Wolfgang McZart, James Paul McCartney, John Winston Lennon, Mick Jagger, Elvis Costello, Little Wilson, Alf Hitchcock, Alf Bergan, Peter O'Toole, Adam O'Toole, Eve O'Hare, Gerald Fitzpatrick, Patrick Fitzgerald, Boss Tweed, Boss Crocker, the Boss, Charlie McCarthy, Charlie Parker, Charlie Parnell, Charlie Connerly, Joe J. MacYes, Aloysius Jennings, Brennus Jordan, Brennus Flahoolah, Ignatius Donnelly, Edgar Cayce, William Casey, J. Edgar O'Hoover, Jakes McCarthy, Jack McCarthy, William Jennings Bryan, William F. Buckley, Jr., Bill Bailey, Billy Bailey, Bilbo Baggins, Mickey Rooney, Art Rooney, Nick McMichaels, Mickey McNichols, Joe Yule, Joe Yule, Jr., John L. Sullivan, Silky Sullivan, Louis Sullivan, John Quinn, Jack Quinn, Quinn the Eskimo, Jack the Giant Killer, Jack Kennedy, George Washington, George Carlin, George M. Cohan, George McMichael, George McGovern, George

Baileyovski, George Bernard Shaw, Henry Higgins, Henry Hill, Hank Tudor, Jerry Powers, Jerry Cooney, Arthur Wellesley, Arthur Godfrey, Art Linkletter, Andy Rooney, Andrew Jackson, Andrew Greeley, Bing Crosby, Bong Bingham, Paddy Breathnach, Paddy Pearse, Pat the Waiter, Sean Eglinton, Sean O'Casey, the Shan Van Vocht, Dante Riordan, Man in the Macintosh, W.B. Yeats, W.B. Murphy, Cranly, Vincent Lynch, T. Lenehan, T. Monahan, T. Shanahan, Nosey Flynn, Nosey Dowd, Nosey Jones, Lips Larkin, Conor Larkin, Larkin O'Connor, Tip O'Neill, Red Hugh O'Donnell, Hugh MacHugh, Fergus MacHugh, Mickey McHuge, Mickey Small, Martin Short, Jim Tallman, Blind Omeros, Blind Raftery, One-eyed Connelly, Wrong-way Corrigan, Nick the Greek Murphy, Roman Riley, Indian MacShane, Murtagh English, Seamus French, Kevin Spain, Sean Fleming, Eamon Flanders, Dermot Holland, Fionn Cornwall, Tomato Can Tomalin, Meatball Mulligan, Boob McNutt, Wacky Wilson, Elmer Looney, Happy Collins, Tom Collins, Mick Collins, George Moore, Thomas Moore, Roger Moore, Les Moore, Dinty Moore, St. Thomas More, St. Kevin, St. Senan, St. Fiacre, Erigena ,Duns Scotus, Johnny Walker, John Jameson, Jim Beam, Arthur Guinness, Rocky Sullivan, Birdy Heeney, Wolfie Coyle, Happy Kelly, Jim Merry, Ned Doheny, Frank Hogan, Joseph Francis Armagh, Jay Gatsby, Doyle Lonergan, Johnny Kelly, Johnny Appleseed, Runt Prunty, Cunty Kate, Charlotte Brontë, Emily Brontë, William Makepeace Thackeray, Eugene Gladstone O'Neill, Niall of the Nine Hostages, Cormac Cas, Cormac McCarthy, Olium Olum, Bill Grace, Murph the Surf, Randall Patrick McMurphy, Pat Riley, Bill Parcells, Tom Kelly, Whitey Ford, Lafcadio Hearn, Billy Yeats, Schemer Burns, Jack Burns, George Burns, Paddy Ryan, Paddy Colum, Paddy Wagon Proudfoot, Paddy Whack Drumgold, Paddy Sarsfield, Patty Duke, Edmund Burke, Edmund Tyrone, Bucky Dent, Bucky Burke, Jack Lord, Séan McClave, Stephen King, Steve McQueen, Stevie Dedalus, Steve Allen, Fred Allen, Gracie Allen, Grace O'Malley, Boyo McGirl, Hairy Mangan, Hairy Arse, the Hairy Lemon, Rock Niblock, Don Warnock, Honey Fitz, Dulce Dugan, Wee Willie Keeler, Ruby Keeler, Druid Presley, Elvis Presley, Pagan Manahan, Foxy Styles, Muggs McGinnis, Skip Mahoney, Slip Mahoney, Bim, Punch Dorsey, Doc Reardon, Spit, Clifford Cassidy, Spike Hawkins, Gypo Nolan, Leo Finnegan, Snap Collins, Lord Killanin, Spencer Tracy, Pat O'Brien, Jimmy Cagney, Eddie Rabbit, Bunny Rabbit, Dirty Henry, Yakima Cunutt, Audie

Murphy, Jimmy Mac, General Charles O'Hara, James J. O'Hara, Terence McKenna, Timothy O'Leary, Chris McCarron, Billy O'Donnell, Gregory Peck, George Carlin, Jimmy Breslin, Frank McHugh, Mickey Featherstone, Jack Amsterdam, Rocky Sullivan, Mad Dog Coll, Ownie Madden, Legs Diamond, Whitey Coonan, Blackie Baldwin, Dinny O'Banion, Bugsy Moran, Muzzy O'Kinch, Crapper Collins, Farter Farrell, Stinky Mahone, couldn't, so why does that narrowarsed beantowner think he can?

They're here! You show them to the product. Their chemist, let's call him Sweny, gives it the cocaine litmus test. Pure Bolivian marching powder, to borrow a phrase from another tuist. They like doing business with you and ask if you have any heroin to sell. You tell them you don't but don't tell them—out of Occamic respect and self-preservation—that you wouldn't even if you had it growing out of your arse.

You try to remember some of the media clichés regarding the phony agon waged against illegal drugs.

Heroin is on the rise. Crack cocaine has become all the rage on Wall Street. Cocaine, once the champagne of drugs, has lost much of its allure among the rich and famous.

And the worst offense of all: the journalistic simile:

Law enforcement officials sadly foresee heroin spreading underground, like the roots of a giant oak, to suburbia.

Fast forward to 1998: Your partner, disheveled, clammy palms, sits on the edge of a bed in a seedy, run-down motel in the Park (the Boss, incidentally, perished in a plane crash in 1997). He shakes black powder out of a bag onto a table spoon, and takes a lighter and heats the tarnished utensil, the liquefying heroin resembles a dying, dazzling star gasping its last celestial gasps. Not really an accurate description. It actually resembles a hissing snake. Your partner transfers the liquid death (overwrought journalistic description) into a hypodermic needle, ties a tourniquet around his upper arm, tightens it, and calmly shoots up.

Movie images. You've never seen anybody fix except on the telly or film. Do they draw blood and mix it with the smack and then inject? Yes, you seem to remember there's something haemal about the process. And don't they make a fist when injecting? And you remember watching a film where a junkie squeezed a ball while shooting up, the rubbery orb dramatically expelled from his hand at the moment of truth as untruth, the saccadic eye of an ersatz Hitchcock tracking its path as it bounces through the universe of a dringy room.

The deal concluded, you make plans for the evening. You think about staying in the City. After all, it's Tuesday, she'll never agree to see you tonight. You don't think you could stand another night at Squares: same old whores, jerk offs, smell of stale beer, not to mention, the enveloping greyauburned mass of carcinogens (a Fabian suicide, you once termed it). Your beloved late, great uncle Tom, war hero, opposite of a lood, liked to say that cigarette smoking is probably not the best thing in the world for you. You would always shake your head in agreement and think how litotic. You think the cigarette companies are facinorous, don't you? You lexiphanic hypocrite, you.

So Squares is out. And Oscura on weeknights is a fooking snooze. The longest day of the year and there's no one to help you spend its golden coin.

When faux Boylan awoke the next morn, as always, he was alone.

Everyman's his own missus!

Later, you see yourself marching by flat iron buildings in SoHo. The Angelica, the film center and café, for which you are bound, is such a construction. So many of the streets down here are cobble stone. You remember that an Irishman, Dan Crimmins, was the contractor who paved the streets of New Amsterdam.

Give us your tired, your poor,
Your huddled masses…

What a fucking lie! The Yanknicks (Brutch, Teutprots, Celtprots, etc.) assaulted Irish refugees (centuries of religious persecution had brought them low) as they disembarked from coffin ships. And yet who loves this country more than their descendants? You'd sooner fly a

124

Union fucking Jack than Old Glory. God bless America! Why not: God bless Ireland! Your grandfather's rejoinder whenever some Amrish fool bestowed a benison upon the good ole U. S. of A.

Know Nothings. Calvinist jerk offs. They were heartless fucks. More savage than the supposed savages. Predestination. Your works are like snotrags. GR is about predestination. One of Pynchon's ancestors, a Calvinist minister, authored a work on it titled (you think) Preterition. A passing over, literally. Calvinists think the Maker neglected to designate those who would be damned, positively designating only the elect.

No freeman needs a formator!

A screaming comes across that little tent of blue Sodomites call the sky.

It's a bird! It's a plane. It's übermensch!
Or is it only your asshole buddies from Planet X going home?

Ninety-two in the shade, you look for shelter. The Angelica can wait. The trembling crossbeam of the bistro in which you take refuge denotes a speeding train below. Irisher John McDonald, you recall, as you elevate a cold one to your lips, built the subway system.

You smile as you glimpse the father of one of your new customers on the box: George Herbert Walker Bush. The sound is turned down, and as you're not a labiomancer, you can only surmise what he's blathering on about. It appears the wimpy fuck is on the campaign trail, addressing what seems to be a cop convention; thus he's *probably* advocating something draconian:

Under my administration cop killers will be drawn and quartered and drug dealers castrated.

They applaud and cheer the Vice President. Hilarious, you think, because your celestial suppliers told you that the Veep, as CIA director, made a zillion drug trafficking and selling banned assault weapons to street level pushers. Still in the business, they say. Very plausible, you think, because they own all the airports in the Lonely Star State. Does the voodoo economist know—or care? Still blathering, you guess the carpetbagging whoreson must be saying something about the importance of protecting children from sexual predators. What a fucking joke! The starry streeters say his name should be Mo Leicester. A *total* bottom, Georgy Porgy, save, the occasional rape of children and ewes, as required by ceremony of the Grand Poobah of a certain, famous secret ossuarial society. Prescott, his father, robbed—as his initiation into said secret society—Geronimo's pocky skull. Pressie, as his male lovers called him, was for a time T. S. Eliot's catamite. In fact, he gave the poet one of his most enduring lines:

Tessie, when you're old and your pants are worn rolled, perhaps you'll begin to see the skull beneath the skin.

Super freak George Herbert Walker Bush, they say, out Caligulas Caligula. They offered you a videotape proving their assertion. You declined the free rental from Captain Video, but, nevertheless, the clerk related every indelible detail. You conjure the Blair-Lee house after dark. The Vice President in bed with a George Washington lookalike. Except the General was much better looking. Smiling, Bar straps on an ebony serpent and rides the Bushian pseudopatrician caboose, makeshift quim, farting, smarting quarse, until, to misecho Milton, all hell breaks loose.

Shit was general all over D.C.

It troubles you that George Og, if they're still in the business, scored from you yesterday. As they say in the cinema: Are you being set up? Maybe he's trying to reform and wasn't packing his usual kilo. Like you, the Bushes can never get busted. Like you, they were given the get out of jail card. They told you if you ever get caught holding, just utter the shibby to the authorities and they'll let you perambulate. Brian William Seamus Walker Jordan. How your Retty friends enjoy their symbolism.

When you think of it, young Bush didn't look so much like a primate, after all. There was a little of that of course, but he has reptilian eyes like the Rets. Speaking of them, what did they tell you is the secret of the universe?

Preconstructionism.

It's making things out of words.

You wonder if they're running the joint? Are the Bushes reptocrats? You check your own eyes out in the brass rail, and think, walking backwards, see you later , alligator.

CHAPTER 10

What do we see: stuck here in the squinting eye of heaven, the light of paradise (a.k.a. the noonday sun) brightly emphasizing the manifestation of Him, things and persons, colored signs intromitted by the senses.

Do the Senses make Sense?

Feeling is the sense that makes most sense to that upright beast called man. Or to define it in a Johnsonian manner: If you can stick your Irish sausage in it, without lubricant, it's an awkward fist, if not, a dubh-door.

Seated at a palehued table on the secondbest floor of the county library, Jordan randomly flipped through Ulysses. Gabler edition! Winedark pages! Perfidious lips to him. No getting this material per vias rectas. Instead, by indirections find directions out. Back and forth, he flipped. The pages blazed with gnosticalfire: What does the oriafiamma say, pyromancer? Thus with the silhouette of a genius' sublime flame cast upon the long canvas of his face, he essayed an interpretation of the flickering words: No speaka da geniush!

A filthy John surprised him:

"Are you reading Ulysses?"

Jordan turned his face over a shoulder, rere regardant, and barked:

"Seemingly."

Hip! Hip! Hooray! One for the Terry Shimmyrag's side.

"Stonehenge of literature," the Englishman intoned. "One must become a Druid in order to decode the pillars of Joycean genius so arcanely erected and eloquently arranged."

Bookwise.

"Have you read it?"

"Seemingly," the Englishman belately echoed, a twinkle in his stony British eyes.

O, my brothers, there's a wee speck of green in our ancient old enemy's seas' rulers snotcolored glazzies.

"I get something new from every reading," Jordan said newly.

Per vias Deasy.

List! List! List! His rattling chain of phlegm alludes to Jacob Marley's karmic forgement.

"It's a writerly novel, to say the least," the Englishmen said leastly.

Grinning, Jordan thumped his book, lightning zigzagged from it, struck and returned. Welcome to the scriptocratic age. The cycle Jammy Vic could nae envision. And if scriptocracy has arrived like a bastard, like a bad simile, my friends, can culocracy be fart away?

"I mean," the Englishman explained, "it's a book written for other writers. Scholars, I should say. Any writer worth his sodium must come to grips with it."

As salty a piece of meat as Lot's wife's arse. The poor woman was sodiumized.

"Are you a writer?"

"Do you know The Rachel Papers?"

Synchronicity up the Junghole. Smarting Anus. Acted in a movie with the mighty Quinn. Screenplayed a Farrah flick. Recipient of a formal first like his John Bull begetter before him. Joe Nathan Motsworthy his royal tutor. Crammers in Brighton readied him for OU. Like his substantial father (fatness being the ultimate substantiality for the roast-beefy English), he too was awarded the Maugham for his first novel. His teeth are very bad. Toothless Amis, the anglo-saxon superman.

"You're a great writer, Mr. Amis," Jordan gushed. "I loved The Rachel Papers and think Money's a masterpiece. I should have recognized you from your photograph on the jacket."

Sycophant! Visibrit! Can't you see he's a history blamer like the would-be gundowner of Pantherus?

Sorry, Nobo. I'm wearing a Kant-See-Back bridle. And I'm no

fig shower!

"I'm such a huge fan. Dead Babies, Other People, Einstein's Monsters," Jordan gushed on, to the apparent delight of his listener. "They're all great!"

List! List! List!

What?

He has a mot for a surname, albeit an English Oxonian background.

Joysus!

He's your Haines.

I'm my own Mulligan.

"I am shocked and pleased that you know them," the Englishman cried. "That you seem to enjoy them is deuced good to hear."

Jordan felt that Amis's mobile brows contrasted with a thoroughly immobile face. Yes, he looks like his lightwrit on the jackie. Pinball wizard, swaddled in roycloth, shirt and tie ominously pale, brightly tenebrous, Bosielipped, cleft in his chin like his handsome perceiver's, a cockholder in that fagdom by the sea, a clitholder over here. What is a book? Nothing but a bunch of words. Unreliable. No wonder why Monsieur Chaucer rhymed word with turd. Words stink like Derrida's derriere. There's no god but language. Language is divinity. Jordan sensed the Englishman's penetralia:

He has swallowed gallons of heavy water

in the tradition of his alma mater...

"I am delighted you didn't," Martin Amis said. "Or else I might begin to think that is how I really look."

Jordan smiled in affable disagreement.

"I'm in awe of your literary accomplishments, Mr. Amis."

"Martin," the author insisted, hand tendered.

"Brian," Jordan informed, unequivocally accepting the Englishman's token of amity.

Hands across the heavy water.

"What a grand library," Martin Amis observed grandly, unconsciously gesturing like a priest bestowing a benison.

"Every library should have a steeple," Jordan proposed.

"Built around a church," Martin Amis enthused. "At least, that's what I've been told."

"That's right," Jordan confirmed. "They didn't want to tear it down completely, so they built around it."

"Judging by the results," Brehon Amis bellowed, "they were right not to. It's a really marvelous library."

Jordan smiled reverently. Built around a kirk. Kirk Patrick. Paddy's church. Colm O'Neill—or was it O'Donnell?—converted the painted ones nearly 900 years before Rory Columbo sailed the ocean turquoise and in turn converted the new painted ones. Genova: new land, literally. Poor maroon bastards! They were a happy lot of heathens before Donny Dove (Dove?) set a brogue on their sandy shore.

This ain't the Taj, paesano, a Sal Mineo looking honest injun informs the admiral. The first bennies. Columbus and his murderous posse. Bene! Bene! By indirections find directions out, as the skewered courtier of Dumbmark dumbmented.

EXTRA! EXTRA! EXTRA! READ ALL ABOUT IT!

WRONGWAY COLUMBUS DISCOVERS QUONDAM ERE-WHON.

"You Riverians are a very reverent lot," the Englishman melodically forged on, laughing Amisly, Englishly, Henghistly, girlishly, churlishly, highly, lowly, in the middle of our lifely.

"Not all of us," Jordan said, rethumping his book.

Martin Amis made a self-satisfied moue.

"Your reverence is for Joyce," he proposed affably. "Libraries are his temples."

The birdbeaked deity, Alighieri, His old fellow. Shakefork: the Holy Gas. Jesus fucking Joyce!

"Should be everybody's," Jordan pointed out.

"Devoutly to be wished," Martin Amis bardically blew.

Hark, Hark, the lark at heaven's gate defecates. Therefore paradise smells like shit.

"If you don't mind my asking," Jordan asked superpolitely.

"What brings you to Toms River?"

River got soul, baby!

Ou! Ah! Ah!

"I'm visiting an old school chum," Martin Amis answered chummily. "Perhaps you know him? Mark Kernow?"

Cornish crew? No speaka da Pistolese.

"Judge Kernow? We belong to the same country club. Joanna's my decorator."

"What a remarkable coincidence," Martin Amis remarked. "Six degrees of separation. I was at Oxford when that Harvard psychologist…What's his bloody name?"

"Milgram," Jordan answered quickly. "Small world phenomena."

"Right! Isn't Jo great?"

Question or statement? Sex degree. The prophet, no poet, advises a spaced togetherness for couples. I filled the space between her legs. Happy Joycemas!

"She's a sweetheart," Jordan answered sweetly. "And she really knows her stuff."

Perhaps not the Kama Sutra, but she's proficient in French, Swedish, Greek, Mongolian, etc.

"That's what I have heard," Martin Amis said amiably. "I'm really happy for Kerns. He's like a brother."

A similized brother is as easily forgotten as a bottle of Visine. He wishes to supplant rugheaded Kernsky. She suspects that is her dull husband's original surname. His petname for his pet is Issy. Middle Earth for beautiful.

"Remember to tell her that I like what she's done with Ferro's."

"I shall. We dined there last night, in fact. She told me that she had recently renovated the restaurant. You must be the Brian mentioned kind enough to have referred Jo. Mr. Ferro, who dropped by our table, vowed his indebtedness to you for recommending her. He hadn't heard of me but declared I'd bet you Brian would. Called you an intellectual."

"Pseudo-intellectual. Rocky's testimony in such matters is biased. We have been friends for years. Plus we're partners in a couple of bars."

"Intellectual by what I have heard today," Martin Amis asserted.

Martin Amis scratched the back of his head as he searched for additional words.

"You own a bar with a rather ominous name, don't you?"

"Oscura and a go-go bar up north," Jordan answered.

"The go-go bar went unmentioned. What is it called?"

"The Shakespeare."

"Are you kidding?"

"Precious Squares. I'm sorry."

"After the Shakespearean metaphor for cunt?"

"You are the only one ever to get the allusion," Jordan laughed.

"I wish I had used it for Money. Talk about recondite! Which of Lear's darlings utter the phrase?"

"Regan."

"Go-go bars are very popular in New Jersey," Martin Amis marked. "I have in my travels, up and down your verdic state, observed many of them," Martin Amis further marked. "With overflowing parking lots, I may add. You must make a mint!"

"I have a lot of partners," Partner Jordan informed. "The bars are a sideline. I'm in advertising."

"Ad canvasser? Thus like pardfooted Poldy, you're here to check out a key logo."

Tilebooks toppled. Jordan sorted through them. The New Alexandria within his messianic grasp. Beware ofs silently recited:

Beware of the Roman horde!

The Danars!

The Holy Office!

The Irish, for all their grievous faults, never burnt book nor witch.

The latter impossible.

Why? Are Irish chicks so frigid that they're fireproof?

I'll take you home again, frigid Brigid.

Let me see? If books burn at Fahrenheit 451, at what temperature would a female direct descendant of Niall of the Nine Hostages burn?

Leave concupiscience to concupiscientists! The reason witches were left uncharred in Ireland was that she would have had to enkindle all of her daughters.

"The only thing I'm checking out today," Jordan said, holding up a book, "is the Skelton Key to Finnegans Wake."

Martin Amis mimicked a snore, pulled up a blond chair, crossed his legs, folded his arms, motioned for the book. Without hesitation, Jordan placed the book in Martin Amis's enthusiastic hands.

Oxy fuck thinks you're not a gentleman. Show him the folded page of O'Hart's you keep in your wallet. You should have introduced yourself as Sir Brian Jordan, not just flahoolah, but also a knight of the bloody realm.

Martin Amis randomly flipped through the book.

His nostrils twitch as if he sherlocks an unpleasant odor: the stench of lucubration. He's Unglish and thinks Joysprick should not be spricken in Joyceland.

Martin Amis brayed, returned the book, saying:

"In my younger and more vulnerable days, I was convinced I could read the Wake like one reads Austen. That is, with the right monograph. I was soon disabused of that notion after repeated attempts at getting past the first chapter without literally falling asleep. It is undoubtedly a work of genius by a genius but—"

Joe Crookedgob, not a crookedgob at all. A Mayo man, thus a bluddlefilth chief. His collaborator was the southie author of The Cardinal.

"I think," Martin Amis thought on, "the monographs are more entertaining than its subject, Brian."

I never gave you cause to call me familiar. Did I?

"Not that entertainment is a measure of art," Martin Amis smilesmirked. "Entertainment is, of course, an equivocal term."

Jordan whetted his knives.

"Derrida argues that all language is an equivocation. We call something onething but mean notherthing or neitherthing. Ding an sich, Kant says. The Wake is an example of wort an sich."

Tomahawk, the phallic automobile he invented for Moolah is gay slang for penis. One of the Beats tapped it for one of their Beatnik works. Moloch whose breast is a cannibal dynamo. Moloch whose hemipenis is a smoking tomb. To be tomahawked, ondit, is to be fucked in the ass. Criticaster Roldy, self-appointed Doctor Ivanovitch of the twentieth century, declared Money phallocentric.

"As a writer," Martin Amis said gravely, "deconstructionism defeats the purpose of my craft."

Smarty A-hole!

Lay on, Macbeth.

I was from my mother's country matters untimely ripped.

"Just as impressionistic painting reduces a picture to five hundred words, deconstructionism reduces a picture to a blur of hands."

Picture yourself in a drunken boat on a river...

Martinamistwohandsablur, concluded:

"The French, it seems, are tribally disposed to blurment."

Gallia est omnia divisa in partes tres.

"Ment, though pronounced differently, means—in their language—lies," Jordan reminded.

Keep on hacking, boyo. This is a cattle raid.

"Spoken like a true Joycean," undaunted Martin Amis exclaimed. "Your master, to whom nothing seems linguistically impossible, asks us to detect a French bug behind the flab of an Irish pol."

Maestro di color che sanno.

"To go back to blurment," Jordan said, "a clever coin. Yet you have to admit, it only shines in the context of what was said before—which proves Monsieur Derrida's point, no?"

Martin Amis laughed.

"I suppose...I mean...I mean to say, I agree with the basic premise."

"In any event," Jordan said, "what you do with language is amazing."

So you opt for tender slaughter. Yours is an abattoir playing Irish airs in the bloodground. Butthead Amis, a reasonable beast whose eyes will follow thou through eternity.

"The poststructuralists would denounce me as an assassin," Martin Amis nasally drawled.

Stiff upper lip. Very nasal! Very posh! Public school means private school in merry old Merry Old. Ope thy mouth, lady. The only time an upperclass Englishman opens his mouth is to admit his schoolchum's chubby.

"The word kills the object," Jordan explicated.

"If they only could kill critics," Martin Amis jicked.

Jordan laughed, saying pointedly:

"Speaking of critics, Harold Bloom says Deconstructionism is the avenue which leads to the street of genius."

"Why not rue? It rhymes with avenue. And, like deconstructionism, it's French. Furthermore, Bloomian Bloom, Whitmanian Shakespearean Bloom, loves the rhymers. He's especially fond of Lord Tennyshite, to one-up Joyce."

Je déteste la poesie cette des rimes comme je déteste la merde.

Martin Amis coughed into his fist, fuming:

"Bloom ignores French poetry. Perhaps he has limited French."

"And less Greek," Jordan queried.

"He ignores Rimbaud out of some insane devotion to Shakespeare," Martin Amis alleged. "I mean," he snorted, "the writer, not the bar. J'allais sous le ciel. Muse! et j'etais ton feal."

Martin Amis touched his lips as if they had conveyeth the word of God.

"I surmise Bloom is a wannabe Englishman."

Je déteste l'anglais comme je déteste la merde. What pretentious assholes! Me and Bobby Amis.

"Blurment aptly describes French poetry," Jordan said, still harping on Martin Amis's daughter.

"A blur leads itself better to interpretation," Martin Amis said,

136

forefinger sketching the nipping and eager air.

Jordan peered upwards in the direction of a gilded skylight. The stairway below it heavening with the argent step of a brother poet back from Tir na Og. Sighted by heartlight, Blind Raftery looked up and noted the white traffic of clouds headed muckwards on an ethereal blue highway.

A destined laevoduction led Bill Barium, not so blind Raftery (Mise Fartery an file), to the deipnosophists.

"Brian," Bill Barium bariumtoned.

Sir Will of the barony of Bariumville in the county of Mayo of the province of Connacht in the nation of Ireland, Europe, eastern hemisphere, world, solar system, fucking Milky Way, welcome to our table.

"Bill," Jordan jordantoned.

Auricular finger plumbing gauche ear, Martin Amis unwaxed poetic, as he awaited an introduction to a ventripotent character exchanging names with Jordan.

"This is Martin Amis," Jordan said with a wristure.

Supercalifragilisticexpialidocious! How fucking femmy. I hope I didn't catch the English flu from Marty Poppins. He seems to be terminally flaccid of carpus.

"I know you admire his work."

Dentelupo admired his chrysopoetics.

"I am a huge fan, Mr. Amis."

"Martin, please. I never imagined that I was so popular in Toms River."

So the Fenian shakes the hand of the Saxon.

"Why don't you join us," Martin Amis said. "We're discussing literature: tragical, comical, pastoral-comical, historical-pastoral."

Jordan laughed, saying:

"Why don't you sit down, Bill. You can play the part of the Player-King."

"Staging the Ghost of Elsinore would be fun," Martin Amis funned. "I refuse to play the role of the arrasdropper, Brian. I don't wish

137

to be run through like a rat."

Bill Barium hemmed. "I'm late for a meeting. Some other time, perhaps?"

Some other space and time. But, please, no rant on Marlowe's authorship of the Swan's firstbest play.

I'll leap up to my god. Who the fuck pulls me down? It's the girl with Godsburgh blazing in her eyes?

A drink! A drink! My kingdom for a drink!

Not e'en the sblood soaked firmament will stand Doctor Feelgood a drink. One drop of the craythure, half a drop, would slake my soul's thirst.

"What about Oscura this weekend," Jordan suggested earnestly. "Drinks on the house, my friends."

"Those Seaside girls," Bill Barium hummed, "would be a distraction to holding a serious literary discussion."

"Isn't that Boylan's song," Martin Amis asked joyously.

Down at Margate looking very charming...

"A happy coincidence," Jordan answered.

"As the song goes," Bill Barium said, "Brian met his girl down in Margate."

"Atlantic City," Jordan corrected. "I was residing in Margate, the next town over. I'm sure Martin isn't interested in the geography of my love life, Bill. Aren't you late for your meeting?"

Jordan grabbed his friend's hand and squeezed affably.

Geographeros might be a good word for it. Slothrop bopped here.

"I am, Brian. Sorry. I hope—"

"I was only kidding, old sport. She'll be around this weekend. It must be love. And just," Jordan chortled, "when I was having so much fun with the girleens."

"She does have remarkable eyes," Bill Barium remarked quite unremarkably. "If I believed in the soul," he continued, "I'd say she was your soulmate. As it is, however, you really couldn't do any better than having such a winsome somamate."

138

Martin Amis stroked his chin and recited in a deepdark voice:

"Still plotting how their hungry ear

That winsome voice might hear."

"Egad! Is that Emerson," Bill Barium asked. "I'm allergic to strawberries and Emerson," he explained.

"Hives on the brain," Martin Amis clucked. "What a funny notion. What about those drinks? I only drink Gilbey's."

"Quite alright, Martin," Jordan said. "Bill here," he continued hoarsely, "is a colapot."

A pleasant smile broke mutely over Martin Amis's thick lips.

"Didn't get that at first," he admitted. "I suppose that I'm a spritopot. Like Kitty Dukakis, I enjoy anything containing alcohol. Anything, that is, except altar wine."

"Veni, Sancte Spiritus," Bill Barium romishly spat.

"Spiritopot," Jordan tried out.

"We are still on for drinks," Martin Amis asked nervously.

Proudest boast. They steal like zingari but cry ninetenths of the law. English pigs. Penitent and not so penitent goniffs. Jordan's clammyhands belied the gelid air of Elsinore. A shaft of light fell on his Mayobroad shoulders. Narrowback is a misnomer. Is it here to take me starward? Fliegen sie mien zum Mond. The extramund is just a shot away! Just a shot away!

"What about my home," Jordan proposed, drying his hands on his pants. "Bill, you promised me you would come by once the renovations were finished. And, Martin, you can drag the honeymooners along."

Me so honee! The Hornymooners. Wait till the honeying of the lune, love. Liquid alliteration.

"I have a fully stocked bar," Jordan giggled, "as one might expect of a publican."

They sit on creepystools at the edge of the universe, hoisting jars, black galaxy expensively blazing like Ada's eyes. Eleven is the number signifying cycle change in the Wake. Issy tends bar. She adds Stolichnaya 50 to an icefilled shaker, shakes and drains the contents into a row of icechilled crystalshotglasses. Stoli is the best vodka because it's distilled from winter wheat. She picks up a shotglass, downs a nun rousing potion, get thee to the stage, her eyes roil with assfuckingdelight.

"Sounds great to me," Martin Amis said. "Any coke or barbiturates on hand? I'm only kidding. I can't speak, of course, for the Kernows. I'm sure they'd love to attend your soiree. They speak of you with great fondness."

Jordan delved into his wallet and produced a garish business card. Sinisterplacedpaddyweed.

"Call me," he said, handing the card to Martin Amis.

"I don't want you to go to any trouble, Brian. And I can't speak for the Kernows. They do speak about you so fondly that I think they certainly would like to get together socially."

"I have to get going, Brian," Bill Barium interjected. "What a great pleasure, Martin!"

More Fenian and Saxon handshaking. Fee! Fie! Fo! Fum! Jordan rose with grace, stuck out his hand.

"I will try to make your causerie," Bill Barium cried, pumping madly the adulterous handle of his countyman.

Act each as a brother and help one another

Like true hearted men from the County Mayo…

Bill Barium corantoed off the stage.

"He seems like a very interesting fellow," Martin Amis phonily phonated midayawn.

"He'll never call me," Jordan revealed with a headshake. "He has an unusual take on the Moor of Venice. He believes Desdemona was guilty of adultery. Not with Cassio but with Emilia. He says when Othello describes her skin as monumental alablaster that it's Will's way of exposing Desdemona as a lesbian. His research tells him that a blaster was Elizabethan slang for a lady of the house that demands sexual favors from her waiting lakin. A man of genius, Stephen Dedalus reminds us, make only volitional mistakes."

"And I always thought," Martin Amis unthought, "that it was just his poor education showing. But I see now, he was just a paronomasiac. Look at her name? I wonder if the source material used such an obviously illogical name for a heroine?"

"In the Hecatommithi," Jordan began, "her name is Disdemona and Iago's name is Alfiero which means literally flagman or ensign. I seem to remember," Jordan rubbed his head. "Alfiero clubs her to death in Cinthio's morality tale."

Iago beat her like a roaneen.

"The Hecatommithi is one hundred and twelve stories told by ten exiles from Rome while on a voyage. Or is it one hundred stories told by twelve exiles?"

"Where are they voyaging to? The Iowa Writers' Workshop," Martin Amis snickered. "On a prairie schooner," he further snickered.

"I don't recall exactly where they were going," Jordan admitted. "They were exiles."

There came to the beach a poor exile of Cimmerian parts. He offered the sunbathers a Cimmerian blessing: May the road rise up to meet you.Blah blah blah blah. And until we meet again, may the light and darkness divider hold you in the palm of his hand.

"My own travel plans include a visit to your club. And certainly the go-go bar! It's a gammastring establishment, I gather? No bush, right?"

"Gamma-string," Jordan echoed. "I call g-strings gamma-strings. Did I steal that from Money?"

"No," Money Amis said. "It just came to me. So it is a bushless premises?"

"We prefer to call it vaginal concealment," Jordan yucked. "I called Squares earlier today and learned from the manager that a recent acquaintance of mine, the vice president's son, George, has been a fixture lately. Whooping it up like a mindless cowboy. I was there the other night but he had already ridden off into the sunset. So strictly speaking, it is—at the moment—or at least the last I checked, a Bushful premises. The girls—I have learned from personal experience—shave—or at the very least—trim their arbustos."

Martin Amis furtively eyed his tablemate's pendulous heaven-hued celtifix: a shimmering earbob bobbing from a fleshy lobe. On that fleshly stage of Eros...

"What is the prodigal son up to? Campaigning for his father? I know you're a publican. But the question is, Brian, are you a Republican? I think you know my politics."

A spectre is haunting Martin Amis. I won't tell him I was a member of S.D.S. Jesus was the first socialist. It is easier for a camel to pass through the eye of a needle, than for a Republican to enter the kingdom of god.

Jay McGod was a great philosopher. Philosophasters of the world unite!

"I voted for Reagan twice," Jordan disclosed. "A friend of mine, Bob Armagh, recently held a fundraiser for Bush in his home. Perhaps Dubya—as his friends call him—is thinking of using my go-go bar as a fundraising venue. Bush fils and Roberto—as Dubya has dubbed him—have become famous for their compotations in the Jersey Shore. I understand from what Bob tells me—he himself a Rothian sexotrope—that Dubya loves the titties bar, as they call them in Texas."

Martin Amis fussed with his slender tie.

"A cockraising venue," Martin Amis opined. "Roth is an unabashed sexotrope. Sexotropic Bush claims he's born again. What would that make him?"

"A failed Christian."

"You called him a recent acquaintance," Martin Amis probed. "I assume you met the heir apparent at a fundraiser."

"I met him in the bathroom of a bar," Jordan admitted.

"Was he doing coke," Martin Amissniffed. "I hear he does bales of the whitestuff."

Martin Amis ruffled his nosewings, searched the pockets of his dress pants, and pulled out the god of this world.

"Eureka! Eureka! Are you holding, Brian? Dear old Ben Franklin," he cried, a fan of bills covering his gob. "A gramsworth of wit in England can be purchased for the one of your dear old Ben Franklins."

"I get the reference, of course," Jordan said, amused at Martin Amis's clowning. "Perhaps if you put your money away, I might be able to help you."

Martin Amis collapsed the fan of fifties and hundreds and slid them into his shirt pocket. He leaned forward and whispered a request into Jordan's uneager ear. The ginbreath of Martin Amis surprised him. Smells as if he has been drinking turpentine. Put but money in thy purse and a gram in my hand. Sansword, Jordan passed Chettle a groatsworth of wit in the guise of a handshake.

"I'll be back in a sniff," Martin Amis cracked. He opened his hand, glimpsed a shining friend, and raced off in the direction of the restroom.

The tinfoil sculpture shining like a sinless thing in the Amisian damppalm. His giddy love concealed within its twisted art. Art for coke's sake! To misquote the Pre-Raphaelite poetlood. The clouds blushed with the setting of the sun. How did he know? Did Joanna tell him? In that nest of guineary she betrayed him. Oh, Brian? Nobody knows where he gets all that cash. They say he's a cokedealer.

Martin ben Amis Elijah, amid clouds of devils, by now, has ascended to the glory of the Bush.

Erythroxylon coca bush. It's a neurotransmitter inhibitor. It prevents the reabsorption of dopamine in midbrain. Substantia Negra was the first name you tried out on your partners as the neonom for the club. They thought it sounded like the name of a black club. Oscura was the compromise. Ironically, its best nights are always the ones featuring black performers. The head of a Jamaican posse, Armstrong Young Laughlin, manages a great Reggae band called Sad Dark Night.

No woman, no cry…

Whirling hesouls, shesouls in the seashore. A shesoul in exquisite fleshcase yagged a book in the eighthundreds. The aisle of dustiny. Quintessence of dust. Dusty literature studies illumined by darts of sunfire thrown by Helios mac Hyperion. Almamate or a nice piece of tail? He got up, stretched, dared to follow the bonny fleshcase into a chiaroscuro painting. She tossed her brownpenny hair, placed a soft hand on her roundverbhips, warmhazel eyes concentrating on a particular tanbookspine: a monograph on Ginny Crown. She can shove it up her brownpenny! (Forgive me, my jeween bawn.) Jordanthoughtsung:

> She had a capallic nog
> and didn't float like a log
> and didn't float like a log…

Back to the barracks! Amisallsniffethout, his prosesteps tend to the table. If Brianeen Levite his mickbeth todday... Every life hath manytoddays when you're a Jet. When you're a Jet, you're a Jet... Jordan sat down a moment before the cokesnortingdirtyjohnny reached for a chair. His fingernails pared, polished, a reminder that he was an English gentleman. A speck of cocaine visible on his freckled nose. Danaric skin. Freckles and redhair are the result of the despised Danish occupation in England according to Brewer Phrase and Fable. Danegeld. Pay through the nose. King Canute killed the Earl of Ulf over a chessgame.

Martin Amissonic:

"Great shit. Some of Bolivia's finest."

"How did you know I was holding?"

"Joanna told me. Don't worry about Mark. He's a libertarian and hates that he has to sentence—"

"I'm not a drug pusher," Jordan assured. "She's a great girl but—"

"I didn't mean to imply that. She only told me that in your capacity as a hedonic engineer, to echo the divine Huxley, that occasionally you come into some gran blanco."

"I hope," Jordan hoped, "that we can keep this confidential."

"I would never say a word," wordy Martin Amis promised. "How much do I owe you?"

"It's a gift," Jordan said. "I'd never sell it. Unsavory, at the very least. Albeit, I agree it should be legalized."

"Well, I am very indebted, my friend."

An aircraft flies under the radar.

"Kinch the knifeblade," Martin Amis announced.

A man—approximately the same age as the deipnosophists—in white and black shorts, jersey and stockings of Hereford United, lean, average height, blackbrownhair and redwhitefosh, invaded Amisspace. Started, Martin Amis fired:

"Jesus, Icke! You're a long way from Coventry. What brings you to the colonies?"

Cheshu Icke's pale Galilean eyes flickered greenfire. The eyes of the bovine emblem of Hereford United evoking sadness in fellow bovine

Jordan.

"Colonies? It is amazing," the man grinned, "what an old Tory Amis the Younger has become. Aren't you expected at Maggie's for High Tea? All the cucumber sandwiches and krimpets will be gone by now."

"Brian," Martin Amis said, "this is the washed up footballer, turned hack writer, erstwhile sportscaster, the redoubtable David Icke. All in all, a brilliant bloke and mensch."

The mensch turned to Jordan, the brilliant turquoise of his eyes surprised him.

"A great pleasure," David Icke Icked. "Amis the Younger is quite a character. One better tolerated after strong drink."

Icke smiled a gummy smile. His handsome face, viewed by Jordan on secondglance as somewhat bonhamish, bobbed like a Corkman in the Dead Sea. Martin Amis's lips poised for anglomachy.

"And you," Martin Amis said in a raspy voice, "are best taken with a tab of lysergic acid diethylamide. Have you seen any lizards lately? Mon Ami Icke believes the world is controlled by an extraterrestrial reptocracy headed by the English Royal Family. He has a book coming out next year that lists the reigning reptocrats. It will be a surprise to the Queen to learn that she's a lizard but our friend Icke is determined to publish his Who's Reptile. Who are some of the people—I use the term lightly—that you include? I hope I made the list," Martin Amis cracked.

"You'll have to buy the book," David Icke said jovially. "You would be surprised to learn that many of our famous personages, past and present, have either been Rept or mindcontrolled by them. Ronald Wilson Reagan is the latter. His vice president is a reptile."

Jordan looked at Martin Amis and they both laughed pointedly.

"We all have the bloody bloodlines," David Icke, with bloodlines in his eyes, bloodied on. "What I maintain, in the Biggest Secret, is that the so-called Windsors have the most reptoglobin. There are scores of witnesses to the Queen shapeshifting on palace grounds."

"If Bess is a reptile," Martin Amis guffawed, "that means she was conceived in the Queen mum's arse."

Martin Amis jested on.

"Vaginarse. Cuntcul. Culcunt...the Queen's mum's bum is

rhyming slang for rum!"

David Icke stroked his cleanshavenchin meditatively, saying:

"You are, of course, referring to the fact that reptile's cloaca—in addition to the obvious task—also serves in a reproductive capacity. The hemipenis is also cloacal."

"When my hemipenis was but a toy," Martin Amis Shakespeared in a festive singing voice.

A clown for all seasons. His flashes of merriment that set the table roaring. Roaring boys! A fool's bolt is soon shot. They call it premature ejaculation of the brain.

"Your poison jests," David Icke said, "act as mithridates. Thus, old boy, I am immuned to your envenom'd foil."

"Like Laertes the Unlucky," Martin Amis cried, "the foul practise hath turn'd itself on me. I'm sorry, Davey. You are probably on to something about the reptilian quality of the Royals—and so-called royalty."

The neocortex is perhaps the result of a virus from outerspace and outertime. It bestowed language and language bestows love. Mammalian brain versus coldsouled reptilian Brian. I love you. The reptile brain squirming in the shadows. What is that word unknown to all reptiles?

David the Icke smiled fulsomely. His opponent, Amis the Younger, tried to match its abundant gleam, but only managed an abbreviated smile.

"Their weekends of debauchery are just around the corner," David Icke Icked mysteriously.

"You mean the illuminati," Martin Amis solved. "The Bohemian Club meets every summer in a grove in Sonoma. I have been invited by one of its directors, Kevin Starr, to give a reading."

"The Bohemian Grove is a place where they perform human sacrifices, engage in the two p's: pedophilia and pederasty. The vice president, Jimmy Carter, Dick Cheney, Kris Kristofferson, and the vice president's Faulknerian son, are the true power in the Grove. Kevin Starr is a frontman. Cheney and Carter are the high priests who sacrifice children to Moloch. Carter is mindcontrolled by Cheney."

Martin Amis shook his head, laughing:

"Hitch told me that last year's grovetogether was rather sedate. He tells me the Creation of Care Ceremony is an unintentional hilarious ecleticism. Starr pulled some strings. Hitch does think that George W. Bush is a drunken moron. He believes he wants to be president someday. But who would vote for such a mess?"

"Don't underestimate the power of the Illuminati to deceive," David Icke reminded. "They actually sacrifice children. Secretly and openly. Kevin Starr is a Druid."

Martin Amis turned to Jordan, placed a soft hand on the American's shoulder, and asked:

"Our friend, Brian, is a personal friend of Georgie Porgie."

David Icke's eyes narrowed.

"Watch that he doesn't introduce you to Cheney."

"Martin is pulling your leg, David," Jordan said. "I met the vice president's son briefly in a bar."

Bohemian Grove? Code White! The Hillbilly is expecting me. I made a large delivery there last year to an enrobed oldfuck in a mask. A faggle of fageese lounging around a grotto seemed at his faggotty call. They may have been minors. One dancing Adamly in a gilded cage. The gayfuck traipsing around in the habiliments of a satyr. He invited me to drop by later that evening for the ultimate party. His card read: W.C. Dearsoil. Which I later deciphered as an anagram of W.C. Arse-Idol. The oldgaybird sounded suspiciously like the vice president. There was an altar erected to the aforementioned Moloch in the drawing room. He was naked underneath his pinksilk robe. His hemipenis intermittently escaping its prissy confines as he gave me the tour of his riverine cabin. The bulleting stream in the rear of the impristine wooded property was, W.C. Dearsoil informed, the Russian River. He asked if I would like to join the party as he panted over a particularly girlpretty boyeen—but I took the cash and sinkapaced out of there. I told my suppliers that I would prefer not to make future deliveries to Mr. W.C. Arse-Idol and they agreed, saying: He's alright, Bry. He thinks he's Sebastian Melmoth. They told me that the Bohemian Grove was where the Kennedy presicide was plotted. The vice president's dark woods more terrifying than my trip to the street where I first met my God and my angel.

147

"I have to shove off," David Icke said, studying his complicated watch. "I'll miss my flight to California. Nice meeting you, Brian."

"And you!"

David Icke's eyes panned the room for visible and unvisible enemies and said:

"I hope we run into each other again, Marty."

Sennet. Exit Icke.

The reptophobe's taut arms swung in unison as he toddled down the apples and pears. The light of the summit brightening his occiput a shade. A moment later, he turned around and ran back up them and retrieved the attache he had left underneath a table in the reference section.

"I have to use the bathroom," Jordan announced.

Martin Amis smiled, untabled a book, turned to Jordan.

"Would you like a pick me up," he snickered. "Or do you have your own," he added stupidly.

Jordan's teeth played the orator. He traveled northwest on Nike Airs that were bought last week in the local mall and unboxed today specifically for his 1.1 mile perambulation to the library. As he entered the glass enclosed forecourt—with its plush redleathercouches, potted tropical plants, and spiraling magazine rack—a beguiling light addressed him. It spoke in Elohimese. If you have Elohimese on you, come into the atrium. The said atrium afforded Jordan a view of the trees north of the unyielding redbrick church steeple; the ones lining the walkway were, for the most part, mature russet oaks. Obviously, he couldn't see the quartet of crimson red bushes in the shadows of the competing royalty of trees throughout the courtyard, but, refuting Berkeley by nose, knew them to still be where they were a small hour ago. He pulled the pine door of the bathroom open and floated in and over to the urinal. He unzipped, brandished his brown boyo, aimed downwards. He placed a steadying palm on the blue tiled wall, humming their song, as his bladder sonorously drained. He zipped up, heard the whirlpool of the automatic flush, went over to the sink, pressed the stainless steel soap pump, saturated his hands with red detergent, scrubbed. He left the bathroom and hurried back to the table. Angstroms again engaged him in celestial chitchat. The visible spectrum, stretching 4,000 (violet) to 7,000 (red) angsts, is useless in differentiating the warmblooded from coldblood-ed, human from reptile. He's the Napoleon of slime! Look! Professor Moriarty oscillating his face like a reptile. He is one of them, Watson. How will we be able to prove he's saurian, Holmes? Elementary, my dear Watson. I'll pull an infrared camera out my arse (Deus ex culum) and shoot the slimey, limey bastard! Jordan sat down at the table next to the possible reptile. Martin Amis closed the book he was reading, smiled, touched his nose in a suggestive manner.

"Where were we," Martin Amis asked with overzealous nostrils.

"We were discussing your hatred of that form of verse architec-ture called rhyme," Jordan recalled, adding after a fat pause: "Nabokov was not a fan of the rhymers. He called them rhyming rabbits."

Martin Amis smilefrowned as he supplied the cauda to the Nabokovian pronouncement:

"They graze in overgrazed pastures."

I saw Harvey on the long and winding road to the stars. He held up a sign, scriptio continua—or because I was traveling at warp speed in a 1983 RX-7 it may have seemed that way—reading:

Ahazeofimagesawaitsyourspaceyeyes…Images   pararhymes with eyes…Pararhyming rabbits hase in overgrazed pastures.

"Shakespeare seems to have renounced rhyming," Jordan pitched in a salesy voice. "At least, a deconstructionist reading of Ham-let points to that conclusion. Horatio chides Hamlet for not rhyming the fourth line of a quartet reeled off by the prince after frightening the king with false fire."

"You might have rhymed," Martin Amis recited knowingly. "Pa-jock might rhyme with was in Zeta Reticuli. That is," Martin Amis, bee-tlebrowed, loudly cried, "if you buy Little Wilson's theory that the Bard was gifted the folios by extraterrestrials. Hamlet, like Bice the tamed shrew of Much Ado About Nothing, was not born under a rhyming planet."

Swollen Bardhead rising out of starched ruff attached to freaky small tunic with oversized shoulderwings. Noveau gentry. His coat-of-arms: Gould, on a Bend, Sables, a speare of the first steeled argent. And for his creast or cognizaunce a falcon, his winges displayed Argent standing on a wreath of coullers. Non sans droit.

"Bloom considers himself the foremost authority on Shakespeare," Martin Amis scoffed. "But he's too dense to have ever made that point."

"I think he's a deconstructionist lost on its silver street. Probably at a pizza parlor or McDonald's," Jordan lowblowed.

"Judging by his ever-increasing Bloomness," Martin Amis sized up with saurian ceannoscillation, "there must be a Häagen-Dazs store or two on the way."

Jordan laughed a fake laugh, the kind reminiscent of the one employed by the lanky Attleborian during a telesales pitch for the old Lucifer's Noose or Parkersburg's Finest.

Greet the world with that word unknown to lizards.

I love you, buddy.

Og Mandino chapter and verse.

It was the lanky Attleborian, bloated Belmarian these days, who first successfully tempted him from nephalism. Don't be a lightweight, buddy. Have a drink, buddy. Cranly's arm. Onan's hand. Dinny Blue's wrist. Ironically, the drunken fuck boasts of being descended from Pilgrims. The Halldweller Famileye (surname later truncated to Hell) came over on the Mayflower. Perhaps not so ironic. That cursed schooner u-turned when they realized they hadn't brought along enough brewski for the voyage (the Halldwellers will drink ye out of ship and boat). Jerry Hell proves they carried the alky gene with them.

Ad campaign Idea:

Old Plymouth Rock: the beer the roundhats turned around for!

Sackers of Drogheda! Go to the fucking dirtiest hell!

Hell was married to Dentelupo's sister, Lori. The bitchcunt, as J.H. calls her behind her big ass, recently left him for a manqué thoroughbred owner and trainer during his stay in a rehab for heroin addiction. Hell was informed of the break-up telephonically (the weekly allowed spousal call): I've left you, Jerry. I've run away with John Pomodoro. He fucks me in the ass and I love it!

"What a downpour," Martin poured forth. "I wish I had brought my umbrella. Who would—"

With bronchitic laughter, Jordan patted the Englishman's twisted back and assured:

"Nothing to worry about, Martin. It's passing by."

He heard the rain impinge upon the concrete walkway. Tympanic footsteps and clamor of those seeking shelter accompanied the moist, proud music of the storm. His eyes celivagous with the appearance of trotter steering, ruddy, fourarmed, Indra Dancer in the eastern skies and behind him, stalking, flapping, that veddy, veddy, windy fellow Vayu.

Lori picked up, toting the kids Josh and Jessie with her, and now resides on a horse farm in a princedom nowhere near the sea (Ocala, Florida) with her expert sodomizer.

It was Lori's oldest brother, Tom, who introduced Hell to heroin. Speaking of Tom, born Gaetano, longtime heroin addict, Vietnam vet, and knowing cuckold (he also hooked his wife, Marie, who happily hooks for their habit), the Dentelupo family hysterically relates that when said brother was filling out a job application a few years ago that he penned in Buster (his nickname since childhood) in the box requesting mother's maiden name. Proving that stupidity is just as funny to the stupid as it is to the so-called intelligent.

"It's stopping," Martin Amis declared upon noting the cessation of serious rain. "You have to agree that Bloom doubles every decade. If I could only get my money market fund to double every ten years? He's absolutely Falstaffian! Fat Jack Bloomstaff—"

"He has heard the chimes of Good Humor at midnight," Jordan broke in.

"He is always saying, to echo the eulogizer of the hooknosed man of Rome, that Sir Jack is the Bloomiest Shakespeare character of them all," the rainwatcher said. "But I see the fat fucking piece of shit more as the dark lady of the sonnets."

Martin Amis stared into the cesious eyes of his viewer and, with a smiley voice, added:

"It's the coke speaking. I'm still angry at him for his neo-Freudian take on Money."

"I came, saw, overcame," Jordan merrily remembered.

"In England," the Englander intoned, still harping on obesity, "we eat badly but, unlike America, where one can obtain a Big Mac, Whopper, Facestuffer, Bellybuster, at every corner, my putative home lags behind in the fastfood race. Like every other race, England has become an also ran. I lived here as a teen and am shocked that wherever you turn there's a set of golden arches. Which is alright, I suppose."

Martin Amis paused to take a palpable hit off an imaginary cigarette.

"I'm dying for a fag. I mean, a cigarette. That must sound terrible to American ears. I'm in the process of quitting. Process is the key word, as any nicotine addict can attest. And your airwave hamburger wars! All beef patty, special sauce, pickle, lettuce and tomato. Where's the beef, indeed? The jingoism! The not so moral equivalent of war. I hope you're not offended that I disparage your profession. I honestly hope you make millions in your field."

"I'm no John Self," Jordan explained.

Séan Féin.

"What does Saint Augustine say about temptation," Martin Amis asked.

"Yield to it," Jordan laughed.

"That's what Oscura Wilde urged," Martin Amis said obscurely.

"I am," Martin Amis said, "as I get older, more near the occasion of sinning than sinning."

"Have you heard Wallace Gray on Lear? He believes the girls, save Cordelia, were molested by their Kingly father. As always, the fool is the wiseman: I have used it, nuncle, ever since thou madest thy daughters thy mothers: for when thou gavest them the rod, and put'st down thine own breeches..."

"If you desire," Martin Amis iffed, "I'll sing the foolishly wise song that follows."

You were best to take my coxcomb. Toynbee is right. The Saxon thinks every fucking thing is a joke. They got fucking drunk on imported usque baugh the night before Hastings and lost their land to the bastard Normans, Norman bastards. At least, we lost it to them because of a nest of spicery and a papal bull.

"I think that would be great, Martin."

152

"I don't think," Martin Amis said thoughtfully, "that I remember it."

Martin Amis raised a stern finger and blanked:

Jordan lifted a mild finger and filled the lacuna with quasi-song:

"Then they for sudden joy did weep

And I for sorrow sung,

That such a King should play bo-peep

And go the fool among..."

Martin Amis howled, miau'd, barked, brayed, belled, yelled, crowed.

"You must," Martin Amis demanded, "at all costs, keep your day job. Priceless. Very funny. Still, we're laughing at a despicable crime, if one agrees with Professor Gray's conclusion that Lear molested his daughters. Bloomstaff, it has been alleged, left Columbia because of his disagreements with him. He calls Wally's deconstructions delusionary. Hearing the phrase in my mind again, it can be construed both ways. Of course, I have read that even during the time of not so chaste Liza Tudor that rod was slang for penis."

Lear leans over a secondbest bed where wee Gonny sleeps. His Krausean corpuscles enkindled by the mild fire of mead imported from cousin realm. His own bed vacant—the Queen long gravecold—the King shivering with concupiscence.

"The deconstructionist can't lose," Jordan said with a shrug. "Ils jouent rouge et noir et vert."

"Have you read Rabelais? A field day for any deconstructionist."

By whose gyronomic circumbilvaginations, as by two celivagous filopendulums, all autonomatic metagrobolism of the Remish Church, when tottering and emblustricated with the gibblegabble glibberish of this odious earror and hearsay.

"I feel in many respects his apologia of the Mendicants is the forerunner of the Wake," Jordan rang.

"My Irish twin," Martin Amis clanged. "Children born in England less than a year apart are called Irish twins no matter their ethnicity," he lightly clanked. "Anyway, my tenuous twin always refers to Kingsley as Gargantua and his slightly older brother as Pantagruel. I'm sorry," Martin Amis stupidly clunked. "You're Irish. I gather that from your name and, of course, from your earbob, that you are of Hibernian descent."

"And my love of Joyce? I am not in the least offended. My father's an Irish triplet."

"Mark is Irish Catholic. The name Kernow is a very obscure one. I love Ireland and the Irish themselves are delightful."

Not a lie! They love Ireland and the Irish so much that they wanted to turn it into their estate and its people into their servants. Or a pasture. It's only teenage wasteland.

"Joyce is undeniably a genius. You would—witnessed by your L.Q. (Literary Quotient)—read and admire the divine Dubliner if you were Serbo-Croatian. He makes even the best writers seem pedestrian, laconic, guileless. He washes his hands—one of them once bussed by Fitzgerald—of bare talent like Hank James."

Literary reference, simile, cliché, simile. I need something more substantial. Suprasubstantial linguistic ascension. He sitteth, he thinks, on the right hand of Vivian Darkbloom. Whom is trying to write like this week? Pynchon or Waugh? If you weren't merely a talent, you could—a la the Emperor of coral and copper snow—have your fucking watercress sandwich and eat it, too.

"In Ulysses and the Wake, he soars to the summit of language," Martin Amis leapt, adding: "In a jet of genius, Joyce leaves in his wake (no pun intended) only contrails of story. As I said in a recent article, Joyce's books are not books one curls up to."

Amisphor, cliché. A gayché. The War against Gayché!

"The true writer has nothing to say. It's the way he says it, as Robbe-Grillet says," Jordan countered, smiling liberally. "If I'm not mistaken," he paused, looked around, moderately smiling now, and closed: "Nabokov was a fan."

"Joyce is the precedent to all reader hating literature."

L'homme qui ment.

"Judging by your expression, you don't agree with me. But the Wake has to be the ultimate anti-novel: unreadable at any speed," the Englishman asserted. "I much prefer the humanity of Lolita: recondite but readable."

Jordan twiddled with his claddagh. A tell.

"I revere both. I think it is so undeniable that…Mailer—I think he put it best—when asked by a television host—he was stumping for his monograph on Miller—whether Miller was as great as Joyce—"

"Was it Don Swaim? He's an idiot. No, you said television, didn't you?"

"Bob Crombie. He was surprised at the depth of Mailer's appreciation of Miller and had to ask him did he think he was the equal of Joyce. Mailer replied: No one's in that league!"

"Joyce is an existentialist writer for the devoutly Joycean reader. If you know what I mean? He assumes no responsibility for what he writes. The Wake is a perfect example of this. It is too bad for us, Joyce seems to say, if we don't know Polish or Danish in order get one of his crosslanguage puns. He might have just as easily written it in Esperanto."

"Eurish, Burgess called it. But," Jordan sighed, "that limits it."

"The Irish really like their stews. Joyce loved to combine disparate verses. A scrap of Dante with a bit of Blake. A prologue to Burroughs's cut-ups experiment. I suppose," Martin Amis exhaled, "the Wake's dreamish is a natural progression for a language mad genius like your God. Burroughs is quite a character. He had a peculiar relationship with language. Satirists always do. Did you ever think Joyce, save for his anti-British rhetoric and renunciation of the Roman Catholic faith, never wrote a serious word? Jocoserious is how someone once described Ulysses. Menippean satirist. Nabokov does perhaps reference the Wake but Joyce references his bête noir Tennyson, doesn't he? Of course, Nabokov despised Tommy Eliot but he uses the music of Ash-Wednesday to frame Quilty's death warrant."

Ashplantwednesday. Somatic and systematic death. I bleed, sirrah; but not kill'd. I still possess skinsense, proprioception, interoception, and for the first time in donkey's ears I've got a woody, thus my somatosensory system is in good operating order, Brewster. Put the deathcap on the American Maeterlinck, Chumsky. Feu! From this time forth I never will gobshite.

"Because you took advantage of my disadvantage," Jordan recited nasally. "Nabokov perceived—I think erroneously—that Eliot was anti-Semitic."

"All Christians are anti-Semites," Martin Amis argued. "Sinners against the light, as Deasy says. Would there be any light in this fucked up world without them? They're the diamonds of humanity. No people come close to matching their accomplishments with the exception of the ancient Greeks. Still, they are despised by Christian, Moslem, Hindi."

"How did we get on this subject?"

"What is the weirdest literary theory you have ever heard, Brian? I mean, one devoid of gaseous vertebrates."

Martin Amis folded his monkey arms, crossed his coltish legs, smirksmiled.

"I prove by syllogism that both Lolita, prey, and Humbert, predator, are scions of Persse O'Reilly. That Irish pol you alluded to earlier."
Martin Amis's lips blossomed into a pinkish purple smile. Your lips are like two petals of grape hyacinth that are twins, which feed among the short and curlies.

"One can prove by syllogism," Martin Amis began to remember the old joke, "that Ray Charles is God. Yet, you pique my interest. But I may as well warn you that if you want to shake my belief that Nabokov hated the Wake you have a stern task before you."

Jordan withstood the blue doubt of miscreant eyes glinting stern under corrugated brows.

"We are often captivated by what we supposedly hate. He may have publicly rejected Joyce's somnopus but there are more references to it in Lolita and Ada than the book he thought of as the finest novel of the 20th century. Ulysses, I mean. I realize that Nabokov often targeted writers by parodying them. Like the parody of Ash-Wednesday availed of by Humbert for Quilty's, so to speak, death warrant. Dostoevski was, of course, a frequent target in his fiction. But the girleen rainbow allusion—seven or twenty-eight—in Lolita—is a loving allusion. And Humbert and Quilty are not only Joyceans, but, moreover, Wakeans."

"Somnopus is a good way to describe Nabokov's opinion of the Wake. He called it a snore—a remedy for his insomnia."

Ulysses thundered closed by Jordan's lightning hand.

"He called its dialect the dialect of a genius. Ada's narrator drives a Jolls-Joyce—which seems to me—the most Wakean of puns."

"Gospodin Nabokov was an incurable insomniac and an acknowledged lover of middle-aged puns," Martin Amis's humorless voice reported. "I honestly think he was telling the truth about the Wake putting him to sleep."

Thou art Pnin Veen and upon this peat bog I shall build my cil.

"It put him to sleep, yes, but in the wake of sleep we call dream, the maze of Lolita and Ada was created. Ada is, of course, Lolita's undeclared companion piece. Remember Humbert tells us that Dolly's real surname rhymes with the one assigned to her in his memoir. Maze perfectly describes the Wake, doesn't it? Ada—a grand relative of Lolita—was born, impossibly and paradoxically, after her exponentially more infamous ink relative. Something only possible in metatemporal fiction such as the Wake or Genesis. Certum est, quia impossibile est."

Martin Amis smiled with good humor, his teeth greyauburned.

"Ada's grandmother Dolly was the daughter of Mary O'Reilly," Jordan informed. "Persse O'Reilly's daughtermother: Vergine madre, figlia di tuo figlio. Both Lo and Ada are sexually precocious and both share the beg srón, little nose, of Dolly Durmanov. Persse haveth childers everwhere! Nabokov's debt to the Wake is enormous. Isn't Earwicker, O'Reilly's alterego, a daughter desirer? Nothing more, as Little Wilson reasons in the introduction of A Shorter Finnegans Wake, than a loyal desire to keep sex in the family. The linguistic vincula between apish Humbert and Humphrey Chimpden Earwicker is undeniable."

Martin Amis laughed kindly.

"Apish Humbert bounded in a nutshell, Brian."

"The infinite space of dreams. The fictive dream, a minor writer labeled it. Is Humbert's memoir but a forlorn dream of its author? Did Nabokov dream of a litter of Lolitas? Did Vladimirovitch see himself king of Humbertland or emperor of Quiltyville?"

"I agree that Humbert envies his shadow—characters are always umbrae of their creators—but Nabokov was no nympheteer."

"He fertilized his brain with Joycean seed," Jordan observed. "Thus the children of his brain resemble Joyce's literary progeny. Dolly rhymes with Molly. Hum, the cuckolded, Bloomlike in his devotion to

Dolly. The Boylanlike Cue: callous bluesoxclockolder of Hoom or—if you like—Blumbert. Of course, unlike his paradigm, he is—if we believe his dying day report—a spermless satyr."

Venomless viper. Fingerless pianist. Nyetaphor.

"No lead in his pencil," the Pen of London Fields and Environs announced.

Jordan frowned at the Englishman's delayed jointpoint.

I say, how uncouth! I had thought Oxford Englishmen were more gentlewomenly.

"All poets feed on other poets," Cannibal Amis stirred. "Joyce was nourished by Homer, Dante, Shakespeare! And by every song John Joyce ever knew. He learned the stream of consciousness from some hack French journalist."

A mess of metaphors mixed with clichés. Give me something more transubstantial.

"Shakespeare hatched other poets' eggs," Jordan hatched. "Kyd's, Marlowe's, Sydney's, Cinthio's, Belleforest's. The latter boosted the choicest cackleberry of them all out from under the rump of venerable Saxo."

"Grammaticus was the source of the Historie of Hamblet but ur-Hamlet's likely quiller was Marlowe or his flatmate Tommy Kyd."

"It doesn't matter who laid the egg," Jordan bickered. "Will gilded it with his golden words."

Non sanz droict! Put Gulden's on it, redwill.

"Joyce is not reader amicable," Martin Amis bickered back. "He is anti-reader, pro-scholar. He's Joyce amicable. His golden words are fool's gold. He screws the prospector with a smile, paring his fingernails."

"His pyrite blends sparkle brighter and more luminously than so-called real gold."

"Bright jimfoolery," Martin Amis smacked. "His god Dante is a writer who borrowed from everything he had ever read."

"Joyce lauds his god with crooked smoke at the conclusion of Scylla and Charybdis."

"You mean Shakespeare? Most Joyceans think Joyce is a Dantean."

"He's Joyspearean," Jordan clarified.

Martin Amis tossed his tie, waxing wroth:

"Auto-god Joyce. Or should I say co-god? Or is it a triumvirate of the sky? A trinity of divinity: Domine Alighieri, filius Joyce and Sancte Spiritus Shakespeare. Nabokov maintained no free man needs a god."

"He also said he was immortal. Other men die, I am not another. Therefore I'll not die."

"And this is the only immortality you and I may share, my Lolita...Lolita is his immortality."

Thou art Pnin Veen and upon this peat bog I will build my parvis.

"Nabokov riles against mere talent. In particular, Henry James. But isn't Lolita an example of talent, not genius? Genius is the only thing that merits immortality."

Nabby adores 225 but detests 224; he adores 900 but detests 800; he adores 144 but detests 145. Which does he adore: 1600 or 1700?

"That long black cloud is comin'," Jordan blackly forecasted.

"Like Rock n' Roll, Lolita will never die. It is a work of genius. Joyce's map and timepiece opus of Victorian Dublin is somewhat of a fictive Baedeker. Genius should transcend spatial-temporal considerations."

Martin Amis paused, sighed and looked, sighed again.

"He is a wonder verbally. Whom could deny that? If the word does indeed kill the object, Joyce spifflicated his hometown with his bon mots—not to mention his mal mots! The former came to him so readily, poetry actually, that he often chose to wield his weapon for the wrong cause."

Jordan cleared his bronchial tubes, saying:

"The definition of a writer is someone who believes everything in the world exists to end up in a book. Joyce believed his books Dublin's raison d'etre."

"I say, Brian. Are you saying your master was a megalomaniac?

Your definition of a writer is bonaroo!"

Gaysprick bka Polari from the lips of a putative anomaly (English heterosexual): When his friend in soccer shorts showed up at our table his eyessayeth: How bona to vada your basket!

"I am serious about the lack of latitude and longitude of his books," Martin Amis rehashed. "He alludes to its lack of space of time in one of Stephen's mental chapbooks."

Saxon Dog! Bursting with inaccuracies. He said: A very short space of time through very short times of space.

"The Circe episode wanders through panspace and pantime. So it is not just Leotidian."

"Circe, I admit, is a glanciful piece of writing," glanciful Martin Amis admitted.

Bright and quick. Carpe verbum! Martin Amis, I hoikphthook in your eek! Londoners are all for turds!

"Ulysses debased epic was begun with Bloom and Stephen's entrance into Nighttown," Martin Amis pivoted.

"You can taste the coral and copper ice cream dished out by Gondolier Rabaiotti on Sraid Mabbot."

"I have always admired that image of stunted Dubliners getting their icy sugar fix in the heat of a midshakespearean night. But you get the point? Joyce like Shakespeare makes so much of nothing. A pushcart metaphored into a Gelato gondola."

"He daedally lifts the lifewand and the dumb speak. He's a Preconstructionist. Things out of words," Jordan explained jocoseriously.

"That sounds, that sounds very much like Paul...Good God! What's his name? His name?"

Echoing himself? Not technically echolalia but close since he's such a fugging solipsist. I hate lethonomia but not the lethonomiac.

"The Report on Resistentialism. Paul Jennings was the bloke's name. Do you know it? Absolutely priceless. Things are against us. A parody of Sartre. Its fictive French philosopher, bearing the apropos surname Ventre, labels the universe as the ultimate Thing. And, as I have said, it is fucking against us. It is really more a parody of French genius than Existentialism. In particular, their uncanny crystalization of a constellation of ideas into logical, diamond hard sayings."

Resistentialism is what things think about men.

"Aphorisms are a specialty of Monsieur Bellow," Jordan bellowed. "There is a great deal of truth in parody. Who hasn't observed the hostility of things toward man? We need no windy philosophaster from the imagination of a Danish ghost to tell us that we are screwed by what Ventre calls Dernière chose."

"The Worldthing—or the Thingworld?—has made us its bitch," Martin Amis bitched in jest. "What did you say the Wake was? You applied Kant's noumena theory. A very clever send off."

"Wort an sich. Das ding an sich, the core of Kantian philosophy, proclaims a posited object's independence from the senses. I suppose wort an sich proclaims a posited word's independence from the reader."

"Another Jennings in our midst. When you write your parody call the pseudophilosopher Kan," Martin Amis closejoked.

Jordan squirmy in seat as he added closetalking to the list of things he detested about the Englishman presently breathing like a ginebriated dragon in his ecaf. A schoolgirl behind a noisy bookcart pushed passed them. Her asstightening with every pushambulation across the sea of carpet. The arsetighteningsea!

"I once started to write a novel with Clare Quilty as the main character," Jordan divulged. "It didn't go very far. That is why I admire what you do. To be brilliant and prolific—as you have been in your career—has me in total awe."

"Don't throw an idea like that out there, Brian. I am liable to steal it. Although I am sure it would be hard to do anything without the permission of the Nabokovs. But it is a great idea. Much can be extrapolated from the Who's Who in the Limelight entry. We know he went to Columbia and worked in, we surmise, advertising, like you, my friend. Did you say you went to Columbia?"

"   I don't remember if I mentioned that. But I did attend Columbia."

"Maybe Mark or Jo mentioned it to me? He was born in 1910, I think? But there's no mention of any service in WW II."

"1911," Jordan corrected with confidence. "Another allusion to the Wake. Eleven is the number signifying of cycle change in the Wake. A dactylonomer's dilemma! If you remember, Quilty was born in Ocean City. My girlfriend's hometown. Well, Rachel wasn't born there but has resided in that princedom by the sea since moving from Pennsylvania in Eighty-One. Her mother works as a carsalesperson in a local dealership. I wonder if Nabokov by choosing Ocean City was bestowing Atlantis citizenship on the author of The Strange Mushroom? Joyce alluded to Ignatius Donnelly in Ulysses and Finnegans Wake. Rachel is very interested in Cayce. Have you ever been to Ocean City?"

"I...I...Ah..."

Martin Amis tried to speak but spat blank. "I am afraid...I...Ah ah...No."

CHAPTER 11

Day had begun to slug itself asleep.

The dark mysterious daughter of semilight wrapped her wanton legs around the traveling stranger; the vermilion slit between her luscious perineum—embers of a near expired day—drawn closed as darkness collapsed its tent over land and sea. The beautiful darkness of a summer evening held him in her outstretched arms.

As he flexed his toes in his flashy black and red sneakers—a model endorsed by a superstar with the same surname—an apposite flashment of lamp lights along the arboreal path occurred simultaneous to a tintinnabulation of church bells.

His lonely, ghostly manor a kilometer away but seemed to the Earl of New Howth—Duke, Duke, Duke, Duke of Ulf—in the gloam as distant as Zeta fucking Reticuli. He stood transfixed amid a row of trees, shadowy and vast, the chromatic Sean Hancock of white poplars illegible in the black ruined air. What is a ghost? Gestures on the air, faint bodiless creatures, under a hollow semblance of form. To free his mind from fear, he sang:

We are spirits in the material world, spirits in the material world...

The balmy breath of a summer night made him think of Rachel. His guilty-as-charged Desdemona. Through spaces smaller than a red globule of Blake's krovvy, he creepycrawled into the amethyst heart of evening. A poet of wee renown proposed that the sky is the soul of the universe. The sun, her cunt. The last glimpse of her cunty like the last glimpse of Erin and Rachel, eternal. Regina Caeli rested her hot arse on the beach. The leucodermic stranger got an eyeful through her holey indigo undies when she gertily opened her dowellic legs.

The red glare of fireworks in post day light lighted Howth Castle and Environs. When the silly cunt limped off into the wings, the whole universe a stage, he pitied her with a Bloomian pity.

L'amour che muove il sole e l'altre stelle. Qui m'aime des bois-sons et me mange.

She bent over in front of him. He loves her too much not to want to do her in her pocky butt. Half. Gibbous. Full. New. Blue. Irrelevant to a tendon strainer. Show him that gorm sul! A thurible swung by an invisible hierophant filled his asymmetrical nostrils with the dense scent of lilies and roses. Tantum ergo sacramentum. Pogue in the dark and never smell. Diffident dicked no longer, Billy Bang banged a lone a long the road less traveled, except in San Fran and Laconia, singing:

A penetration once again!

*

Day spread out on the earth like a knocked-out pugilist on the canvas. Goodnight, sweet Prince Nelson Rogers. And may a flight of doves cry thee to thy rest.

After being knocked out for the count one should expect significant damage to the part of the brain which deals with visuospatial processing. Namely, the lobus parietalis.

Rolf Sleepwalker walks.

Perhaps the unconscious mind allows one to open the Blake-Huxley door of perception. The lucid dream of the infinite agnostic. A proposed grafitto: If Nietszche was right, God sleeps with Joe Pesci.

*

Neal is the Latin pronunciation of nil. Erigena, in the spirit of Irish fun, called God nihilum. Thus Johnny Irish dared to preach the nothingness of God. For his brilliance, his students poked out his red verbs eyes with their pens. The unblinking eyes of Grendel or Gardner or some other monster stared at Jordan. Think of God as a soul. Does God have a soul? You asked that once before, didn't you? A soul to know itself would have to have a second gnosticizing soul, and a second a third, the third a fourth, etc., etc. What else do you have for me? If you are to know your heart, it must first be broken. Sounds like fortune cookie wisdom or a Quotable Quote from *Reader's Digest*. They used drive a stake through the heart of a suicide. As if a suicide's heart wasn't already broken. Whom said that, Irish Nobodaddy? An affable lemony smelling cuckcold.

If everybody had a heart

Yours would never be broken

Ginny Stephen did herself in, didn't she? She drowned herself in the murky Ouse in imitation of Ophelia. All because the dirty Eblanite had murdered her lingua patria. Help! cried lean unlovely English. Seamus mac Sean, being of less than sound eye but of very sound ear, heard the rodentine squeal loud and quare, and with fiery quickness thrust his ash sword through the arras of respectability. Dead for a ducat! A fishy pond the best place of rest for the English Sappho. A pity they had to dredge her out of deathless Aphrodite's arms. All Italian men claim to be Lesbians. The walker serenaded the stars:

The ghost in you

she don't fade

I want to be haunted by the ghost

haunted by the ghost, haunted by the ghost

He faced New Howth's wrought iron gate, defined it Johnsonianly, swung it open, couranted through it. Incidental ferric contact caused his brain to roil with mnemonic lightning:

Brennus piled his sword and torc onto the scale. The vanquished brood of Aeneas objected. The Flahoolah laughed a wry laugh. "VaeVictis!"

Lupetti! If Remus had murdered Romulus, the duck of Stratford-on-the-Avon would have quacked:

Friends, Remans, and Countrymen!

They stole iron swords from the Gauls. The nuclear weaponry of the epoch. They purloined most everything else from Greeks and Phoenicians. They swindled half of Rome and credit for the aqueducts and the invention of cement and the arch from the Etruscans. Co-opted Christianity from a band of disillusioned Jews. Amici, Romani, Paesani, lend me your sphincters. Oh, that way madness lies.

CHAPTER 12

Confined in a room of saucy doubts and fears, Jordan had traveled from the reverse side of Time merely to be. Le bheith nó gan bheith. He explored beneath the teal tee flowing over his omphalos. Blemished bellied like the son of man. Flesh and bone prison. The body is the womb of the spirit: a casing of molecules useless to God. More on his useless molecules later. Not his thinking. Books, one after another, side by side. He larded his lean mind with the fat thoughts of others. Are you thinking your thoughts or are they thinking you? A Cartesian-Newtonian with a Freudian beard proposed that. The Forum. The Area Center, Society Hill. Spectacles! You start out kissing a stranger who becomes her. The fair daughter of a man who makes you feel heaven sired. Apotheosis in her arms. This happens to all of us. Tristan. Mark. Blazes. Poldy. Even Rick. Whom chopped down the heavencherrytree of stars in mud-eternity. I cannot tell an untruth. Philosophers are not gods. Jesus was a philosopher. He's an anodyne if you believe he's the savior. I believe in him. Does he believe in me? Love Jesus only. Become his spirit bride. Don't become too alarmed, fellow. That's only an air-drawn dagger pointed at the throat of your manhood. What's that? I see, it's a fleshy dactyl. A dilemma for tailors. Informed by a particularly incompetent one on the happiest day of his life, to echo il Corsicano, that he'd always be impossible to fit with dress slacks due to his, so to speak, misalignment. No impediment to her performing oral sex on him. A chemistry of stars in the crossing eyes of Rachel as she knelt down and milked him of his essence. In the end, she had turned his pizzle into a teat. Sword into a plowshare. Thus he became the mother of their story. Its unconscious begetter, off to the side, paring his dirty fingernails. Gametic syllables. Zygotic words. The first sentence, its heartbeat:

sixbuildingsablur, the seventh we see through a glass, darkly.

Step on the pedal that lifts the lid of the stainless steel receptacle. A neogod glimpses his own reflection in a gleaming can as he steps on the petal and lets go of a mysterious thing hanging from his latex fingers. The air whistles as a fetus falls thirty-two feet per sec per sec. Clangthump. Nuncle Billy's lump of love. He should have kept his joyspear in his pocket. Poor, bovine thing. When he stumbles, she whets her knives. A slaughter's smile.

A callused hand is all that remains. The neogod—realizing his mistake—retrieves the fetus from the steel universe it has been consigned to like a nullius filius. He bloweth lifeth into its nostrils and the piece of him revives.

*

Jordan looked up, spiritus mundi flashing in mocking mirrors, he closed his eyes and welcomed the adiaphane. Why isn't she lying next to me? What day is it? Inniu. It's always today. That is, unless he had slept a perfect circle in time, as Air Dunne argued in *Nothing Dies*. That would make it de Domnaigh. Of couse, it could be a case of pseudotempoblepsia.

Tripping and sunny, Rachel tripped over the céad míle fáilte doormat. She smiled her embarrassment away, greeted her mirror image, pressed the bell. The impressive green door was incised with a Celtic cross, despite her bid for a carved ankh.On her white neck she wore a sparkling ankh! Very much like an alien.

He answered the door, smiling, a blue towel flung round his neck stolewise. Rachel took the end of the towel and wiped off a splotch of shaving cream underneath his nose. His eyes brightly inquisitive as she played with the ends of the towel.

"I bought you a Braun," she pouted. "Why don't you use it?"

"I—I don't know," he stammered. "I should've," he admitted. "I certainly wouldn't have so many nicks," he cried, as he stroked his chin and neck. He made a funny face and picked her up. Nymphetine. One zero four. He drew foamborn Aphrodite to his breast, sighed like Monsieur Lance ap Lot. Spumescenthearted, his eyes bubbled:

Little lamb

Here I am.

Her frothy reply:

Come and lick

167

My fat dick.

With anxiety, he put her down. Thirty-two feet per fucking sec per fucking sec. He redacted: white neck. He feasted on her and the feast moaned with pleasure. She appeared to be saying: Voici des fruits, des fleurs, des feulles et des branches ... and here's my heart: bluddle-filth rare, the way you like it. He systematically picked all the fruit in the orchard and ruthlessly drove her heart into the abattoir of his soul. Soon we all hear the drone of—Don't say it! The drone of the Drone. Le breith. The droning drone droning out all other drones. Le bheith. Cartesianically Newtonian. Newtonianly Cartesian. The two of them burning in the crude oil of his animal magnetism. Le bheith. A phrase, in Mid-Eternal Mancunian, descibes the traction of their pelvises: a bit of the old in-out in-out. Le bheith. All because—as Olcott never sang—a piece of heaven fell out God's vaporous eye and he called it Cuntland. What a terrible craic on the birthland of his ma and da. As for him, he was from its longitude and latitude untimely ripped. He's a Yank, made with American molecules. Bog fuck America! Fuck the Yanks and drink their wives, to quote Shane the Bard. They greeted us with rocks, bottles, sticks, fucking sneers. They exploited us from the beginning. They made us fight their wars. We built the subway. McDonald. We paved Broadway. Crimmins.

*

Giggling gurgles gurled.

The speed of dark couple lounged in jacuzzic bliss. Dolce far niente dolce far niente dolce far niente nient. Jordan had telestically lured her into the bubbling lough in order to cleanse her second best mouth. Painted roses ready to be plucked. But first, a poll on the question of whether zu essen oder nicht essen.

KIT MARLOWE

(wearing an eye patch and a bloody doublet)

Perhaps I'm misreading the question. But drinking from the river of Hell won't quench a culoteer's dirty thirst.

EDMUND SPENSER

(wearing a tiara)

Not a Spenserian stream of nectambrosia but deadly victuals.

STEVE NUNZIO

To me it's a slice of pizza with anchovies.

CHAPFALLEN SKULL A.K.A. FRANK FLATULENZA

No comment. But that said, I think women in full panties are much sexier than those who wear thongs or g-strings. Here's a poem that validates my argument: Her inscrutable crevices where pleasure prevaricates, like a monkey in heat arguing for a meritocracy of lust.

JACK KENNISTON

A sin against priapus, they saith. And a sign that a man's not gayeth.

THE AUTHOR PEGEEN

My soy snapper will unpack any man's colon. Even gay men like Brian.

BWSJ

I've had as many women as Liberace.

Is BWSJ a tendon strainer as it has been insinuated?

FRANK DENTELUPO

(displaying a tube of lubricant)

What the fuck is that?

Assfucker.

(snickers, squeezes lube into an unidentified flying anus)

My wife's asshole is wider than the Grand Canyon, thanks to me.

We mean a male's ass. He fantasizes about making Rachel's brother his catamite. Get it? He wants to fuck Rachel's brother in the arse. Fire into the brown, to quote Commander Grant.

FRANK DENTELUPO

You're a queer English cocksucker to say something like that about my best friend.

Re: Dentelupian amicoship. Fast forward to the night of December 31, 1988. Leather jacketed Dentelupo planks down the stairs, Jordan toddles behind him.

Let's see what BWSJ is wearing this summer day in the final year of the clownship of the symmetrically monickered Ronald Wilson Reagan.

Colorized as a winter, handsome leucoderm, BWSJ should eschew dressing in black, else he might be mistaken for a ghost. Actually at this moment, he's naked except for wearing Rachel's painted roses on his face. One surmises BWSJ is using her roseate panties as a hot compress. One further surmises, for the purpose of relieving a hangover. But after drying off, BWSJ, keeping with the geistic theme of the day, puts on a gray linen sports jacket by Smithy the ghost.

FRANK DENTELUPO

Now that was a queer cocksucker!

BWSJ stows a letter along with a red velvet gift box in one of the large pockets of his bright, baggy short-sleeved shirt. The letter reads:

Dear Rachel,

A touch of your molten lips transforms my dream world into a reality burning brighter and fiercer than fantasy's white hot fire. A new world is created in our lovemaking's wake. A place of light and elevation, dry rain, blue green snow, platinum grass, constant rainbows, warmish 0000000 breezes, pleasurable pain, happy sorrow. I call this place: your eyes: a place where my body merges with god's soul. You are God! You are space and time made directly perceptible to my heart. My hopelessly adolescent heart! The brightest stars are only dim imitations of your celestial magnitude. You are the Alpha and the Omega. You are eternity. You are all. I am nothing but ask you to come away with me and everything with me.

Bry

Rachel slipped into new pair of white panties, so pale they made her tan abdomen and tanner legs seem darker and more delicious than complete nakedness had suggested. The conjecture jeans she squeezed into acted as a clever endorsement of her posterior. How cute she looked in her little white Nikes: rolling iambs going nicely with the Mersey beat of Brian's Yeah! Yeah! Yeah! heart.

CHAPTER 13

Clings and clangs, creature creecries, the boardwalk round with them. The dirty tongue of a filthy daughter of a dark wild wagging at everybody. No place for a supposed übersoul like her.

"Do you want to get a drink, Brian?" Rachel solicited, her hand wrapped in his sweaty palm.

"Yeah," he answered, aglow with embarrassment. He let go of her hand, wiped his sweaty palm with a pristine handkerchief yanked out of his back pocket, smiled curiously, as the blush faded from his face. "It would be nice to have a few drinks," Jordan added, regrasping her hand. "We'll drop by Oscura."

As they descended the ramp to the street, he nosed the scent of tomato sauce and seared animal flesh amidst an invisible cloud of garlic. Garlicity annoyed him. Everywhere in the Heights and Park during the summer. He recalled his connection with Ferro, whom reeked of it A.M. and P.M., as if he were a human loaf of garlic bread.

A pleasant walk, a pleasant talk, along the promenade to Edenville. Will they do the coupler's will? Will they knit their Deoxyribo Nucleic Acid onto a beautiful insubstantiality? Insubstantiality, dreamy light of life, consubstantial with flesh and blood. Their melded blood to be carbonated by holy gas. Will they? The answer proclaimed in the derision of the ocean waves:

Fuckno! Fuckno! Fuckno!

Colored pills. What color today? A different color for each cycle. The pill in her bloodstream by now, for hours. Morning ritual. Orange juice used to wash it down. Dead Sea. No speranza for his sperm. Might as well make her brother his catamite. Edenville but a fata morgana for them. Seaside Heights will have to do. A sterile promontory. Confused, he looked out at the Atlantic. The expressive skies, silky beach, and brilliant ocean, of little importance if she doesn't love him. Hadn't the demiurge, billions and billons of years ago, as Carl Sagan told him in a dream, sculpted the fucking whole thing for them?

They float to the Boulevard as a feather is wafted downward from an eagle in flight, nescient gods falling to earth. Those who will not kneel down to us are allotheists. And to those faithfully kneeling, please no theophagy. In the beginning, the horrible music of humanity is sordino, but soon half creation, pictures without sound, becomes full when the volume is pumped up by whomever is in charge of audio. Pump up the volume! Cars honking. Deafening. Screeching tires. Aural shit. Garlicky nest like Ferro's. Stinking garbage dump. Every sense assaulted. She's different. She's a fragrant piece of heaven. Lori Dentelupo thinks Jews stink because a Jewish dentist she once fucked stunk. Stunk like a disappointed simile, Lori? A race of hypocrites. Yet they're all bad actors, aren't they? Fama volat! They spread the fetor Judaicus rumor but ignore their own aglic stench. What a streg! Streg is the apocope her poppa uses to describe her. You know what that means, Bry? I do, Tom. It means witch. He's always surprised a Mick knows so much Italian. He was shocked I knew his fellow Nap, Billy Marconi, was half Mick. Gugliemo's mother was a Jameson. Tom's no genius but his wife is as dumb as a pet rock. Her maiden name, Giovedi, means Thursday. No intelligent clan could be surnamed thus. What's the adage? Thursday's child has far to go!

ITALIAN RETARDS OUT CRUISING. The IROC, along with garlic, ubiquitous in the Heights this year. There goes one blackly by. There goes a sanguine one. It puts one in mind of a globule of Remus' blood. O, my brothers, through spaces tinier than a drop of a globule of Blake's blood they creepycrawl after the Master's white bum into eternity of which this fucked-up world is but a shadow. The here and now, the diving platform from which the future plunges to the past.

Jordan and Rachel waited for a light to change. It changed and they walked across the street. A Firebird parked in observance of a light preferred a familiar beat. No thank you, Tony, I hate Bon Jovi. And the Boss too. Sadly, I was born in the USA. Fuck New Joysy. O Jamesy get me out of here.

Down they continued, greeted on their descent by brutish mater, which proved they were on the wrong side of Maya Angelou. Oscura, a three-story amalgamation of cement, sandstone, and lime, situated on the corner of Porter Avenue and the Boulevard, blighted the streetscape. Who was responsible for its design? Frozen muzak. The architect of record: I.M. Scheisse. The day is fucked, and darkness falls from the sphincter of night, as shit is squirted earthward from a sacred pigeon in flight. It missed them, but hit the bibleblack hood of a parked IROC.

Jordan sighed as he led a lump of organized matter through the side entrance of Oscura, an obligatory nod to muscular doormen. As he is one of the owners, no need to check his companion's ID (slightly underage). The club opened early in the afternoon in the warmer months but would not become really busy, usually, until at least eleven. Oscura had bars strategically located throughout the premises. Tonight they'd become rivers of commerce. Trickle down. Trickle down. Trickle down. Trickle down. Voodoo economics according to W.C. Dearsoil a.k.a. C.W. Arse-Idol. Behind a drab fusion of mahogany and formica, a short, plump man stood smoking, oblivious to the carcinogens invading his lungs. He tugged the cuff of his frilly white shirt, removed a speck of ash from the insignia blue dress pants impossibly stretched at the waist by his buddha belly, fat swaying as he poured a row of shots. Shade sagapawing and magapassing in Hades. Buddha mouthed the words to a lugubrious song playing unnoticed in the background:

And I'm never gonna dance again

Guilty feet have got no rhythm.

They take a spot along the bar, east of the sun, west of the moon, waiting for the bartender to see them. En attendant Pierre. Finally.

"Groove," the bartender called out, bowing, for there is no disguising the majesty of a fallen god. He scurried over to them, smiley, puffy, laughy.

"Pete," Jordan sang out, tendered hand, "I believe you know Rachel." Pete nodded happily. Rachel smiled curtly. Jordan's and Pete's very different hands allied. The bartender grinned, rubbed out his cigarette in a glass ashtray. He almost immediately recigaretted.

"Do you mind," he asked, for a millimoment decigaretting.

"Of course not," Jordan chimed. Pete frisked himself for a light. Eureka! He snaked his nicotine-tainted fingers down a cavern and pulled out a book of matches. He smoothed the cover a bit, struck a match, contemplated the flaming spunk, ignited the Marlboro ridiculing his gob. The bartender puffed on the cigarette with an oral fixation his boss found strange.

"What can I get you," he asked.

"I'll have a Corona, Pete."

Jordan turned to Rachel. "White wine, honey?"

"Red," she muttered. Pete poured Rachel a full-bodied glass of Cabernet. The mixologist knew the finest crystal would accentuate the taste of the wine. Pete also chose a glass with a rounder, wider bowl. In theory, this would allow the wine to breathe. Oenophiles enjoy pathetic fallacy. Chardonnay in a shot glass allows it to piss. All for nought, the mixologist knew, because Rachel typically took but a sip of her drink.

"Do you want a glass, bro?" Pete juggled glass and bottle, as he awaited Jordan's command.

"Just the bottle," Jordan informed. "If Rachel will permit it," he added. Rachel smiled. Jordan detached a brand new one hundred dollar bill from a gleaming money clip and pressed it into the bartender's slick palm. Sorry to see your abbreviated lifeline. The gods will make it up to you. First off, take this trash from my hand. A visual reverberation of Precious Squares. 'Tis something, nothing, Alfiero says. I say put money in thy purse. Take my money, that slave to a thousand, but he who filches my eunym, bro, I'll hit them with my geld laden purse. What is it? 'Tis a wanton burning away the supramatter of my bejewelled soul. My emerald green spirit. Revenant of my green self.

"Bro, you're an owner now. You don't pay. Here, take this back."

"Keep it, Pete. For your always excellent service."

Pete meditated on the cash. A Hellenic Siddhartha contemplating his omphalos, nirvanic with the thought of clutching over thirty thousand drachmas. Yassoo! Pete took a noisy hit on his Marlboro. "Bro, are you sure?" Pete turned to Rachel. "What a guy! He's the best! Too generous." Pete inched centimeters closer to Jordan, stuck out his compact hand. They gipped hands sixty style. "Epharisto poli, bro."

Translated: *Go raibh maith agat.*

"You're welcome, Pete. Has Rocky made an appearance this weekend?" Jordan's voice had become hoarse by striving to speak above the music. He squeezed a lemon into his cerveza. Remember the San

174

Patricios.

Pete coughed. "Rocco was in last night, bro. He asked whether you had been around." Pete coughed an encore. "Let me get you the phone," Pete said, searching below the bar. A few seconds later, he plunked the black desk phone, mouth piece segued by the receiver, on the bar. "Call him, bro."

Probably out spending the trash he owes me. Atlantic City, here I come. "That's alright, Pete. It's not important. I'm having lunch with him tomorrow. Talking tonight would feel like work."

"Never on Sunday, bro?"

"Mercouri," Jordan replied.

"Yeah, bro. Well, I'm a Greek who works when he can get it. Shuckin' and jivin'." Pete danced a silly, amorphous set of steps. He punctuated the clownish routine by high fiving Jordan. His boss heaved with laughter. Feste. Fool. Sirrah.

"Where've you been hiding yourself, bro? I never see you around anymore."

"I've been busy. Rachel lives in the Atlantic City area," Jordan explained. "A little to close to the casinos. If you know what I mean, Pete."

"I'm a Greek, bro. Gambling is a real problem. I'll let you and Rachel have some privacy. If you need anything give me a holler. Gettin' busy, bro," Pete concluded. The bartender made his way down to a few recently arrived customers. Jordan's eyes tracked Pete's blackbrown occiput to the other end of the horseshoe configured bar.

Myrmidon. Passionate eyes flowed over Rachel. I love her face. Her nose, she hates it. Those two freckles, didn't see them before. Newly formed on the trip over here, I suppose. Her nose is mountainous. Thinks it's because of her Jewish blood. The Irish often have what could be termed a Semitic nose. Farrell's Lonigan's describes his nose as almost a sheeny's nose. Harold Bloom reacted hysterically to my criticism of his criticism of Studs. Those freckles do look distant and lonely way up there. Are they climbing up or down Sinai? It doesn't matter, she's fucking amazing. I know she'll never leave Rick. Something metaphysical, misological, won't allow her to leave him. For me? A fucking fraud. I know she'll never be mine. Do I really want her? Do I want anybody? I

175

was informed on my trip to sráid na realtaí that on the eve on her thirty-ninth birthday earth will be smashed to smithers like Tennyson's bottle. Twenty-five fucking to one. Bottle of Smoke.

Who the fuck selects these songs? The D.J. will be here soon and it will be more sonomerde. Dance fucking mixes. Music was invented by Jubal O'Cain to confirm loneliness. Music was invented to pave romance. Music was invented to sever, temporarily, the mind's tongue. God's unofficial coroner insisted life wouldn't be worth fardel bearing without music. The Great Gaels of Ireland are happy warriors but sad harpists. Jews and the Irish similar in their enjoyment of unhappiness. Bars were created for cryptozoes crying in their cerveza or uisce beatha or vino. Lonely people talking to each other make each other fucking lonelier.

Isophrasticism: everyfuck repeating everyfuck. Democracy of language, cliche, undermines the aristocracy of expression. I shall become a Lord of language without being tried as a sodomite.

*

Jordan tugged at his earring. The ancient Irish believed heaven's color was silver. Perhaps because Ireland had very little gold. He glanced at his expensive Swiss chronometer. Guinea and gold was an alliterative synonym for Irish Nobo. What a hater! The Swiss are a bunch of yodeling yahoos. They aren't that bad. They threw in with Willem. Dafoe? No, Nassau. The Helvetians are Celts akin to the Welsh. Blast the Taffies! The Nation for which bend sinister was devised.

I'll make a pilgrimage to Fluntern next Bloomsday, Irish Nobo. Put Joycewax on Billy Blaca, Brian. Irish Niebo, then. Nilbudner 15, Loondoner love. Basque not in the fickle sun of glory, Jinko. Do you have sledded Polack on thou? 30, love. Match called because of literary whim.

Jordan ogled the familiar callipygee of the barmaid. He thought his proclaimed basherter's fundament not dissimilar architecturally to the barmaid; however, unlike his present love's bellecul, he did not look at her shapely buttocks conamorically, only brenningly.

Jordan faced the bar, confronted a mirror image of a mirror image, reached for his drink. The fountains mingle with the river.

*

Frank Dentelupo turned his Grand National onto a desolate come-to of ills. Cookman Avenue. Its name seemed benignant for such a malignant thoroughfare. He had snorted a gram of coke on his melancholy way up from Barnegat and had already begun to Gionse, as Brian Shakefork would pitch it.

Stopped at a light, he inspected the bibleblack hood for bird shit. He smiled. It was as pureblack as his hair. The light changed and he raced to avoid another. He should feel elated, as he was minutes away from being handed the fat take from Fat Joe's. Instead, he felt as shitty as the time his partner had screamed at him in front of a roomful of salesman. Bry was infuriated at him because he had caused a talented salesman to quit. Dentelupo kept on calling the salesman fat. Worse, at the time, the salesman owed Bry ten large, as Rick Masters would pitch it.

A few hours ago, in search of a lost Bry, he had made the mistake of calling Rachel's number. He believed she could inform him of his partner's location. (Bry, as his wont, had turned off his beeper.) Dentelupo hung up when Rick—Rachel's cuckolded boyfriend—had answered the phone. The fuckhole immediately dialed return call. Dentelupo realized it was Rick calling back, so he answered in a stage Chinese accent: "Hong Kong Gardens!" Predictably, Fuckhole Rick gullibly, racistly screamed: "You called the fucking wrong number, Charlie Chan. Don't call here again."

Dentelupo now worried that if Rick noticed the return call charge on his monthly bill, he might recognize Dentelupo's number. Rick hated Dentelupo over an incident occurring six years ago. Back in the early eighties, Rick was a small-time weed dealer who worked as a messenger in the same, now defunct Atlantic City telephone sales office, managed jointly by Jordan and Dentelupo. Dentelupo, who also dealt pot, had fuckhole front him a few ounces when his source was incarcerated, but later refused to pay for it, claiming the weed was bogus. Jordan eventually made good on Dentelupo's debt. Notingham quit his position and has ever since made no secret of his hatred for Dentelupo.

Paranoid Jordan might think his partner was trying to promote Rachel's pussy. Who knows how he might react to it? Fucking paranoid Irish fuck might break up their partnership. He'd beg his forgiveness if he had to. Brian did have a forgiving nature.

He parked in front of Fat Joe Uzzi's Faust's, the raunchiest go-go bar in New Jersey. At Faust's, unlike Precious Squares, the girls showed everything, including their cunts. Customers routinely shoved bills and fingers up the vaginas of dancers. They had been closed down and fined by the ABC for obscenity violation but Uzzi had finally found a way to bribe a high-ranking official in the ABC and no longer worried about being closed down. What hypocrisy? After all, prostitutes openly worked the streets in Asbury Park.

Dentelupo, gut sucked in, chest out, strode into the bar with a proprietorial gait. "Tell Joe, Frankie's here," he commanded to an army of bouncers. A gargantuan black doorman ran back to Fat Joe Uzzi's office, returning a few moments later. "You can go back," the giant informed in a resounding baritone. Dentelupo gave the giant a contemptuous look and started for the back room.

*

Jordan peered into the dark air. He found her amid giddy flutters of light. Eden's penultimate brightness, Herr Mangan. Looking on his love with soft eyes, his gaze turned ardiseyed when one of his gender, slight, stylish, proffered his rhythmic hips to her. Wisely, she rebuffed his crude pelvicity and danced away, alone, along a different light-punctuated darkness. Far off in anti-terra, I see her dancing with the gods. He faced the bar, confronted a mirror image of a mirror image, reached for his drink. Poor me, poor dogsbody. The pessimist held his half empty bottle to his red lips, pulled its cool, slick trigger, his darkhead jerked backwards. A moist bullet to the cerebrum. It erodes copper. A sure Mick killer, lager. Uisce beatha is the saving of us. It polishes our cuprous insides. Jordan stared at the drained bottle loosely cupped in his hands. Someone approached him. The someone: Dae, friend, former love (exactly a thousand daynights older than Rachel). On this particular daynight, his ghostlove of two summers ago flickered before him in fluorescent white bicycle shorts and bare midriff. He watched, listened, reflected, as her superfluous lips flapped brightly in the dusk. A nasty prefigurement took life in a dirty mind. Fellatrix. Interpreting the flames, Jordan nodded. She swiped the bottle from his vague grasp, twisted her lean torso in the direction of the garbage, tossed the empty away, it shattered, she grimaced, laughed.

A lovely drunkenness the French call it. J'attends, engulfed in

178

rising ennui. Bighair brings me another. "Thanks, Dae. When you get a chance, I'll have a shot of Jameson." Leggy blonde proceeds to lope over with my water of life. Anna Livia Plurabelle to the rescue. How her retroussé nose differs from Rachel's. Which one was designed for soixante-neuf?

"Dank u."

"You're welcome, Bry. I've got to... We'll talk. Rachel's really, really cute."

Jordan smiled. She flies away in mid-conversation as bartenders do when duty calls. I am sure it is her conceit that I drink and coke it up in order to coagulate a hemorrhaging begun in my heart by a ruthless extrication of her rodentine claws. I do admit the way it was handled was rather bloody. Don't misjudge me because of these kind eyes, mesmoiselles. I am no Monsieur Moullason. Fucking chatté actually invited me to dinner in order to meet her new lover. The fucking nerve of the Dutch cunt. Fucking whore! He threw back his whiskey like a cowboy, took a swig of beer. The gracious loser that I am, I picked up the check. She invited a friend for me. At the end of the evening, her future (I hate to think I was cuckolded) presented his semi-white hand and said some awfully nice things to me before going off into the moonrise with my erstwhile girlfriend. It didn't cause a single white night. Interesting to witness your own cuckolding. In a way, it spares one of any dark imaginings. Il moro di Veneto should have been so lucky. In any event, I had a pocketful of groove to console me. Her friend blew me in my car for a few lines. How did that Dutch whore know I wouldn't become Lizzarrabengoan? By the end of the night, I was quite happy to be rid of her. She got rid of mustachioed, muddy-pawed Pasquale Mezzobianco a few months ago. She claims Pat has turned to substance abuse since she's dumped him. Vain Dae Vandersuck believes coking it up is concomitant to her banishing a monkey from her bed. He's probably celebrating his liberation from her tyrannical twatdom. You're nothing compared to Rachel.

He rubbed his eyes. I'm drunk. Dae's alright. Has a big head to go with her big hair because she once slept with Bon Jovi. Listens to his garbage when she works out. Told me she's having an affair with Michael Bolton. I think he's that ugly singer who was sniffing around her last week. She doesn't frenzy my Krausean corpuscles. I suppose I don't excite hers. I honestly like her. She likes me because I'm a gentleman. Good manners can be a curse. Fuck it! I'd rather be home reading. That collection of Mallarmé I picked up in New York is deuced good. I think he's much better than William Butler. Proves the Lychfield lexicographer was spot on about the children of Miles. We're a fair people.

Mon coeur qui dans les nuits parfois cherche `a s'entendre.

How I hate this place. Sonomerdic dance mixes through the ears and into the soully soul. Quick! Somebody shoot the greasy DJ. He's Ferro's doublegoer down to the hirsute knuckles.

I'll block it out. Sweet hour of twilight. Who shall now lead the scattered childers forth, and long-accustomed bondage uncreate? Byron with a wink to Joyce. Knowest thou the castle that beetles over the moananoaning sea of troubles? English poets suck, Bill Barium says. Willing irrumators, he joshes.

The Bry Jordan Cosmos has become astroless. I can't make her out in the absence of light. There's no key, but the end, to release me from my Irish Catholic mind. A mind like Mangan's. A reconciler of dichotomy. Knowest thou the castle that beetles over the winedark pelagos? The Dionysus dark Liffey begins to bear me away, Taddy. Joyce found his book of flowers on Manganificent dichotomy. Telemachus at Elsinore. Doublends jined. Beyond the ken of Latin or Londoner.

He prosaically dispatched the rest of his mickocide. Dae logolessly served him another. Rachel is so many things, that like god, she is no thing. The Dauphin in the Hiberno-Dano tragicomedy by Liam Mac-Shakespeare calls his uncle-cousin no thing. Jordan buried his face in his hands. Stage directions very scant in his plays. Roldy says out of his arse that LLL is a mini-Wake. Of late, and I know not why, I have lost all my mirth. He disinterred his clownish countenance, staringforth. What do I see? I see the dance floor. I see extradimensional Rachel receding into drei dimensions. I'm seeing things again. Jordan searched his pocket. A line! A line! My kingdom for a line. I am not Richard Crookback, nor was meant to be. Bosworth Field is bluddlefilthy. Frankie Rosencrantz and Rocky Guilderstern sleep with the fishes.

He took a sip of beer. I snorted my first line four years ago in West Virginia. It has a delayed reaction. Nose to midbrain. Nasus te ipsum. Rachel wants to unnose herself. If she leaves Rick, I'll pay for a rhinoplasty. Never, Rachel. I love her srón mor. A tit job perhaps after she has our kids. She's not going to leave Rick. But why? Believes he's her son in another life. Jews are incestuous in flesh and spirit! Is that you, Irish Nobodaddy? It is, my son. Where have you been? I almost felt sane. Or maybe it's the absence of that neurotransmitter inhibitor in my midbrain? Coke causes a cacoethes loquendi among its users. Does it cause one to hear things? Or see things?

Jordan finished his beer. A fronte praecipitium a tergo lupi.

"Bry!"

"Bry!"

Dentelupic voices. They pat his Padraic back. "Mike! Anthony!" Jordan exclaimed, shaking hands with his partner's fratelli. "What brings you here tonight, guys?"

"Free drinks," Mike Dentelupo replied.

"Of course," Jordan said.

Mike's eyes grew preternaturally large. Anthony's weaselic eyes remained lifeless under a prehistoric brow.

Jordan groped Anthony's biceps. "Working out, Ant?"

"A little," Anthony answered.

"Dae," Jordan called. She takes their order, serves them. On me, of course. They speak Dentelupese to her and she answers them in Daeish. They drink, she flies away. They try their lingua on me, I shake my head knowingly. I understand it but only vainly speak it. Mike calls for shots of Tequila. Dae returns, serves us. I offer up a toast in Brianese.

Mike Dentelupo and Anthony Dentelupo poured salt on their paws, licked, drank.

"Whatever the fuck that means," Mike Dentelupo boomed.

"It means death to the queers," Jordan explained.

"Even Ant," Mike Dentelupo cried.

"Fuck you, Mike. Bry, he told me if he went to jail he was gonna get a bitch to fuck in the ass. No lie, Bry."

"You're my bitch! Bitch."

"Fuck you, Mike!" The brothers glared at each other.

"Boys," Jordan diffused. He shook their shoulders affectionately.

"Let's have a few more drinks. Rachel will be over here in a few minutes and so let's be on our best behavior."

"Where is she, Bry?" Mike asked, searching the dance floor.

"She's dancing," Jordan answered. "See," he directed. "The cute blonde."

"She's really cute," Anthony said earnestly.

"Thanks, Anthony."

"She has a Jew ass," Mike said.

"Mike," Anthony exclaimed. "Watch what you say."

"Goddamn it, Ant. Bry, I mean that as a compliment."

"Of course. Of course."

"Let's have another drink," Mike said. "On me. We have to get going. We have to meet Frank at the Headliner. He's has a few grams he promised me for souping up his car. Are you packing, Bry? I'm Jonesing like a motherfucker!"

"I never pack when I'm out with Rachel," Jordan explained.

"Come on, Bry. You're telling me you don't do a few lines with your girlie girl?"

"She's really not much of a partier, Mike."

"A gram," Mike pleaded. "You have to have a gram," he insisted.

"Mike," Jordan exclaimed. "I'm buying." Dae served them a round, they farewell hugged. Jordan waved goodbye as Rachel walked his way. Mike smirking, waving. Mike ran back and alone and whispered in Jordan's ear. A few moments later Anthony shuffled over.

*

Dentelupo ripped from Fat Joe Uzzi's manzic fingers the weekly receipts of their coke business. His, Fat Joe Uzzi's, Jordan's, et al. The amber light of the gray office illuminated the spur of industry crossing the narrow thoroughfare of Dentelupo's palm. Dentelupo's harpy lips curled in delight as he concentrated on the cash. Also delighted, Fat Joe's fat eyes coruscated like dark gems.

Dentelupo whiffed the fiat currency before rudely shoving the bill underneath Uzzi's bifurcated schnozzola. "Fuck, Joe," Dentelupo cried. "This smells," he groaned, taking another whiff of the bill, "like it was up a twat. A dirty one!"

"Ain't no clean ones over here," Fat Joe Uzzi fatly rejoined.

"You ought to know, you dirty pussy eating guinea motherfuck-er," Dentelupo said, smiling.

"Guilty as charged, paesano," Fat Joe Uzzi said, as he stuck out his tongue for Dentelupic inspection. "Want to smell that new girl?"

"By the look of your fucking tongue," Dentelupo observed with humor, "you'd been eatin' asshole again."

"I get a little confused which end I'm eating, Frankie. As you know," he said, "it tastes like battery acid." Fat Joe Uzzi laughed.

"I don't! You fat perverted fuck, you." Dentelupo howled with laughter, faded a playful left to Fat Joe Uzzi's ginormous gut. Fat Joe Uzzi shook his monstrous face in a joyous, monstrous choreography of flesh. Fat folds of his fleshy neck fatly unfolding with every explosion of laughter.

*

Jordan anatomized his melancholy with the dull knife of drunk-enness. If I can't bend heaven, I'll move hell. He pulled up a seat, sat, turned around and faced the darkness. Never turn over. He laughed the scornful laugh of self-disgust. He went on laughing. New Jersey: You can't beat us because we're shaped like a fetus. Laughing, he glimpsed the goldtrimmed, pitchblack face of his Movado. He adjusted its leather band. O accurst craving for AU. Am I the only goddamn idiot to notice his surname is an anagram of Roma? He was a Cisalpine Gaul, who, they say, spoke Latin with a brogue. Fama volat! Jordan stood up, tapped his foot to the music. Hell is paved with lawyers' skulls. It's easy to go down in the dirt, night and day, the gates stand wide, to retrace one's step back to the upper air, there's the rub, Will. Jordan shaded his eyes. Out of the darkness like a meteor, Rachel speeds towards me. Semi-speeds. Woody Allen once said a Jewish American Princess never moves fast except in a mall. Beauty's light in my eyes. One flash of in the Club, Professor Khayyám, confirms the existence of another world. Who said douse thy candle light and you'll see divine light? An optimistic Hamlet Hamlet-son? Someone proposed the prince was really princess. God hath given you one face and you make yourself another. I say he was a Dublin Dane. Yes, by Saint Patrick! I always thought one had to die to really see God.

No split infinitives and no need to unsheath thy bodkins, she is near. Jordan remembered their first romantic date: She seemed immolecular in the inconstant light, a spirit more than a body, a parody of flesh and blood. We talked of our future. I'll write something in ten years, I boasted as I carved my bloody entree. In ten years. Jordan checked his right shirt pocket. I'll give it to her now the Dentelupi have gone on a coke and cul conquest in some other part of the shore's universe. Mike, I wasn't saying I didn't have any because Ant was present. Frank is holding. Find him. I'm sure he'll share it with you. I told you I never do groove when I'm with Rachel. A Jew ass. You said that already. No, I'm not mad. You guys are like brothers. Mike, I don't. I'd give it to you if I did. Frank has it all. He's meeting Rosa at the Headliner, as you know. Tell him I'll call him tomorrow, tomorrow, tomorrow. His banjo eyes played a sad refrain as I repeatedly told him I didn't have any. You sure you're not packing, buddy? Why don't cokeheads believe you when tell them the first time? Ant, more interested in some Sunday sodomy, told him to stop asking me. More farewell hugs. Tendon strainers! Beware of the Neapolitans, boyo. They're Greeker than the Greeks! Was Alighieri Aliqueeri? Guelph sounds like the sound one would make if one was being cornholed, doesn't it? Will I ever hear guelphs from Nealish lips? Nel mezzo del cammin di nostra vita, I came to a dark wild because the straight way was passé. Di qua, di la di giù, di su li mena. A dirty, hopeless circle! A sterile promontory. I'll not abandon speranza for my sperm. Dead Sea scrolls up your arse! Klismaphiliacs like it that way. And even though my surname symbolically signifies a termination of my DNA, I know somehow our melded acids will melt the frozen space of now in order to propel the resultant flesh and blood, soulsheath, through eternity. Mid-eternity, anyway. Jordan threw his arms out like a net, and, with the tenderness of a saint, fished Rachel out of a sea of illusions. She smiled with subtle madness. You have taught me to be a piscatore of apparitions. He drew his catch to his breast, smelled her hair, kissed her lively mouth. Heaven blazes into my head with a touch of her lips. Jordan reembraced her, licked her sweat-drenched neck as if it were a lambitive. "Stop it, Brian," she moaned. Jordan smiled enchantingly at the enchantress. "My salt lick," he joked, stallion nostrils flaring. Why did she look back? Sodiumized like Mrs. Lot. As salty a piece of meat as Lot's wife's arse.

"Who were those guys with you?" Rachel asked.

"Frank's brothers."

"The really short one was saying something as I was approaching. He seems like a jerk."

"Not seems," Jordan said. He concentrated on the imprecision of her features. A strangeness to her beauty. The kind Pater championed. Some may say a rather poor reliquary for those sacred eyes. Her Giocondic smile. "Do you want a drink?" he asked in a loud but tender voice.

"Ice water," she hoarsely whispered.

Dae fetches a glass of ice water for my hydropot. Hydropot fakes a grateful smile. Barmaid fakes a smile back. Two androvores eating men like air. The two engaged in soixante-neuf wouldn't excite me. They peel forth from apple-red lips words deadly sweet. I'm starting to sound like Lawn Tennyson or some other bardaster. Jordan looked around the bar. He saw fair women speaking to men with, for the most part, Sicilian coloring. Glaucous-eyed sisters sing their minds away, shrivel their swarthy skin, pile their bones. Tie me to the mast, Omeros mac Seoigh. He picked up his bottle. Je bois donc, je suis. He drank. Folamh. He gave the bottle a disapproving glance. Heaven has become mute. He hiccupped, set the empty down on the cardboard coaster. LA CERVEZA MAS FINA. Rachel claimed his arm. Dae disposed of the empty, removed a bottle from the cooler, raised it to mid-heaven. The telepathy of drunk and barman. Of course I want another. Another and a better world. A world where poetry is legal tender. Dae served him and barmaided away.

Rachel's face collided benevolently with Jordan's face. His heaven-colored earring swung like Mesmer's watch. Braid's chronometer, forsooth. They kissed: gasoline of animal magnetism pumped into the tank.

Rachel, sheepishly, sleepily: "I love you."

CHAPTER 14

The clack of chips against chips in his pocket serenaded him as he wended his way through an illusion framed by the flesh, bone, and blood of our great mother. With fond sadness, he recalled a nursery rhyme his teacher-mother used to recite to him as a child:

> The Sun's lovely bride
>
> gives us all a free ride...

He stopped, sipped his drink. The mild fire of Jack Daniel's kindled his Krausean corpuscles. Machines playing machines. He considered them castle rats. They sensed an ailuric presence and appeared nervous. A mouser intersecting their rodentine paths. Cursing subverbally, he glissaded past them and started in the direction of the cashier. The shrill, dolorous ringing in the backsound muted the rattling of chips in his pocket. He walked to the cage, unpocketed the chips, musically slid them across a versicolored counter to a pair of two-toned hands. Chubby fingers erected the chips into color-coordinated stacks spread across a marblescape like Martello towers.

"You having a good afternoon," the she-teller proclaimed, revealing a gap in her smile resembling his own.

"It seems that way," he roared, smiling.

Hans, the ruddy-swarthy blackjack dealer, waited for Notingham to erect his bet.

"Vivty dollar minimum, zir," the dealer informed. No longer a twenty-five dollar game, he would have to add five reds or remove the green and boldly put a check in play. A black tribute to his testosterone. Soft. I'm always hard at the table prior to a winning hand. With a snap of his thin wrist, he scooped up the insufficient bet from the circle halfway between first and second base. His so-called lucky spot.

"Play by me."

A screaming comes across the cesious felt table, as the dealer's fingers launch a blur of cards: black smoke and red glare in the players' green adjective eyes.

"I knew it," Notingham exclaimed. "They always bring in a new dealer mid-shoe when they want to blow up a table." The sound of defeat rattling in his pointy ears: chips being carted off and stacked in the tray like plastic casualties of war.

"I'll be back," Notingham announced, gathering up his winnings. "Save my spot, bitte."

The dealer shot a clear chip into Notingham's so-called lucky spot. Notingham departed.

Grand Master Bobby Fischer, every ounce and pound of his manzic bulk ensconced at third, grinned, shuffled black and orange chips, muttered esoterically:

"Who does that guy think he is? Tyrone Sloproth."

Second based Professor Don Harold Bloom emitted a cognizant yuck.

"Alluding to GR at a twenty-one table is as ridiculous as a pig wearing a yarmulke. By the way, Grand Master Bobby, it's Slothrop. A Pynchonian pun on Scythrop. Peacock's loving parody of Shelley."

"Schuffel!"

Professor Don Harold Bloom signed a marker with a borrowed pen. A cigar smoking Carny-garbed maneen named Jim Merry stood midway between the professor and swarthy-swarthy Rocky Ferro who scowled as he sat at first. Grand Master Bobby Fischer, also penning a marker, sat slumped at third. Don Harold Bloom, humming Wagner, read the name on the laminated gaming license attached to the dealer's pale shirt.

"Hans Wiezwei," Professor Don Harold Bloom exclaimed, Shakespeareanly asiding: "I know there's a significance to that name but Bloom has yet to arrive at it. Belatedness!"

A cocktail waitress handed Professor Don Harold Bloom a glass of seltzer and he handed her a chip in appreciation. He drank the seltzer in one gulp, burping voluminously at conclusion. Smiling, he lifted an arse cheek and volleyed a fart heard round the table.

"Sorry, gentlemen, but Bloom had a plate of beans at Plimpton's cookout yesterday."

Swarthy-swarthy Rocky Ferro angrily pointed at the cigar smoking Carny-garbed maneen named Jim Merry and screamed:

"Nobody can smell shit with that cheap cigar he's smoking!"

"An offence that smells to heaven," Professor Don Harold Bloom opined, inhaling a plume of crooked, vaporous material through a set of gigantic nostrils. "I daresay Bloom's farts even smell better than that ignited pernicious weed."

"That doesn't mean," Ferro cried, "you can continue farting and stay at this table."

"That's right," the cigar smoking Carny-garbed maneen named Jim Merry interjected, "this is a no flatulence table."

"Not to worry, I think I'm out of ammunition," Professor Don Harold Bloom assured, again lifting an arse cheek. "See, nothing! In the old days, I'd engage in farticuffs with the Great Edmund Wilson. Old Nobobunny, we called him. We'd meet out on the town and he'd boom: 'Bloom, you old sissy, let's go culo a culo.' Some arsenal he had."

Grand Master Bobby Fischer shook his sanguine head and began a whispering rant:

"Paronomasia. Metanoia. Tuism. Pasigraphy. Macarism. Lestobiosis. Jentacular. Crenellated. Deipnosophist. Prelector. Spatchcock. Transom. Autognostic. Autotheist. Cartesian. Newtonian. Einsteinian. Geromorph. Microclimatic. Dactylonomy. Spondee—"

"Metrical foot of two long syllables," Professor Don Harold Bloom interrupted.

"Greek for libation," Grand Master Bobby Fischer sanguinely explained.

"No doubt libation was synonymous with lubrication," Professor Don Harold Bloom humorously posited, as he watched swarthy-swarthy Rocky Ferro's dark lips being kissed by dark liquid.

Grand Master Bobby Fischer occulted a smile.

"Surely, you know A View of a Pig, Professor," he said, no longer able to conceal his glee.

"Indeed I do," Professor Don Harold Bloom said.

At another high minimum table, Notingham counted his chips. Red King's Pizza can get someone else to deliver tonight. Alan will understand. He wants us to go in on a franchise together. Rachel would like that. The Jew in her appreciates proprietorship. Alan says if we can get up twenty-five we can buy the one planned for Marmora.

*

She wants us to be something. We are, aren't we? An us is what they strive for. The day we first met in the arcade, she was a ripe grape, ready to fall for the mere shaking of the vine.

He doubled on eleven and took a hit from a dealer whose small black eyes buttoned her Far Eastern face. Dealt a perpendicular ace of spades, he shook his head in undisguised disgust. Fucking gook! Six showing. Still have a chance. The dealer drew to a seventeen and subsequently swooped up his initial bet and double down. He scraped a smooth cheek with the plastic yellow shuffle card, tossed it in the direction of a man resembling a bulldog. The bulldogman said something like he'd try to give it a good cut. The cynanthrope tried to engage him in conversation, but after losing a hundred bucks on one hand, Richard Lowe Notingham boiled with anti-socialism.

She spoke in a voice so faint I could scarcely hear what she was saying. She was on the edge of seventeen. A time in a girl's life when bright, unused beauty still plagues her in the mirror. Her eyes: blue fire before a kiss.

A young man with a long humorous chin sat down at firstbase, a horsechoke of hundreds pressed between his palms, youthful eagerness in his eyes.

Loser. Losing is contagious. Get up, Notingham. This rich fuck can afford to donate to Herr Trump but your pizza-delivering ass can't. He has caviar between his teeth. With a grunture, Notingham directed button eyes to save his spot. He got up and began a march through the casino. I should shit and book. I can come back later. Walking by her in the arcade that day, her eyes in the glass made me dizzy. I envisioned myself removing her little hand from the joystick and putting it in mine and like an old-fashioned movie star leading her in slo-mo back to my room. I don't remember the date but it was autumn or late summer. Why does she want to get married? I really can't stand her fucking silences when I tell her we have to wait. Notingham continued his constrained march through the carpeted Land of Nod. East of Farewell. He entered the bathroom and glided over a white marble floor to a black marble toilet stall. He kicked the door completely open. Before squatting, he peered through the stall openings. Nobody. All alone. Nobody. The king is in his courtinghouse. Enthroned on the cuckstool, he picked up a throwaway and began to read the classifieds. Massage and more given by young ravenhaired Greek goddess co-ed. Call Aphrodite at 821-1111. His bowels, gravid with yesterday's catch, groaned as its net unfurled, brown fish sonorously flopping out of it, his own stink rising to meet his asymmetrical nostrils. He wiped his ass with enough paper to wipe a giant Siggie's ass.

"Scheisse! It doesn't take a Charles Einstein to win at blackjack," Notingham whispered to the brown leviathan swooshing out of Berkeleyan existence.

*

Rachel wrapped her arms around Jordan's trunk. "You're wasted," she risibly declared.

Jordan countered: "The gods made the world for joy."

Go raibh maith agat, Grendel Meister!

"For their own," she rejoined, turning around until her hips and buttocks presented themselves to his groin. She closed her eyes, swayed to the pulse of a hypnotic dance mix. Jordan placed his hands on her hips. She looked back and smiled his chivalry away. When his Feste thing rubbed against her mesial groove, she began a grind he thanked Eros for. Groove Jumping. Get thee a breech pad, Pharaoh's daughter. I fear I am more Neapolitan than the Dentelupi tonight. Their recurring malediction: Vaffanculo! I'm euhung and she has Devil given arse.

It used to be, speaking of the napoletani, every time I was making love to her, I'd envision myself as Giordano Bruno burning at the stake. Last year she was regressed and learned Rick was her spiritual son. You're wading barefoot in a creek. Tuism must be the route to the past life highway. She participated at the advice of her psychic in order to conquer her pnigophobia. Smother me amárach. Let me live tonight! She thinks in one of her past lives she was a nun knocked up by the Nolan himself. Jews and Protestants think our rectories and convents are

190

brothels. Was Ricky boy the product of their clergic lust?

In a fioric field, actually a dirty Roman street, an elevated Monk stares with obdurate eyes at the soul of the world. Roasting in Roma, did he cry out like a forsaken son? Did he wish he was the stuff dreams are made of as he fried like the devil's brother? Jesus, Jordy declared, only seemed molecular. Perchance to seem, as mac Hamlet opined to other mac Hamlet. The docetist seemed immolecular in the inconstant stake-light. Never, my son, fly too close to the truth with wax balls.

The planetgirdedsun shines to succor flowers seeded by his blood. Planetgirdedsuns, if the street of stars wasn't pseudoblepsia. My name is a stealthy backward tribute to the tuist. Thou art born in Nola, a province outside the capital of the south, to an ancient clan much respected in the Christendom. I pillowshared my vision with her and she advanced the theory that I might be the Nolan reincarnated. Poor bastard. I'm burning. Paris is burning! Molten Molly is to blame. The goddess of flames ignited my loins with one rub of her Titanic butt. Nobody—Jesus H. maybe?—could think pure thoughts who looked upon her ass. The last refuge of a failure, as W.C. Arse-Idol chuckled. The mighty Jordan flows into the ducat Dead Sea.

Jordan's expression changed from subtrist to silly. Jewess ass, Mike Dentelupo means. What an absurd name. Wolfteeth. He's banjo eyed like Eddie Cantor. Her fundament is heavenly round. Titanium butted Rachel: Do you take butthead Brian as your loyful bedded husband? You could break a hardboiled egg on my girleen's pleasing bottom. Diamond hard. Numero uno on Moh's scale. If she swore, Pogue Mahone, Shamie, I'd gladly kiss those perfidious winedark lips. Strong curtain. Incidental music. By curtaining my parboiled eyes, I build, with mortar of luminous black, a house of dream: dwelling place of vain imaginations; its terrace affording a view of the playground of the heavenbeasts.

My pen is poised for poetry. I scribble in the dark a message. Illegible. Shouldn't the scribbler know what the scotograph says? Jordan quickly opened his eyes to a semidarkness punctuated by nervous light. Where am I? Where are you, my friend? Somewhere über the rainbow. What the fuck! The seat of consciousness mightn't be located in the ceann at all. It might be down the block or up the Hershey Highway, hers, for all we know, or it might be on that street of stars you always blather on about, or a locker in Port Authority? Who knows? It might be up the nose, boyo. Or up the twat? Or up in smoke?

What formed her? The same thing that formed everything: the shuttle of molecules. What do you see under the glass? I see double helices moving among big concepts.

Jordan inspected the dance floor. It recalled for him the Hellish storm of Canto V. Whirling hesouls, shesouls in the seashore. Forget them. Every inch of her ass is a miracle. Women are like ponies. You never know if one is a jady coppaleen until you ride her. I prefer a bumpy ride. Relationships might be decided by astrology. You need an amber halfmoon for harmony. Why do I feel so attracted to her? I might even eat her brown apple, my friends. Jordan downgazed. Looks as sweet as Irish sorrow. Critics differ on the taste of Dead Sea fruit. The funniest one I have ever heard is that it tastes like battery acid. I hear a lot of men enjoy their lovers playing the rusty trombone. Ed egli avea del cul fatto trombetta arrugginito. No rusty trombonist, my jeween bawn. She does enjoy performing oral. Lovers of the lollipop, Jim Merry says. This is so much better than to be stung for one swift moment. Wilde doubted pleasure's ability for longevity. Perhaps pleasure ceases to be pleasurable after a while? Voglio più!

Firstlips. Secondlips. Thirdlips. But do I have the key to open the door barr'd with gold? Perhaps this dirty dance on the polished floor of Nova Antonia is to inform her dance partner that the door is already open for dirty business. Do you know whether she'll stay with you tonight? If you leave me tonight, my Carmen-cita, I will kill you. Don't leave, Rachel. She'll say: Bry, I must. I'll say: I understand. But before you go, we'll have breakfast at Tiffany's. A gold anklet bracelet with 5 pt diamondhearts. Lox and Murder. The new mystery from Jessica Arrowmaker. To kill her—to kill anybody—is only a merciful release of an invisible Patrick McGoohan pent in walls of flesh. Life has no meaning the moment you lose the illusion of being eternal. Sartre, I'm not prepared to leave the mudwomb yet. None of us benefit from dwelling in the tissue of physical illusion. It might be expected after performing such an act of charity, smothering her with a pillow pulled out my ass, that I'd do the same for my own soul. Le bheith nó gan bheith. I shan't increase myself to vapor. I'll suffer dermic imprisonment a while longer. A long while. No death penalty in the Empire state.

Why didn't we drive to the City tonight? We could have stayed at a five star hotel and had dinner at The Four Seasons. A veal T-bone, heirloom potatoes, mushroom ragout for Monsieur and roasted turbot prepared in a lemon-thyme sauce for mademoiselle. And of course, une bouteille de blanc, une bouteille de rouge. We could have caught a midnight movie at the Angelica. El Topo is the best or the worst film I have ever seen. Translated The Mole, albeit a deranged Deconstructionist film critic you know maintains it should actually be translated The Awkward Person or The Klutz. El Topo turns its audience into tunneling rodents searching for the sun and other stars. While in wintry Zembla—where they shout: Translators are traitors!—it ended up as the ridiculously obscene Gospodin Cunthand on the marquee.

Driving over the bridge, I saw a thin wire of lightning in the sky, that thing referred to as expanse in the malscribed folio of this world without end, Amen. The trees—white poplars—were restive spirits the day we first kissed outside our Spanish restaurant, the Moorish Wall. The aloof sun emoted brilliantly when our mouths collided like a trillion stars. Ajo undetected, my love, on your wooing breath. Tipping her tepping her tapping her topping her tupping her. She looks back and is instantly sodiumized like Ms Lott.

Last night's sallow filet mignon was as salty a piece of meat as Lott's wife's arse.

This feels like the final entrancement, as the neoplatonists describe the reunification with nothingness.

Sign, scriptio continua, your name across my heart. I'm writing mine, sorrily, boustrophedonically, if you will. No balls, I mean. Side by side, like oxen that go yoked. The yoke is on you. I'm a fugging bull! This morning at six minutes after eleven, I proved my genitals to be in good operating order. A come rainbow to rival the panspermia. Resurgam. Thanam o'n dhoul. D'ye think I'm dead?

Prima facie passion. Her walk, a socalled verse of steps, reveals a true goddess. In her arms I experience apotheosis. Still, I retain a nostalgia for the mud.

I'm bluffing. The dawn terrifies me. Prince Harry's camp was full of eosophobes like me. Why am I such a Berkeley 'unt?

She turned around, kissed him. They glided over to the bar, her hand wrapped in his. "I'm as banjaxed as a Lord," he whispered.

"What?"

"Drunk," he explained. "Excuse the Irishism, my love."

"Do you do coke, Brian? Dawn is convinced you're a coke dealer."

Jordan's eyes exhibited rage. "She should mind her own business," he groaned.

"I know, Bry. She's a yenta."

*

Notingham handed a red chip to a cocktail waitress. She smiled a thank you. He sucked down a rum and Coke, contemplated the corpsewhite hands of the dealer. Midhand, Fat Harold Bloom sat down at first.

"Beautiful," Fat Harold Bloom puffed when the dealer broke. "More of that, Patrick."

"Pat has been treating us alright," Notingham volunteered.

"Is that right, Patrick?"

The dealer laughed without mirth. "Don't tell anybody," he said. "But I'm getting buried today."

Fat Harold Bloom snorted. "Excuse my schadenfreude. I'm assuming you're Irish. Some of the dealers have tags with fore and surname but you only have your … What's your surname?" Fat Harold Bloom's pendulous cheeks rocked with anticipation.

"McFade."

"Are you from Atlantic City?" Fat Harold Bloom probed.

"Ocean City." The dealer broke again.

"Princess Grace's and Clare Quilty's birthplace," Fat Harold Bloom reported as his fat fingers erected an ebony ziggurat in his betting circle. "I'll try to get back some of those Mary Fitton's eyes deposited by yours truly in the teeming coffers of Monsieur Trump."

"You realize, man," Man Notingham laughed, "you're tempting the gods with your Tower of Babel." Notingham sighed. "What the fuck!" Notingham added a black story to his bet and the dealer belatedly proceeded to deal.

"Don't worry, young man," Fat Harold Bloom comforted. "I have an autographed copy of Thorp's *Beat the Dealer*. Very dog-eared, I assure you." The dealer asked for a hand signal from Fat Harold Bloom. "The game is vingt-et-un," Fat Harold Bloom cried, pounding the table.

Grand Master Bobby Fischer, his right arm claiming an exquisite bare shoulder of an exotic slaveen, rumored to be a Croatian princess turned prostitute, a lateral descendant of Franz Josef I, that the Grand Master had valiantly semi-liberated from a Montecarlo brothel only a little month ago, managed a Bloomhating smile as he passed the table of destiny. Bloom o'Bedlam commanding atop a horse of air espied nothing but the felt universe created by an egomaniacal demiurge. The Grand Master buzzed the slaveen's incarnadine lips without pausing his prosaic gait. It had also been tattled that his lover—prior to her stint in the world's ickiest profession—had been mind controlled by none other than Pindar Rothschild, as the Baron bills himself in illuminatic circles, who had intended to present her to the Pope as a childbride, but K.W.— having his Polish sausage set on a hermaphrodite—rejected his Babylonian brother's gift and subsequently married a shehe from Connecticut named Ann Coulter in a Black Mass held in the subterranean Saint Peter Basilica, officiated, it has been reported, by the Reverend Billy Graham. As a result of the Pope's rejection, Irina, her peaceful name, was bartered by the Baron to a Montecarlo pimp for a newborn boy. Shortly thereafter, the Baron allegedly snapped off the babe's head with a caimanlike bite.

Catches his shreiks in grails of gold!

That evening, unanimously black like the events about to be delivered by the polluted womb of Time, fiend Pindar served baby tartare to his guests, Babylonian brothers all, including his double first cousin, Patrick Hitler, Esq, Bob Hope, Bob Heinlein, Malcolm Forbes, Boxcar Willie, John F. Kerry, Richard Cheney, Pat Robertson, Donald Rumsfeld, John Self, Tad Allagash, and W.C. Dearsoil. Triskaidekaphobes would have been right to have forecasted that it would be l'ultima cena for one of the aforementioned lizards. Did Heinlein grok his impending death? One could have easily glarked it. That is, if Heinlein had consulted the First Lady's stargazer, Quigley-Wiggly, whose Jyotish is undeniable. Heinlein surely would have declined the invitation. The wealthy science fictioneer was invited to the dinner by Cheney, as it doubled as a political fundraiser. Cheney, the heartless, soulless oldcoldbrainer, supposedly felt guilty—on occasion reptocrats access the mammalian brain—about inviting Heinlein, who suffered a fatal heart attack the following day, apparently an allergic reaction to baby tartare. Thus Dick the lick, as the Thai lady boys call him, playing Iscariot the Obscure, attempted to hang himself from an eponymous tree, large shrub actually, but for some reason, Cheney ended up only blowing his load. Cursing his good bad luck for not falling victim of what has been termed carotid sinus reflex death. Strangely, Cheney was not moved by the thought of infanticide and cannibalism. Maybe a case of Caiman tears for another caiman. Perhaps it wasn't an attempt at suicide at all, but, instead, autoerotic asphyxiation by a well documented erotomaniac. It has been reported that Cheney—in his younger and more vulnerable years—enjoyed being cornholed by the infamous Hung Gallery. Such is the hedonist mentality of the Babylonian brotherhood, or as the kenning Anglo-Slavics would call them, cockroads. Faugh-a-ballagh! Clear the rocky road to dirty dear Eblana.

"Here, Mr. Bloom," the pit boss said as he handed Fat Harold Bloom a slip of paper.

*

The little bar, at which Jordan stood drinking, overlooked the ghostly dance floor. He turned around to monitor her movements, angered whenever male revenants invaded her dancespace, shooting them down with a gunmetal stare. Nunc est bibendum. His head convulsed with a shot of apple. He wiped his sticky fingers with a napkin emblazoned by an Irish Brigade officer in a red Stuart uniform and a black velvet tricorn, earnest in eye and long in profile, a reminder that we gave our best blood to the Continent. The logo of a company founded by a wild goose. Jordan rediscovered Rachel. She motioned to him to join her.

Come dance with me

in breezy, sleezy, garlicky Seaside

He laughed, shook his head. Another wild goose, Monsieur MacMahon, replied: J'y suis, j'y reste. She stuck her tongue out at him a la gamine. He turned around and smiled at the mirror. Silver goddess: flashes of lightning viewed in the undiffused light promoted her being status. If he worshiped in ambient lighting, his worship squared when she danced on the edge of the universe. Stay. He recalled in images and borrowed words how he had taken the hillock velveted with delicate moss at six minutes past eleven this morning. Cock crowing. Cuckooing. Je te salue, ô vermeillette fente. My ghosteen enfleshed with the touch of my flesh. Let us walk from fire unto fire. The bon mot of a wild colonizer of boyeens. Der blaue Engel: Men cluster to her like Melmoths to a boy's posterior.

*

Martin Amis: a gin and tonic welded to his palm, a maroon fag moored to his thick lips. He unfagged, extinguished the butt on a wedge of citrus somehow confined to a glass ashtray. The fate of his eurosmoke turned him giddy. Giving the back of his hand—a topography of freckles and liver spots—the sidelong glance of a stranger, he grimaced. The opisthenarologist ignited another cigarette. His epidermis didn't seem to belong to him anymore. Alien flesh! It caused him to wonder how he had come to this point of preexistent future. He remembered entering the atramentous maw of a sandstone creature; he also remembered paying ten dollars for the privilege of being devoured by it. All because he had joined a queue of Eloi forming outside a building. For Amis refused to be an outcast from life's feast, even if it meant he'd end up as its main course.

Anglo-Saxon bluddlefilth rare!

He shoved his alien hand in his alien mouth, closed his eyes, imagined himself as diner and dinner at the ultimate dinner party. Jesus Amis meet Jesus Judas. Kiss me, Jude. There's witchcraft in your lips!

A familiar reflection in the mirror above the altar of a petty Dionysus engendered the infamous Amis smilesmirk. Undiffused, Amis thought Amis apish. He scratched his pale pate and muttered:

"A very low primate, indeed. He could scratch the bottom of his feet standing up."

He gulped down his drink, like a stream in a grotto, it swept him through caverns of unfathomable sadness. I feel my life's star dimming. The poet in love is a twone fool; (a) for loving; (b) for saying so in weeping poetry. But for whom does my pen weep? It weeps for the girl with strawberry lips and the humid kiss of a vampire. For whom? For the girleen of fourteen whom shortly thereafter became a ghostess.

197

A petty Dionysus served Amis another.

"Thank you, Peter."

"You're welcome, Bro."

*

Seated in the far corner of Herr Trump's New York styled delicatessen, Fat Harold Bloom interred his flabby face in a book. Molly's secret parts in whiffing distance. Also noseward: the wooing scent of pickle brine. His blue lips pursed. "A gherkin! A gherkin! My kingdom for a gherkin!" An over-parodied line, Roldy. Forgive me, Papli.

A set of ill-fitted dentures smiled gelbly as Nell, the waitress, with fiery quickness, served the gelbic smiler a hot pastrami sandwich. He smacked his indigo-violet lips, attacked the sandwich with whetted incisors, swallowed with delight. He grabbed a napkin and swiped at the mustard oozing from the corners of his mouth without diverting his eyes from the page.

Un jardin des chemins bifurquants. Lingua est contagium ex caelum.

The feminine sheaths unfurled before his eyes, assisted by forefinger and thumb, reminded him that even the pansagacious Stratfordian was humped by words.

Language is what, Roldy? It is god, Papli. God? Don't you mean a ghost? Unrealible. In the kitchen of the mind, some dilectophagic scion of the so-called Babylonian diaspora koched up the delicious anti-theory of textual neutrality. "Delicious! Delicious! Delicious!" Fat Harold Bloom critiqued, swiping his mouth with a fistful of napkins again and again. He downed an entire glass of seltzer in order to extinguish the fire engendered by the spicy mustard applied to the pastrami. A Bloomian eructation followed. Fistful of napkins still in hand, he blew his Spenserian nose.

Fat Harold Bloom, a sensate flesh, envied the insensate shadows cast upon the pages. Still, Malbecco flipped forward, looking Spenserian.

"Chemistry of stars," he mumbled agnostically. If he had one tenth of the monographs, stranded on the shelves of his bookcase, that do no work today, he'd locate the source of the brilliant phrase and lap

198

up the milk of its meaning. "More honor for the professor."

He pressed a median finger to his mouth and ejaculated: "Eureka!"

As he shifted out of neutral, the ancient mariner navigated his way past the basilisk of theory, and the whirlpool of allusion, before docking at a glistening port. Looking with lust on the callipyge of page 179, Fat Harold Bloom saw, in the golden dream of reading, an archdruid's laudatory plumes of smoke widening the nostrils of snubnosed and hooknosed deities alike. He caressed the smooth flank of his adulation, rested his eyes.

Reading and noshing is the only ataraxy declared the posterior lips of the bloated disciple of Epicurus: Prrrp! And though his body was a center of meanness daynight, when his rheumy baby browns scanned the pages of great work and/or yellow teeth chomped on an excellent gherkin, the impossible was made possible, finally: Fucking aponia!

Fat Harold Bloom popped up from his chair, wobbly, canescent, clammy, he collapsed and died without allowing the book to drift out of his grip.

CHAPTER 15

The advert read a 1976 vair colored BMW in mint condition, low mileage, asking I forget! I promptly rang up the owner, a woman sounding New Yorky and ethnicky (hard g's a giveaway according to my father), whom I guessed to be mid-way through her life's journey. She assured me of the absolute treasure she was allowing to slip through her fingers (like the base Judean etc., etc., I thought). I told her it was essential that the automobile be in excellent running condition, as it was my intent to drive across this variegated land (the good old U.S. of A.) following the tireprints of a late, faded lepidopterist, the subject of a series of articles for the *New Yorker*. I informed her who I was: Kingsley Amis's son. She hadn't heard of either of us. Still, she seemed impressed. She asked me the names (American usage amuses me) of the books I had written. I told her I didn't think she'd recognize any of them, but nevertheless proceeded with a rapid fire intonement of titles.

"I think I know that one," she enthused. "Because—"

I tried to make an appointment to see the Beemer the following day, but Stridentsand (apt, I assure you) insisted I come right over because she had had a lot of inquiries and could not promise it would be available tomorrow. I told her I'd be over in a jiff (my feeble attempt at Americanese).

So there it is again. That word. For me, it is a bridge I am none too eager to cross. Thus I left the first bridge unfinished. (Joyce's definition of a pier as a disappointed bridge resonates in my psyche when I think of all the unfinished projects of my life.) Because (that fucking word again!) I wish to tease you, I will conceal from your sight a little longer the white beach on which I set my tale.

Synchronicity was defined by Jung as meaningful coincidence. He offered the following example:

Adolph orders a blue car, but on the day of the death of an immediate family member, is delivered a black one instead.

I only bring this up to alert those attuned to such things that Amis fils has had his ever-loving fill of meaningful coincidence. As the poet says, our fates are born in the stars. And why not? Like the stars, our lives are scattered, dying hallucinations.

The skies appeared aloof, as I got out of my rented sedan. An improbable day for the heavens to plummet into the stygian muck. But then it occurred to me: Beyond every bright horizon, there's an Enola Gay flying unannounced. I knocked on the door. The word beg—for no apparent reason clanging in my mind, like that poor bastard in the story by Bowles. Something Episode? When she opened the door, wearing mini-shorts and a halter top halting very little, Amis was sold. All I could think of, as my baby blues descended and scaled her rosy bareness, was how I was going to make her my somamate, how indeed? Mais Amis, she's only a little girl, I thought. But what a little girl! A sexual savant if I had ever seen one. I close my eyes and conjure a figure more beautiful than one ever created in marble by Mike Angelo. O my Basherter, that I might again plunge into pure delight and know your ghost lips. Alas, my soul has been consigned to the cold heaven of remembered love.

It was then and there, in nosing and earing distance of the big sea dividing our nations, that I learned of angels with smiles of infinite whiteness. In a princedom by the sea. In the birthplace of the second murdered playwright and Princess Grace of Monaco. A summer of breathing its air changed Amis. Nymphets became a narcotic for me. Well, one nymphet. All confessionals derive from the creased thought of memory, folded again and again, like cerebral origami. Perhaps the only way to look at things properly is to look at the shadow of things? The shadow has, as Mallarmé sings, symbolic powers. Memories tucked away in the convolutions of the brain, according to Freud, act as occulted enemies of the psyche. Robbe-Grillet said: "The true writer has nothing to say. What counts is the way he says it." But I digress.

As I peer into the dull eyes of the past, I see a girleen of fourteen, amidst blonde latitudes, five-two in flip-flops. I want her. She wants me. Two impediments: a foolish law and Stridentsand. After learning there was no Mr. Stridentsand in extant (thirty years her senior, ah it runs in the family, he dropped dead years ago—in no doubt connubial bliss—leaving them shekelless), I decided to take the cow by its de trop tits and initiate a romance. Stridentsand's breathy responses to my wee talk informed me she was panting to unpant hunky Amis. Soon I was her lover-lodger with Blank (the ineffable name for me) horizontally on the horizon. Incidentally, I did purchase the Beemer. Money problems had forced her to sell her "baby." Ever since Blank's father had shuffled off his mortal coil, things had been tough. She was even forced to go to work, like a buonaroba. In the process, she became the first saleswoman in the history of a local car agency (Kosher BMW and Mercedes Benz). Working mom gave lounging, writing Amis ample opportunity to romance Blank. And very often, hypochondriacal Stridentsand would stay home to nurse whatever malady she was imagining, urging her paramour to take her little daughter—they were new to the area and Blank didn't have many friends—to the boardwalk for some cotton candy and amusement rides. Amis would be friends enough for Blank. For when Madame Bernhardt bowed out, I played my scenes with an exquisite ingénue. Blank, the greatest actress of generation X, took over the role in shining fashion. How I remember those balmy nights filled with balmy kisses, crazed caresses, and more. In princedom by the sea. Some would call our liaisons sordid and disgusting. But for a man like me, who sees the world as a grain of sand and heaven as a wild flower, what could I do? I plucked her, and like a buzzing fiend, imbibed her fioric soul. Death is always too close to voice regret. We are soon enough plunged into the shadow's chill. Blank's body was an isle of tender secrets that I solemnly excavated. I view life differently than most, hyperaware of the not so delusionary abyss to the north. Pascal's gauchephobia a mystery to a high church Englishman like me. I fear what's a head of us. I saw the abyss ahead of me, that's why I thrust her body between it and Amis. It actually brought it closer.

When I departed for England—all along I knew I had to go back—Blank appeared unaffected. Now, like that demented Frenchman, I move my abyss about with me. Because my heart has become an immeasurable void enveloping my soul. Does Amis have a soul?

I have this recurring cauchemar. It involves apish Amis's rescue of Blank from the bottom of the ocean. Strangely, I have never learned to swim (my brutish father considered not being able to swim the physical equivalent of illiteracy), but in the aforementioned dream, I swim like an eel and save my beloved from drowning. But she's actually not drowning. She's like anemone skipping along the bottom of our great sweet mother. I sense I shouldn't remove a bewitching revenant like her from the other—obviously happier—side of the veil, but, nevertheless, proceed with the retrieval. Thus I awake with tears of blood in my eyes.

Once amid one of her vampire kisses, I had breath enough to breathe: I am I plus you. She smiled a soulbright smile that lights my path to this day. How close I come to uttering my God's sacred name.

The vile bodies answering my lust these days, with the smellfulness of their lady lakes, make me sick. If society allowed, I'd sooner relieve my lust via a catamite than climb aboard a vessel en route to the noisome chaos called a woman's body. The smellessness of Blank's virtual mare clausum delighted me, as, no doubt, the breath of Aphrodite would. Amis says: girleens or boyeens or no noting at all!

Like a Mick who eschews public drinking for the sake of appearance, but drools every time a dram is poured for somebody else, I avoid the English cliché of fop, albeit reveling in the mysteries of Anglo-Hellenic pursuits.

Dreams. Dreams. Dreams. They forecast the future sometimes. Religion is to blame. The servants of the heavenbeast grease us with guilt and roast us on a spit of shame in the hope of making us more palatable fare for their master. In His cause, they preach against a voluptious life. Well, I expect to be the antithesis of sirloin when I show up on the great pig's plate. A fat laden soul not even fit for his dogs. That's why sinners live longer than saints. Either way the pig will get us! Demophagy is his favorite thing. Instead, I hope he'll just whirl my fractured molecules into the void.

Aboard the TWA flight for Heathrow and my putative home, I began thinking of—as the engine hit the high note it always leads off with—the Lennon (sans McCartney) song titled God:

Blank is a concept

by which we measure our pain

The song drones on—after making some important points about apotheosis—to declare:

The dream is over

What can I say?

A dream God lives only as long as its worshipper remains asleep. I awoke sometime during the summer of 81 to find that my dream God, despite unparalleled nymphetry, lacked an essential part of anatomy to satisfy Amisian sexuality. Allow me to explain it in another way. Amis's love is consistently heterosexual (I have never loved another the way I love Blank), his lust: habitually homosexual. Doctors term this condition Oxonanism (defined in a recent *British Medical Journal* as "adjunct heterosexuality"). The condition affects, for the most part, seemingly heterosexual men (husbands, fathers). It is particularly prevalent—as had already been suspected—amongst the upperclasses of England (Oxonanism is a portmanteau of Oxonian—a graduate or undergraduate of Oxford—and Onan—a biblical symbol for sterile sex). Needless to say, I fit the profile. It all began at Oxford. It was there I first played the game—excelling, so to speak, at both sides of the ball—Greeks and Cheeks.

Amis: tall, semi-dark, handsome girlizer (let's call a rake a rake), as queer as one of Splangler Arlington Brugh's (a.k.a. Robert Taylor) jockstraps. Heavy water to swallow but true (heavy water is Oxonian for come and the title of my very first story), and Blank, nay, a litter of Blanks, couldn't cure my innate phallolatry.

The lacunae in this manuscript are many. I have never intended for it to stand as an entire record of Amis's summer of 81. After all, the gospels leave out more than they include. My best friend Hitch, an enormously talented journalist, once posited, speaking of literary technique, that if Joyce had been one of the gospellers—a funny notion, really—we all would have been treated to Christine bowel movements. (Dark eucharists to signify the shite of the savior!)

I have been withholding a bit of information from you in an attempt to prolong the climax of my memoir. (Blank's gospel, actually.) A literary butt plug, we'll call it.

Yes, there was another playmate all along. One with the adjunct equipment needed to play Greeks and Cheeks. A thirteen-year-old brother with a penis the size of Blank's uncircumcised nose. (I enjoyed that her nose felt penile against my face when we kissed.) The walls of Stridentsand's rented home were paper thin and in the whispering darkness I swore I heard Blank's brother's penis tapping a message on the wall like some homosexual Morse code. We became lusters (my love for Blank remains constant). We were found out. Not by Stridentsand but my beloved Blank. What a saint she is! No recriminations, no threat of criminal prosecution, no threatening to tell mamma. I well up with tears to think of her sacred eyes being besmirched by the sight of her little brother rudely excavating her amant Amis.

CHAPTER 16

Lights basso, a rather tender cut of Faith—at present her favorite album—softly breathing in his ears, engendered in him a mood which could only be described as amative. Foolishly, he tried to sing along:

You are far

When I could have been your star

You listened…

Earlier, music pulsated, lights flickered, blackwashed walls mirrored his partners' alleged souls. The soul is the second conceit, a fat atheologist constantly tells him.

The existence of the soul is as dubious as a simile's power to transform a dishonest bawd into an honest beauty or a dirty anus into a clean machine, very strange. Penny Lane. He fell like a dead man falls sans fall. Dizzy emperor of ice cream. Ah! The seeming random logosity of a hurdling poet hurtling past us like a speeding dysenteric speed freak. Let us return to our mutton.

It was as if he had entered a portal to the underworld: the inverse of paradise, a glimmer of green, here and there, to remind him of primal lost, splashes of red to complete the hellish canvas. And on the fringe of the Dalian vision, Rachel, like a perverse Madonna, watches as one of dearest sons of the mud is carved by an infinity of devils: Dentelupo, Ferro, Hundsheim, church, state, family, race, gender.

Euge Onegin! Euge Twogins! Euge Threegins!

Rachel purloined a glance of her Fendi watch. "It's getting late," she observed, adjusting its gold bracelet. "I mean, it's getting early."

Jordan mused a reply. Le pont du jour.

The mad sun igniting dark waters as it chases the roseate moon from Howth and Environs.

"Toms River will seem as desolate as the moon," he said. "We'll

206

watch le pont du jour from the Gazebo."

"Come again?"

"The bridge of day, rosy-fingered dawn."

"Don't you have to go to work tomorrow?"

"I have a clear schedule. Frank and Carrick can handle things. Croix avec moi a l'autre côte. Oui? Mademoiselle?"

"I wish I had your job."

He laughed stagnantly. "I have decided to divest my interest in the bar."

Her brow knotted. "Oscura?"

"Precious Squares."

"Oh, the go-go bar."

"Yeah, the go-go bar."

"Why? It makes you a fortune."

He caressed her cheek. "It's such a sleazy place. I think it's time to get rid of it."

"Brian, I really have to get going."

"Let's go."

"I have to go home, Brian."

His forehead became suffused with deep color.

"Toms River is your home. Our home."

"Brian, please."

"Before we came here tonight," he said in a calm voice, "we sat in the garden, shaded by that huge black knotted tree, the sweet Liffey serenading us, talking, making plans for our supposed future together. If I'm permitted to ask: Where's that forever you always talk about?"

"What?"

He mimicked her voice: "I promise when I stay it will be forever." He laughed savagely.

"Brian, don't."

"Croix avec moi a l'autre côte. Oui?"

"I don't know what I'm saying yes to!"

Her eyes drink up my joy, unparadising me. Say yes in any fucking Indo-European language and you'll catapult us to realms of light not seen with molecular eyes. Say fuck you and I might become Lizzarabengoan.

"Cross with me, Rachel."

"Didn't we already," she joked with a smug point across the room.

"Fuck you, Rachel. Fuck you! Is it a fucking joke to you?"

"Don't, Bry." She reached for him but he squirmed away.

"I feel Baudelaire's piss yellow serpent crawling out of my heart. It has nested there ever since I fell in love with you. So don't say ondt gracehopper. What bitter knowledge—"

"You're not making sense," she broke in, her eyes downcast, as she wiped away his drunken spray from her face.

"French poetry isn't to your liking. Huh!" Jordan tapped his forehead. "And I know you sure didn't get the Joyce reference. But you like the impression," he said in a French accent. "The fucking isophrastics say imitation is the sincerest form of flattery. Maybe I can put on a dress and pretend to be you, huh? This way I won't be so fucking lonely in that fucking house. The fucking house you begged me to buy. Buy it, Bry. Buy it! O Satan, prend pitié de ma longue misere." Deep color returned to his forehead, as if sparked by his pyrogenic words.

"You're being mean, idiotic and disgusting," Rachel concluded, matter of factly.

"I'm sorry, Rachel. I'm drunk." He attempted to wrap her in his arms but she twisted away. "You can leave. I'd never stop you."

She hugged him. "I'll stay. I wouldn't leave you when you were so upset."

"I'm sorry. I'm terrible at rejection."

"Rejection? I'm not rejecting you, Brian. I need more time. It's very close to happening for us."

"You talk as if it's a real estate deal. I ..." Jordan turned away, looked down at his shoes.

She rubbed his shoulder with a naked tenderness. "Love isn't a Dance Club," she cried, suppressing tears. "It's the everyday mind-numbing dull moments of a relationship," she continued. "He has always been there. I'm not saying you won't."

I'll be somewhere with someone sometime or nowhere with no one no time.

"Do you know what I'm saying?"

"I'd do anything for you."

"I really haven't decided. You're asking me to change everything in my life overnight."

He appeared more perplexed than disappointed.

"What we have is great," she went on in a somber voice. "It feels dishonest sometimes but I know I couldn't be doing this without love. I love you very much. Sometimes I want to be with you so much it drives me crazy. But I realize it isn't that easy."

"It's easy, Rachel. Stay tonight. Forget everything else. You love me. I love you. What else is there?"

With eyes whose pale fire was snatched from the sun, Rachel noted the impressive symmetry of Jordan's face: squarish jaw, fortic chin with a prominent clitoris holder, Cartesian forehead demarcated by lush, ominous brows, large ears with fleshy lobes, luminous eyes, petite srón.

"Sitting with you in the garden today," he boomed, "it seemed as if you had finally decided."

Choose me. Choose me. Choose the as if over user. Choose the lovable skink stuck in the cosmic stink. Choose the man whose abyss is brightened by his own suffering.

"After all, God was with us. You know, like the old days."

The sticky gust from the east: Lilith calling Adam back. Collier's screech owl: a bonny redhead, her pleasing geometry free of attire, except for a stylish reptogod sarong. In other words, the true uniter of the fucking dust spun race, Snake Plissken, resides about her waist, in the middle of her fortunes.Privates we! Both Strawberry Lil and Rachel Bawn are flat as one of Fitzgerald's flappers.

"God is everywhere."

Shall I tell her about sráid na realtaí? She must already know, no? Favete linguis. She never exclaims, reddens. Sic itur ad astra. She's already on the street waiting for me. Schwarmerei, why? It works on the masses, doesn't it?

"God is a deer that hunts us, goes the Irish American proverb," he replied audaciously.

"We're God's prey," she dartled.

Blue bullets of love pierce my heart. Schwarmerei, why? Amantes sunt amentes.

"The proverb is a pun on the pronunciation of the Irish for deer. To go back to what I was saying, Rachel. In the garden today, everything formerly dull became vivid. Flowers took on hues I never knew existed and scented the air with Edenic perfume. Adam Kadmon in the arms of naked Heva. Alright, Lilith in a string bikini."

Purusha whose mind is lunar, eyes solar, breath aeolian and very bad.

"Time usually holds me in a bear grip, but today I sensed a timelessness similar to the one Adam must've enjoyed. I never suspected those late-arriving billows of white and pink clouds—I remember you called them floating cotton candy—were concealing the descent of God's azure soul into the stygian muck. Because if you leave me tonight, any night," he sobbed, "the bright day was a lie."

"I won't leave," she whispered, wrapping her arms around the cry baby.

CHAPTER 17

The phone on the marble top end table—Alec Frankenstein's brain jolted to life by coursing volts of electricity—rang godlessly. Jordan read the caller ID, rubbed a vast corrugated brow overhanging perplexed eyes, answered.

"Hello."

"Bry."

"Rick. What's up?"

"Rachel's left me. She called me a few weeks ago and told me she wasn't coming home. The next day I received a letter with her engagement ring. Fuck, I don't know what to do. I thought she'd be home by now."

"Rick, I'm sorry."

"I think she might be seeing Frankie. Is she?"

"What? Absolutely not. Frank's seeing a dancer."

"His home number was on our return call list. I recognized it because I don't know anybody else with a Barnegat number. Why would he hang up on me?"

"He was probably looking for me that night we all went to the casino. Who the fuck knows? Maybe he was going to apologize for stiffing you years ago. He's jealous that we hang out."

"Are you sure? You haven't called in weeks, have you? Are you hiding something? Some fucking girls like grease balls."

"I'm telling you, Rick—"

"Rachel might be trying to hurt me by going away with someone she knows I fucking despise. Stolen by that little greaseball. Maybe she's doing blow. I know you and that greaseball sell the stuff."

"I'll excuse that fucked-up remark because of your situation." Jordan hung up, breathed a stealthy exclamation. Rachel was still in bed.

211

The luxurious territory of a four-poster made her resemble—in vulnerability and smallness—a famous lepidopterist's daughter.

Jordan's mouth twisted into a grimace. Frank, what was he up to? He never gives Rachel a first look. And Rachel doesn't like guys with big noses. He's such a dumb fuck. A real jerk-off. He probably thought he'd find me through Rachel. I wish I could tell poor dogsbody. I'm a poor dogsbody too, but I'm a pedigree. You Irish-hating fucking mutt, the Irish fucking gangster has stolen her, but in the last word in stolen-tellen the Bardaster Purblind Brian cannot fuck and tell. Much to do about noting. Yet, Jordan no longer wanted to beat the samekh out of Notingham.

VENIVIDIVICIAMORVINCITOMNIA.

Diapason! In a quaint but sexy rhythm, a postmodern diva—in a pale side-panel tennis dress, racket in hand—descended a Jordan curve of burgundy-colored carpeted red oak stairs. She certainly has coolness. Sheets of icy sound unpeel every time she walks into the room: Trane's masterpaean to Monk: J'ai sang-froid.

He would have to tell her about the call. Why can't he tell Rick the truth? Fucking Frank. Maybe the vaffanculist was trying to do her—and in the process—me—in the ass. Rachel might have come on to him. Or maybe she's been making the beast with two backs with him behind my back, all the long, as Stanley Clemens would say. Frank would never make the approach. He was probably looking for me. O misery! Fuck it! I'm not an old black ram topping a whitehot ewe. If she's fucking anybody but me, I'll make jealousy suck the meat it dines on. A tragic loading of many beds. This morning, faced down in a fluffy pillow, in that intermediate state lying between sleep and consciousness, hypnagogia, they call it, I remote viewed the perverted fucks at the Bohemian Grove. The smell of blood and ouns in the woods cries out. Kids, whose faces decorate the milk cartons of a totalitarian state, raped and sacrificed by the global elite. Moloch smiles Canaanitely. Last summer, in a sylvan compound along the Ruskie River, he had made the acquaintance of W.C. Dearsoil:

The monster threw open the rustic door, judged him through a failed equilateral triangle formed by forefingers and thumbs. He collapsed the phalangic isosceles and scorched: "Dr. Feelgood, I presume."

"Rachel, Rick called. He thinks you're with Frank."

LATETANGUISINCULUS.

"How did he get that idea? I mean, I don't remember ever mentioning a word about Frank."

"Frank called your number and hung up and Rick rang it back with return call."

"Why would Frank call my number?" Rachel asked, the blue confusion of her eyes a visual exoneration of the charges implicit in his voice. "Did he ask you if you knew anything?"

"I told him you're not, you're not with Frank. I didn't tell anything. I wanted to tell him, Rick, she's with me, but you have for some reason forbade me from doing so. Forbade Christ! What a bad British drawing room drama my life has become."

Jordan looked away. Mirror mirror on the wall. The bronze girandole in the anteroom remained candleless, a charade, a joke. He returned his gaze from the bitter glass to eyes full of pulse-quickening iridal light. Divine blue lights that hypnotized everyone she met.

"Rachel, we should tell him," he added.

Her pale blond hair avalanched over one clavicle and the motion she made of ushering it back in place, a kinesthetic rubric in the text of her seductive book of body language, instilled her audience with the feeling expressed by that word known by all song writers.

Everything she does is magic. Eee oh oh …

She pinned back her feathery, heatherlocklearish locks with a bright scrunchy produced from racketless hand. Her eyes blazed as she straightened the path of rubies strung from her neck.

Everything she does is magic. Eee oh oh … Magic! Magic!

"Rick would plague us to no end if we told him. He'd try to ruin what we're trying to establish. My mother and brother won't tell him anything. They hate him. He'll find out eventually, of course. But by then, it won't matter as much."

Jordan laughed. "I see you're ready to play at Wimbledon, Ruby Tuesday."

"You said we were going to the country club for breakfast. Unless our plans have changed."

"Nothing has changed. I play a third-rate game of tennis."

"I'm third rate," she opined. "You're fifth rate. I'm not going to wear the ruby necklace during our match," she protested.

"No, wear it. I am pretty bad. So don't beat up on me." Jordan de-racketed Rachel. She stepped on his bare feet, kissed him on the mouth. The doorbell rang.

*

Richard Lowe Notingham paced the kitchen. His anger multiplied with every step. He took a swig of a bottle of Jack. The leg pocket of his olive-green cargo pants bulged. He had deposited huge amounts of cash in them. Eleven thousand in hundreds, fifties, twenties, tens. The door bell rang. It had to be Dick Schiller, the gun dealer. Notingham opened the door. "What took you so long?"

Tallish, boyish, longish and shortish blondish-haired Dick Schiller smiled, as his prognathic face preceded—by a long millimoment—a lean body across the threshold of an unhappy abode. A casual dresser, Schiller wore neutral-colored khakis and a gray customized tee with a bright silk-screened quotation:

VIRTUE IS AN EMPTY ECHO

IF THERE'S NO SOUL

Richard Lowe Notingham was in no mood for thickly applied existentialism. Schiller, a direct descendant—he constantly boasted—of scriptocrat Friedrich Schiller, coughed repeatedly into his pink fist. He was Notingham's first cousin on his mother's side. Schiller squeezed the wings of his aquiline nose, exhaling sonorously: "So cuz, how are you holding up?"

"Not too fucking good, man," Notingham said, gesticulating with the bottle of whiskey. "Want a drink?"

"I'm good," Schiller answered.

"What's that supposed to mean?" Notingham pointed to the quotation on his cousin's shirt. "I guess those are the fucking words of your great-fucking-grandfather."

His cousin resumed coughing. "It's Schiller but I altered it to give it a Sartrean twist, cuz."

"You're a poet and didn't know it!" Notingham smiled. "I feel very hostile to the hostility today, Dicky boy."

"You're an existentialist, after all," Dick Schiller cried.

"You're the man, cuz," Notingham affirmed with a hand slap.

*

Jordan located a pair of brown penny loafers in the hallway, eased into them, and opened the door. Whom else? Dentelupo removed his Oakleys, displayed trademark coprophagic grin. Jordan often felt odium for his partner's inappropriate flexing of zygomaticus major. One may grin and grin and be a villain.

"Brian! Rachel! Headed for the country club," the portal-straddler observed.

"Yeah, we're going to have breakfast and play some tennis. We need to talk about something, Frankie. Let's take a stroll in the garden." He turned to his tennis partner. "Rachel, I'll be a few minutes."

"Sure." Rachel trotted up the stairs.

"Andiamo, Frank."

Jordan blundered out the door behind Dentelupo. The rolling English drunkard made the rolling English road. All roads lead to Toms River. They strode into the sun via a slate walkway, adorned by pale mimosa petals, in the direction of the state of the cash gazebo: air-conditioned, stereo, cable telly. I shall gaze at how beautiful money is! A red cedar jewel in the garden of the Fitzi-Continis. On the back of a charming anguine we go down in the sod, Monsieur Belvedere. See beauty in rose, dandelion, whatever flourishes in the melancholy soil of her fair rape. A tribe of Salix babylonica bowed when Wilhelm Meister sinkapaced by.

The River Lady paddled past Lilith's and Adam Kadmon's, from swerve of bay to bend of shore. Potentillas along Nova Howth, caged and bound, attracted an army of buzzing suitors in the midmorn air.

A slew of cochleashattering metaphors and similes rattled and rolled in his mind's asshole. The sky was a sleepy blue curtain until it was torn by a dagger of lightning. The motionless sky begged to be roused into action by Maxwell's silver hammer. The sky was as lifeless as a dead bard's simmies and nuts but was reanimated by a set of jumper cables attached to Tennyson's testicles. A blue bodkin of lightning hacked open the breast of the heavens, 'sblood and 'swounds! Sound of fallen Heavenbeast. Crasheth! Boometh! Goodbye Charlie! Gott ist fur einem Dukat tot! The Levite will leave me one day just as she left him. A Futurist watched as the sky turned a hazy shade of shit blue. 'Sdeath! I say, we will have no more similes or metaphors or another serious word.

"Sit down, Frank. Do you want a drink? Help yourself," Jordan urged with a belated gesture to a cooler. Dentelupo shook a declination. Jordan sat down on a padded wicker chair but Dentelupo settled on part of a bench across from him.

"What's up, Bry?" Dentelupo's gaze intensified.

"Rick called a few minutes ago. Get this, Frank. He thinks Rachel is with you. Thinks she's with you?"

"Why would he think something like that?" Dentelupo's voice expressed the apparent confusion in his dark eyes.

"Did you call him and hang up?"

"I did, Bry. A few weeks ago. I needed to get hold of you but he answered instead of Rachel. Bry, I'm sorry. I knew it might cause a problem. I don't know what I was thinking. You always get the wrong idea."

"Should I?"

"Bry!"

"Well. I can't understand why Rachel won't let me tell numb nuts that she's with me. When we get married ..." Jordan paused. "He'll find out." Jordan looked at the bench sitter with kindness. "We're going to the Country Club to play tennis and for some sustenance and hopefully much libation." Jordan laughed at the pretension evident in his words and diction.

"I'll let you two honeymooners enjoy the day free from unwanted company. You'll soon enough get sick of each other. Like every other couple."

*

Rachel lounged on Jordan who in turn lounged on a divan in the parlor of their well-appointed, recently restored Victorian home. Rachel liked to think it had the charm of antiquity without the accompanying wear and rust. In fact, everything about the house seemed perfect to her.

After all, Brian had hired a decorator to see to all the details. She feared he had spent too much restoring and furnishing. Brian wasn't a millionaire. Or was he? She remembered Rick had once asked him: "Don't you ever run out of money?" Her present lover smiled and looked away. She didn't know what Rick had meant until he told her later. Was Brian an Irish gangster? Last night, as they dined in Seaside, in the patio of Sir Kyles, a hoodish guido walked by his table and screamed, "If it isn't Pablo Escobar of the Jersey Shore!" Brian was evidently upset, glared, but said nothing. Rachel had asked him: "What's that about!" She was startled to learn the hoodish guido was a police detective. Brian had told her: "I know him since we're kids. He thinks I'm somekind of a wiseguy because I'm involved with Ferro in Oscura. I'd love to punch him out like I did in high school."

Was Brian a criminal? She didn't know. Nor did she care. She became wet over the thought of fucking a big-time coke dealer. One getting away with it. She only knew she enjoyed the status of living in an undeniably magnificent home. Every time she looked around the house, it was like a preview of heaven. A constellation of beautiful things shone in her eyes. Their home was a material paradise.

How she loved the shelves and shelves of objets d'art. In particular, she was gaga for the array of romantic treasures, like a soapstone figurine of a little girl and her dog resting on the cherrywood fireplace mantel. Her eyes panned the room with continued admiration for this or that. Such as a swelter figure of a little boy; a cast-iron lion cub; a sanded majolica bear; a pair of decorated Irish vases brimming with silk yellow roses. To the left of the fireplace, a Staffordshire ceramic dog guarded, with Cerubusian zeal, these treasures. Farther off to the left, a walnut table with a black marble inset displayed a girandole to die from, as her mother would say. She studied it a moment. It had power. It took her away from herself. Beauty could do that to a person. Only lower species are unappreciative of the beauty of a starry night. Higher ones too. From her trip to the avenue of lights, she learned celestial beauty goes unnoted by the extradimensionals. But most of the time, of course, she didn't believe she had traveled metatemporically, metamolecularly. She was bleeding from her anus upon waking the morning after her trip. They always probe the backdoor of their abductees, they say. She further studied the astral light. The Moonrace, the Selenians, her captors told her, are the most dolorous blokes in the entire universe because they are polluted by the sadness of the human race, as their home is the repository of all the tears shed and sighs emitted on earth. With a curious and curiouser smile, she envisioned the white light of her soul passing through its hanging prisms, while a gilded Athena whispered something sagacious in her ear. Not Pallas at all but a pontificating Brian.

Rachel rolled off his lap and sat next to him. "That's got to feel better," she said.

"You're like a feather wafted down from an eagle in flight," he said, laughing. The Persian sofa, which at present supported them, was a rather enterprising construction of tufts, buttons, brocaded fabrics, fringe, and tassels. Joanna, the decorator, boasted she hadn't seen a divan to rival it. In many ways, Rachel thought the entire parlor suite unrivaled. Seventeenth-century Lady's chairs provided an Old World elegance. A set of blazing black horsehair chairs assigned it a distinction.

"I have to get something upstairs," Rachel chimed. Jordan watched as she vanished through an incised oak door with a sterling silver doorknob.

*

Richard Lowe Notingham parted a flowing red sea of wavy locks and passionately bussed the tasty nape of a young beauty. With a tongue moistened by a small ice cube lodged between his equine teeth, he proceeded to scale up and down, down and up, the ensellure of the young beauty. Her mouth pressed against the pillow of a disturbingly fragrant and jangly bed, the young beauty emitted muffled groans of appreciation with every glossal incursion. Kissening glistening yellow-smellons of her plumprump, he paused reverently at a barely traversible abbreviated space, wormhole, rabbit hole, brown eye!

"Why did you stop?" the young beauty cried.

A whiff of voider: grecian loins ignited and whirled into flames. Robed in the fire of concupiscence, Notingham laughed, licked, laughed, licked, laughed, licked, laughed, licked, laughed, licked, laughed, licked, laughed, licked, laughed, licked, laughed, licked, laughed, licked, laughed, licked, laughed. He urged his speckled snake into abbreviated space, wormhole, rabbit hole, brown eye of the sturm und drang, trapdoor, holy of holies, cul de sac, dead sea, dead end, deadwood, blind alley, blind spot, muck, mire, impasse, puzzle, bind, blackbox...

The red locks: faux: a fall purchased in the mall. Underredneath, the young beauty's pale oak hair was a clever truncation of Rachel's longish, feather cut. The ass very much like a mamma called Rachel. Very much like a mamma. The old in out in out made new again by the addition of her brother's black hole of Ocean City and penis the size of Rachel's uncut nose.

Notingham's penis imploded in his demimondaine's cavern of jocoseriousness with a burst of light and lust. Cries of fulfilled desire, a detonation of deadly delight, passionate pain, and other trite alliterative synonyms for the lust that dare not speak its name, as the demimondaine exploded a copious amount of the sown Wildean seed upon blue cotton sheets purchased at the mall yesterday. Pulling out, Notingham, who had finally begun a perusal of *Ulysses* last week (Rachel's deserted copy had generated impetus), laughed, muttered: "Fagenbite of Inwit."

"What?" Mark Neal asked.

"Nothing. I was just saying how good it was in German."

"You speak German?"

Redheads have more fun. A red sea of troubles. Mein betrunkenener Dummkopfvater. I ought kill the little sissy. The fucking little faigeleh. Played his rusty trombone. I should shoot the little sissy for refusing to tell me where Rachel's hiding. Has sex with her boyfriend but remains true to her wishes the boyfriend not be informed of her fucking precious whereabouts.

*

In his dream, she vanished through a drawn portiere, never ever returning from ten and one dimensions.

Ten and one is the loneliest number that you'll ever do...

The portieres, colorful velvet tapestries, whose removal he contemplated daily, were numerous throughout New Howth. Very Victorian, the decorator had assured him. He was no stuffed shirt, no Victorian. He was fucking bloody parvenu. He wished he had razed the fucking damp, musty manse and had a modern home erected over the ossuary of Injun Tom's tribe. The servants' quarters above a barn without animals—and most of the time without servants. Ma and Pa Kettle, as he called them, lived off premises. They worked sparingly, Ma Kettle cooked for them on occasion and Pa Kettle spruced up the property. He liked his privacy. Their true surname was Applegate, the name of the first family of Toms River and environs. Relatives of Injun Tom, no doubt, as all the locals were alleged to have Tom's Deoxyribonucleic Acid. Injun Tom hath greatgreatgreatgrandchilders everywhere.

Interestingly, one of the portieres depicted a wigwam around which headdressed natives stood schmoozing with a band of musket-bearing Pilgrims. They no doubt had an Applegate in the band of fowlers, a common English surname, albeit the Applegates in his employ were—in his opinion—somewhat phenotypically Wampanoag—or more accurately Lenni Lenape. Do you have Algonquin on you?

Money! Jordan certainly had a lot of it. Advocates of supply side economics would be bolstered to know that Jordan cleared millions, nearly monthly, from his share of his Hedonic Engineering enterprise. Tax free. The night after Rachel had agreed to live with him—thus finally giving up the geist of her relationship with Notingham—Jordan—her new official boyfriend—had begged her forgiveness for having to leave her the next day in order to travel to Houston for business. She told him she understood but would be lonely and couldn't wait until he got back. Jordan had to meet Hundsheim's son, T.J. (Thorstein Johannes), who was back from Switzerland—a week earlier than expected—with the funds that had been electronically deposited by their clients in a numbered Swiss account. A cliché on the order of a Robert Ludlum thriller, the numbered Swiss account, but nevertheless, the way Hundsheim set it up. As for T.J., he was a perfect courier as he carried Interpol credentials (Special Agent for North America Drug Importation Task Force), as well as being fluent in German. Messrs. Jordan and Dentelupo regarded him an asshole.

Jordan converted oodles of cash (as Rachel pitched her lover's liquid affluence), when he could, into real estate, blue chip stocks, precious metals: a pirate's chest of the coin upon which the sun never sets: the British Gold Sovereign: Jockey George front and center, the Windsors' forefather reverse. They were also Pandas and Maple Leafs and Kangaroos lining the chest. Naturally, no coin of apartheidal realm permitted. Pirate Jordan smiled when he thought of the gold and silver coins at his disposal. He also dabbled in philately and, of course, a bibliophile, he had a spectacular book collection. All paid for in fiat currency. His loins ignified with one gaze into the omphalos of Silas Marner Jordan.

Niatross Jordan paced the room. The books stacked on a nearby table included volumes of Hume and fellow empiricist Bishop Berkeley. The latter will admit no object; the former no subject. The latter admits only the immolecular; the former only the molecular.

Wry laughter filled the room. The laugher walked over to an exquisite side chair, plopped down in it. Gilt incising bahblahblah. Joanna called it a fine examp (she abbreviates evthin') of Franco-Anglo Renaissance revival. Her toric confession that she's a cheater wasn't a fucking revelation. After all, I had my schmeckle in her judge's-wife-to-be ass. Cheated and fucked and sucked her way through school. She's a lying cunt. Nonetheless, I do like Auggie's and Billy's work. Jordan got up and tried the spiffy Morris: adjustable-backed, wood-frame chair with wheels. Its loose-cushioned back and padded arms suited his mood more than the Potter and Stymus. One could traverse eternity with this one! He wheeled forward a few meters. I went half mad with poetry on that day. Belated Bloomsday or Happy Boylansday. Well, if this is poetry it is very easy to write. He popped up and went over to the liquor cabinet, removed a bottle of Jameson. He returned to the Morris, sat down: a burnished autochariot with its coordinates set for the city that never wakes. Prelude to quaffment, he gripped the bottle like a football about to be passed, pumped fake in the direction of a vintage oak shadowbox grained and hued like his begetter's begetter's coffin. Photograph of grandgetter in Feinian garb preserved for a posterity devoutly to be wish'd.

CHAPTER 18

As he sped redly along Cookman Avenue—the speeder's central nervous system stimulated by a crystalline tropane alkaloid imported all the way from la via delle stelli—Asbury Park seemed the lowest, darkest and farthest place from heaven. Ironically, a limey voice within the car proclaimed the opposite:

Heaven and Heaven…

His car trembled at a light, limbs and shape of a putative female crossed to the other side of the drag: a queen like the one he had had as a serviceman in Thailand. First dishonorable discharge. Second. Turn her over and you'd never guess. Felt as good as sheep cunt. Maybe he'd come back later and pay the little sweety a visit. The light changed and his borrowed wheels broomed east. The streets, stained with mystic horror, were quiet except for the babble of radial tires. He noted the swarthy disposition of the Atlantic. His father had made his way across it years ago. The pilot reconnoitered the landing strip: the target: an idling black Grand National. He guided his car into a propinquitous space. In eyeshot, earshot, noseshot: the black steeds of Neptune galloped plangently, fragrantly. The driver swung the door open, dingdingding, eased out of a plush bucket seat, slammed the door closed. With a trace of mischief in his smile and step, he approached the Grand National. He tapped the tinted window on the driverside. The aphotic window vanished and a face rich in melanin appeared. The face, young, outlined by dreadlocks and topped with a multi-colored cap, belonged to a minor hedonic engineer in the employ of the syndicate.

"Mon," the multi-colored cap wearer exhaled. Dentelupo's leather paw swatted a tendered hand.

"What, are you too good to get out the car, you ganja-smoking motherfucker? Jesus!"

Dentelupo's black claws guided a gray halo voidward. "Stinks like shit."

The multi-colored cap wearer coughed a laugh. "We didn't recognize the car, mon."

"You have the take, Marley?" Dentelupo asked uncordially.

Hedonic engineer X handed an obese envelope to hedonic engineer Y.

"A pretty good week," Dentelupo guesstimated.

"We made shit this week, mon. We need a bigger cut."

"No can do, Marley. A deal's a deal in America."

"Mon, you owe us. You didn't give us nothing for ripping off that faggot in Uzzi's parking lot."

"I paid you five bills, you sack of shit."

"We could have been killed. He had a gun. We had to let him suck our dick."

"You loved it!"

"Maybe we should make a deal with Ferro. Tell him how one of his partners put us up to ripping off one his dealers."

"He'd serve your eggplant ass with parmigian, you ganja-smokin' queer cocksucker."

"He'd cook your guinea ass too."

"Alright. Alright. How much more do you need, Marley?"

"Thanks, mon. We'd never rat you out. If you could throw us…"

Dentelupo stopped him in midsentence by shooting him twice in the temple. As anticipated, the suppressor he had purchased from a Jamaican posse leader, Laughlin Armstrong, reduced the sound of gunfire to the sound of a cap pistol. Dentelupo examined the cylindrical device attached to the barrel of his Beretta as he contemplated shooting the victim one more time. He checked his clothes, face, neck, gloves, shoes, face again, for a trace of blood, bone, brain. Nothing.

Starless, the firmament seemed a lie until he noted that the near total darkness was trimmed by a haunting ribbon of moonlight.

The moon was the first movie screen. Put in the sky by God to entertain and enlighten us. His friend's clever remark years ago. A different person of late, he recently black Irishly observed: We're God's furniture; when we wear out, he carts us out to the curb like bulk trash. His friend said things like that when he was having trouble with that no-good cunt. Which was all the time. If his friend was correct, well, then, he had destroyed a piece of God's furniture (albeit a worthless chair) and would have to pay Rowdy Roddy Piper. Isn't murder, technically, like robbing God? It didn't matter. Our fates were decided long before we were slapped into existence. It was Marley's fate to be killed by a guinea. Who would kill him? Blow Frankie from Belmar away! Who started all of this? Who was the fuck who slapped God into existence? Certainly not an Italian midwife with a fat ass and a mustache. With a throbbing pain in his gulliver, he got into his car and drove away. A couple of Fire-golds before spatchka and he'd be fine in the morning. Despite the head-ache, he'd return his friend's fiberglass chariot only after he had thor-oughly scrubbed every centimeter inside and out. His fucking friend would never know it was gone. His friend trusted him too much. He'd burn his clothes just in case an infinitesimal amount of the Rastafarian's blood had splattered on them. He'd toss his sneakers in the Salvation Army's donation bin after washing them off at the self-service carwash on Route 9. Prepared, he had stuck a pair of Nikes under the seat. He was glad he had said ariverderci to Diane and their whining son. Rosa came over the other night and he fucked her hard. She said one night she'd even let him fuck her in her ass. She enjoyed the helplessness of it. As he turned onto Route 35, he began to feel sleepy. His headache was now compounded by intestinal discomfort. He laughed outright, when, as anticipated, his anus—sounding like a Dantean trumpet—blew an odiferous note: a B-flat major: the anthem of a galaxy fart, fart away … A Satchmo, his friend called such resonant honeys. He pressed a button on the door panel and the driver's front window opened. The resultant cool air abated his sleepiness and dissipated the procrastinating fart odor as well. Without delay, he put both hands on the wheel, steered down a ramp. His father, a retired overland truck driver, believes only pussies drive with the window up. His father's cruelty toward his mother leapt out of his memory. Six fucking boys and not one of them had the co-gliones to stop him. A midget, barely five feet tall, still not one of them stepped anywhere but backwards. His sisters claimed poppa impropri-ety. Dentelupo's mind ignited into a bright fire of hatred, but above the flames, like a Roman laudation, rose a smokey tribute. A disgusting drunk, degenerate gambler, perverted motherfucker. He's like his father. No fuckin' good like him! He thanked God.

*

You bounced down the stairs, looked for Rachel in the parlor, not there, decided she must be in the kitchen. The space not occupied by her reminds you of the inferior universes within the universe. You were apart for a week, what did she do? Dance. She admitted that her friends took her out. What? A night of hip proffering to celebrate her grandmother's passing. Ellis said it was the same thing as fucking. Even a first-degree relative, like her mother, didn't sit shiv'ah. No leather shoes for mourning Jews!

The floor resonated with uncertainty with each heavy step of the monster in your black alligator loafers. Meanwhile, you dreamed you were a schmetterling floating through the air knowing nothing at all of Brian William Seamus Jordan. You admit a dreaming, a perceiving, but deny the dream and dreamer.

Jordan found her at the table, a bowl of cereal under her blunt chin, a newspaper under her monumental nose. You dared to sit down next to her. She said nothing. You could see she was in a mood. The radio droned in the background, top forty, a girl not yet twenty-one, of course she has limited taste. Your lips moved but emitted no sound. The boiler coughed, a repairman would have to be called, defective from the moment it was installed. Still, heat circulated nicely throughout the house, the curtains in response, trembled like weak spirits. The movie theater of the mind, where perceptions pass, repass, glide away, and mingle in an infinite variety of postures and situations.

You had, indeed, sat down across from her. You had, in fact, observed she was in a mood. The movie theater metaphor should not mislead you, what, what? After all, the mind is constituted only of perceptions. You don't have a notion of what place is or what materials are used in the composition of things. You're as ignorant as God and as stupid as the devil. Spirit or material, everything has an unreliable tag attached to it. You looked around the room, took inventory: white plastered walls, oak quarter sewn kitchen cabinets, an ovate two-leaf ornately carved oak dining table, a lordly refrigerator. Philosophy is a flower of the intellect that blooms latest. Cousin Jordan, you'll never be a philosopher.

225

You had, in fact, jounced down the stairs.

"Good morning," he muttered, as he sat down. She muttered, continued reading.

"What's wrong?"

She handed him the newspaper. He was, as they say, all over it. The motherfuckers had leaked his name as a suspect in an execution-style murder in Asbury Park. His attorney had assured him his name would not be released to the press. Wasn't he released uncharged? And didn't he have an unimpeachable alibi? He was in Boston at the time of the murder. To go back to your alibi, Brian. Again? Why were you in Boston? I was attending a NORAID fundraiser. Oh, you mean that fucking front for the IRA? You don't have to be the triggerman to go up for murder. I was at the same table as the Mayor of Boston and the president of the state senate. The children of Ireland will not be allowed to fall prey to British Military miscalculation. The troubling thing is, troubling thing, the troubling thing is, is that the victim, the victim had your business card in the glove compartment of his car. Your card. My card? A red Corvette with a New Jersey tag was seen speeding away from the crime scene. My card? Which one? Jordan spread three disparate business cards across the nicked-up table. Which card? The investigator eyed the troika of business cards, ran his hands through his ill-dyed head, and tapped the card for Oscura. The card was pitch black, front and back, with fancy silver lettering. Maybe the victim held a party at Oscura or bought me a drink. I give my card out to a lot of people. Jordan envisioned it snowing business cards. He thought in hackneyed movie images most of the time. An investigator showed him a picture of the murdered man (premurder). A Rastafarian? A Reggae band performs weekly at Oscura. Was he a musician? He's in the same line as you. Was, I should say. He got the inference. Advertising? A drug dealer. Ha! Ha! Ha! Jordan's attorney protested excessively. Jordan tried to remain emotionless but his palms became pools of perspiration. He dried them on his chalkwhite Dockers. Your alibi checks out but we're going to keep your car a few days. We figure a coke dealer has a fleet of cars. Confident he would be released without charges, he smiled. I bought a Range Rover last week. He had angels—devils—protecting him. The teflon Mickey. The allegation about his occulted profession, however, was disturbing. His clients wouldn't appreciate the president of their agency being accused of coke dealing and murder. Allen, none of this will hit the papers, will it? Of course not, Bry.

"They spelt my name correctly."

"That's not funny. Is it true?"

"You can't think I'm a murderer?"

"I know you're not a murderer. But are you a coke dealer?"

"Dealing coke isn't any different than selling liquor."

"I love you, Brian, but I couldn't stay with a coke dealer."

"You must have known, Rachel?"

"I gave you the benefit of the doubt. If I asked you to give up dealing, would you?"

"Jesus Christ, Rachel. It's a larger issue. One I don't dare touch on."

"What are you talking about, Brian? You're talking down to me. You're being evasive."

"Rachel, I didn't kill anybody and have no idea who killed that poor bastard in Asbury Park. I have been cleared. I'm going to receive a personal apology from the Prosecutor."

"What happens if someone comes after you? Or me?" Rachel trembled, sobbed.

"I'm untouchable and because of that, so are you." Jordan got up and hugged Rachel. If only he could tell her the unbelievable truth.

*

March 28, 1986: Driving on a dark road outside Florence, New Jersey, lost for miles (the Turnpike his destination), he was pulled over by a squad car. A trio of graysuited officers, tendering an assortment of federal, state, and local law enforcement credentials, superpolitely insisted that he accompany them in their vehicle. As he sat in the backseat in the dark, save for a dim overhead light, he felt as impotent and confused as Joseph K. All day he had experienced jamais vu. Cognitive result: he was a bundle of axons. He recalled that it was a day of legendary spiritual journey, Good Friday. Perhaps the fear of imitating Gis and Alighieri—namely the concomitant somatic disconnection—had engendered his lethotopia.

A sharp turn catapulted a book onto his lap. He raised it up to the exiguous light for a better look. *Finnegans Wake*, the eternal book. It must have rested next to him, unobserved, like a quiet truth. If it had been the so-called holy folio, it would have been marked a theodore. But Joyce was no less a miracle to any thinking man. He read aloud until he fell asleep.

He awoke from a dream only to be ushered into another dream: the dream of a man, presumably, the wearer of his skin, seated at a wooden table in a poorly illumed room, a light trained on his boyishly handsome face, as the aforementioned trio questioned him about his erewhonabouts during someone's dark night of the soul. Because he refused to answer their questions, they, via formal fallacy, concluded his guilt.

If BWSJ thinks of his girlfriend's brother's arse when he fucks her, then he is homosexual; he is a homosexual. Therefore, he thinks of his girlfriend's brother's arse when he fucks her.

Affirming the consequent: If p then q : q / p.

The trio weren't coppers, as Cagney would put it. They were Zeta Reticulians. It appeared that the dreamer had been transported to the street of stars (which its citizens call sráid na realtaí), that place where life is not flattened into three dimensions, but his abductors assured him they would have him back in his bed before rosy-fingered dawn had squeezed the balls of the Jersey Shore.

He was feted like an Irish chieftain that night. Portions of the Wake—the Zetas worshipped Joyce—were recited by a troupe of actors, as Séamus O'Seoigh looked down from an elevated box. BWSJ kissed the hand that wrote *Finnegans Wake*. The author and the abductee drank at a hendecagonal bar, all night along, with Shakespeare, Archdruid Berkeley, Joe Nathan Swift, et al.

The official name of the street of stars was Lindolinda. They gave him the key to the city. A plastic keycard. He read a prepared speech from a teleprompter:

Cén fáth nglacann sibh, na Giúdaigh, lenár gcultár, ár gcreideamh, agus ár dteanga?

The Zetas, despite contrary reportage, are a wonderful race.

Their planet—tarnally bathed in platinum sunshine—is a giant mead hall. Their lexicon is devoid of a word for rain. They have rehabs for those suffering from sobriety. BWSJ drank and did line after line of coke with his hosts. He may have been rectally probed. They maintain cocaine casts a magical shadow with symbolic powers over the mind. He suspected they must have read the French Symbolists. They convinced him to go to work for them dealing coke. They'd supply it to him free of charge. He'd become rich and powerful and his scions would rule over nations or at least the Irish Riviera.

He awoke on the floor, not bed, tickled by Eos, his barreltone chest crushed by an incubus of typescript pages. The pages scattered across the hardwood floor when he jumped up. Torpid, he theorized that a succubus, earlier described, metaphorically, as an incubus, must have sucked the typescript pages from his hemipenis. Alright, from his juicy malroot. He gathered them, one by one, and attempted to put them into manuscript form. Hours later, seated at an oak rolltop desk, BWSJ finally achieved page order. Approximately 5000 words, he came to refer to the manuscript (previously incubus)—as a report, although it was, in fact, a Menippean satire. As expected, BWSJ gave his zygomaticus major a major workout as he read the said report, said Menippean satire: a risible play-by-play of his trip to the street of stars and an even more hilarious forecast of the consequences.

CHAPTER 19

Midtwenty, callipygian Joanna Kernow crept down a long hallway in a black Halston gown. N.J. Road, who lounged, almost effeminately, on a gray Victorian fainting sofa, a needlepoint pillow fluffed underneath his head, tracked her acatalectic verse of steps on a black and white security monitor mounted in a corner of a decorative ceiling. Her black Gucci handbag, which swung at her side—contrary to her confident spondees—iambically, had been a gift from her client, ardorless amant, and, at present, sort of remote viewer.

He recalled their plan to travel to New York in order to hunt for objets d'art which would complement the furnishings of his riparian mansion. No need to conjecture the intent of the tightness of her Conjecture jeans that gray February morning. The upside-down triangle on the back pocket prophetically symbolic. Apophenia. She was his dedicated interior decorator about to be married to a local superior judge. He had met them the previous spring at the country club. There was something izmenic about them. She wore a black leather mini-skirt up to the pipik! Apt, as the country club is the omphalos of local society. Her mouth: a big red lie he had delighted in kissing that monumental day, as they stood at the foot of the scimitarine red oak stairs. A painting of a tragic Irish princess in the hallway reminded him of his beautiful decorator. Joanna possessed the fluorescence, fine cheekbones, prominent nose, and regal bearing requisite of an Irish princess. Her nickname in college was Issy because of her habit of asking her girlfriends the sexual preference of available pretty boy classmates: "He's cute! Is he gay or is he straight?" You won't play the sad sailor for her. You love another, you think. Because of your knowledge of the classics, it bothers you that her betroth is named Mark Kernow. Synchronicity. He adjusted his torc, twirled his noble moustache. He had long maintained the best thing she had ever acquired for his home was a very good copy of the Dying Gaul.

N.J. Road stood indecently close behind her. Puissant pike evident, he rubbed her coccyx to make her chatté purr. She whirled around, breath burning, lips gliding. Their tongues connecting, briefly, their disconnected souls. "I want you," the big red lie whispered amid an ear bite. Their spirits touch in silhouette.

Good Friday 1986, a wooded area in western New Jersey, somewhere near Florence, rather disoriented, as you travel the Constant in a silver RX7 on your way back from a failed date. If her breath smells like fish, what does her cunt smell like? The curse of the Irish: overly efficient olfactory bulbs. She did have a great arse. Legs too thin to support it. You will regret not smacking your azure balls against it, boyo. Tuxtax. Tuxtax. Tuxtax! Later we see you committing self-incest. Tuxtax!

Nel mezzo del cammin di nostra vita. The white line in the middle of the road flutters like a ribbon of coke stretching eternity. You're fucking lost, aren't you? Morpheus begins to spread his veil of uncertainty over the world as soon as you shut your eyes. Your car transmogrifies into a flatbottom skiff. You hear the susurrus of sails luffed by Zephyr. Your stylish dark hair levitated by the affable breeze. Just as Adam's costal endowment served as the building block for the first sinner, from some misplacing of your thigh, a naked girleen materializes in the boat. You breathe in deeply and opine: "Heaven's breath smells wooingly: a very ancient and fishlike scent." You kiss her girleen gob with your thirtysomething lips, your mouth descends her undulating bronzed abs until you arrive at her most precious square of sense. With closed eyes, held breath, and a small amount of shame, you eject your skinkish tongue, your eyes uncurtain upon discovering the girleen had been infibulated.

You laugh. As ye sew, so shall ye ream. By indirections find directions out. You turn the girleen around and lick her cuvette d'or until she mysteriously disappears in midmirk.

The skiff, curragh, Kon-Tiki, transmogrifies back into your car, engine babbling like a newborn in a cradle of bulrushes, as it fumes noisily and noisomely into the night.

What happened that evening, boyo? The purple robed night strolled the sky with the moon gripped in his hand like a softball about to be hurled out of existence. Purpurated gonads obviously lead to purple prose.

It begins to pour a menagerie, as your mother would say. The windshield wipers slapping the shite out of space's long time companion. You can't see a fooking thing, can you? You oneiric bastard, you. Tell yourself again what happened in those dark woods. Were you made to quelph like the alleged crooked podestà of Firenze? Your gobshite theory posits Durante was sodomized by a mysterious woodsman in lupic clothing on Good Friday 1300.

That dark night of the soul you were pulled over by cops for speeding, weren't you? The officers were actually Grays from Zeta Reticuli. Lost, you found yourself on the street of stars! That place, as you say in your memoir in progress, where life is not flattened into three dimensions. The triumvirate of officers, their beastly surnames telepathically embroidered on their shirt pockets, requested in oral triplicate that you accompany them. You remember a pleasant mist spraying in the backseat of the squad car. The mystery mist caused you to dream the dreams you dream when you have shuffled off your mortal coil. You awoke later in a four poster in a gleaming palace. You rubbed your eyes as you prepared to travel the soft white silence of a seemingly interminable expanse of marble leading to a lambent door which glittered like the door to paradise. You opened the door cautiously, crossed the threshold, one parsec at a time, and glissaded down a corridor to great acclaim from a host of anonymous citizens. You suppressed their ovation with a royal hand signal, as a ravenhaired beauty escorted you to the head of an endecagonal dining table. Rapping it like a drunken Norman baron, you determined it was oak. You were, in a word, famished. Without ordering, you were served your absolute favorite meal: baked, blighted potato and filet mignon, bluddlefilth rare. Later, you drank a few jars with your God, James Joyce. The trade paper edition of *Finnegans Wake* found in your car, purportedly, your passport to sráid na realtaí. Because the starry streeters are devoutly Joycean, espousers of the Wakean *wort an sich*, opposed to the Kantian *ding an sich*, you were given the key to the city. Mounds of cocaine, a river of Irish whiskey, a litter of Lolitas…and an intriguing proposition. Also, you were probably subjected to a rectal probe. Perhaps because you were going to have money coming out of your arse. Chrysopoet N.J. Road. If that is your real name?

The proposition was more of a fiat.

Let there be white!

They'd supply the product, you the customers. You'd be able to keep all the money generated by the enterprise. You were assured not to fear arrest or prosecution. You'd have complete immunity no matter what you were caught doing. Omniregent, they run the planet. Naturally, you inquired why N.J. Road? They produced the copy of *Finnegans Wake* which they had found on the seat of your car. They quickly opened it to a passage which explicitly alluded to you (270:19). Logomancy by your God! And you had always thought it was a coincidence that your name was written in the Book of Books.

Why the white stuff? Pink stuff, really. Erythroxylon coca arbusto. You should've guessed it was the color of the trap that many men are gladly ensnared. Some women too. It's the agents it's cut with that imparts its famous blanche and smooth constituency (it's chunky to start out with). They explained it in a very convoluted manner.

Language is a virus from outerspace, literally. That the neocortex is the result of said virus—a gift from them to your supposed species in order to advance your civilization, provided you are, in fact, human. Moreover, language bestows an emotion known to all Homo sapiens.

Why did they wish to punish your race (there is only one, after all) by getting as many members of it as they could fucked up on extragalactic rock?

They told you they were doing it mainly because your race has, largely, rejected *Finnegans Wake*. As a result, Avernus would be paved with the ignoblest neurotransmitter inhibitor of them all. You agreed to become one of their paviors. You remember the motherfuckers a little differently than other abductees. Most abductees speak of them as gray, neotenous creatures. They describe them as having large aphotic eyes and heads many times the size of humans. Some religiously inspired abductees portray their abductors as aligerous, coniferous maniacs intent on speciocide. Devils, in other words. They are angry at us, sure, but you are sure they don't intend on killing your alleged species. You remember them as having, for the most part, cesious eyes and thinker foreheads. You called them grays, for lack of a better term. In truth, they are very fair. They are what most people would deem very Nordic looking. Meaning, they are often tall and blond. They have long noses, usually. Better to look down on the paragon of animals.

Standing naked in front of him, her back to a cherry framed cheval mirror, he was strangely enthralled by her reflected ensellure. All roads lead to Sodom. He waved her over to his big brass bed. She flashed *il cornuti*, as she slithered over, the scent of her nest of spicery arrived a moment sooner than her creamy, perfumed murderous body. She looked him in the eye, smiled. "You like what I've done? I think it's my best work."

He nodded, preoccupied with erotic navigation, squeezed her phytophagic roes, eased her face down on the mattress, rustling the red charmeuse sheets, in order to make his approach a tergo. He felt the warm reception of her awkward fist, fluidly thrusting in and out of its theoretical grip.

"Fuck me you ox," Joanna screamed.

"Oxen can't fuck," N.J. Road informed as he continued to plow, irony noted, somewhat boustrophedonically.

"Fuck me like I'm a fucking whore!"

Tis pity she's a whore.

All harlots were virgins once.

Phil emerged from Gobbler's Knob in Punxsutawney today and saw his shadow; thereby sentencing you to six more weeks of discontent. What's in the near present for you and your moll? Molls. Weeks and weeks remain of staring out the bedroom window into the gray reality of the garden, the Welsh bard's green fuse only a rumor.

Why did she call you an ox? Who does she think she is? Talking to you like a stable boy she's bedding. Kate the Great once gave her favors to a steed. Just because you're hung like Kelso she thinks you're going to whinny for her. Of course, Kelso was a gelding and you're a ridgling. You'd love to redirect your malroot to an exponentially narrower via. The road less traveled, to quoth the Rhymer. Propelled by latent misogyny, the "ox" increased pelvic thrust, fresh streams of pleasure ran through her, murmured her moans. Flesh arrows puncture your prostate, you look for but see no rainbows, as the gong of your dong sounds.

N.J. Road collapsed in bliss. The mantel clock chimed eleven, six minutes slow, N.J. Road calculated. The grandfather downstairs had struck eleven precisely at the time of penetration.

He had expected Joanna. "Let yourself in," he had told her earlier on the phone. Everything of any taste and elegance in his home had been acquired by her. The alchemy he had employed to obtain the everything created a moral dilemma. Even though he no longer held the beliefs of his Iar Connacht ancestors, hyperduliacs, he felt the consequences of his actions made him a looderheramaun. A disgraceful sinner, literally. A murderer, atheist, dope dealer, etc. The sinner sat up, checked out his hair in a gilt edge wall mirror, the centerpiece of a brass and crystal girandole. The sinner seemed immolecular in the undiffused light.

Perhaps the result of the inconstancy of reflected candlelight? Or perhaps a premonition of your impending physical doom? Technically, there is only one form of worship which can result in molecularless bliss. You learned the term for it from Summa Theologica, latria, which accords the highest honor to the heavenly God. You say bugger off, heavenbeast. Nothing to fear but man itself! For the tank is empty. Siphoned off a gallon at a time. So Yahweh, Nobodaddy, the Force, can just whirl your fracted molecules voidward.

N.J. Road collapsed next to his conquest. Joanna's airborne ass having crashed landed the moment he had ejaculated.

You said nothing for the longest while. The panspermia of the multiverse credited to Gugliemo Pellegrino was surreally performed by you at this moment in alternative time and space. This room with a purview is your zoo and Joanna is pornstar for the day. Philopornosophical, you follow her every dictate.

"What just happened?" N.J. Road asked. Joanna laughed nervously as she straightened her feathery dark locks. Her smoky blue eyes always appeared sleepy.

"I don't know," she tittered, rubbing her bedmate's smooth cheek. "Felt good." She kissed him adamantly on the mouth. "You're too Catholic, honey." She popped up on her knees, adding: "Let's get high! Do you have any weed?"

"I have coke," N.J. Road said.

"Coke! Fuck, I'm psyched."

N.J. Road pulled up his black boxers and jumped out of bed. He rocketed out of the room, toddled downstairs. Joanna hopped off the bed naked and ran to the bathroom. As she sat on the toilet, she listened to bare feet scurry across hardwood floors. Wiping herself with care, she flushed, stopped to wash her hands. The sink had yellow daisies, blue morning glories, and yellow buttercups painted inside the basin and roses painted on the pedestal. Fired onto the white porcelain to insure the impossibility of erasure. N.J. Road had opposed its overt femininity, but relented when his decorator had argued "Chel will love it." Chel being his Daisy Fay. Garish as Gatsby, he did like the 24k gold faucets.

Chel was a petite blond with empyrean blue eyes. She was engaged to a gambling addict, a quondam friend of his, and someone who owed N.J. Road thousands of dollars. He had pleaded with her from their first kiss to run off with him. Last week, Chel spent a day with him at his newly renovated home and promised—on his tearful imploration—to consider his offer. They made love in three different rooms. He presented her with a 14k white gold bracelet studded with that allotrope of carbon very popular with her sex. The blue fire of her eyes lighted the way from concupiscence to love, a pilgrimage he had been reluctant to make. He would never love Joanna. She was a jaunt.

Joanna recumbent alongside recumbent N.J. Road. He sniffed the heady aroma of an inadequately extinguished maroon Gitanes in a Baccarat ashtray on a marble top teak and rosewood night table. A near empty bottle of Hennessy XO rested on his chest. The recumbent couple had toasted each other, repeatedly, and snorted lines of coke, fucked three times in addition to the precoke fucking. She smoked a cigarette to ashes postfucks except the last one, which she rubbed out with most of her expensive smoke in extant. Paris is burning! Pricey designer perfume splashed in strategic somatic areas that went unnosed by him in the friction of passion, the noncorrosive sublimate of temporal heaven, now registered in the proboscis like a sharp jab. Poison and poisson in the air! "What a doll," she had exclaimed when he allowed her to smoke in his bedroom. She knew he wasn't misocapnic but had heard him say Chel had detected the presence of a smoker in the bedroom during her last visit. Chel knew he didn't smoke. N.J. Road had fucked a concatenate smoking barmaid earlier in the week and Chel, with her superior olfactory bulb—her late father had, after all, been Irish—was still able to accuse him of entertaining "a filthy cigarette smoking whore" in the bed he had just thrown her down on. "The others are only nepenthes," he had explained. The speed of light lovers changed bedrooms and positions: "Let me get on top," Chel had requested of alphaic N.J. Road. "Alright."

"Be a teddy bear…" Joanna commanded incompletely.

"And what," N.J. Road sighed.

"I'm thirsty. Can you get me an Evian from the fridge, honey?" Her lips puckered for a kiss.

N.J. Road felt the bedroom morphing into a bear trap. He wouldn't take the bait. No more kisses. "Sure." She punched him affectionately in the arm, presumably for ignoring her labial trap. No matter how he beat his wings, his cock of fire would not rise again for the slut of Babylon. What time is it? It's 11:32 a.m. in sráid na realtaí.

You want her out of your bed, pronto. You fear you are in a Pinter play. Overcast, befitting an afternoon in early February, you squint to see what your conquest honestly looks like. She might be a saurian Mata Hari. They always seem to know what you're up to! They don't employ you. You're an independent contractor. When the sun drips its luminous paint across the canvas of the room, you begin to see her differently. Her chin's a little pointy. You wonder if she practices stregheria? Her makeup attenuated by perspiration and insincere saliva exposes at least a half a decade. She's probably lying about her age! She may have some Babylonian blood. Like a lizard, she likes it in the culo. Never misocapnic, instead agliophobic, you hate the trace of garlic in the thank-you buss for fetching her a bottle of water. She's part ancient old enemy, isn't she? All the water in Wye cannot wash her majesty's tomato sauce out of her pody. Nunc est bibendum! You offer her a pull on the bottle, hydropot declines, you finish it in one gulp. You wipe your mouth with the back of your hand. You wait for her to take her leave. Eternal moments tick. You decide to tell her about your trip to Heterotopia.

N.J. Road looked straight up: the 11-foot-high bronze tile ceiling ornamented with tesselated polygons were not her idea. She had desired a Japanese motif, but her client chose the geometric design from the catalogue. "Not suitable for a Vic," she had counseled. It was no use. Chel was keen on the polygons. Now, after months of being out of contact, Joanna wanted to see her former client.

"Honey?" It was Joanna's voice on the telephone. As he spoke to her, he divided the jacquard white lace curtains and peered outside. Winter, as a bad memoirist once pitched it, had come out of from the shadows of the north, like a Viking wielding a battle axe. His head jerked back as a sonorous arctic blast shot through the barren trees and bushes, subjugating them to its will, triggering a metamorphosis of the smooth turquoise river into a violent lead-colored stream. Hanging up, he cachinnated: "It's snowing in the Devil's stomach!"

She came into the room as N.J. Road fussed with his hair. He needed a haircut and a shave. "Hello, honey."

"Joanna!" N.J. Road arose from the sofa. He kissed his guest's heavily rouged cheek. "You look great," N.J. Road exclaimed, hugging his former decorator. "What are you all dressed up for," he asked, with an occulted smile. "A political fundraiser?" She diplomatically extricated herself from the fond restraints draped over her shoulders. She took a graceful step back. With an indeterminate expression, she delved into her handbag, removed a .22 pistol, pointed it at her host.

N.J. Road smilesmirked. "I wish I had more than a robe on," he groused. "Wearing a robe, sans underwear, when one is found shot to death will appear very tacky." He filled the silent room with bronchitic laughter. He attempted to lower himself back on the sofa, but Chum *fils* convinced him to remain standing. "I think," he began, "they were right to call it," he stared back to where he had lounged, "a fainting sofa." He threw back his head in prolonged, nervous laughter. "Maybe dying sofa," he emended. "The melancholy gray sofa incarnadine with the blood of this just person."

"I hear Chel has picked up and gone back to Ricky," Joanna said coldly. "Did she tell you why, honey? It might because you always sound as if you're high."

"She felt like she was being smothered. A Desdemona complex, they call it. Very boring, don't you think? A better question is why you're going to blow my head off?"

"Who said I'm going to blow your head off?" Joanna shuffled

a step closer in her 11-cm black heels. Without looking, she produced a suppressor from her purse, adeptly attached it, and pointed the enhanced barrel in the direction of his genitals. Her ophidian grace was the ocular proof. Izmena! The slither of a loveless reptile.

"Not in the balls," N.J. Road protested.

"Your robe's coming undone, honey."

N.J. Road cinched the sash of his borrowed robe. "Joanna, put the gun down. Please! You realize I'm dead already without Chel."

Chel had finally consented to leave her boyfriend and move in with him. N.J. Road joyfully moved large shipments of cocaine for the extraterrestrial cartel. They'd call him every week and tell him a sammy full of cocaine would be in a particular locker in Port Authority. They'd FedEx him the key and he'd pick it up when he had a delivery scheduled. He had a solid base of customers, mostly small-time dealers with Westy or Camorra ties. Since his suppliers required no valuable remuneration—they were doing it in the spirit of Starish fun—he and his partner, Ted Lupone, became millionaires. They bought a go-go bar and part of a nightclub in Seaside Heights. He purchased his riverside estate, the most expensive property in the county, with the cash he made pushing coke. N.J. Road had been given a verbal get out of jail card by his handlers. Not the MKULTRA courtesy phrase, Code White, but the blended literary allusions (a result of his handler's reverence for Joyce): A screaming comes across that little tent of blue sodomites call the sky.

N.J. Road got to use said card in a scene resembling a bad movie, when cracking a suitcase full of yeyo open to the fervid eyes of a troika of putative buyers in a Waldorf-Astoria suite, a slew of Feds barged into the room, guns out, profane clichés flying. N.J. Road turned to them, obviously a sting operation, and uttered the aforementioned Pynchon and Wilde melded phrase. The cowboys holstered their guns, shook their heads. He smiled, peered down at the diaphanous bags of cocaine stacked in the suitcase like ghostly bodies, thudded the sammy shut, zippered it up, nodded to the pigs, and departed. Standing in the middle of the wheel of life, he muttered: "Zeta Reticuli, here I come!"

Chel left him because of his jealous rages. He received the news of her departure telephonically. There was resolve in her voice. She was banishing him from the realm of possibility. N.J. Road gave up the apparition. He stopped making deliveries for his suppliers. He refused to leave his residence. Instead, he occupied his days and nights writing his memoir, viciously titled "Scarring Penuel." A silly exercise in tuism in the mode of Giordano Bruno's risable autobiography: You are born in Elizabeth, New Jersey to Hiberno-Catholic immigrants. The happiest day of your life is the day you made your First Holy Communion. You would experience a different communion decades later.

"Are you saying killing you would be redundant? You often accused me of making redundant purchases. What did you say? How many girandoles does one need, Joanna? You were right, of course." She stooped down and ran a long silky black evening glove along the dusty surface of a coffee table, while alertly keeping her eyes on her prey. "You need a maid to come in, honey," she quipped, inspecting the glove. "Enough white powder for Mark to send you away a long time. This home is in a drug free school zone," she teased, giggling as she rose slowly to her designer-shod feet. "Chel once confessed to me," Joanna went on, "she found it hard to believe you had made so much money selling ads for police publications. I told her it's rumored that you're a coke dealer. That excited her, honey." Joanna stroked a sallow cheek with her gun. She looked ill. "I have AIDS," she blurted, smoky blue eyes darkening to a subtrist violet. "Mark gave it to me. He's gay."

"I'm sorry, Joanna," N.J. Road said earnestly. "Labs make mistakes. I read there's been a rash of false positives of late. That's why multiple tests are recommended."

"I have AIDS, honey." Joanna sighed. "How many times do I have to tell you?"

"Are you sure?"

"Dead certain," she replied with a strange mirth.

"I'm really sorry, Joanna. But what do you want from me? I'm very confused why you're threatening my life. So please stop fucking around and put the gun down."

"I was contacted by your suppliers," she exhaled. "They have cures for the incurable. You're fucking with the wrong people. Well, whatever they are? Telling them to go fuck themselves is very rude, honey. But what worries them," Joanna confided, "is that fucking memoir you've been writing. I understand I'm portrayed less than flattering.

They want me to destroy it."

"I have it upstairs in my desk drawer. Burn it! It's not very good. Nobody would believe a word of it, anyway. My brother believes I'm being mind controlled. He thinks the 'aliens' are CIA operatives masquerading as Zeta Reticulians. I can easily discredit my account by adding, quite erroneously, that they love strawberry ice cream. Rocky Road is their favorite. This will make it seem as if my trip to la route jaune de brique was merely pseudoblepsia. As I said, I have the manuscript upstairs."

"You do," she said, pointing to her head. "Have it upstairs, literally. You remember everything. Everything but what's important. I thought you loved me."

"At present, I don't think I'm capable of discussing our relationship with any degree of honesty. After all, you have a firearm."

"Too bad for you, honey. I don't think you'll get another chance."

"Quel dommage," he intoned wistfully, adding in a high-class British accent: "By the by, Joanna. Some of those painted flowers in the bathroom sink have begun to wear off. You owe me a morning glory and a yellow daisy. I am prepared to accept an amaranth in exchange." N.J. Road curtailed the British accent. "I accept your bullet-doux with open arms," he bellowed, spreading his arms out in a silly imitation of Thomas à Kempis.

The beautiful and beastly merged in her face prior to pulling the trigger. Feu! A bullet struck N.J. Road directly in the heart. The syncopated red deluge that streamed from the wounded heart anointed the oriental rug with thick gore, while a big pink bubble with jejune connotations formed on his lips, grew to the size of a toy balloon, and burst. He neither flapped nor heaved, but fell back brown occiput down onto the sofa, gliding, sliding, subsiding in a purple heap.

CHAPTER 20

Winter had rearrived from North Armorica. Maraoínn an geimhreadh.

A murderous chill assaulted Dentelupo as he stepped out of his car. He shivered, zipped up his black leather bomber jacket, mused the unfulfilled moon. The dragon belched a white exhaust upon a violet haze flung from the mind of Hypnos or Henry James. At the end of a walkway, lined by swooning hedges, shimmered a white Victorian. Its steeples resembled alert felid ears against a backdrop of sylvan darkness. The lawn: a darkened stage to wind choreographed crumbling leaves. Fortune cookies sans quasi-wisdom. Brian Confucius say: Never turn over, my dear...

A searchlight enabled the invader to ogle the swerve of shore, as the choppy, lead-colored river hummed its last bars before an imminent silent frost.

Dentelupian neatsleather rhythmically struck the slate snake—as his friend had christened the recently laid serpentine walkway—of late a via dolorosa for Gis of Elizabeth (Can any good thing come out of Elizabeth?)—until he reached the base of the stairs of a nostalgic wraparound porch. He placed a firm palm on the handrail, planked up the wooden steps. The house appeared busy. Lights on in every room. Color signs flickered from a mute big-screen television. Upstairs the Psychedelic Furs pleaded in stereo for temporal perversion:
Let it stay forever now let it stay forever now

An overhead yellow light revealed all sixty-six inches and one hundred and sixty pounds of Dentelupo. He was greeted by a duplicate in the glass storm. Albeit, one with a sheeny's nose. He hated Jews and could not understand his friend's obsession with Rachel. She was a fucking Jewish-American Princess. He'd love to fuck her in her Jew ass. His friend has been distant and unloving lately. Did he blame him for what happened? She left his friend the day after the story palpably hit the local rags.

BUSINESSMAN QUESTIONED IN MURDER INVESTIGATION

By H.S. Levey

TOMS RIVER—The prosecutor's office questioned local resident Brian W.S. Jordan, 35, as part of their investigation into the execution-style murder of a Jamaican man in Asbury Park last week. Authorities speculate the murder is related to an ongoing turf war between drug dealers in the shore. Details of the crime remain sketchy.

Authorities claim Jordan, owner of the ultra-popular nightclub Oscura in Seaside Heights and a go-go bar in Old Bridge, Precious Squares, is a known coke dealer with ties to the Gambino crime family.

In the last few years, Jordan has received numerous civic awards. In 1987, he was awarded the Governor's Medal for community service. Over the years, Jordan has donated generously to local and national charities. Last year, Jordan held fundraisers for President-elect Bush at his residences, here, as well as his posh standardbred farm in Excelsior. A longtime harness racing enthusiast, Jordan owns two-year old New Jersey Sire Stakes pacing champion Molten Lead, as well as distaff champion Molten Molly.

Jordan's ad agency, Odyssey Advertising, Inc., located in Keyport, publishes the *Law Officer News*, official publication of the Reserve Police Officers Association. When reached for comment by phone, the Executive Director of the R.P.O.A., Lieutenant Charles G. Hundsheim, was adamant in his defense of Jordan.

"Brian would never have anything to do with those bums," Hundsheim said, referring to the mob allegations.

Yesterday morning, Jordan's 1987 red Corvette was impounded by the Prosecutor's Office. A search of Jordan's office in Keyport was also conducted. A spokesman for the Prosecutor's Office stated the search of Jordan's home was a matter of procedure. "We confiscated the suspect's financial records to check for anything out of the ordinary," the spokesman said.

Jordan's attorney, E. Allen McDougal of Lavallette, claims his client was away at the time of the murder and has an "iron-clad alibi." Jordan has refused comment.

Did his friend suspect he was the murderer the pigs were actually looking for and therefore responsible for Rachel's departure? He would try to regain his friend's love tonight. He must have Brian's total trust for the plan to work. After all, what's going down later was for the best. He hasn't been happy since he met that little twat. He does love his friend, but like any man, he loves himself (a) more (b) so much more that he actually hates himself (c) unnaturally (d) longtime…

He espied through diaphanous silk curtains a spectacularly lighted and decorated Christmas tree. A noble fir purchased at a great expense by the master of New Howth Castle and Environs. Dentelupo also glimpsed a solid gold menorah atop a mahogany end table. His friend had blown a fortune on the Jewish piece of junk in a desperate attempt to celebrate what he had labeled Chanukahmas.

Feetstoops of ancient old enemy announced his presence. The underdarkneathian stooped to tap the head of a marble Dying Gaul. His friend really knew how to waste money.

Dentelupo bent a forefinger in the direction of the bell. The impressive ash door was incised with a Celtic cross that Dentelupo, ever the pagan, read as a fucked-up lower case t. Puzzled by it, he frowned. Why not a big J for Jordan?

CHAPTER 21

Richard Lowe Notingham applied a grey cloth to the barrel of a .38 snub-nosed Smith & Wesson revolver. The chambers empty, he cocked the hammer and repeatedly squeezed the trigger. With his free hand, he pulled a folded sheet of stationery out of his shirt pocket. He unfolded the paper and read aloud a handprinted epistle:

12-31-88

Dear Rachel,

I know it will be difficult to understand what I have done (if you are you are reading this, my love, I have been victorious in ridding the earth of the vicious dog abductor of my soul). Please, don't weep for the scum. He was a pimp and a drug dealer and deserved what he got (a ball of lead with his stupid, lousy name on it). Did he hook you on drugs? That's the only logical explanation I can come up with why you ran away with him to his filthy den. I blame myself. I should have been more attentive. Forgive me. If you are right, we will meet again in another life. I will again look into the eyes of the most constant blue, again kiss a mouth like two cherries. I curse the remaining moments of my life, my love, for allowing a treasure worth the world to slip through my fingers. Goodbye and love always, Richard…

Notingham folded the letter twice and slid it into a white envelope addressed to Rachel. He put the pistol to his temple, squeezed the trigger. "After I finish the fucking cur, and whoever tries to interfere, I'll blow my brains out," he whispered. "Like the man says, I'm a fucking existentialist!" An epicritical spasm, lumbar, caused Notingham to wince. "It won't be too fucking hard to say fucking farewell to this body." Existentialist Notingham reached in agony for a bottle of Jack on the counter. He unscrewed the top, contemplated the dusky liquid, placed a yellow pill on his tongue, washed it down. His intention was not to eliminate the pain, but to regulate it to a less specific, protopathic sensation, a devoted, monotonous friend.

WFAN SPORTS RADIO buzzed in the background. The scores and banter about upcoming contests no longer mattered to him. Concerns about such things vanished with her departure. He became a gardener weeping for a dying rose. As for his companion, WFAN, Notinghan was grateful of the Schmoozer's intervention last night because by continuing a little longer, he could free Rachel from the mad dog holding her captive. He thanked Jack for the lovely numb feeling. A shot could solve every problem, his father used to say.

CHAPTER 22

Magnums of chilled Dom rested on a table decorated with freshly cut flowers.

Most of the vampires in the party preferred red wine. Vampire Dentelupo forkrang a goldrimmed glass and toasted his partner, Vampire Jordan, with a guinea red. Dentelupo's new brother-in-law, Vampire John Pomodoro, a drunken klutz, unleashed a red river on the white tablecloth with a grand gesture. A familiar, assisted by vampires, mopped in vain. The stain elicited a smile from the toasted Vampire.

"It's official: you're flagged, John," Dentelupo's goumad Rosa said with a smile.

"I told him he can't drink," Dentelupo's sister Lori growled.

As expected, Oscura was decorated with brightly colored balloons. Party streamers hung everywhere. Noisemakers rattled incessantly. Jordan has always viewed New Year's as a step closer to the void. The negentrope didn't necessarily think this was a negative. Last week, he directed the black walls of the club be painted hellred and stenciled with quotations. Jordan squinted and read a rather optimistic one:

NOTHING DIES!

J.W. DUNNE

Yet, nothing could cheer the jejune jack off. Save, for a laughing synchronicity.

AN EDACIOUS MAW—WITH THE GRAVITATIONAL PULL

OF A BLACK HOLE—SWALLOWED EVERYTHING IN ITS DARK
PATH.

WILLIAM BARIUM

"John," Dentelupo's sister screeched. "Stop fucking making a glutton out of yourself. You're getting so fucking fat, you have bigger tits than me."

Still cheerless, Jordan laughed a mocking little laugh.

New Year's Eve was the one night Oscura served food. Incongruous for a dance club. Something oddly postmodern Guy Lombardo about it. Jordan, nauseous, turned his attention from his crowded plate: the prime rib seemed sallow and disgusting. He'd needed to get high. Nunc est snortum!

Through a distorted prism of cocaine and alcohol, he'd watch a demiurge malleate a new place, material without being real, where stupid ghosts, breathing dreams like air, drift ignorantly about—like that specter floating toward him through an amorphous existence of grey quotidians.

In the bathroom, behind a caliginous stall door, a Vampire in a Savile Row dinner jacket snorted a few lines of white powder. To his dismay, John Pomodoro grabbed Jordan's sleeve on his return to the table of bloodsuckers.

"You know I'm in the horse business," Pomodoro needlessly informed. " I own a thoroughbred farm in Ocala. I might ship a few up north this spring and understand you have boarding farm. Lori says I should ask you about boarding them at your place. I can't pay a lot."

"It's a harness racing facility, John."

"That's alright. I just need the stalls for a few months. I have applications for stalls at Monmouth."

"Anytime. We have plenty of stalls. I wouldn't think of charging you."

"Lori told me you'd probably say that. If you ever need any stalls in Florida," Pomodoro iffed, ripe with confidence, "you can board them at our farm."

"Thanks, John. I'll keep it in mind."

"Did you hear the one about the…"

Jordan nodlaughed.

" One man's meat is another man's poison," Pomodoro gushed.

Jordan's laugh deadened. He remembered a similar punch line of a joke he only half recalled. One man's meat is another man's poisson. It involved a gay Nazi performing oral sex on a mademoiselle he believed to be a monsieur.

"Remember, Bry," Lori's husband cried, every word drawn and quartered, "when they used to open Freehold's infield for the public?"

"Yeah, I remember."

Remembrance of journuit past: the day cooed, but the night shivered with a radical noise, as they played in the master bedroom. Lights left on, her angel ass bare temptation to his urban eye. Voyeurs with green veined, ovate faces pressed against the panes.

Keen, keen Jordan noted the dalliances of puppets. Fugging marionettes smoked fugging cigarettes. Blue smoke clogged the air. Goofusses preen before the specula of flipped-up compacts. Redundant faced betrayers of men! He cocked an airdrawn pillow, uncocked.

"Because they have that thing," Pomodoro went on in an inarticulate attempt to explain the Faustian hold of a Judasean circular piece of heaven scented like hell peehole.

He needed to get higher. Nunc est bibendum! Jordan drank a few glasses of champagne. Silent, he evaluated his date. Messina Siciliano, notwithstanding sirenic nomenclature, was a poor siren. Her glaucous eyes offered no allure for New Howth's master. She was Rosa's Italian born cousin, a cosmetologist and part time go-go dancer. Jordan thought her a faccia brutta. Singsongo, she whispered with hivestung lips a whorish proposition, but, because he had plugged his ookos with beeswax, her siren's song was all just pops and buzzes. People say she looks like a young Sophia Loren. A zaftigophobe, Jordan's loins remained cool at the prospect of knocking his lower sconce against such a de trop lump of flesh. Tuxtax! Tuxtax!

Jordan dabbed his mouth with a napkin uncoiled from his lap and, without a word, retreated to a little bar near the exit. Dentelupo's brow displayed its typical ridges of confusion. He shook his head in unbelief, tossed his napkin on the table, and, also without word, followed his disgruntled partner. Jordan loosened his black tie, ordered a double whiskey. Dentelupo took off his dinner jacket, placed it on a stool.

"For the record, you didn't," Jordan asked. Jordan downed his whiskey. "I must seem like a real asshole the way I got up and rushed over here. I'll apologize to everyone later. Sometimes I don't blame Rachel for leaving me. She probably had her fill of assholes. Rick and I are two of the biggest assholes in history. You know he thinks Rachel ran

249

away with you. Still thinks she's with you. Can you believe that?"

"He's an asshole, Bry."

"But I have been acting like one since she's left. I shouldn't have left the way I did. It was very rude."

"People understand, Bry. Look what you've gone through. Messi is a real whore. Are you gonna fuck her?"

Jordan begged the question. "What the fuck is it with Lori's husband? What a slow-talking, boring fuck! Where did Lori find him?"

"She's bleeding him. She ruins all of her husbands. I mean, if they're not ruined to start with. Remember what my father said about her when she came back to Belmar: Here comes fucking trouble."

"Lori's alright," Jordan asserted. "It's funny the way she picks on him."

"She's a real bitch. I was glad you got up. Gave me a chance to get away from the guinea bitches. John's the biggest guinea bitch of them all."

"Maybe I should fuck him, Frank. After all, I better get used to fucking men if I'm going to jail."

"If you grab his check, he'd let you. Cheap whore. Stop saying you're going to jail, Bry. Allen told you the investigation has cleared you. Thank god."

Dentelupo had gained his partner's confidence. The plan: Armstrong beeps him when he's in position. Dentelupo asks to be excused in order to phone his son. Returning, he tells Jordan that when he had hung up, the phone rang and it was Rachel. She sounded frantic. She said she'd meet him at his home in fifteen minutes. She said she'd explain everything when she saw him. Please, tell Bry I love him. There would be no holding him back. He was now in the hands of fucking god and Laughlin Armstrong.

*

A greycoated hunter traveled under an arch, stepped onto a dance floor, polished marble of Nova Antonia. His righthand pocketed, happiness soon, quarry sighted, he read the writing on the wall:

THE STARS TURNED OFF IN MID-ETERNITY,

A COLLISION OF WORLDS LOOMED,

LIKE SUPERMASSIVE BLACK HOLES

DRIFTING TOWARD A VIOLENT MERGER.

VIVIAN DARKBLOOM

Jordan noticed him first. His gun and gummy smile aimed at Dentelupo's back. Jordan immediately lunged at the gunman, wrestled him to the floor, the revolver went off, a bullet sailed into Jordan's adolescent heart, instantly transporting him to the eternal silence of infinite space and time. As the shooter tried to get up, beefy bar personnel pounced on him, the gun squirting out of his hand, as his skull mortally cracked against the implacable marble. Without cunctation, Notingham joined his inadvertent prey on the infinite side of paradise. Dentelupo just stood there—as still as his partner—feeling—if he could—like Romulus after he had killed his fellow suckling; like the Buchanans; like Kinbote. Some tomorrow he too would shimmer into impalpable blackness—but for now he would beat on—almost envious of the voidward waste of souls.

*

ENTER ARMSTRONG

Void quiet, Oscura, white chalkings of the authorities glowed pink in the infant red sun, a shadow of a man lifted a shadow of a glass to a shadow of lips—all withering away with the waning darkness. A tall figure blazing blackly, clad in a mail of gold chains, approached the creature back from the shadows.

"Pour yourself a drink, Laughlin," Dentelupo commanded.

Armstrong reached over the bar and retrieved an unopened bottle of Chivas Regal. He used his teeth to break the seal, unscrewed the top, and drank a gallus potion that would rouse a friar.

"Fuck, Laughlin," Dentelupo ejaculated. "That's eleven-year-old Scotch. I said pour yourself a glass. I thought you Rastafarians only smoke ganja, chrome dome."

Armstrong smiled abundantly. "No Rasta ever shave his head, you dumb wop." Armstrong rubbed his smooth scalp, laughing. "God help you, mon. What the hell are you gonna do without him? He was smart, mon. Never one bust. I'm happy I didn't have to do it."

"He wasn't that smart. He's dead, ain't he?"

"He saved your life, mon. What's wrong with you?"

"All this shit is his fault. He nearly got me killed, Laughlin. All for a stupid whore. I was tired of listening to his shit. Are we gonna talk business?"

www.ingramcontent.com/pod-product-compliance
Lightning Source LLC
Chambersburg PA
CBHW050505260626
47157CB00004B/1192